WALT DISNEY'S
Donald Duck in
TRICK OR TREATMENT

THERE'S NOTHING DONALD LIKES BETTER THAN TRICK OR TREATING ON HALLOWEEN –
OH, BOY! LOOK AT ALL THIS CANDY! THE LAST BLOCK WAS THE BEST ONE YET!
I'LL SAY! MY BAG'S STARTING TO GET HEAVY!
MINE, TOO! WE'RE TIRED, UNCA DONALD! LET'S GO HOME!
D 2005-358

BUT THIS IS THE BEST TIME TO TRICK OR TREAT!
WHAT? IT'S AT LEAST 9:00! WE'RE PRACTICALLY THE ONLY ONES STILL OUT!

EXACTLY! PEOPLE GIVE EXTRA CANDY WHEN THEY KNOW THERE WON'T BE MORE TRICK OR TREATERS!
FORGET IT! WE'RE NOT GOING ANOTHER STEP!

GO ON HOME, THEN! I'LL TRICK OR TREAT BY MYSELF!
THAT'S NOT A GOOD IDEA, UNCA DONALD!
YOU SHOULDN'T GO OUT ALONE ON HALLOWEEN!

AW, THERE'S NOTHING TO BE SCARED OF BUT FAKE GHOSTS AND CARDBOARD GHOULS!

WHAT A BUNCH OF PANTYWAISTS! THE ONE NIGHT OF THE YEAR WHEN PEOPLE GIVE FREE CANDY AND THEY WANT TO GO HOME!

"MYSTERY LANE"! I KNOW I HAVEN'T BEEN DOWN THAT STREET YET!
SQUARE ROAD
MYSTERY LANE

IT IS SPOOKY OUT! MAYBE THIS WASN'T SUCH A GOOD IDEA!

AW, I'M JUST BEING SILLY! ANYHOW, IF I RUN HOME NOW, THE BOYS WILL NEVER LET ME FORGET IT!

WHOA! IF I WERE GOING TO DRAW A PICTURE OF A HAUNTED HOUSE, THAT'S WHAT IT WOULD LOOK LIKE!
BUT THERE ARE JACK O'LANTERNS ON THE PORCH, SO SOMEBODY'S GOTTA BE HOME!

TRICK OR TREAT!

A TRICK OR TREATER!
YEAH, WELL... IT IS HALLOWEEN!

SNIFF! DON'T I KNOW IT!
YOU'VE BEEN CRYING! WHAT'S WRONG?

THERE'S A BIG HALLOWEEN PARTY TONIGHT! I SO WANTED TO GO BUT I DON'T HAVE A DATE!

IT'S THE SOCIAL EVENT OF THE SEASON! MUSIC, DANCING, LOTS OF TREATS!
LOT'S OF TREATS, HUH?
I'LL GO WITH YOU, IF YOU WANT!

THAT'S VERY KIND! BUT I DON'T EVEN KNOW YOU!
DONALD'S THE NAME! DONALD DUCK!

I'M BELLA! YOU DO SEEM NICE! WERE YOU REALLY SERIOUS ABOUT GOING OUT WITH ME?
WELL, SURE!

ALL RIGHT THEN! JUST ONE THING!
YOUR COSTUME NEEDS A LITTLE SOMETHING! HERE, PUT THIS ON!

HOW'S IT LOOK?
SNAP!
VERY CLASSY! OKAY! LET'S GO!

WOW! WHAT A PARTY! PEOPLE REALLY WORKED ON THEIR COSTUMES!
OH, YES! MY FRIENDS JUST LOVE HALLOWEEN!

AND I'M BEULAH'S BOY-FRIEND, COUNT GLOBULA!
GOOD NAME! I'M PLEASED TO MEET YOU!

MIND IF I BORROW YOUR DATE FOR A BIT? I'D LOVE TO SHOW HIM THE GARDEN!
NOT AT ALL! HAVE FUN, DONALD!

SOON –
GOSH, THIS IS QUITE A GARDEN! I'VE NEVER SEEN PLANTS QUITE LIKE THESE!
THEY'RE INTERESTING, AREN'T THEY?

BUT NOT NEAR AS INTERESTING AS YOU, CUTIE PIE!
HUH?

BEULAH! DONALD!
COUNT GLOBULA!

EXACTLY WHAT DO YOU THINK YOU'RE DOING OUT HERE WITH MY DATE, SIR?
JU-JUST ADMIRING THE FLOWERS!

WAAK!
SNAP!

YAAAAAGH!

JUMPIN' JACK O'LANTERNS! THAT WASN'T LIKE ANY FLOWER I'VE EVER SEEN!

SAY, PEOPLE ARE CARRYING PLATES! THOSE MUST BE THE REFRESHMENTS BELLA WAS TALKING ABOUT!

OH, BOY! A SNACK IS JUST WHAT I NEED!

WHAT'S THIS? EYEBALLS? FRIED BUGS? AND THAT PUNCH LOOKS LIKE -ULP!- BLOOD!

DONALD! THERE YOU ARE!
I GUESS THINGS COULD ALWAYS GET WORSE!

MY SISTER SURE DOES HAVE GOOD TASTE IN MEN!
I'LL GO FIND HER AND TELL HER YOU THINK SO!

NO REASON TO RUSH OFF!
SO! THERE YOU ARE!

AFTER MY GIRLFRIEND AGAIN, ARE YOU?
NO, NOT AT ALL?

ALL I'M AFTER IS A LITTLE SNACK!
HEY, BUDDY! THAT'S MINE!

YAAAH!

I'VE HAD ABOUT ENOUGH OF THIS FREAKSHOW! I'VE GOT TO FIND THE WAY OUT!
BOOM PA!
BOOM PA!

THIS LOOKS LIKE THE DANCE FLOOR! MAYBE SOME REASONABLY NORMAL-LOOKING PERSON WILL TELL ME WHERE THE EXIT IS!

ER, EXCUSE ME, MA'AM!

YES?
WAAAK!

HAAAAALP!

THERE YOU ARE, SILLY BOY!
HOOF! NOT YOU AGAIN!

BETTER GET USED TO IT, LOVERBOY! WHEN I LIKE A GUY, I DON'T TAKE "NO" FOR AN ANSWER!
BUT WHAT ABOUT COUNT GLOBULA?

AW, DON'T WORRY ABOUT HIM!
SORRY, BUT I THINK I'D BETTER!
GRRRRR!

EEP!
I WARNED YOU TO STAY AWAY FROM HER TWICE, DUCK! THAT'S CHANCE ENOUGH FOR ANYONE!

LET HIM GO, GLOBULA!
WHAT?

BUT HONEY BUNCH!
HONEY BUNCH NUTHIN'! I'M TIRED OF YOU BUTTING IN! WE'RE THROUGH!

ZAP!
THROUGH, DO YOU HEAR ME?

AS FOR YOU, SWEETIE, GET READY FOR A WHOLE LOTTA LOVE!
YIBZEE PIBZEE POP!

WHAT?!
BWANG!

HAVEN'T YOU HEARD, SIS? IF YOU WANT OTHERS TO LOVE YOU, YOU HAVE TO LEARN TO LOVE YOURSELF!

OH, MY GOODNESS!

POOF!

BELLA! MY DARLING!
GLOBULA! YOU'RE BACK!
OH NO! DON'T TELL ME HE'S IN LOVE WITH *YOU*, TOO!

DON'T WORRY! COUNT GLOBULA WON'T THREATEN YOU ANYMORE! HE ONLY ACTED THAT WAY BECAUSE HE WAS ENCHANTED!
ENCHANTED?

SEE, COUNT GLOBULA IS *MY* BOYFRIEND! BUT MY SISTER IS INSANELY JEALOUS OF EVERYTHING I HAVE, AND SHE CAST A POWERFUL LOVE SPELL TO STEAL HIM AWAY!

GUESS THAT'S WHY YOU DIDN'T HAVE A DATE TONIGHT!
EXACTLY! BUT WHEN YOU CAME TRICK OR TREATING, I THOUGHT OF A WAY TO WIN HIM BACK!

I KNEW THAT WHEN SHE SAW YOU, SHE'D TRY TO STEAL YOU WITH THE SAME LOVE SPELL SHE USED BEFORE!
THE SPELL CAN ONLY ENCHANT ONE PERSON AT A TIME, SO COUNT GLOBULA WOULD BE FREE!

AND THEN I'D BE THE ONE GOING GA-GA OVER BEULAH!
THAT'S WHY I GAVE YOU THE MEDALLION!

IT REFLECTS A SPELL BACK ON WHOEVER CASTS IT! ALL I HAD TO DO THEN WAS MAKE SURE THAT THE FIRST PERSON BEULAH SAW WAS HERSELF!

LOOKS LIKE IT WORKED LIKE A →HEH!← CHARM!
YUP! MY SISTER WON'T BE STEALING ANYONE'S DATE FOR A WHILE!
I LOVE YOU SO MUCH!

SORRY ABOUT THE UNPLEASANTNESS, OLD SPORT! ANYTHING WE CAN DO TO MAKE IT UP?
HOW ABOUT GETTING ME HOME?

I THINK WE CAN MANAGE THAT! TAKE CARE, DONALD! AND HAPPY HALLOWEEN!
SNAP!

POOF!
HUH! THIS IS EXACTLY WHERE I LEFT THE BOYS!

WOW! THIS IS TWICE AS MUCH CANDY AS I HAD BEFORE!

WHO CARES? I JUST WANNA GO TO BED!

THE NEXT MORNING –
OH BOY! NOT ONLY DID UNCA DONALD DECIDE TO SHARE HIS EXTRA CANDY, HE GAVE US ALL OF IT!
IT'S STRANGE! CONSIDERING HOW WELL HE DID, HE DOESN'T SEEM VERY HAPPY THAT HE DECIDED TO TRICK OR TREAT ON HIS OWN!
THE END

BRER RABBIT VISITS THE WITCH

BRER RABBIT, AIN'T YOU FEELIN' WELL? YOU LOOK **MIGHTY, MIGHTY BAD!**

I GOT TH' **MOPES**, BRER TURKEY BUZZARD!

W OS 129-05

TH' **MOPES**?
THAT'S RIGHT, AN' TH' ONLY WAY TER GIT RID OF TH' MOPES IS TER GO SEE **AUNT MAMA-BAMA BIG-MONEY!**

YOU MEAN T-T-TH' **WITCH** THAT LIVES IN TH' **S-SMOKIN' HOLE** IN TH' MIDDLE OF TH' DARK SWAMP?
THE SAME!

BUT TER **GIT** THERE, YOU GOT TER JUMP SOME, HOP SOME, FLOP SOME, SLIDE SOME, CREEP SOME, LEAP SOME, HOLLER SOME....

... AN' EVEN **THEN**, IF YOU AIN'T KEERFUL, YOU WON'T **GIT** THERE!

YET BRER RABBIT GETS THERE!
TH-THAT'S TH' P-PLACE! I SMELL TH' SMOKE, AN' I SEE TH' SMOKE!

OH, AUNT MAMA-BAMA BIG-MONEY! IT'S B-B-BRER RABBIT! I C-C-COME TER GIT YER H-H-HELP!

UP FROM THE SMOKING HOLE COMES THE WITCH!
WHY SO, BRER RABBIT? WHY SO?
I GOT TH' MOPES!

I'M LOSIN' TH' USE OF MY MIND! THERE'S NO SMARTNESS IN ME ANY MORE! I'M SKEERED TH' BIG CRITTERS MIGHT NAB ME AN' SKIN ME!

I'LL BRING YER SMARTNESS BACK, BRER RABBIT! JEST DO AS I SAY!
I'LL DO AS YOU SAY... ANYTHING YOU SAY!

THERE SITS A SQUIRR'L IN THAT TREE! GO FETCH HIM FOR ME, BRER RABBIT!

HMMM! IF I CAN'T COAX THAT BUSHTAIL FROM THERE, THEN MY SMARTNESS IS REALLY-TRULY GONE!

THIS JOB CALLS FER AN EMPTY SACK...

... AN' THESE TWO ROCKS!

WHAT'S THAT?
BLUP!
BUT BRER RABBIT SAYS NOTHING!

WHO'S THAT?
BLUP!
BLAP!
BUT BRER RABBIT STILL SAYS NOTHING!

BLUP!
BLAP!
BLAP!
SPEAK UP! WHO'S THAT?
IT'S BRER RABBIT!

WHUT YOU DOIN' IN THAT BAG, BRER RABBIT?
I'M CRACKIN' HICK'RY NUTS!

HICK'RY NUTS! MM-MM! KIN I CRACK SOME, TOO?
SURE ENOUGH, BRER BUSHTAIL! GIT IN TH' BAG WITH ME!

AND BEFORE YOU CAN SAY HOPPERGRASS, BRER BUSHTAIL IS INSIDE THE BAG...

..AND BRER RABBIT IS OUTSIDE THE BAG!
HEYO! AIN'T NOTHIN' IN HERE BUT ME AN' SOME ROCKS!

WELL DONE, BRER RABBIT... WELL DONE!

WHAT NEXT, AUNT MAMA-BAMA ?
KING LION IS OVER THERE SITTIN' UNDER THAT TREE!

TAKE SOME ROPE AN' TIE HIM TO THE TREE!

B-BUT THAT LION COULD MAKE MINCE-MEAT OUTTA ME WITH TWO CHOMPS OF HIS TEETH!
NEVER-THE-LESS...

...IF YOU WANT ME TER CURE TH' MOPES, YOU GOT TER DO IT!
YESSUM!

I FEEL LIMP AS THAT LEAF THAT'S TUMBLIN' THRU TH' BREEZE!

TH' LEAF... TH' BREEZE... THAT'S IT!

OOOO! LOOK OUT! OOOOO!
BRER RABBIT! WHAT'S TH' MATTER? WHERE YOU GOIN' WITH TH' ROPE ?

I'M GOIN' TER TIE MYSELF TER A TREE! YOU BETTER TIE YERSELF TER A TREE, TOO, KING LION!

SEE TH' LEAVES FLUTTERIN' THRU TH' AIR! THERE'S A HURRICANE-STORM BLOWIN' UP!

A HURRICANE-STORM? BUT I DON'T HAVE A ROPE TER TIE MYSELF TER A TREE! WHAT'LL I EVER DO?

YOU BETTER RUN... REAL FAST!
I'M TOO OLD TER RUN REAL FAST!

THEN DIG A HOLE AN' BURY YERSELF, KING LION!
IT TAKES TIME TER DIG A HOLE, BRER RABBIT! I AIN'T GOT TIME!

THEN YOU'LL JEST HAVE TER LET TH' HURRICANE BLOW YOU AWAY!

PLEASE, BRER RABBIT! LEND ME A PIECE O' YER ROPE! TIE ME UP TER THAT TREE, TOO!

FOR YOU, KING LION, I'LL DO IT!
YOU'RE SO GOOD TER ME, BRER RABBIT!

WELL DONE, BRER RABBIT... WELL DONE!
WHAT NEXT, AUNT MAMA-BAMA?

THIS TIME YOU GOT TER DO SOMETHIN' **REALLY** HARD! IN TH' FOREST AN **ELEPHANT** ROAMS ABOUT!

GO FETCH ME A TUSK FROM OUT HIS SNOUT!
AN ELEPHANT-TUSK!!/!

B-B-BUT I AIN'T EVER LAID EYES ON AN ELEPHANT! HE'S TH' **BIGGEST CRITTER** ON **EARTH!**
DON'T **ARGUE** WITH ME!

YOU SAID YOU'D DO **ANYTHING!** BUT MAYBE YOU AIN'T **SMART** ENOUGH! IN THAT CASE, I'LL GIT **BRER FOX** TER FETCH IT!

OH **NO,** AUNT MAMA-BAMA... **NOT BRER FOX! I'LL** FETCH IT... **RIGHT NOW!**

WHEN BRER RABBIT REACHES THE FOREST, HE HIDES IN A TREE AN' WAITS AN' WAITS UNTIL...

HERE HE COMES... FLOPPIN' HIS BIG EARS, AN' SWINGIN' HIS LONG SNOUT! WHY, HE... HE... HE'S **BIG AS A HOUSE!!**

HOWDY, BRER ELEPHANT! MIND IF I ASK YOU A PERSONAL QUESTION?
WHAT'S THAT, LI'L RABBIT?

IS IT TRUE WHAT KING LION SAYS? HE SAYS YOU'RE TOO BIG TER BE VERY STRONG!
HAW! HAW!!

ME NOT STRONG? WATCH THIS!
CRACK!
CREAK!

PSHAW! THAT WUZ EASY!

EASY? WATCH THIS! I'LL PULL UP TH' WHOLE TREE!

AN' FLIP IT THRU TH' AIR LIKE A FEATHER DUSTER!

SHUCKS! THAT WUZN'T MUCH OF A TREE! SEE THAT BIG, ENORMOUS OL' PINE TREE THERE?

I BET YOU AIN'T STRONG ENOUGH TER KNOCK THAT ONE DOWN!
YES, I AM STRONG ENOUGH!

WITH THAT, HE STARTS A-RUNNING...
I'LL SHOW THAT RABBIT A THING OR TWO!

AND CRASHES INTO THAT ENORMOUS PINE TREE WITH HIS TUSKS!
KERBLASHITY
BLAM!
KERACK!

WHEN HE COMES TO, THE TREE IS STILL THERE...

...BUT HIS TUSK ISN'T THERE!
HEE! HEE! HEE!

AUNT MAMA-BAMA BIG-MONEY, I'M HERE! AN' I FETCHED TH' ELEPHANT TUSK LIKE YOU TOLD ME!
THAT YOU DID!

WHAT YOU WANT ME TER DO NEXT?
NOTHIN'! AN' DON'T WORRY 'BOUT LOSIN' YOUR SMARTNESS!

IF YOU WERE ANY SMARTER THAN YOU ARE RIGHT NOW, YOU'D BE TH' RUINATION OF TH' WHOLE, WIDE WORLD!

SO BRER RABBIT FEELS MIGHTY, MIGHTY FINE!
I AIN'T GOT TH' MOPES NO MORE!
End

WALT DISNEY
presents
DONALD
DUCK
WHAT LUCK! THERE ARE BUGS ON MY VEGETABLES!

I'LL HAVE TO GET THE BUG SPRAY AND KILL 'EM!

THIS STORE SPRAY HAS SPOILED! I'LL HOP IT UP WITH SOME TURPENTINE AND STUFF!
FLEA OIL
OIL
ROACH POWDER

PHEW! WOW! WHAT A CONCOCTION!

THIS SPRAY OUGHT TO KILL ANYTHING!

WAK!

HO! HO! HAW!
IT SURE KILLED
YOUR TURNIPS!
MUZZLE YOUR SNICKERS! I'LL LICK THOSE BUGS YET!

WHILE UNCA' DONALD IS MIXING HIS NEW SPRAY, LET'S GO DOWN TO THE COSTUME STORE! I'VE GOT A SWELL IDEA!

WE'LL DRESS UP TO LOOK LIKE BUGS, AND GIVE UNCA' DONALD THE SHOCK OF HIS LIFE!

WE'D LIKE TO RENT SOME BUG SUITS
FOR A FEW DAYS!
LIKE THAT UP THERE!

THIS SPRAY WORKS BETTER! I DON'T SEE THE BUGS DYING, BUT THEY LOOK PLENTY SICK!

THERE! THAT'S FINISHED! TOMORROW I'LL CHECK TO SEE IF ANY BUGS SURVIVED!

NEXT MORNING!
HO HUM! TIME TO GO SEE HOW MY BUG SPRAY WORKED!

WHAT'S THAT NOISE COMING FROM THE GARDEN? SOUNDS LIKE CHEWING!
CHOMP! CHOMP!

GREAT JUMPING JAYBIRDS! BUGS AS BIG AS WOLVES!
CHOMP!
CHOMP!

THEY MUST HAVE BEEN CAUSED BY THE SPRAY I USED YESTERDAY! IT MADE 'EM GROW!

I MUST GET THE MAYOR DOWN HERE TO SEE 'EM! I'LL GET SOME NEWSPAPER MEN, TOO!

OH, WHAT BUGS! I'LL BE FAMOUS!
CHOMP! CHOMP!

OKAY, BOYS! TIME TO HIDE THE BUG OUTFITS AND GET OUT OF SIGHT!

SEND YOUR STAR REPORTERS AND CAMERAMEN OUT TO MY PLACE RIGHT AWAY! I HAVE SOMETHING IMPORTANT TO SHOW THEM!
EDITOR DAILY GAB

HIS HONOR THE MAYOR OF OUR FAIR CITY
PRIVATE
HURRY OUT TO MY HOUSE, YOUR HONOR! SEE MY GIANT BUGS! THEY'LL MAKE THE TOWN FAMOUS!

THOSE BUGS ARE BIG AS HORSES, AND GETTING BIGGER ALL THE TIME!
BIG AS HORSES— FANCY THAT!
I BET THE BUGS ARE ALL IN THAT DUCK'S HEAD!

THEY'RE RIGHT HERE IN MY GARDEN!

GONE! THE BUGS ARE GONE!
PROBABLY GREW SO BIG THEY HAD TO MOVE TO TEXAS!

THEY WERE RIGHT HERE, BUT I DON'T SEE ANY TRACKS!

BUGS AS BIG AS HORSES WOULD LEAVE DEEP TRACKS! MR. DUCK, YOU HAVE LED US DOWN HERE ON A FOOL'S ERRAND!

BUT I SWEAR I DID SEE THOSE BUGS! I DID!
NEXT TIME YOU SEE THEM, BRING THEM TO MY OFFICE! GOOD DAY, SIR!

RIDICULED AND DISGRACED, DONALD SEEKS SOLACE IN SOLITUDE!
MAYBE I DIDN'T SEE THOSE BUGS! MAYBE I WAS ONLY DREAMING!

CHOMP!
CHOMP!
THAT CHOMPING—! THAT SOUNDS LIKE—

THE BUGS! THEY'RE BACK IN MY GARDEN AGAIN!

THE MAYOR SAID TO BRING 'EM TO HIS OFFICE! I'LL GET A NET AND CATCH 'EM!

EVEN IF I ONLY CATCH ONE BUG, IT'LL PROVE I'M NOT CRAZY!

GONE! THE BUGS ARE GONE AGAIN!

WHAT'S ALL THE FUSS
ABOUT BUGS,
UNCA' DONALD?

YOU KIDS GET OUT OF SIGHT! I'VE GOT SOME GIANT BUGS TO CATCH— AND THEY'RE VERY SHY!

IF I CAN FIND MY BEAR TRAPS, I'LL CATCH 'EM, THOUGH! YOU WATCH!

WE'VE SURE GOT UNCA' DONALD GOING HAYWIRE!
HE'LL BE IN A STRAIT JACKET BEFORE LONG!
HAW! HAW!

NOW, WHERE DID I LEAVE MY TRAPS?

I'LL LOOK BEHIND THESE TRUNKS!

WHAT'S THIS? .... LOOKS LIKE A BUG COSTUME!

I SEE IT ALL NOW! SNORT! SNORT!

THOSE KIDS! I'LL PEEL 'EM LIKE SPUDS!

SPLAT!

THAT CRACK WAS AN OMEN! IT MEANT I WAS DOING SOMETHING WRONG!

I GET IT! I WAS GOING TO WALLOP THE KIDS FOR LAUGHING AT ME, BUT THE WAY TO GET EVEN IS TO TURN THE JOKE ON THEM!

THIS WILL REQUIRE SOME CRAFTY PLANNING!

LATER!
DID YOU FIND THE TRAPS,
UNCA'
DONALD?
NO! I'VE FIGURED OUT A BETTER WAY TO GET THOSE BUGS!

IF THIS SPRAY DOPE MADE THOSE BUGS GROW INTO GIANTS, IT'LL ALSO MAKE BIRDS GROW!

SO I SPRAY SOME ON A BIRD — AND TOMORROW MORNING HE'LL BE BIG ENOUGH TO CATCH THOSE BUGS!

UNCA' DONALD IS GOIN' COO-COO!
TEE! HEE!
HE'S A SUCKER FOR A GAG!

THE KIDS ARE LAUGHING THEIR HEADS OFF AT ME! HO! HO! HO!

NOW TO SNEAK DOWN TO THE COSTUME STORE AND RENT A BIRD OUTFIT!

NEXT MORNING!
TIME TO GET INTO OUR BUG SUITS AGAIN!
YEAH! NEVER A DULL MOMENT!

POOR OL' UNK!
HE'LL STRAIN HIS EYES LOOKING FOR HIS GIANT BIRD!
AND WE'LL STRAIN OUR SIDES LAUGHING! WHAT A GAG!

WE'LL CHOMP EXTRA LOUD THIS MORNING!
ALL SET!
LET'S CHOMP!

CHOMP!
CHOMP!
CHOMP!

CLACK!
CLACK!
CLACK!
?
?

DID YOU HEAR A CLACKING SOUND?
YES! IT SEEMED TO COME FROM UP IN THE TREE!

CLACK! CLACK!

GREAT SNAKES! A BIRD AS BIG AS A HORSE!
THAT SPRAY DOPE REALLY WORKED!

HEH! HEH! HEH! NOW WHO LAUGHS? HEH! HEH!

RUN FOR YOUR LIVES! THAT BIRD MEANS BUSINESS!
SNAP! CLACK!

MANY BLOCKS LATER!
CLACK! CLACK!

I CAN CATCH THEM ANY TIME, BUT THIS IS MORE FUN! ON WITH THE CHASE!

WE CAN'T KEEP RUNNING MUCH LONGER!
LET'S STOP RUNNING AND START SCREAMING!

STOP! STOP, MISTER BIRD!
WE'RE NOT BUGS!
WE'RE BOYS!

LOOK!
WE'RE NOT GOOD TO EAT!
SOB! SOB!

SO YOU THOUGHT YOU COULD LAUGH AT YOUR UNCLE DONALD AND NOT LIVE TO BE SORRY!

UNCA' DONALD!
OH, THANK GOODNESS, IT'S YOU!
WE THOUGHT YOU WERE A REAL BIRD!

NOT SO FAST, ME BUCKOS! YOU WON'T BE SO THANKFUL WHEN I'VE FINISHED SPANKING YOU!
OH, MY LANDS SAKES ALIVE!

THROCKMORTON, GET YOUR GUN! A GIANT BIRD IS ABOUT TO POUNCE ON THOSE HELPLESS LITTLE BOYS!

I'LL FIX HIM —THE OVERGROWN CROW!

BANG!

BANG! WHANG! BOOM!

LATER!

UNCA' DONALD, YOU'RE NOT GONNA
SPANK US,
ARE YOU?
OH, NO! NOT AT ALL!

I'M GOING TO GET EVEN WITH YOU A BETTER WAY! EACH OF YOU GET A BLOCK AND A HAMMER!

NOW START KILLING THE BUGS IN THE GARDEN... ..ONE BUG AT A TIME!

PUT EACH BUG ON A BLOCK AND HIT HIM WITH THE HAMMER! WHEN YOU'VE KILLED ALL THE BUGS IN THE GARDEN, YOU CAN START ON THE APHIDS IN THE ROSEBUSHES!

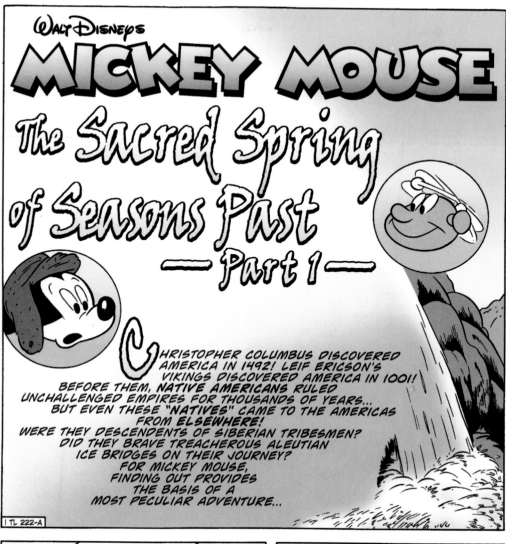

Walt Disney's

MICKEY MOUSE

The Sacred Spring of Seasons Past

— Part 1 —

CHRISTOPHER COLUMBUS DISCOVERED AMERICA IN 1492! LEIF ERICSON'S VIKINGS DISCOVERED AMERICA IN 1001! BEFORE THEM, **NATIVE AMERICANS** RULED UNCHALLENGED EMPIRES FOR THOUSANDS OF YEARS... BUT EVEN THESE **"NATIVES"** CAME TO THE AMERICAS FROM **ELSEWHERE!** WERE THEY DESCENDENTS OF SIBERIAN TRIBESMEN? DID THEY BRAVE TREACHEROUS ALEUTIAN ICE BRIDGES ON THEIR JOURNEY? FOR MICKEY MOUSE, FINDING OUT PROVIDES THE BASIS OF A MOST PECULIAR ADVENTURE...

1 TL 222-A

ALL RIGHT, LAWN! TODAY YOU AND I HAVE A HAVE A DATE WITH THE HEDGE CLIPPER!

TIME FOR THIS UNCTUOUS WEEDERY TO TAKE LEAVE!
CLAT! CLAT!

THERE'S ALSO THAT TERMITE-INFESTED NIGHTMARE OF AN OAK TREE...

HEY, MICK! HOW LONG YA GONNA LEAVE THIS OLD EYESORE STANDING?
OH! HIYA, HORACE!

I MEAN, IT'S CUTE IF YER INTO "YEAR-OLD UGLY!" BUT IT'S WAY PAST ITS PRIME!
SO HOW TO KNOCK IT DOWN?

LEAVE IT TO OL' HORACE HORSECOLLAR, PAL! I'LL GET MY TOOLS!
WOW! THANKS LOADS, HORACE!

AND THUS...
-GNNGH!-
B-R-RAZ-Z-ZZ!!

VOILA, MICK! TALENT LIKE MINE IS—
CRE-E-E-AK!!

CRASH!
SUFFERIN' CATFISH! MY KITCHEN!

EHEH... OOPS? UH—DON'T YOU WORRY NONE, MICK! I'LL GET THIS FIXED IN NO TIME FLAT!

AHA! THIS'LL PRY THE CRAZY THING LOOSE!
I'LL CHECK FOR ANY DAMAGE TO THE KITCHEN!

WHEW! TH' PORCELAIN'S OKAY!

NRGH!!! GIVE, YOU INANE SPROUT!

ALMOST...

NO PLANT CAN MAKE A MONKEY OUTTA—

MeEEE!
BOING!

COMIN' THROUGH!
WHA—?! HOLY COW!!!
KA-RASH!

SWEET CHIBA, MAN! WHAT'S THAT MONSTER MADE OF?!
MAYBE I OUGHTA CALL SOMEBODY...

FORGET IT, MICK! THIS PARASITE HAS RANKLED MY IRE!
GOOD GOSH! I BETTER HURRY!

I'M POSITIVE MY INSURANCE DOESN'T COVER "ACTS OF HORACE!"

HEY, MICKEY!!!

TAKE A GANDER AT OL' "WIDOWMAKER!" AIN'T SHE A BEAUT?!

AND NOW...THE PIECE DE RESISTANCE!

A WEE DAB OVER HERE...
"WEE"?! IS THAT POISON?
NOPE! SOFT-ENER!

AND NOW—ROUND TWO!
HE'S NUTS...

PERHAPS!
CREAK!!!

BINGO!
R-RIPP!!!!!

JUST LIKE PULLIN' BABY TEETH!
CRASH! BAM!

BABY TEETH?! YOU'VE YANKED THE FOUNDATION OFF MY HOUSE, YOU LUNATIC!
!

HEH! GO FIG!... WHO'DA THUNK ALL THOSE ROOTS WENT BENEATH YOUR HOUSE?
YEAH, HORACE! GO FIG!

AHEM! I—
HORACE HORSE-COLLAR, YOU HAVE THE FINESSE OF A NUCLEAR TYPHOON!

DON'T SWEAT IT, MICK! I'LL POP BY TOMORROW AND FIX EVERYTHING JUST FINE!
"DON'T SWEAT IT," HE SAYS! MY POOR HOUSE IS TOTALED!

HUH! GARDEN GNOMES COME IN **BLUEBERRY?**

WOW...I HAVE ***GOT*** TO STOP DRINKING STEAK SAUCE...

PERHAPS ***I*** CAN BE UFF ASSIS-TANCE?

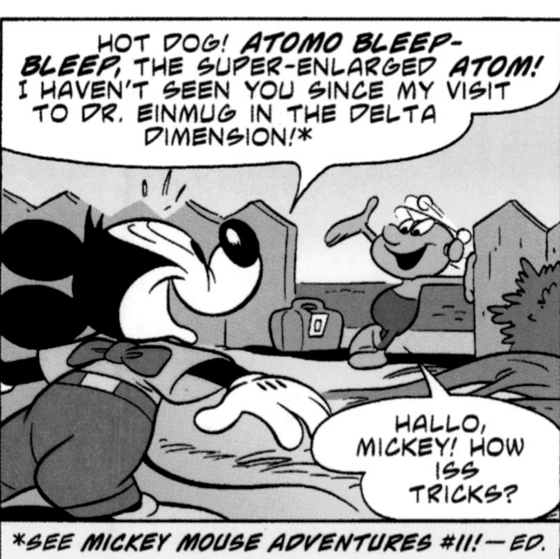
HOT DOG! ***ATOMO BLEEP-BLEEP,*** THE SUPER-ENLARGED ***ATOM!*** I HAVEN'T SEEN YOU SINCE MY VISIT TO DR. EINMUG IN THE DELTA DIMENSION!*
HALLO, MICKEY! HOW ISS TRICKS?
*SEE MICKEY MOUSE ADVENTURES #11! — ED.

THIS ***IS*** A SURPRISE! WHAT BRINGS YOU HERE, ATOMO?
DER DOCTOR SENT ME ON ***HOLIDAY!*** I FIGURED I'D VISIT YOU!

WHAT'S THIS?! AT EXACTLY THE MOMENT THAT MICKEY UNEARTHS THE POUCH...

?
AHH-ROOOOOOM PAAAAH!

FIRST MIDGETS, NOW CAVEMEN? WHAT DID I EAT?!

CIRCUS SMIRKUS!
• Sensational Sights to See! •
GRAND OPENING TODAY!

HAW! FOR A MINUTE, I THOUGHT I'D FALLEN OFF THE TURNIP WAGON!

MICKEY AND ATOMO MAKE AN ODD DISCOVERY!
C'MON IN, PAL! FIRST WE'LL GET THIS THING CLEANED OFF—

THEN WE'LL SEE IF WE CAN LEARN ANYTHING NEW ABOUT ITS ORIGINS!
ODD INDEED!

JUST THINK, ATOMO! THIS POUCH COULD BE A VITAL LINK TO TIMES PAST!
HM! "VITAL LINK," YOU SAY?

...ATOMO? WHY THE SPIT-TAKE?
ZING! ZAZZ! IT ISS NOT SPIT! I'M BLOWING MINE MESONS OVER IT!
ZING! ZAZZ!

DER MESONS HELP ME CARBON-DATE DER LEATHER'S AGE... DOWN TO DER MONTH!

ATOMO, THAT'S AMAZING!
DANKE! 0.071 ≥ 82 - √12 (COS β + SIN ∝) Δ/π = ...

BLEEP! DERE! DER POUCH ISS EXACTLY 15,372 YEARS UND FOUR MONTHS OLD!
SWEET! NOW THAT'S WHAT I CALL PRECISE RECKONI—

JIMINY CRICKETS! 15,372 YEARS??!

YE CATS! THIS DILLY-WHOPPER DATES BACK TO PALEO-INDIAN DAYS! BUT—HOW COULD LEATHER POSSIBLY LAST THAT LONG?

IT'S THE FIND OF THE CENTU
GIFF IT HERE! HAFF YOU SEEN ITS ODD MARKINGS?

LET US PEEK AT DER STRANGE TREASURES DOT LIE INSIDE!

ELEVEN PUMPKIN SEEDS!...
HMF! LOOKS LIKE TRASH, NOT TREASURE!

AHH-ROOOOOOMPAAAH!

AHH-ROOOOOOMPAAAH!
VOT ISS DOT AWFUL RACKET?
AW, PROB'LY THE TRASH COLLECTOR!

JOOST IN TIME! AUF WIEDER-SEHEN!
WHA— ATOMO, WAIT!

I DIDN'T MEAN IT REALLY WAS TRASH! *PUFF!*

SORRY, MISTER! MY PAL DIDN'T REALIZE WHAT HE'D DONE!

15,372 YEARS... ATOMO, THIS PROVES EVERYTHING! DO YOU KNOW WHAT THIS BAG IS?
BLEEP! COW REMAINS?

HOLD THE PHONE! THAT GUY IN THE GARDEN...THAT WASN'T THE TRASH COLLECTOR! HE ALMOST LOOKED LIKE...NO, IT COULDN'T BE!

VANISHED IN THE BAT OF AN EYE! WHO WAS THAT STRANGE FELLA?

LATER ON!
WHERE ARE WE GOINK, MICKEY?
TO A REAL ANTIQUE DEALER! MY FRIEND CHIEF O'HARA HAS A COUSIN WHO CAN PROB'LY HELP!
1313

HEATH O'HARA III
Antiques Bought & Sold
HERE WE GO!

CAREFUL, CHAPS! YOU'RE TREADING ON THE ORIGINAL STAIRCASE OF ADMIRAL NELSON'S FLAGSHIP!

YOU MUST BE MICHAEL! COUSIN SEAMUS HAS TOLD ME ALL ABOUT YOU!

UH, "MICKEY." I—
NOW MORTY, I SIMPLY MUST SHOW YOU MY RAREST ANTIQUITIES!

THIS MULTILINGUAL DICTIONARY DATES ALL THE WAY BACK TO THE TOWER OF BABEL! ISN'T THAT SPIFFY?

2,000 YEARS OF EGYPTIAN PYRAMIDS WERE BASED ON THIS SCALE MODEL! ISN'T THAT DELICIOUS?
?

THIS MUSKET BALL HAILS FROM THE REVOLUTIONARY WAR! ISN'T THAT FANTABULOUS, MANFRED?

AND THIS...BLAH, BLAH...
"MICKEY!"
MR. O'HARA, I—
ZIZZ!
ZAZZ!
AUTHENTIC MING DYNASTY VASE
Circa 1423 A. D.

NOW JUST OVER HERE, MONTY...
"MICKEY!" YIKES! CALM DOWN, MISTER!

YOUR COLLECTION'S SWELL AN' ALL, BUT I ONLY REALLY CAME HERE...
AUTHENTIC MING DYNASTY VASE
Circa 1423 A. D.
POSTWAR CANDY DISH
MADE IN TAIWAN

...TO ASK YOU FOR YOUR APPRAISAL OF THIS POUCH!
OH...IS THAT ALL?

AHEM! HOW ANTICLIMACTIC! THIS RATHER SMELLY...BAUBLE... IS WORTH EXACTLY NOTHING!

BUT MY PAL ATOMO SAYS IT'S 15,372 YEARS OLD!
OH! AND I SUPPOSE YOU KNOW ITS MONTH AND DATE OF MANUFAC-TURE TOO!
BLEEP! SURE!

I'M SORRY, MARTIN, BUT I'VE NO TIME TO WASTE ON SUCH GAUDY TRINKETS!
"MICKEY!" C'MON, ATOMO! WE'LL GO ASK SOMEONE ELSE!

CAREFUL, MICKEY! YOU'RE DROPPING DER PUMPKIN SEEDS!
AW, NUTS...

P-PUH-PUMPKIN SEEDS?!!

BUMPIN' PURPLE UGLIES! IT CAN'T BE! EXACTLY ELEVEN IN COUNT?
Y-YEAH! WHAT'S UP, MR. O'HA—

MERCIFUL KITTENS UP A GUM TREE! TO THINK I NEARLY SENT YOU AWAY!
NAPOLEON'S TINY CHAIR (CUTE BUT REDUNDANT)

HEATH O'HARA RECOVERS FROM HIS SHOCK TO WEAVE A BAFFLING TALE!
MEN, YOU HAVE STUMBLED ON THE SOLUTION TO A GREAT MYSTERY—THE BEGINNINGS OF NATIVE AMERICA!

PRIOR TO COLUMBUS OR EVEN ERICSON, THE MISNAMED "INDIANS" HAD ALREADY SETTLED OUR CONTINENT!

COMPARE THESE TWO IMAGES AND YOU WILL NOTE A STRIKING RESEMBLANCE!
1000 B. C.
EARLY AMERICAN
1000 B. C.
MONGOL PEASANT

WE BELIEVE THAT THE DAWN OF HISTORY SAW MASS MIGRATION OVER AN ICE BRIDGE...FROM THE TIP OF ASIA ONTO WHAT IS TODAY ALASKA!
ASIA
ALASKA
NORTH PACIFIC
NORTH AMERICA

I'VE HEARD ABOUT THAT THEORY! BUT WHAT ROLE DO MY POUCH AND ELEVEN STALE PUMPKIN SEEDS PLAY?

WELL...YEARS AGO, A CHEYENNE CHIEFTAIN SOLD ME THIS—AN ANCIENT ILLUMINATED COWHIDE PICTURING THE MIGRA-TION!

SEE? IT DEPICTS MONGOL MIGRANTS VISITING A WATERY LANDMARK EN ROUTE!

TO MARK THEIR FIRST ARRIVAL TO THIS "NEW WORLD," THEY BURIED A WONDROUS TREASURE IN A DEEP PIT!

BY MEANS OF A PRIMITIVE BUT INGENIOUS MECHANISM, THE PIT WAS SECURED AGAINST THIEVES!

SUPPOSEDLY ELEVEN PUMPKIN SEEDS WERE THE KEYS TO RE-OPENING THE PIT! STORED IN AN INDESTRUCTIBLE LEATHER POUCH...

...ASSEMBLED WITH A MAGIC GOLD SEWING NEEDLE!

THIS IS THAT POUCH! IT CAN FIND US THE TREASURE—AND PERHAPS EVEN THE NEEDLE, HISTORY'S OLD-EST GOLD ARTIFACT!
RATTLE!
RATTLE!

OMIGOSH! PROOF OF EARLY AMERICA'S ORIGINS! BUT HOW CAN WE LOCATE THE PIT?

THAT'S THE BEAUTY OF THE BAG...A **PERFECT MAP** OF ALASKAN TERRAIN! MY GUESS: THE **NORTHERN SLOPE!**

HOT DOG! IT'S TIME FOR A **TREASURE HUNT!**
JOLLY GOOD! I SEE WHY SEAMUS LIKES YOU!
WOW!

FOLLOW ME, MATTHEW! I HAVE ALL THAT WE'LL NEED IN THE NEXT ROOM!
"MICKEY!" AND THANK YOU, SIR!

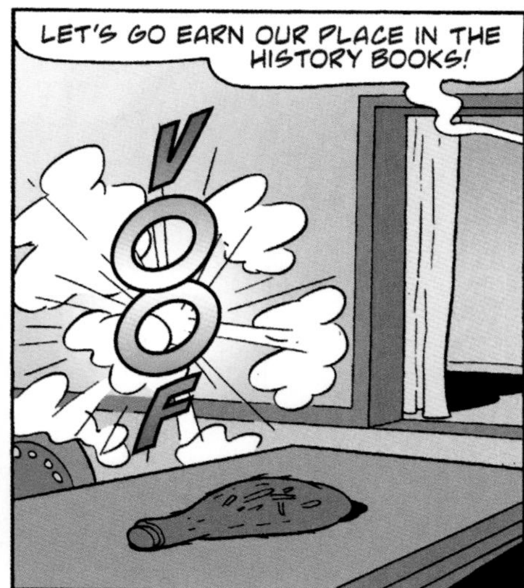
LET'S GO EARN OUR PLACE IN THE HISTORY BOOKS!
VOOF

WITH THESE WARM THREADS, ICE AND COLD SHALL BE BUT A MERE TRIFLE!
ROOOOOMPAAAH!
AND HOW!
BLEEP!

SAY, MEL...WHAT IS THAT AWFUL RACKET?
"MICKEY!" AWFUL RA—?
"ROOMPAH!"
OH, NO!

HOPPING YELLOW BLIMEYS! THE POUCH IS GONE!
OW-W! I KNEW IT!
ACH! MICKEY, LOOK!

FIGURES! IT'S THE WEIRDO FROM MY FRONT YARD!
SNATCHING AWAY OUR KEY TO NATIVE AMERICAN PREHISTORY!

OH, DEAR! IF HE ES-CAPES, ALL IS LOST!
HEY! WAIT! HOLD IT!
CRA-A-SH!

I SAID WAIT!
SCREECH—
GROAN!
SCRATCH!

CRACK!
WHAT?!
THE STAIRS!

THIS RATTLETRAP IS FALLING APART!
SKRASH!
BOOM!
PHOOEY ON YOUR CHEAP WOOD, ADMIRAL NELSON!

HERE! USE THIS PHOENICIAN SAIL-ROPE!
IT'S TOO STEEP TO CLIMB!
HURRY!

AND TOO OLD TO HOLD US ALL!
SNAP!
THUD!

TRY THESE ANCIENT PRE-COLOMBIAN VASES...
PANT! ALMOST... MADE IT...

AWP! NO DICE!
#$!% USELESS AN-TIQUES!
SKRANCH!!
BLEEP!

YEESH! YOUR SHOP'S STARTING TO LOOK LIKE WORLD WAR FOUR!
IT'S NOT IMPORTANT! THAT TREASURE IS EVERYTHING!
BLEEP!
HERE ISS HOW WE GET OUT!
CATAPULT CIRCA 1500 A. D.

HEATH O'HARA III
Antiques Bought & Sold
?

SIR, HAVE YOU SEEN A BIZARRE CHAP TRAIPSING ABOUT?
FUZZY CLOTHES, BIG NOSE...

UH, A "FUZZY" GUY HEADED THAT WAY THREE MINUTES AGO!
QUICKLY, MOE! TO YOUR CAR!

"BIZARRE," EH? AND THOSE GUYS THINK THEY'RE NORMAL?!

HE CAN'T HAVE GONE FAR!
FASTER!
WE'LL GET HIM!
1313

THERE'S THE CHURL UP AHEAD!

STOP THE CAR, MAX! WE'LL COL-LAR HIM ON FOOT!
"MICKEY!" NOW TO TO SEE WHAT'S WHAT!

THAT ALLEY IS A ***DEAD END!***
WE'VE GOT HIM NOW! ***HALT,*** RASCAL!
WAIT!

HERE'S WHERE YOU GET YOURS, SKIPPY!
HAND OVER THAT POU—

SLAM!

VISIT ALASKA!
North to the Future

AM I NUTS...OR DID OUR "CAVEMAN" JUST VANISH INTO THIN AIR?!
"VISIT ALASKA?!" IRONY, GO TO POT!

THIS IS A DISASTER!
NO POUCH! NO TREASURE! NO HOPE!

153 CENTURIES OF EARLY AMERICAN HISTORY VANISH INTO AN ALLEY! I FEEL SICK!
GET IN LINE, BROTHER!
I HAFF AN IDEA!

IT ISS NOT MUCH, BUT I CAN RECONSTRUCT DER MAP WITH MINE MESONIC MEMORY...

HUH? YOU CAN WHAT?!
AFTER I CHARGE MINESELF UP! MINE ENERGY ISS A LITTLE BIT LOW!

ATOMO, WE'LL GIVE YOU ENOUGH ENERGY TO POWER DETROIT!
LOOK, MILTON! A **CAFÉ!**
Chez la Froo-Froo

WAITER!
YAHS!
HURRY! WE'RE IN A RUSH!

OUR PRECOCIOUS YOUNG FRIEND NEEDS AN ENERGY BOOST, POST-HASTE!
YAHS!
Menu

I SUGGEST BRAISED QUAIL KNEES WITH TRUFFLE AU GRATIN AND VICHYSSOISE!
UM, SIR...I NEED **ELECTRICAL** ENERGY!
Menu

HMPH! DO I LOOK LIKE **CALISOTA POWER?** 110 OR 220 VOLTS, BOY?
220, PLEASE! DANKE, HERR WAITER!

OF ALL THE PECULIAR SIGHTS TO SEE...
NOT SO PECULIAR IF YOU'RE A SUPERSIZED **ATOM!**

SLURP!
ZING!!!
ZAZZ!
ZIZZ!
GULP!

-BLEEP!- AH, TASTES LIKE DER CHICKENS!...SHALL WE, CHUMS?
AND HOW, ATOMO! LET'S DO THIS!

THAT MESONIC MEMORY SURE IS SOMETHING!

HE DID IT! HE DID IT!
GO, ATOMO BLEEP-BLEEP!

HEY, MON-SEWER! HOW ABOUT THE CHECK?

-SIGH!- A BUCK FIFTY PLUS TAX...SIR!
THE DING-DONGS YOU MEET IN A JOB LIKE THIS!
-HEH!-
THANKS, MISTER!

MEN, IT IS ESSENTIAL THAT WE REACH ALASKA BEFORE OUR VANISHING BANDIT!
BUT IMMEDIATE FLIGHTS COST AN ARM AND A LEG!

IF WE STILL HAD MY POUCH, I COULD CONVINCE PROFESSOR DUSTIBONES TO LOAN US A PRIVATE PLANE! BUT WITHOUT IT—

MERRILL, MY BOY, YOU JUST SOLVED OUR PROBLEM!
"MICKEY!" I DID?
1313

YES! A COLLEGE CHUM OF MINE OWNS AN AERONAUTICS MUSEUM!
SWEET! SO YOU CAN GET US A PRIVATE PLANE!
BLEEP!
1313

WHOM DO YOU SUPPOSE OUR THIEF IS, MERCER?
"MICKEY!" DUNNO FOR SURE...

"BUT MY GUT TELLS ME THE GUY MAY BE SMARTER THAN WE'RE GIVING HIM CREDIT FOR!"

A LITTLE LATER!
AERONAUTICS MUSEUM
1313
PULL IN HERE, MAYNARD! IT'S BEEN AGES SINCE I'VE SEEN OLD BRUTO!

BRUTO FILIBUSTER, YOU OLD SCAMP!
HEATH O'HARA... AS I LIVE AN' BREATHE!

REMEMBER THE TIME WE PUT ITCHING POWDER IN THE SWIM TEAM'S SHORTS? RIOT!
OR WHEN WE LET GREASED PIGS LOOSE IN THE CAFETERIA!

BRUTO, I MUST GET TO REMOTEST ALASKA AS QUICKLY AS POSSIBLE! GOT AN IRON BIRD FOR ME?
ON MY HONOR, HEATH!

YOU GET MY BEST MODEL... I CALL 'ER THE "SCREAMING METAL DAREDEVIL!" RUNS ON KEROSENE AN' SKUNK OIL!
SPLENDID, PAL!
GOOD GOSH!

SOON!
GODSPEED, FELLERS! HAVE FUN IN ALASKA!
ARRIVEDERCI!
BOOM!
CRASH!
BANG!

ISN'T IT UPLIFTING TO FLY THIS WONDER?
YEAH! IT'S A WONDER THAT IT'S LIFTING US UP!
BLEAT!
BONK!
BANG!
ROAR!
SCREEEEEECCH!

AND SO OUR HEROES FLY TO THE ALASKAN WASTES UNAWARE OF THEIR STRANGE CARGO...

WHO IS THIS MYSTERY MAN? WHAT IS THE SECRET OF THE POUCH? WILL MICKEY, ATOMO, AND HEATH REACH THE TREASURE FIRST? ALL THAT AND MORE TO BE FOUND NEXT ISSUE IN... "THE SACRED SPRING OF SEASONS PAST" —PART 2!
To Be Concluded!

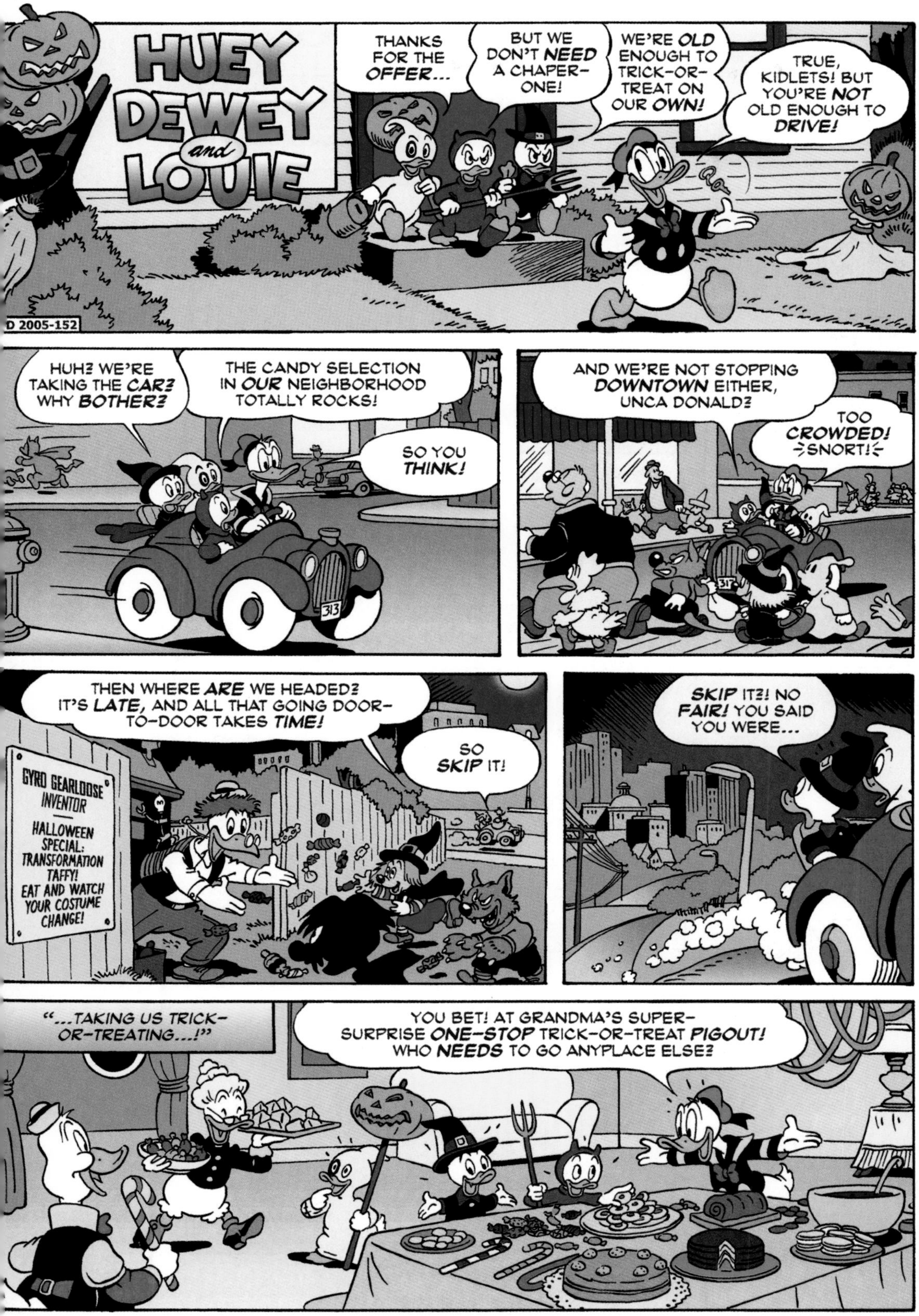

HUEY DEWEY and LOUIE

THANKS FOR THE *OFFER...*
BUT WE DON'T **NEED** A CHAPERONE!
WE'RE *OLD* ENOUGH TO TRICK-OR-TREAT ON OUR *OWN!*
TRUE, KIDLETS! BUT YOU'RE ***NOT*** OLD ENOUGH TO ***DRIVE!***

D 2005-152

HUH? WE'RE TAKING THE ***CAR?*** WHY ***BOTHER?***
THE CANDY SELECTION IN ***OUR*** NEIGHBORHOOD TOTALLY ROCKS!
SO YOU ***THINK!***

AND WE'RE NOT STOPPING ***DOWNTOWN*** EITHER, UNCA DONALD?
TOO ***CROWDED!*** SNORT!

THEN WHERE ***ARE*** WE HEADED? IT'S ***LATE,*** AND ALL THAT GOING DOOR-TO-DOOR TAKES ***TIME!***
SO ***SKIP*** IT!
GYRO GEARLOOSE INVENTOR
HALLOWEEN SPECIAL: TRANSFORMATION TAFFY! EAT AND WATCH YOUR COSTUME CHANGE!

SKIP IT?! NO ***FAIR!*** YOU SAID YOU WERE...

"...TAKING US TRICK-OR-TREATING...!"
YOU BET! AT GRANDMA'S SUPER-SURPRISE ***ONE-STOP*** TRICK-OR-TREAT ***PIGOUT!*** WHO ***NEEDS*** TO GO ANYPLACE ELSE?

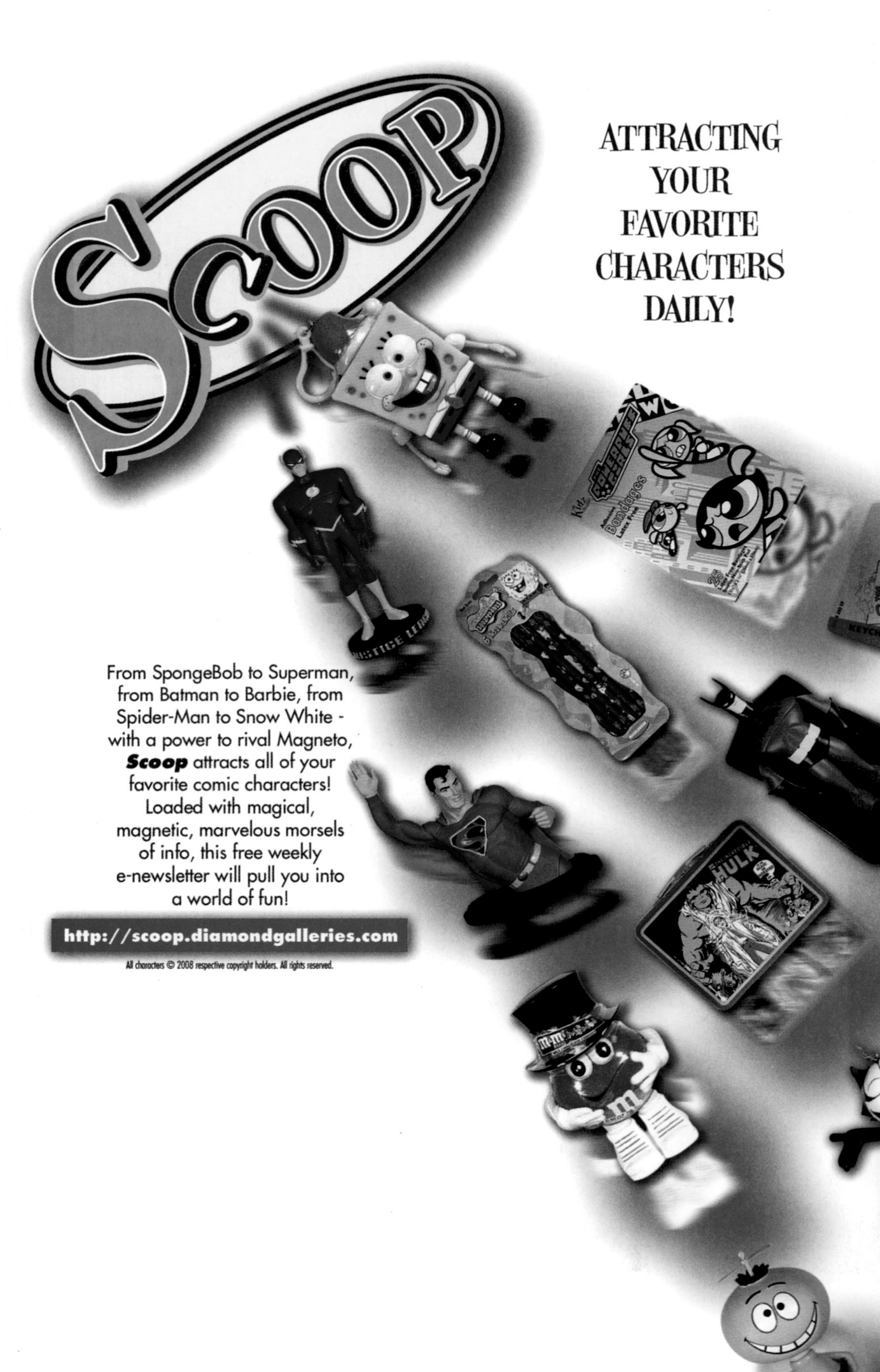
SCOOP
ATTRACTING
YOUR
FAVORITE
CHARACTERS
DAILY!
From SpongeBob to Superman,
from Batman to Barbie, from
Spider-Man to Snow White -
with a power to rival Magneto,
Scoop attracts all of your
favorite comic characters!
Loaded with magical,
magnetic, marvelous morsels
of info, this free weekly
e-newsletter will pull you into
a world of fun!
http://scoop.diamondgalleries.com
All characters © 2008 respective copyright holders. All rights reserved.

100 SECOND GRADE SKILLS

Thinking Kids®
Carson-Dellosa Publishing LLC
Greensboro, North Carolina

Thinking Kids®
Carson-Dellosa Publishing LLC
P.O. Box 35665
Greensboro, NC 27425 USA

ISBN 978-1-4838-3117-6
02-044178711

Table of Contents

Table of Contents

Skill 16: Adding 2-Digit Numbers

Directions: Follow the steps to add.

Step 1: Add the ones.

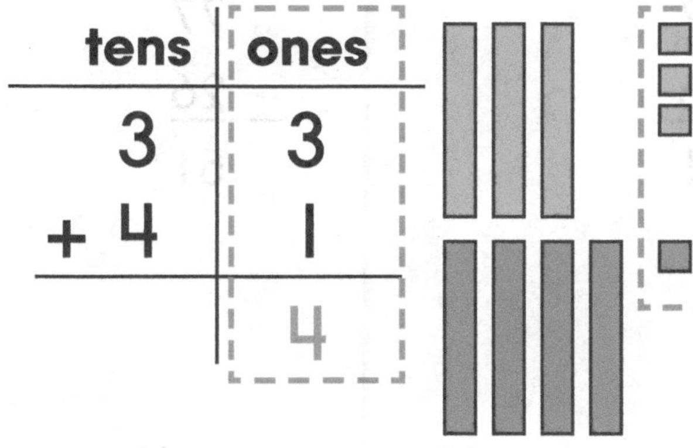

tens	ones
3	3
+ 4	1
	4

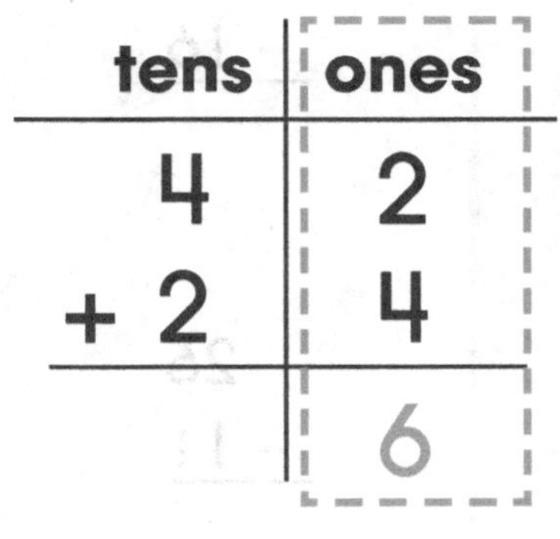

tens	ones
4	2
+ 2	4
	6

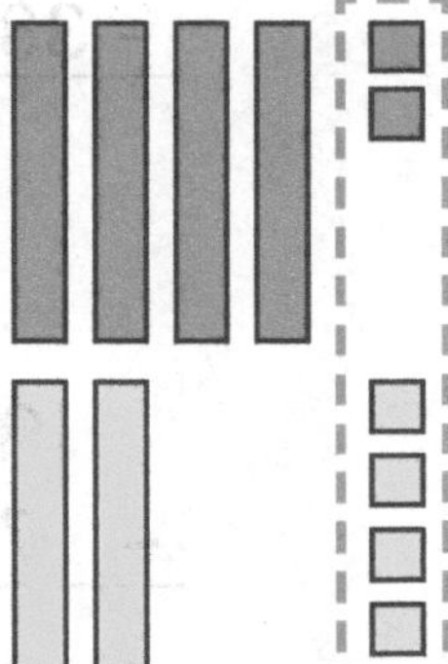

Step 2: Add the tens.

tens	ones
3	3
+ 4	1
7	4

tens	ones
4	2
+ 2	4
6	6

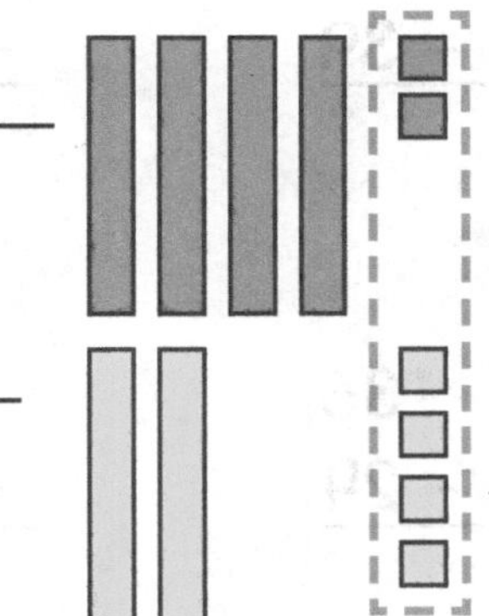

$$\begin{array}{r}24\\+\,62\\\hline\end{array}\qquad\begin{array}{r}72\\+\,11\\\hline\end{array}\qquad\begin{array}{r}38\\+\,61\\\hline\end{array}\qquad\begin{array}{r}11\\+\,26\\\hline\end{array}$$

$$\begin{array}{r}37\\+\,42\\\hline\end{array}\qquad\begin{array}{r}15\\+\,23\\\hline\end{array}\qquad\begin{array}{r}33\\+\,51\\\hline\end{array}\qquad\begin{array}{r}10\\+\,30\\\hline\end{array}$$

MATH

Skill 17: Subtracting 2-Digit Numbers

		First, subtract the ones.	Then, subtract the tens.
77 - 26	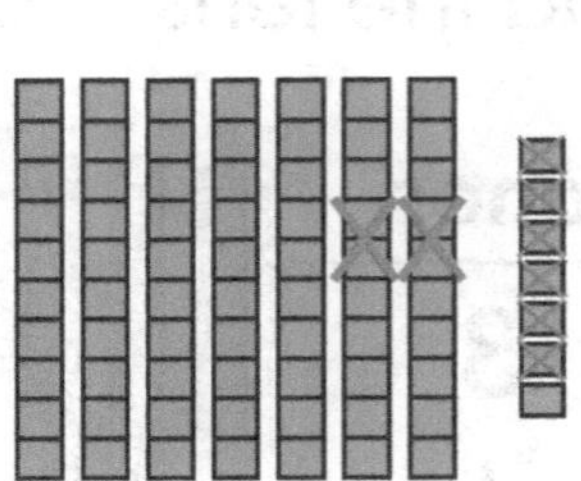	77 - 26 1	77 - 26 51

Directions: Subtract.

49 - 39 10	87 - 6	79 - 63	59 - 38	68 - 16
36 - 24	78 - 25	28 - 14	19 - 7	26 - 11
54 - 40	42 - 12	95 - 62	67 - 41	74 - 50
92 - 81	77 - 17	35 - 5	82 - 51	86 - 64

Skill 17: S btracting 2-Digit Numbers

Directions: Fo he steps to subtract.

Step 1: Subtrac ones.

Step 2: Subtract the tens.

tens	ones
2	8
– 1	4
	4

tens	ones
2	8
– 1	4
1	4

tens	ones
2	4
– 1	2
	2

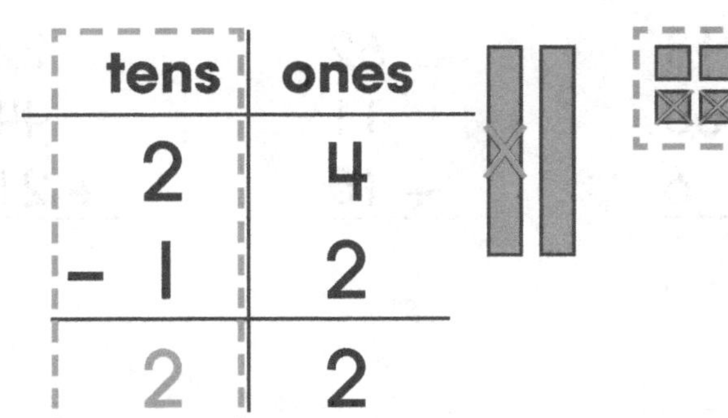

tens	ones
2	4
– 1	2
2	2

$$\begin{array}{r} 24 \\ -\ 12 \\ \hline \end{array} \qquad \begin{array}{r} 59 \\ -\ 34 \\ \hline \end{array} \qquad \begin{array}{r} 77 \\ -\ 44 \\ \hline \end{array} \qquad \begin{array}{r} 85 \\ -\ 24 \\ \hline \end{array}$$

$$\begin{array}{r} 57 \\ -\ 23 \\ \hline \end{array} \qquad \begin{array}{r} 87 \\ -\ 33 \\ \hline \end{array} \qquad \begin{array}{r} 61 \\ -\ 30 \\ \hline \end{array} \qquad \begin{array}{r} 96 \\ -\ 16 \\ \hline \end{array}$$

MATH

Skill 18: Adding Three Numbers

		Add the ones.	Add the tens.
23 44 + 12		23 44 + 12 9	23 44 + 12 79

Directions: Add.

13 50 + 6 69	62 11 + 15	22 44 + 21	30 10 + 9	22 32 + 42
44 23 + 20	16 40 + 12	71 12 + 4	33 20 + 6	12 20 + 33
12 40 + 4	36 20 + 13	25 32 + 1	11 16 + 20	32 12 + 22

Adding Three Numbers

Directions: Solve each problem.

Jesse has 11 .

Lynn has 13 . Paul has 25 .

How many  do they have in all? 

The toy store sold 13 in October,

16 in November, and 22  in December.

How many  did the toy store sell in all? ________

Tom puts 7 , 33, and

30  on shelves. How many toys

does Tom put on shelves in all? ________

The toy store has 33 , 25,

and 11 . How many of these toys

does the toy store have in all? ________

Andy has 14, Linda has 23,

and Jason has 30.

How many  do they have in all? ________

MATH

Skill

19: Counting and Writing 150–199

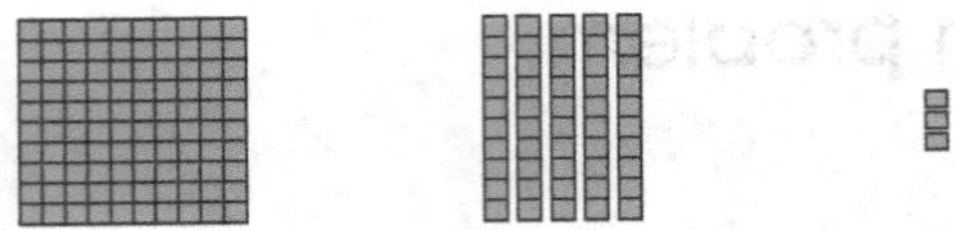

1 hundred + 5 tens + 3 ones = 153

Expanded Form: 100 + 50 + 3 = 153

Directions: Write the number and its expanded form.

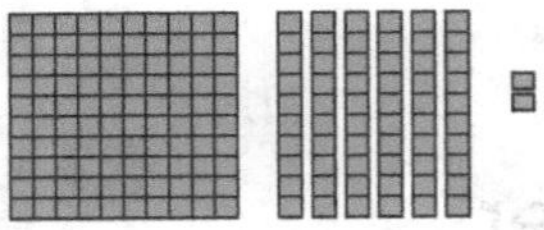

162

100 + 60 + 2 = 162

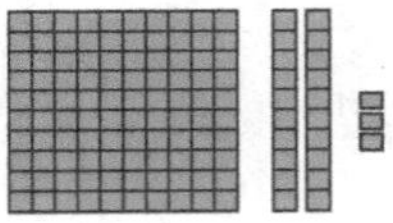

____

________ + ________ + ________ = ________

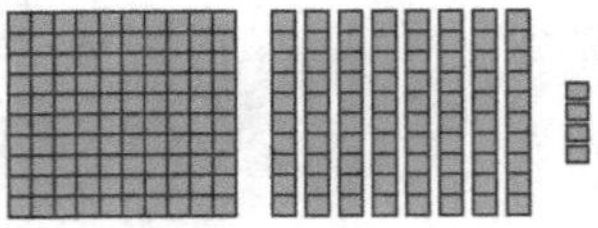

____

________ + ________ + ________ = ________

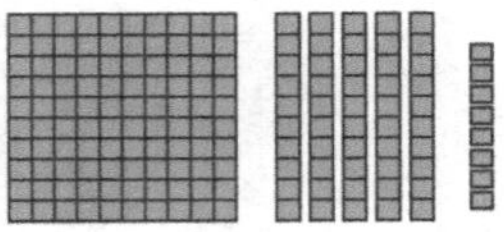

____

________ + ________ + ________ = ________

MATH

Skill 19: Counting and Writing 150–199

Directions: Write the number and its expanded form.

____

__________ + __________ + __________ = __________

____

__________ + __________ + __________ = __________

____

__________ + __________ + __________ = __________

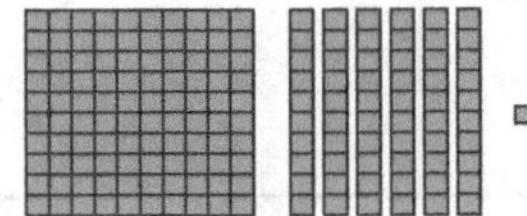

____

__________ + __________ + __________ = __________

Skill 20: Counting and Writing 200–399

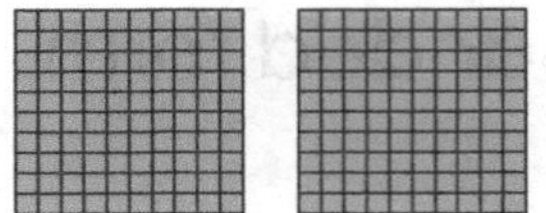

200
Number Name:
two hundred

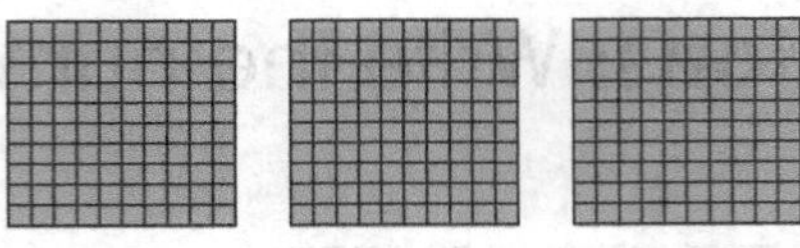

300
Number Name:
three hundred

Directions: Write the number and the number name.

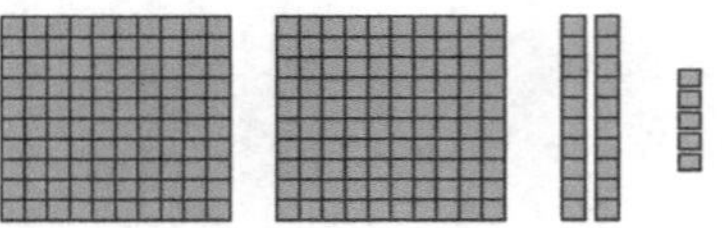

224

two hundred twenty-four

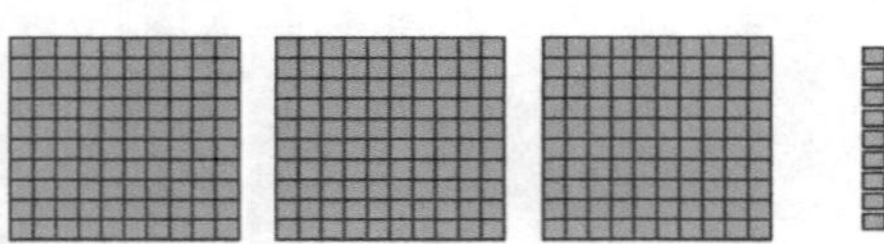

____

____

____

____

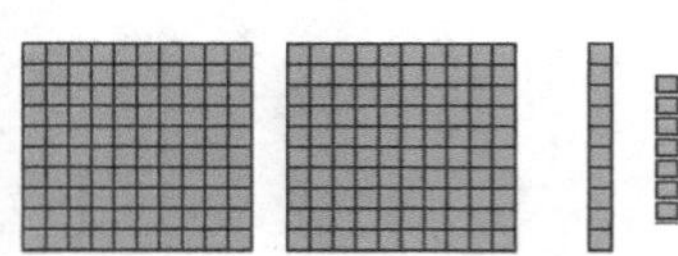

____

____

Skill 20: Counting and Writing 200–399

Directions: Write the number and the number name.

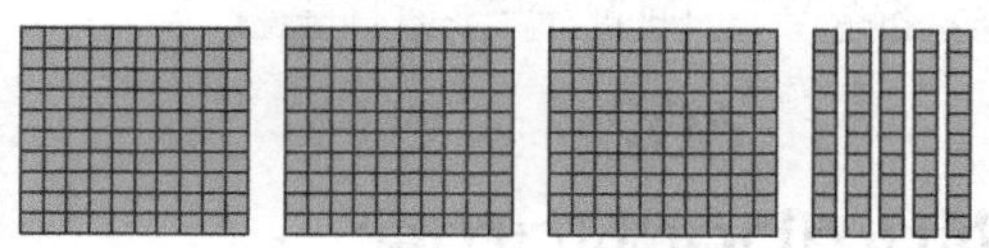

______

____

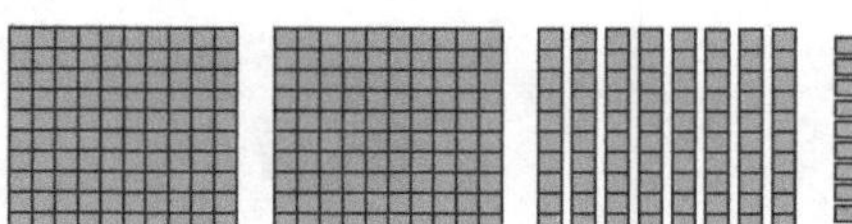

______

____

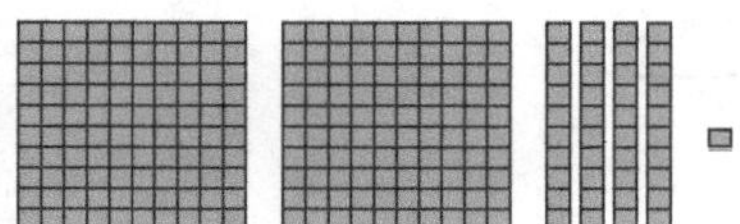

______

____

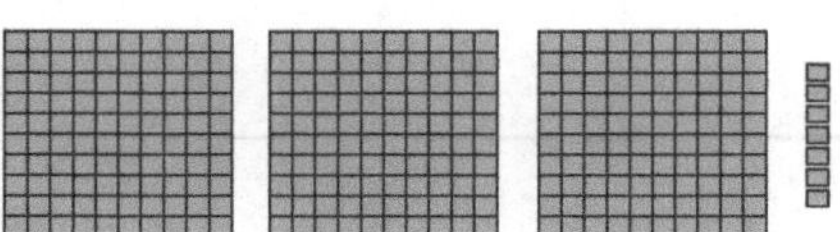

______

____

MATH

Skill 21: Counting and Writing 400–699

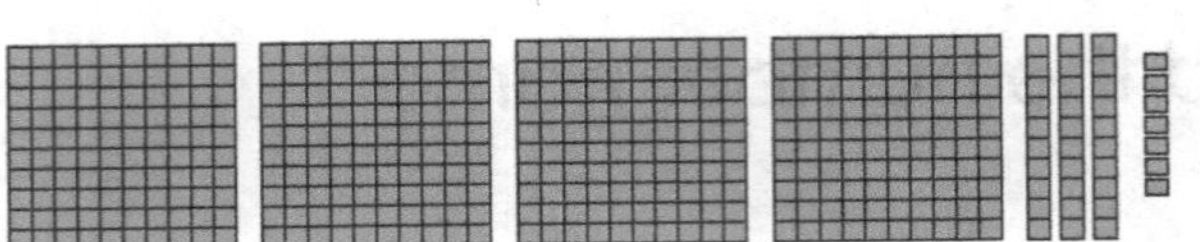

437
Number Name:
four hundred thirty-seven

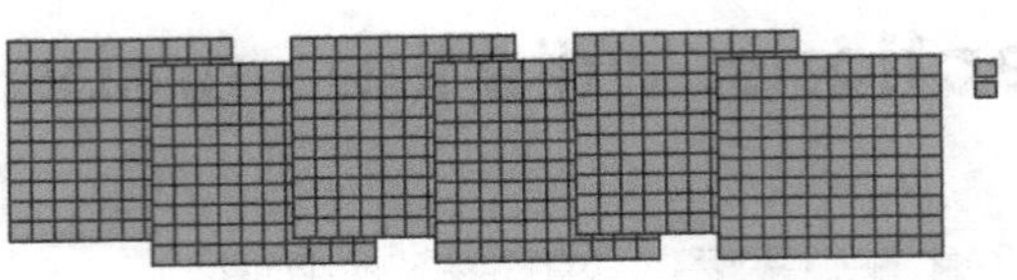

602
Number Name:
six hundred two

Directions: Write the number and the number name.

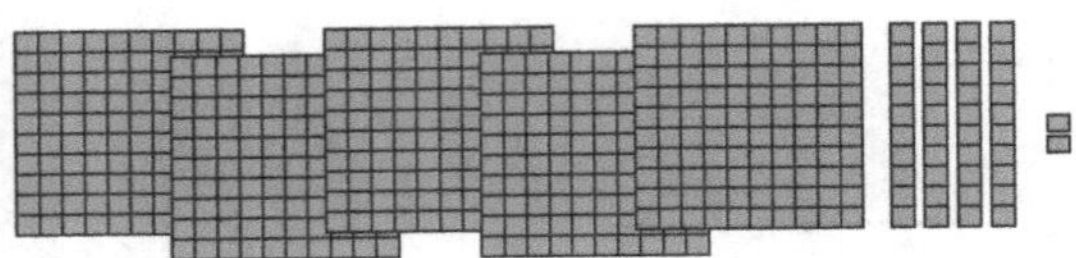

542 ________

five hundred forty-two ________

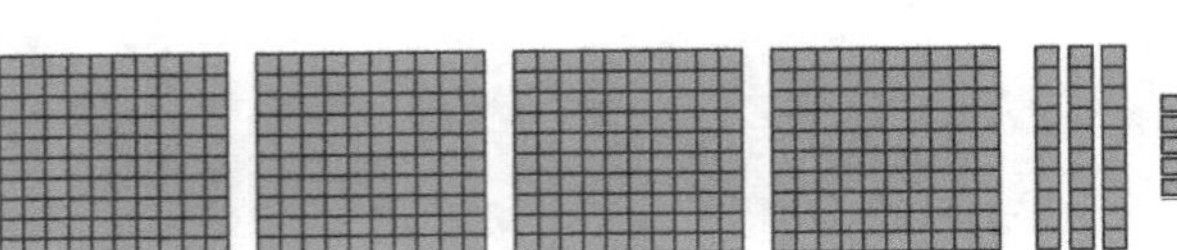

____

____

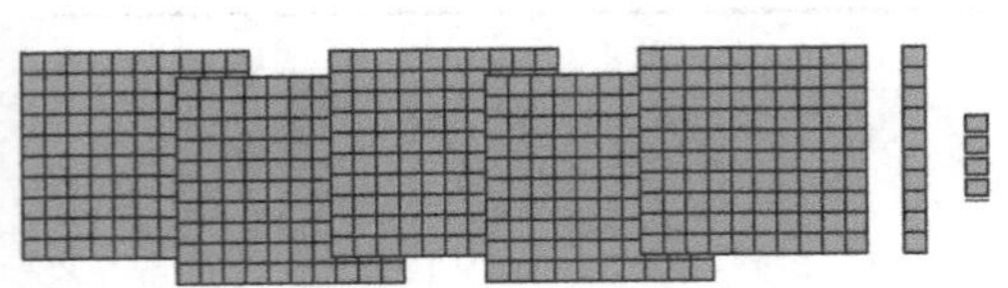

____

____

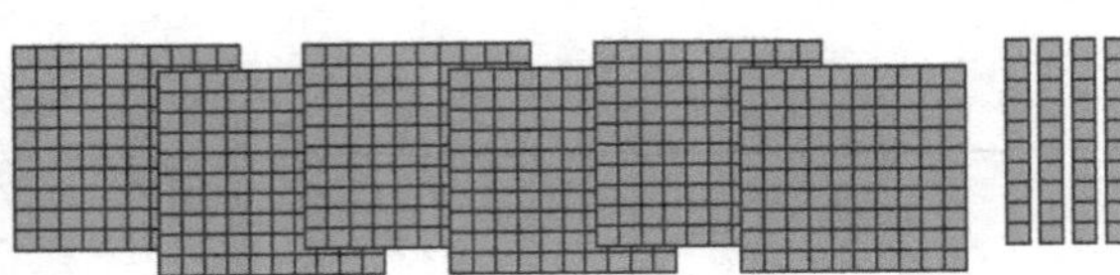

____

____

Skill 21: Counting and Writing 400–699

Directions: Write the number and the number name.

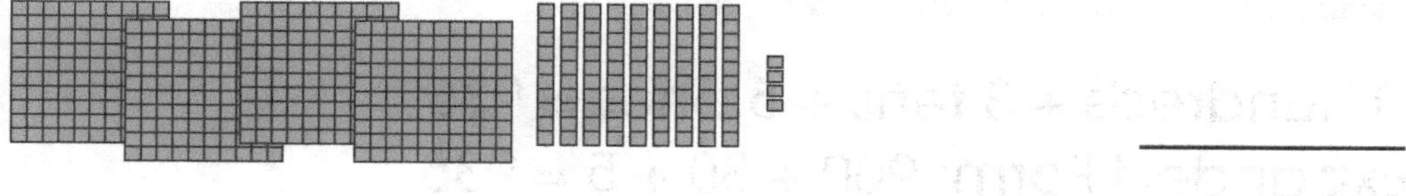

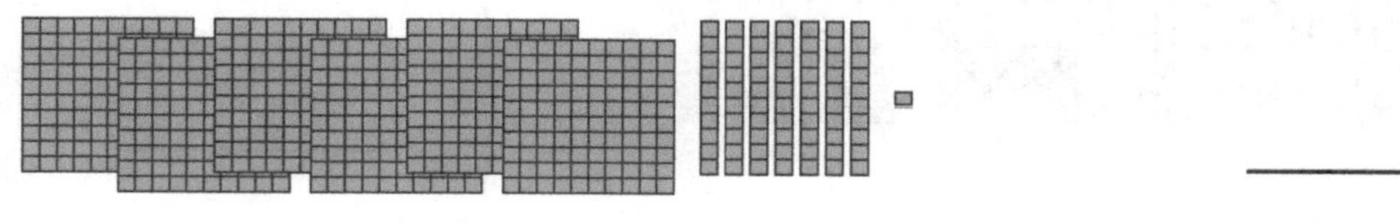

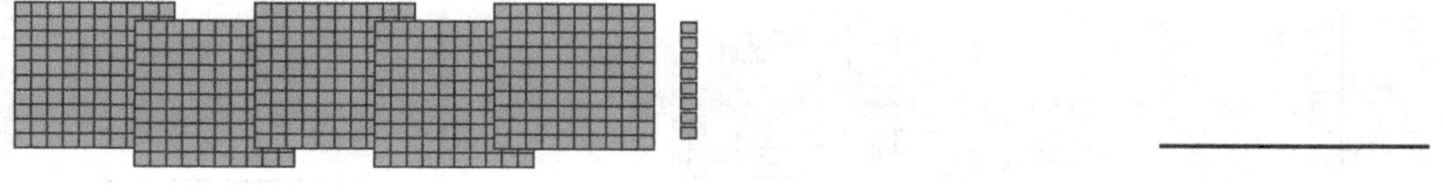

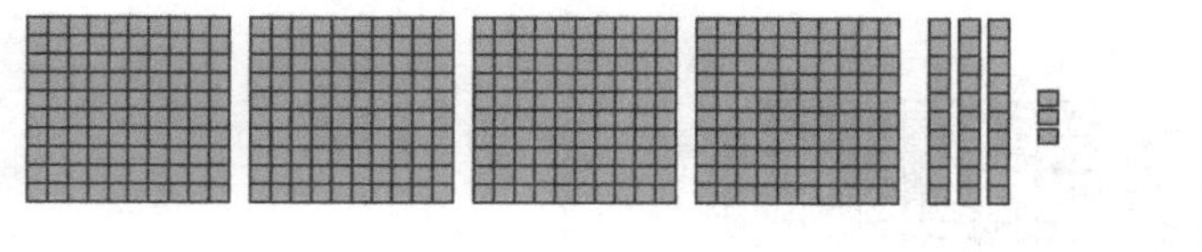

MATH

Skill 22: Counting and Writing 700–999

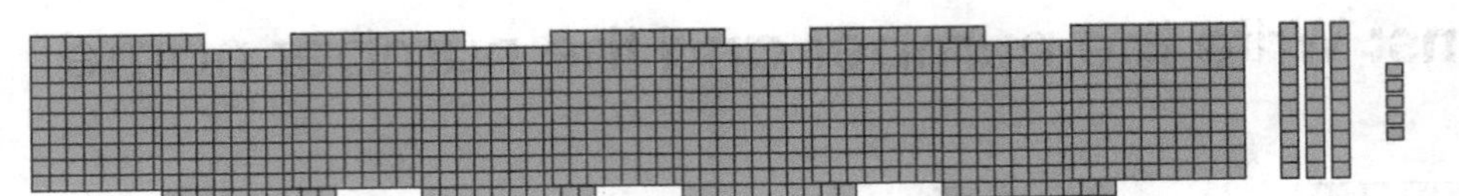

9 hundreds + 3 tens + 5 ones = 935
Expanded Form: 900 + 30 + 5 = 935

Directions: Write the number and its expanded form.

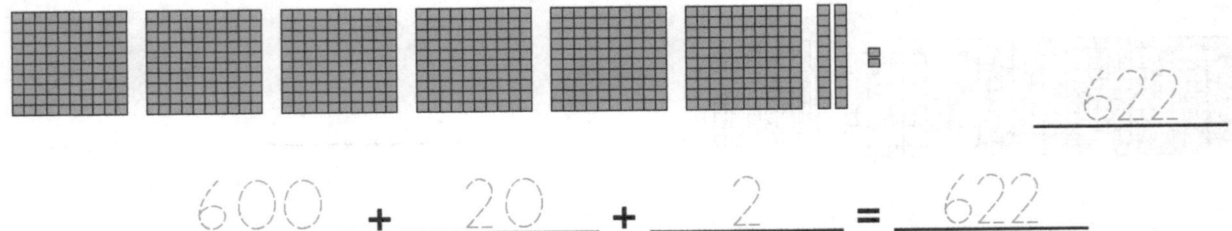

622

600 + 20 + 2 = 622

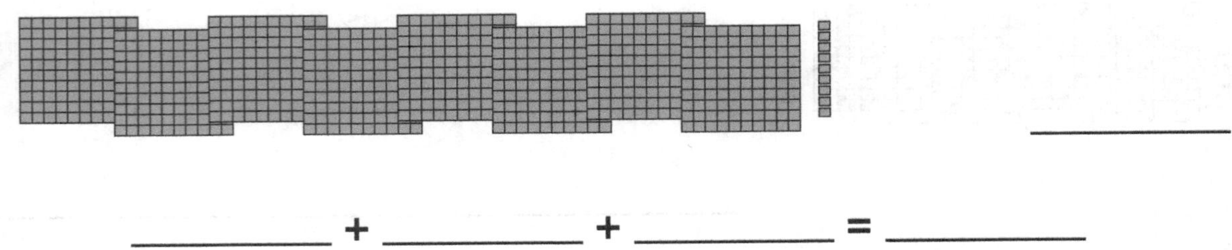

_____

_____ + _____ + _____ = _____

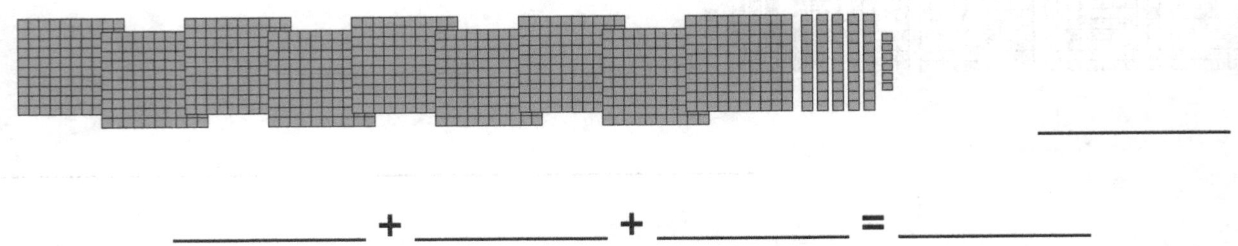

_____

_____ + _____ + _____ = _____

MATH

Skill 22: Counting and Writing 700–999

Directions: Write the number and its expanded form.

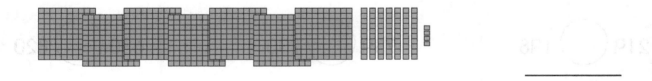

______

______ + ______ + ______ = ______

______

______ + ______ + ______ = ______

______

______ + ______ + ______ = ______

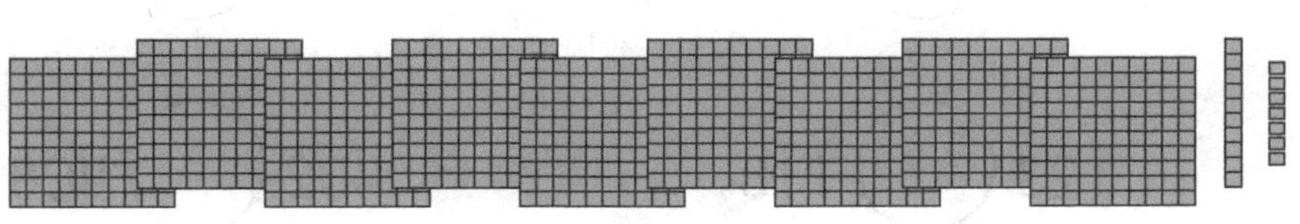

______

______ + ______ + ______ = ______

Skill 23: Comparing Numbers

403 (>) 362 Compare hundreds. 4 is greater than 3. 403 is greater than 362.

739 (<) 761 If hundreds are the same, compare tens. 3 is less than 6. 739 is less than 761.

801 (<) 803 If hundreds and tens are the same, compare ones. 1 is less than 3. 801 is less than 803.

Directions: Compare 3-digit numbers. Use > (greater than), < (less than), or = (equal to).

831 (<) 843	127 ( ) 119	504 ( ) 504
567 ( ) 564	306 ( ) 401	535 ( ) 535
219 ( ) 198	739 ( ) 730	630 ( ) 820
436 ( ) 379	923 ( ) 925	407 ( ) 610
354 ( ) 453	802 ( ) 792	236 ( ) 401
902 ( ) 911	123 ( ) 118	402 ( ) 408

MATH

Skill 23: Comparing Numbers

Directions: Write >, <, or = to compare the numbers.

886	◯	542	130	◯	13
119	◯	109	903	◯	309
984	◯	984	153	◯	153
578	◯	587	600	◯	300
907	◯	709	999	◯	799
534	◯	990	865	◯	568
760	◯	760	712	◯	233

Skill

24: Adding and Subtracting 3-Digit Numbers

Decompose numbers to help you add three-digit numbers.

```
                 210
               + 125
200 + 100 =      300
 10 +  20 =       30
  0 +   5 =        5
                 335
```

Decompose numbers or use other methods, like place value blocks, to help you subtract three-digit numbers.

```
                 465
               - 223
400 - 200 =      200
 60 -  20 =       40
  5 -   3 =        2
                 242
```

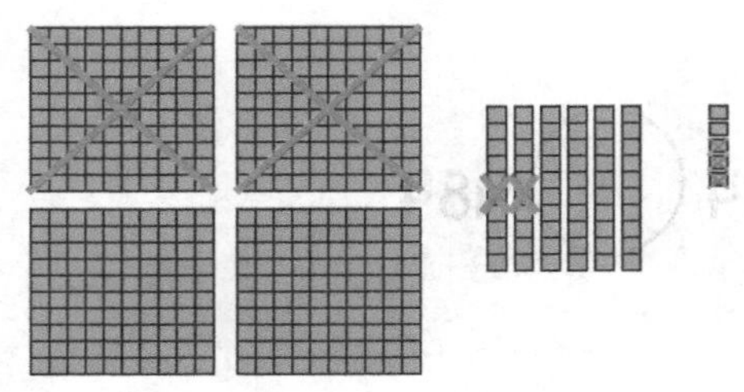

465 - 223 = 242

Directions: Solve each problem. Show your work.

```
  2 2 7
+ 1 3 1

_____ + _____ = _____
_____ + _____ = _____
_____ + _____ = _____
                _____
```

```
  3 3 1
+ 2 5 6

_____ + _____ = _____
_____ + _____ = _____
_____ + _____ = _____
                _____
```

MATH

Skill 24: Adding and Subtracting 3-Digit Numbers

Directions: Solve each problem. Show your work.

$$\begin{array}{r} 777 \\ -\ 211 \\ \hline \end{array} \qquad \begin{array}{r} 852 \\ -\ 751 \\ \hline \end{array}$$

$$\begin{array}{r} 516 \\ +\ 142 \\ \hline \end{array} \qquad \begin{array}{r} 427 \\ +\ 221 \\ \hline \end{array}$$

$$\begin{array}{r} 653 \\ -\ 412 \\ \hline \end{array} \qquad \begin{array}{r} 749 \\ -\ 513 \\ \hline \end{array}$$

$$\begin{array}{r} 688 \\ -\ 533 \\ \hline \end{array} \qquad \begin{array}{r} 495 \\ -\ 253 \\ \hline \end{array}$$

MATH

Skill 25: Checking Addition With Subtraction

To check

215 + 109 = 324,

subtract 109 from 324.

```
  215 <----┐
+ 109      |
  324      | These should be
- 109      | the same.
  215 <----┘
```

Directions: Add. Check each answer.

```
  157      625      312      710
+ 212    + 111    + 105    + 225
  369
- 212
  157
```

```
  301      461      712      351
+ 215    + 218    + 263    + 611
```

MATH

Skill 25: Checking Addition With Subtraction

Directions: Add. Check each answer.

714 + 291	317 + 111	581 + 318	300 + 547
612 + 319	863 + 112	411 + 120	425 + 444
459 + 130	603 + 202	252 + 130	711 + 148

Skill

26: Checking Subtraction With Addition

To check

982 − 657 = 325,

add 657 to 325.

$$\begin{array}{r} 982 \\ -\,657 \\ \hline 325 \\ +\,657 \\ \hline 982 \end{array}$$

These should be the same.

Directions: Subtract. Check each answer.

$$\begin{array}{r} 720 \\ -\,150 \\ \hline 570 \\ +\,150 \\ \hline 720 \end{array} \qquad \begin{array}{r} 423 \\ -\,197 \\ \hline \end{array} \qquad \begin{array}{r} 125 \\ -\,92 \\ \hline \end{array} \qquad \begin{array}{r} 983 \\ -\,657 \\ \hline \end{array}$$

$$\begin{array}{r} 300 \\ -\,179 \\ \hline \end{array} \qquad \begin{array}{r} 456 \\ -\,291 \\ \hline \end{array} \qquad \begin{array}{r} 119 \\ -\,104 \\ \hline \end{array} \qquad \begin{array}{r} 321 \\ -\,83 \\ \hline \end{array}$$

MATH

Skill 26: Checking Subtraction With Addition

Directions: Subtract. Check each answer.

$$\begin{array}{r} 592 \\ -463 \\ \hline \end{array} \qquad \begin{array}{r} 259 \\ -147 \\ \hline \end{array} \qquad \begin{array}{r} 519 \\ -120 \\ \hline \end{array} \qquad \begin{array}{r} 540 \\ -320 \\ \hline \end{array}$$

$$\begin{array}{r} 192 \\ -\ \ 86 \\ \hline \end{array} \qquad \begin{array}{r} 710 \\ -447 \\ \hline \end{array} \qquad \begin{array}{r} 683 \\ -419 \\ \hline \end{array} \qquad \begin{array}{r} 719 \\ -532 \\ \hline \end{array}$$

$$\begin{array}{r} 919 \\ -457 \\ \hline \end{array} \qquad \begin{array}{r} 687 \\ -250 \\ \hline \end{array} \qquad \begin{array}{r} 912 \\ -609 \\ \hline \end{array} \qquad \begin{array}{r} 542 \\ -327 \\ \hline \end{array}$$

MATH

Skill 27: Telling Time to the Hour

3 o'clock
3:00

Both clocks show 3 o'clock, or 3:00.

Directions: Write the time two ways.

7 o'clock

7 : 00

_____ o'clock

___:___

_____ o'clock

___:___

_____ o'clock

___:___

_____ o'clock

___:___

_____ o'clock

___:___

MATH

Skill 27: Telling Time to the Hour

Directions: Write the time two ways.

_____ o'clock

_____ : _____

_____ o'clock

_____ : _____

_____ o'clock

_____ : _____

_____ o'clock

_____ : _____

_____ o'clock

_____ : _____

_____ o'clock

_____ : _____

_____ o'clock

_____ : _____

_____ o'clock

_____ : _____

_____ o'clock

_____ : _____

MATH

MATH

Skill 28: Telling Time to the Half Hour

8:00
8 o'clock

8:30
half past 8

9:00
9 o'clock

Directions: Write the time two ways.

half past 4

4:30

half past ______

______ : ______

half past ______

______ : ______

half past ______

______ : ______

half past ______

______ : ______

half past ______

______ : ______

Skill 28: Telling Time to the Half Hour

Directions: Write the time two ways.

half past ______

___:___

half past ______

___:___

half past ______

___:___

half past ______

___:___

half past ______

___:___

half past ______

___:___

half past ______

___:___

half past ______

___:___

half past ______

___:___

MATH

Skill 29: Telling Time to the Quarter Hour

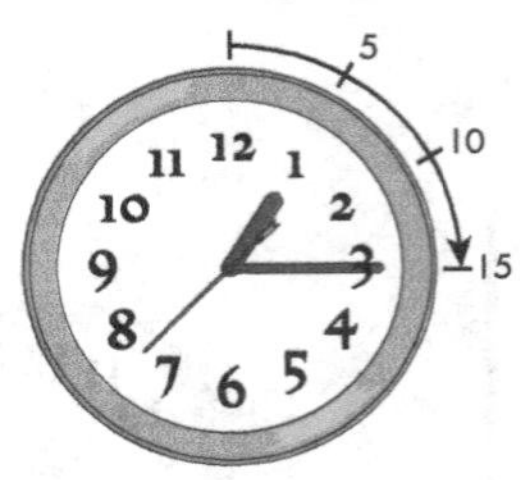

1:15
one fifteen

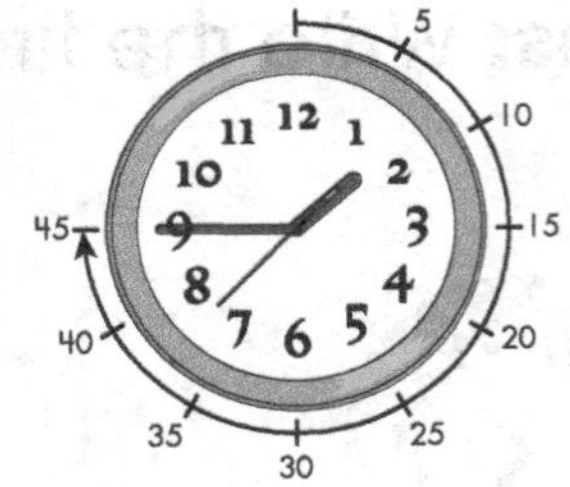

1:45
one forty-five

Directions: Read the time on the first clock. Write the same time on the second clock.

6:45

:

:

:

:

:

MATH

Skill 29: Telling Time to the Quarter Hour

Directions: Read the time on the first clock. Write the same time on the second clock.

Skill 30: Estimating Length in Inches

An **inch** is a unit of length.

Directions: Use the ruler to measure each object below to the nearest inch.

inches 1 2 3 4 5 6

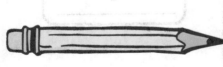

about ______ inches

about ______ inches

about ______ inches

about ______ inches

about ______ inches

about ______ inches

MATH

Skill 30: Estimating Length in Inches

Directions: Estimate how many inches long each object is.

inches	1	2	3	4	5	6

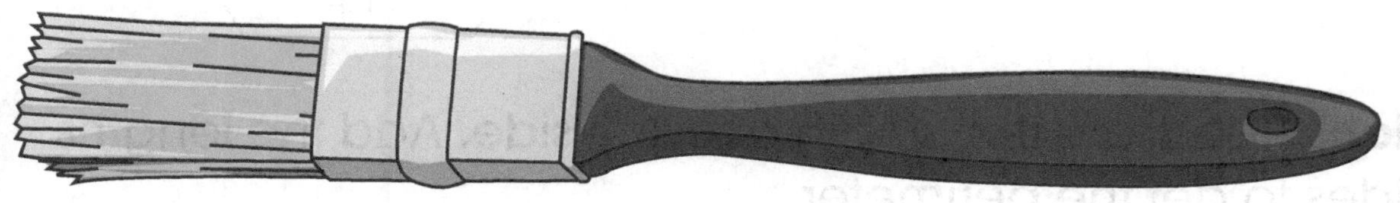

about ______ inches

about ______ inches

about ______ inches

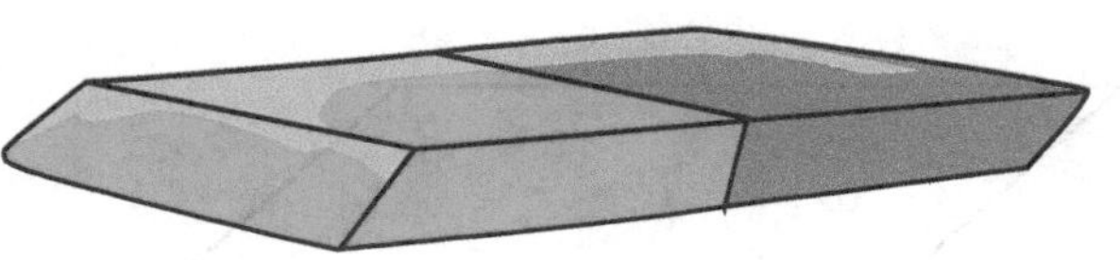

about ______ inches

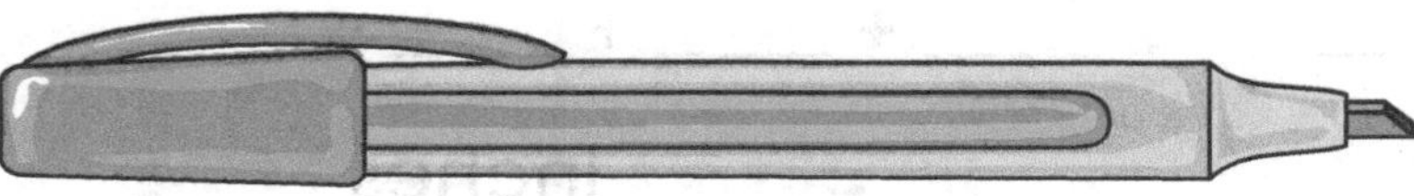

about ______ inches

MATH

Skill

31: Measuring Length in Inches

Perimeter is the length around an object.

The perimeter of this hexagon is
1 + 1 + 1 + 1 + 1 + 1 = 6 inches.

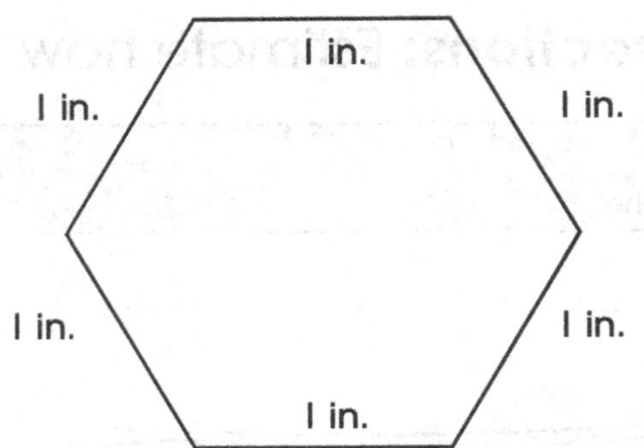

Directions: Measure the length of each side. Add the lengths of all sides to get the perimeter.

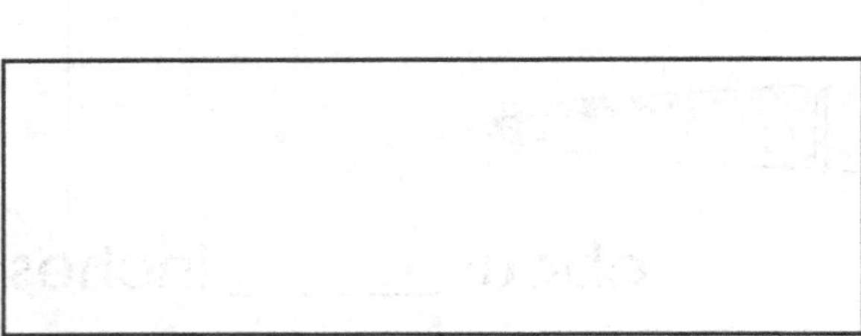

3 + 1 + 3 + 1
= 8 inches

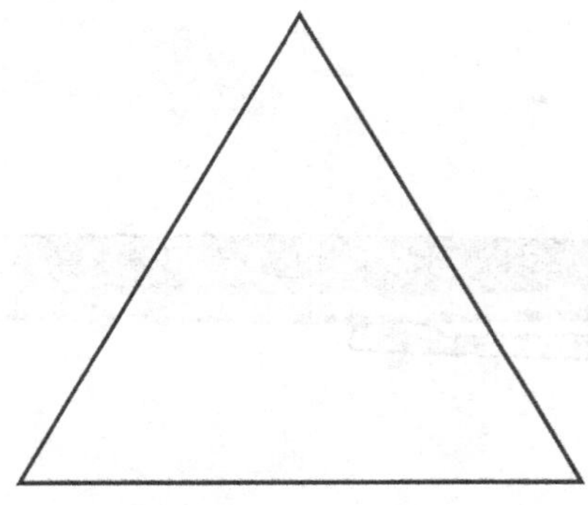

____ + ____ + ____
= ____ inches

____ + ____ + ____ + ____
= ____ inches

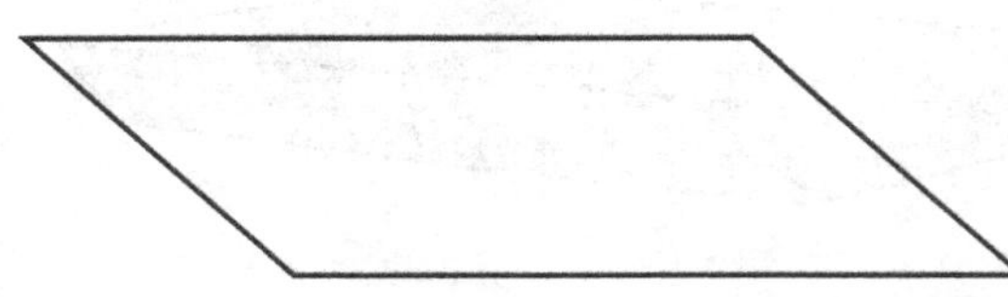

____ + ____ + ____ + ____
= ____ inches

MATH

Skill 31: Measuring Length in Inches

Directions: Write the length of each object in inches.

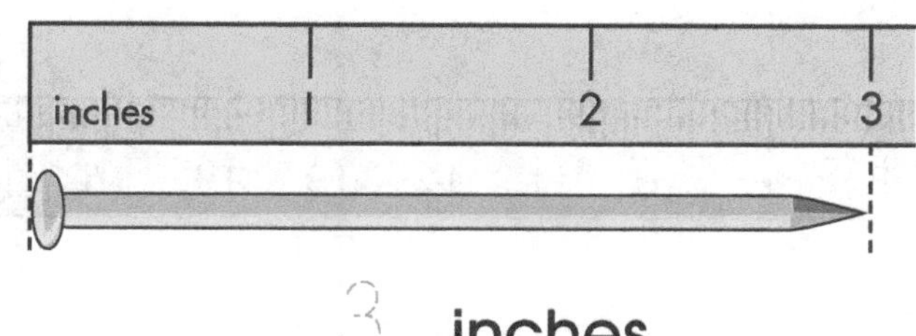

__3__ inches

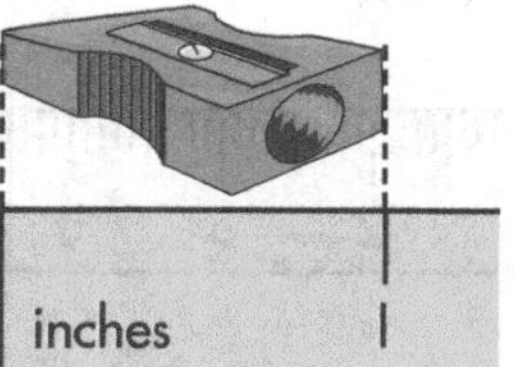

____ inches

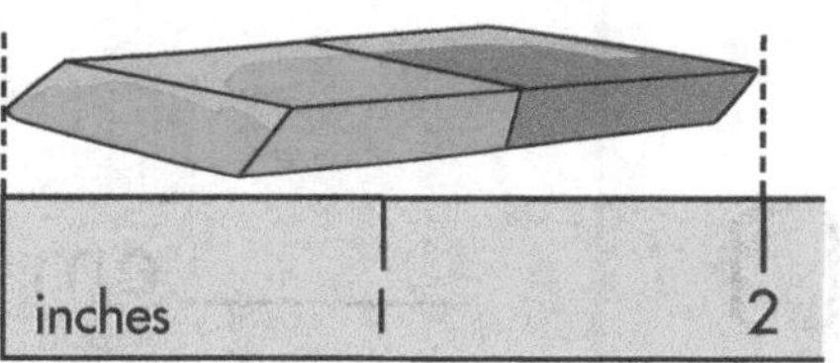

____ inches

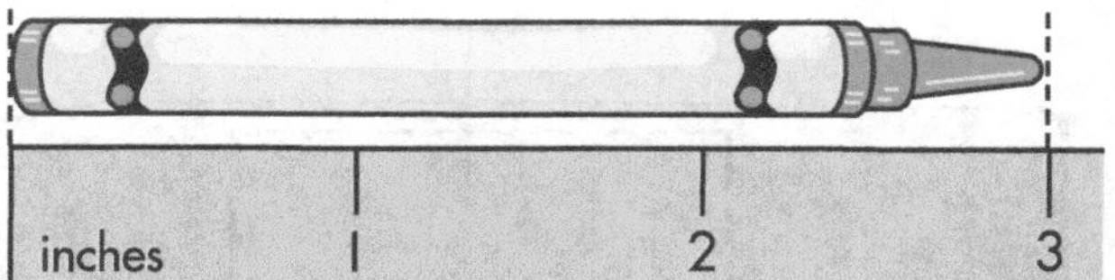

____ inches

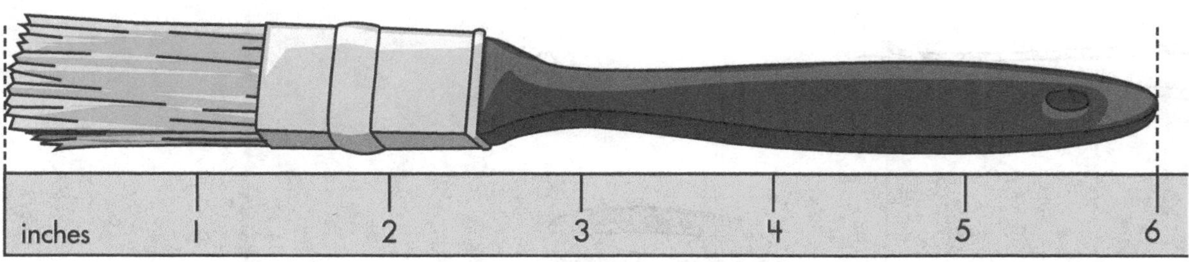

____ inches

Directions: Use an inch ruler to measure length.

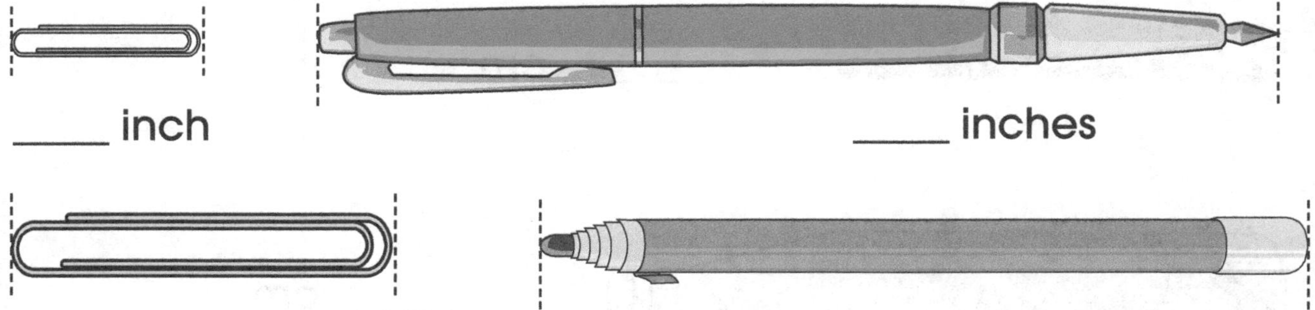

____ inch

____ inches

____ inches

____ inches

MATH

Skill 32: Estimating Length in Centimeters

Directions: Estimate how many centimeters long each object is.

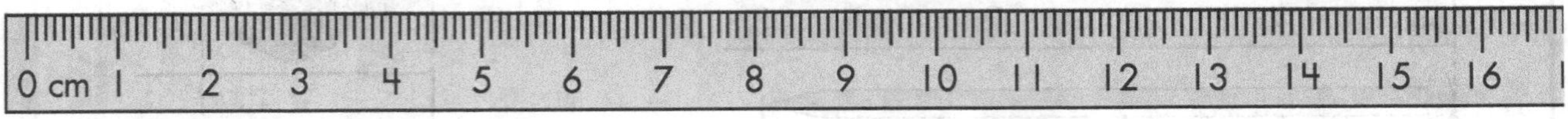

0 cm 1 2 3 4 5 6 7 8 9 10 11 12 13 14 15 16

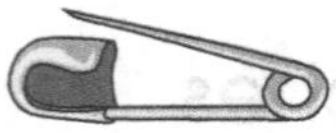

___2___ cm

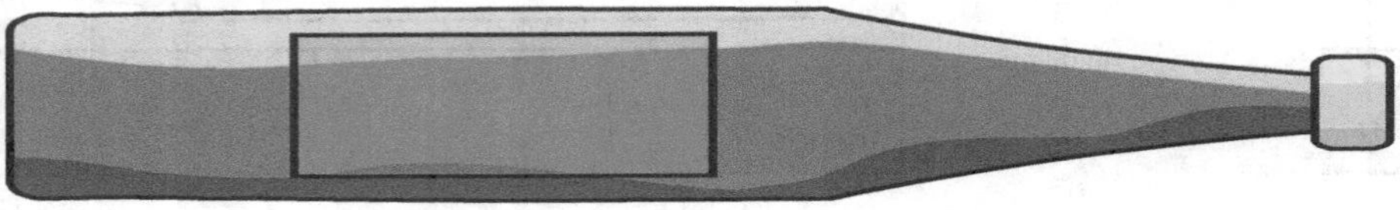

______ cm

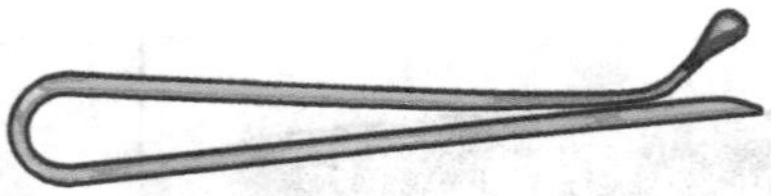

______ cm

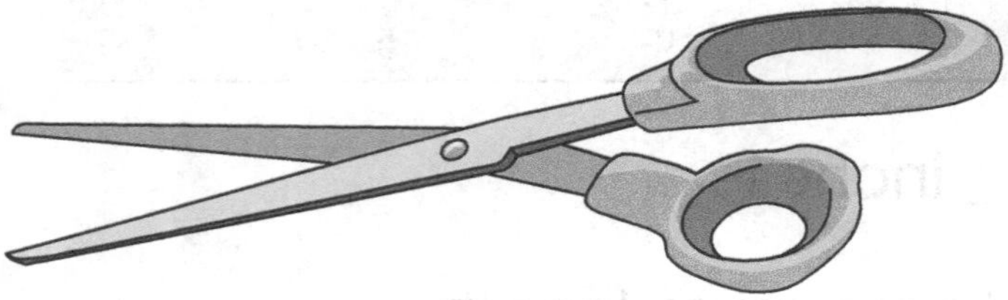

______ cm

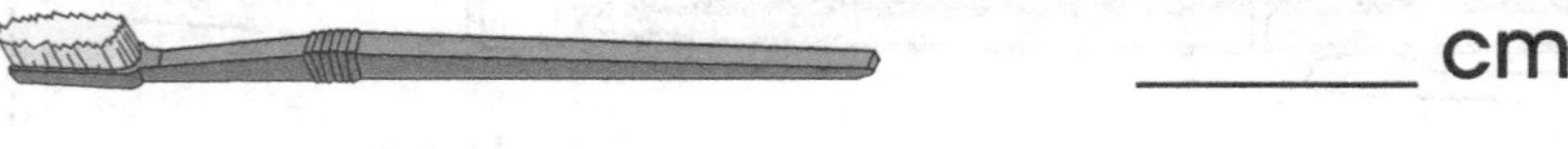

______ cm

______ cm

MATH

Skill 32: Estimating Length in Centimeters

Directions: Estimate the length of each crayon in centimeters. Then, write the numbers 1–5 to show the order from shortest to longest.

	Length in cm	Order
	_______	_______
	_______	_______
	_______	_______
	_______	_______
	_______	_______

Draw a crayon measuring 6 centimeters.

Draw a crayon measuring 11 centimeters.

MATH

Skill 33: Measuring Length in Centimeters

You can measure perimeter in centimeters.

The perimeter of this triangle is

3 + 3 + 3 = 9 centimeters.

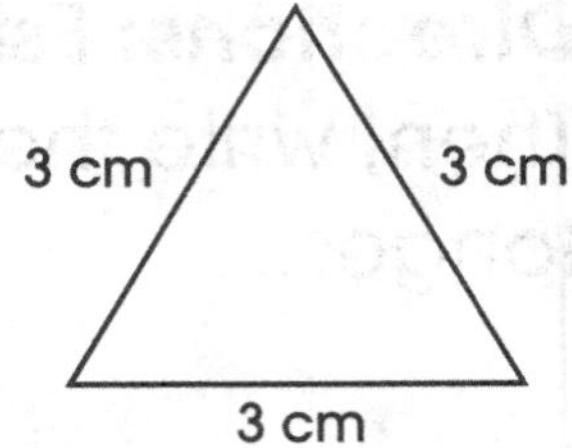

Directions: Measure the perimeter. Add the lengths of all sides.

6 + 2 + 6 + 2

= 16 cm

____ + ____ + ____ + ____

= ____ cm

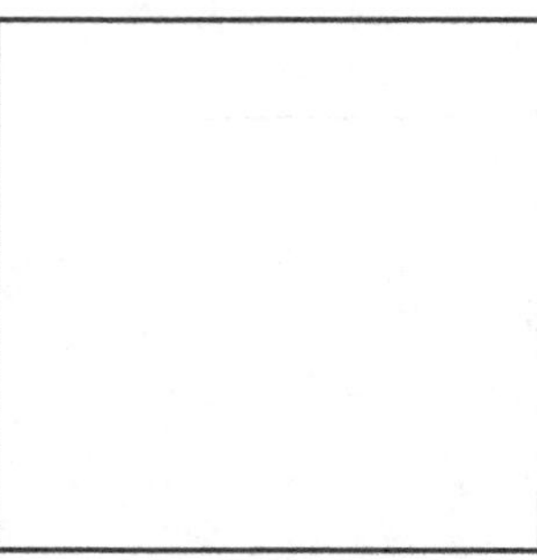

____ + ____ + ____ + ____

= ____ cm

____ + ____ + ____ + ____

+ ____ = ____ cm

MATH

Skill 33: Measuring Length in Centimeters

Directions: Write the length of each object in centimeters.

_____ centimeters

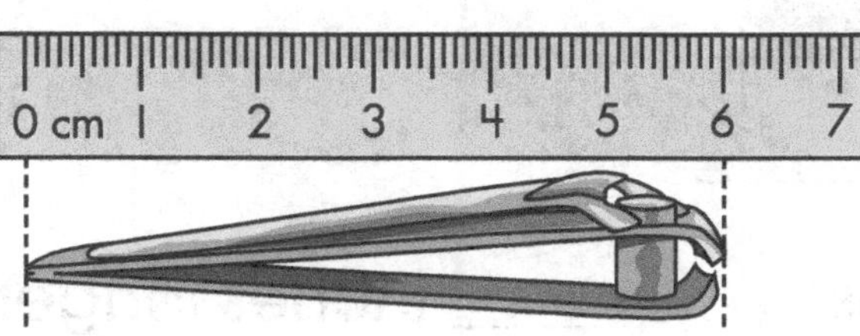

_____ centimeters

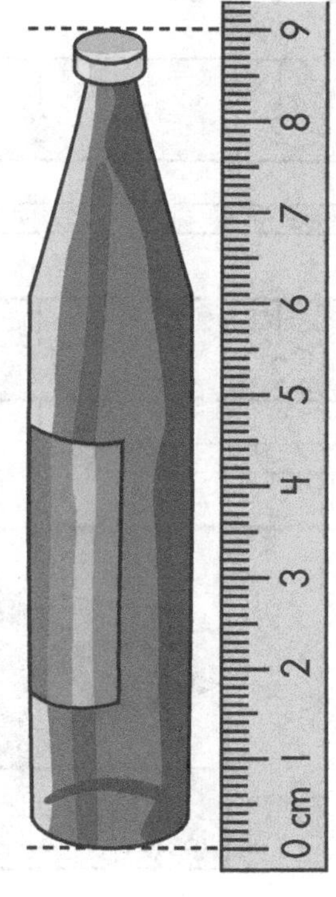

_____ centimeters

_____ centimeters

Directions: Use a centimeter ruler to measure length.

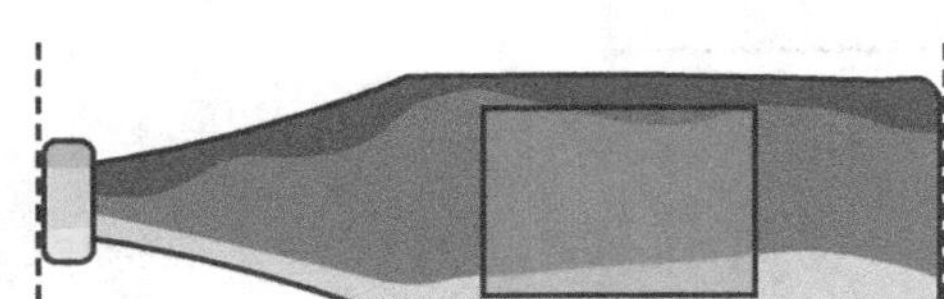

_____ centimeters

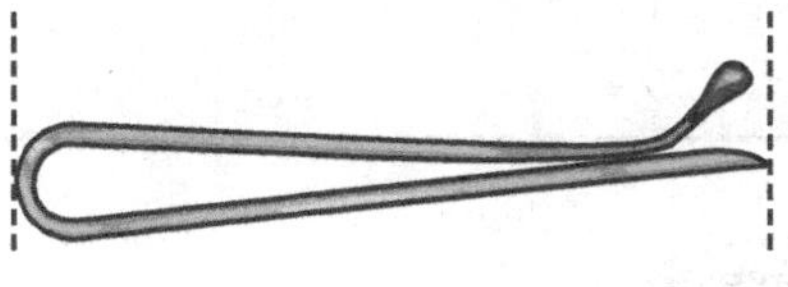

_____ centimeters

_____ centimeters

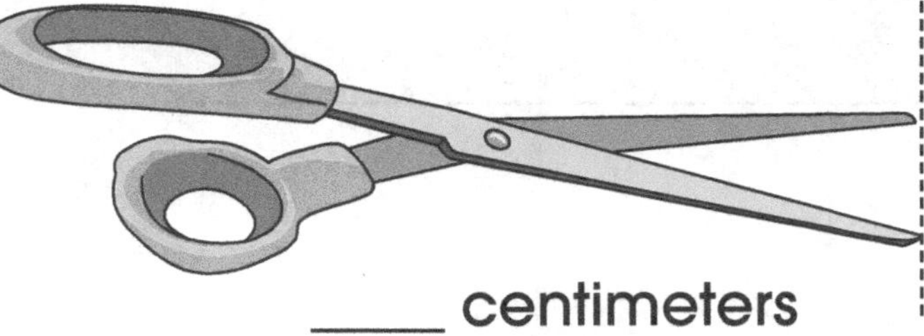

_____ centimeters

MATH

MATH

Skill 34: How Much Longer?

Directions: Measure each object. Tell how much longer one object is than the other.

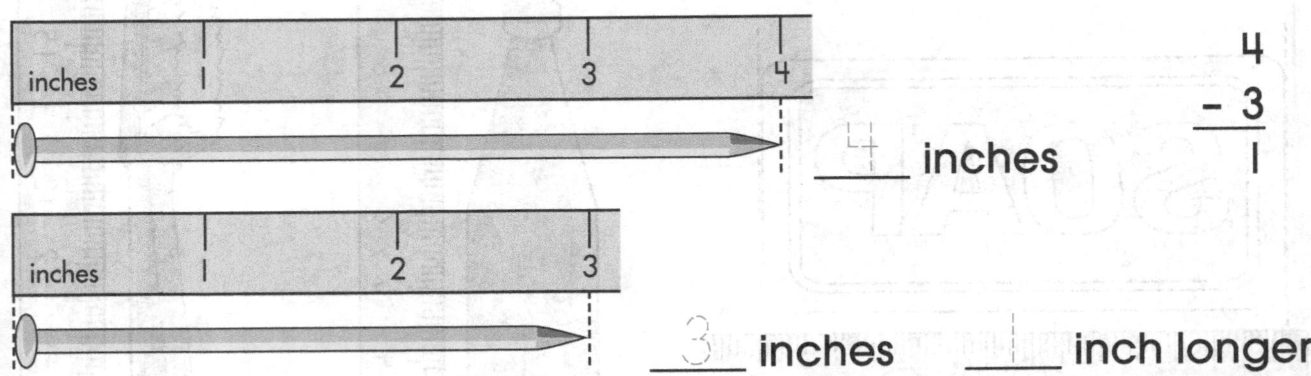

4 inches

3 inches

4
\- 3
1

1 inch longer

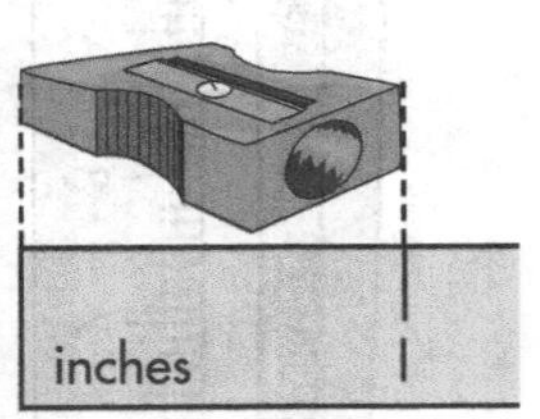

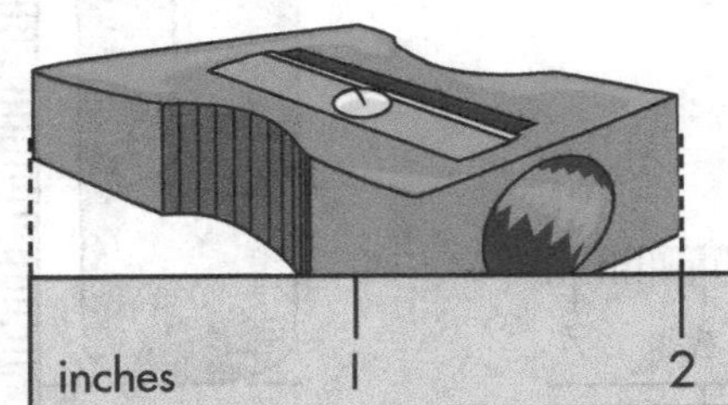

____ inches ____ inches ____ inches longer

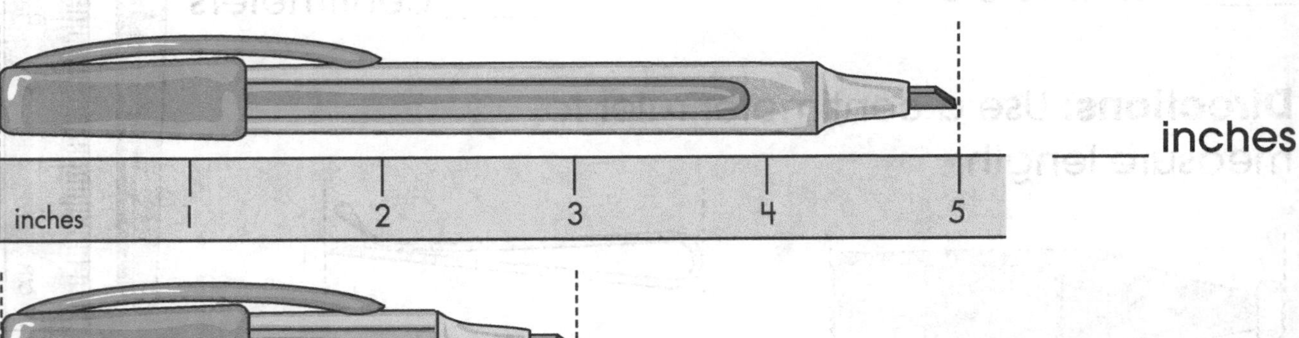

____ inches

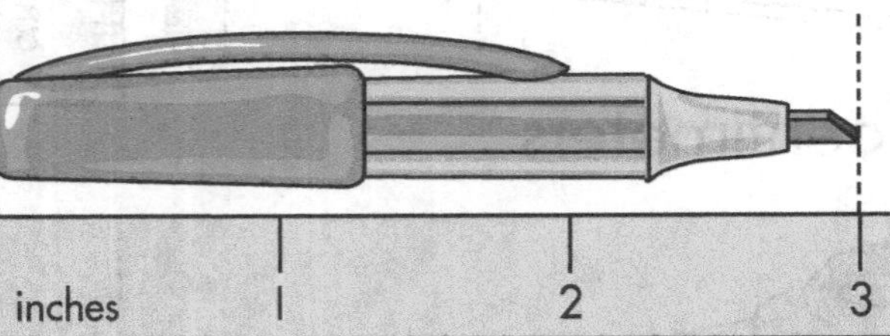

____ inches

____ inches longer

Skill 34: How Much Longer?

Directions: Measure each object. Tell how much longer one object is than the other.

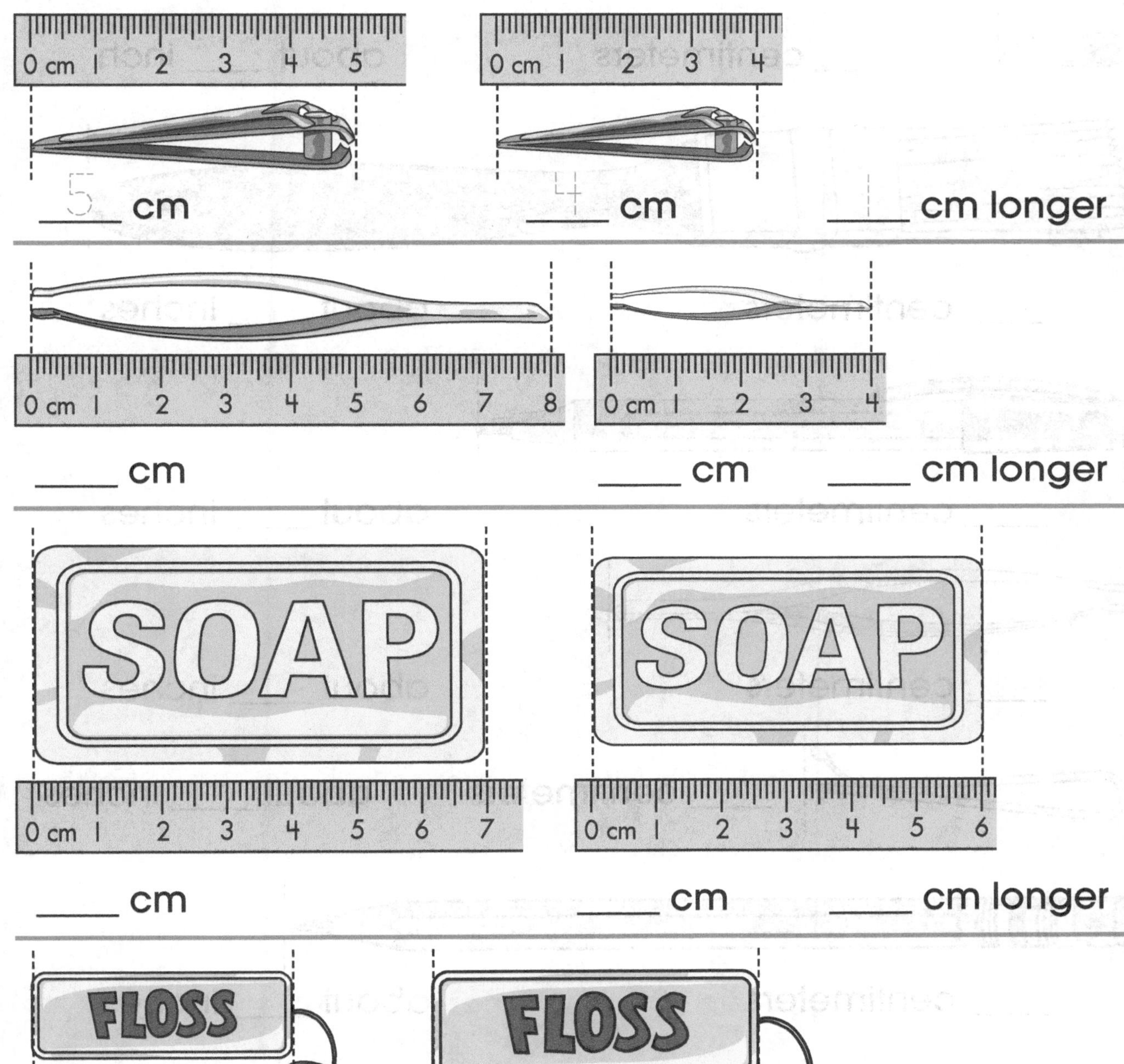

____ cm ____ cm ____ cm longer

____ cm ____ cm ____ cm longer

____ cm ____ cm ____ cm longer

____ cm ____ cm ____ cm longer

MATH

Skill 35: Comparing Measurements

Directions: Use a ruler to measure each object in centimeters. Then, measure again to the nearest inch.

____ centimeters about ____ inch

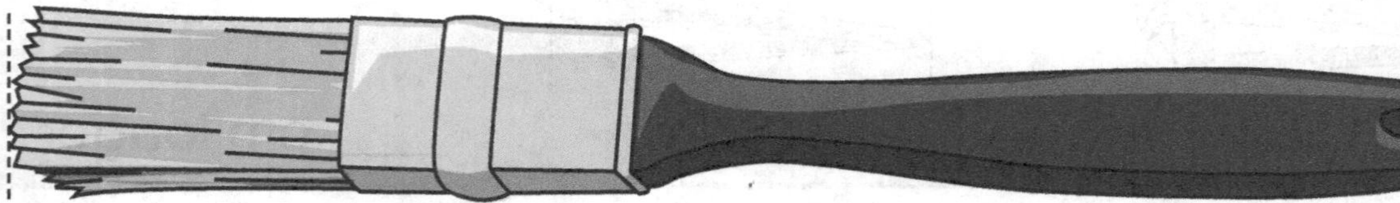

____ centimeters about ____ inches

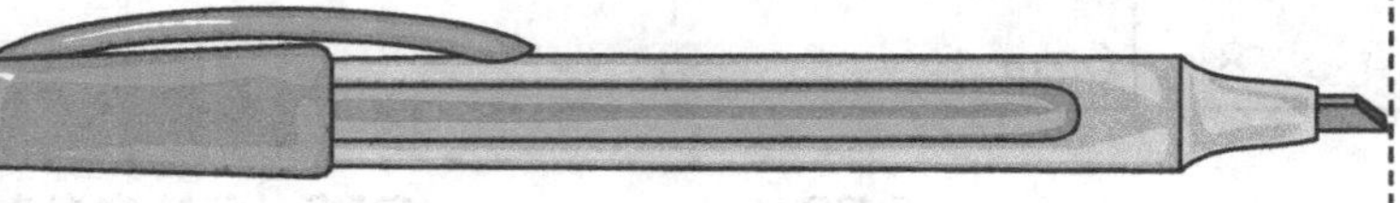

____ centimeters about ____ inches

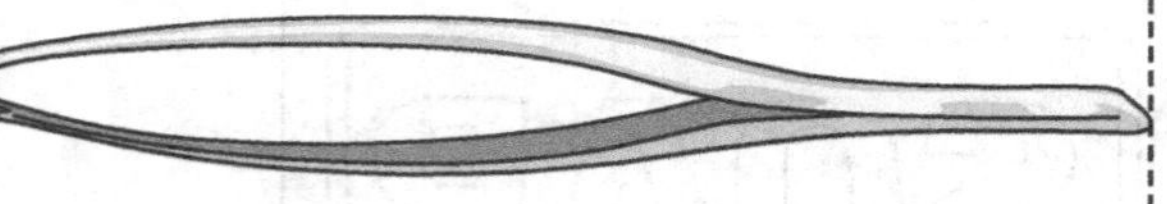

____ centimeters about ____ inches

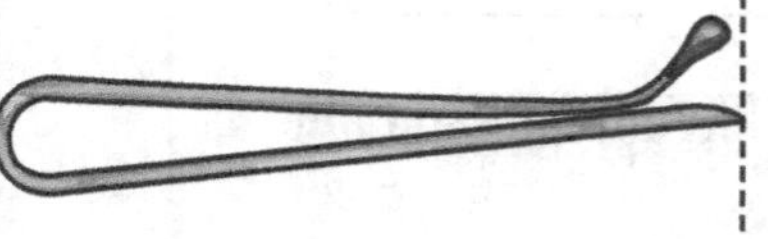

____ centimeters about ____ inches

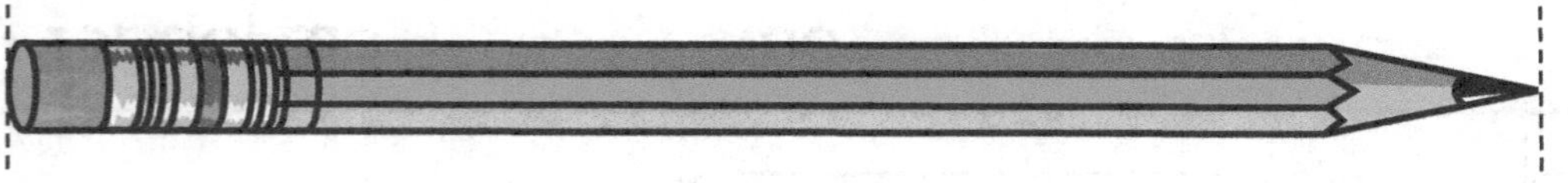

____ centimeters about ____ inches

What do you notice about the measurements in centimeters compared to those in inches? ______________________

What explains this? ______________________

MATH

Skill 35: Comparing Measurements

Directions: There are three pencils in each problem. Use a ruler to measure each pencil to the nearest half inch. Write the measurement next to each pencil. Then, write 1, 2, and 3 on the lines to put the pencils in order from shortest to longest.

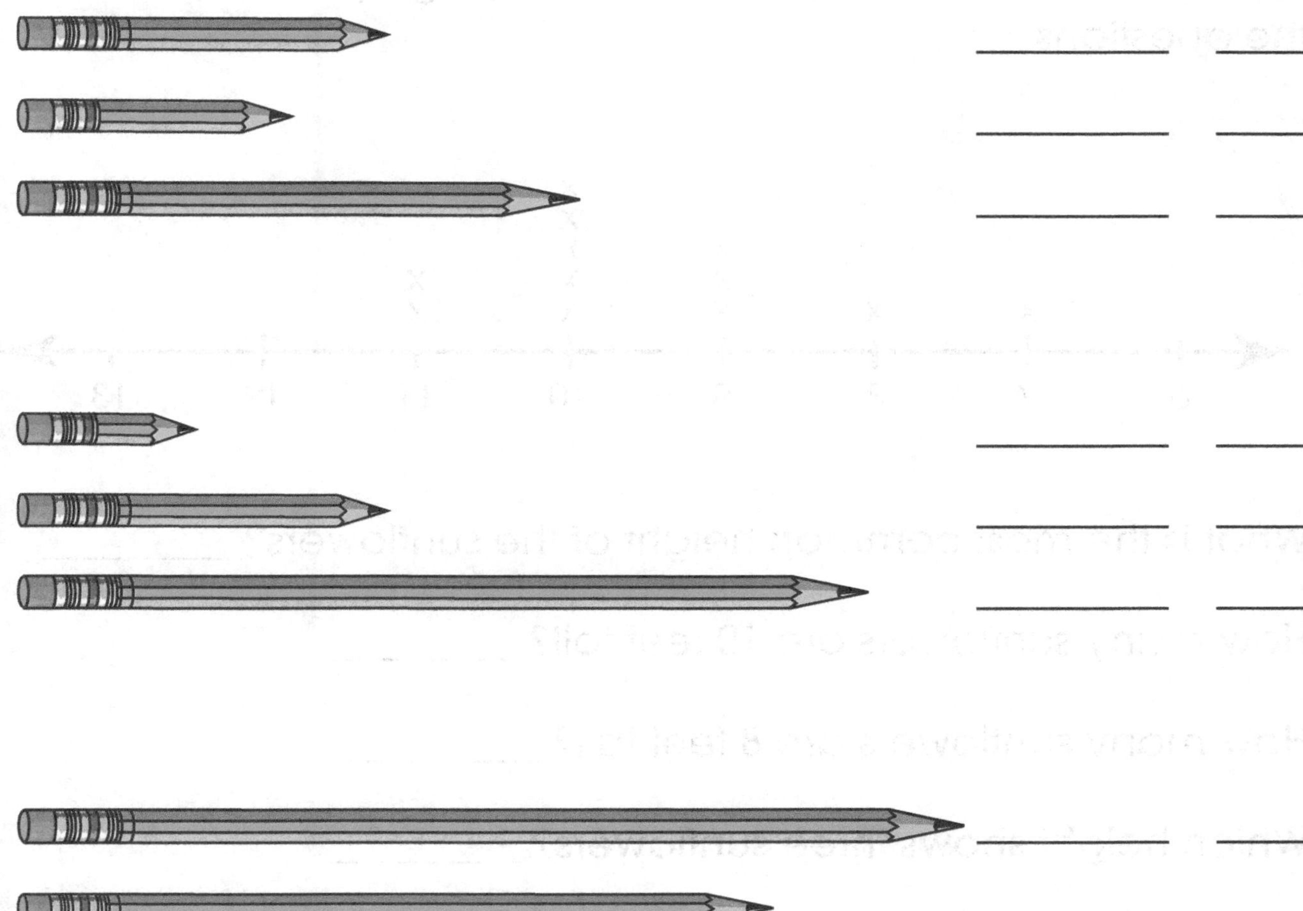

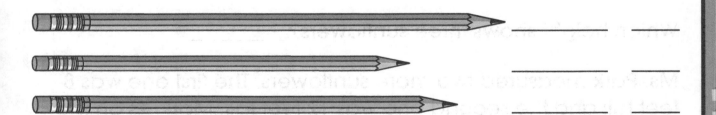

Guess the length of your shoelace in centimeters. Now, measure your shoelace. How close was your guess?

____

Skill 36: Line Plots

A line plot uses a number line and Xs to show data that has been collected.

Directions: The line plot shows the height in feet of the sunflowers in Ms. Park's garden. Read the graph and answer the questions.

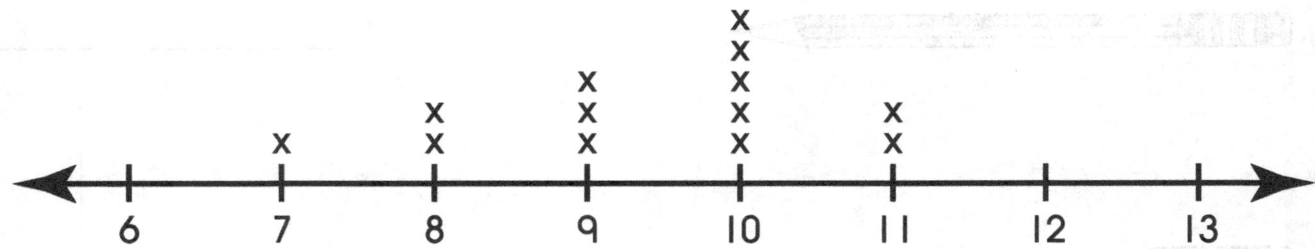

What is the most common height of the sunflowers? __________

How many sunflowers are 10 feet tall? __________

How many sunflowers are 8 feet tall? __________

Which height shows three sunflowers? __________

Ms. Park measured two more sunflowers. The first one was 8 feet tall and the second one was 12 feet tall. Mark **Xs** on the line plot to add the sunflowers to the graph.

Skill
36: Line Plots

Brooke made necklaces of different lengths to sell at the school carnival.

Lengths of Necklaces

16 inches	18 inches
20 inches	17 inches
16 inches	16 inches
17 inches	19 inches
18 inches	16 inches

Directions: Use the data to complete the line plot. Answer the questions.

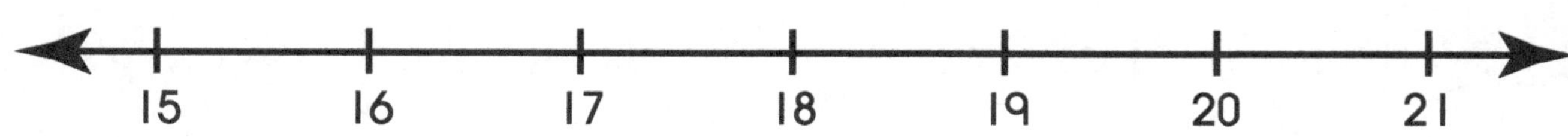

What was the total number of 16-inch necklaces? ________

What was the total number of 18-inch necklaces? ________

Brooke made one more necklace that was 20 inches long. Graph that necklace on the line plot.

What was the total number of necklaces that Brooke made? ________

Skill 37: Making a Line Plot

Directions: Mrs. Rivera's class planted beans. After a week, the class recorded the heights of the sprouts. Use the following data to make a line plot in the space provided. Answer the questions.

Bean Sprouts

Height in centimeters	Number of sprouts
3 cm	4
4 cm	7
5 cm	6
6 cm	7
7 cm	3

Which two heights had the same number of bean sprouts?

____

How many bean sprouts were 7 centimeters in height? ________

What was the total number of bean sprouts? ________

How many more bean sprouts were 5 centimeters than 3 centimeters in height? ________

MATH

Skill 37: Making a Line Plot

Directions: Create a line plot based on the measurements below.

6 centimeters

4 centimeters

3 centimeters

5 centimeters

12 centimeters

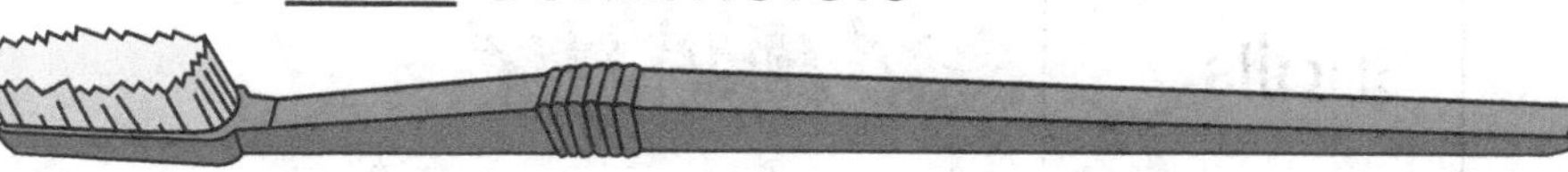

2 centimeters

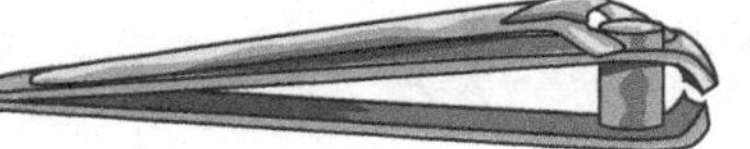

5 centimeters

5 centimeters

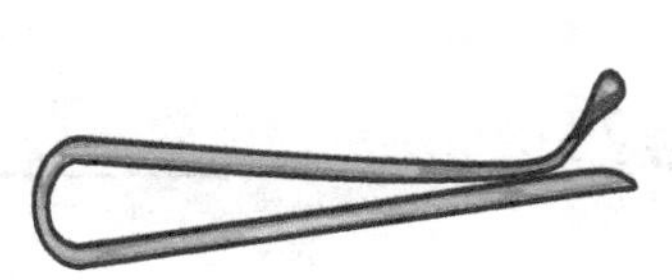

4 centimeters

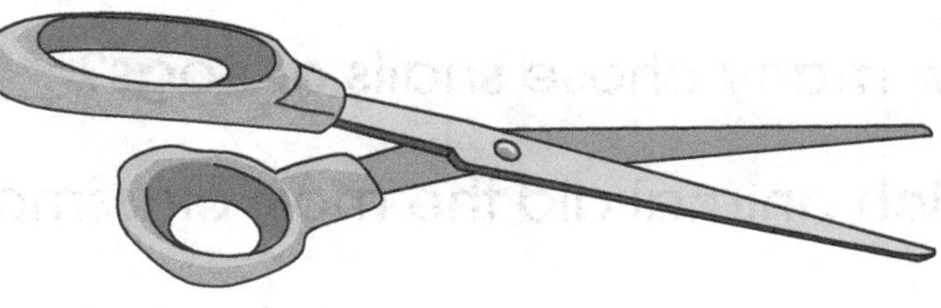

9 centimeters

X (above 6)

1 2 3 4 5 6 7 8 9 10 11 12 13 14 15

MATH

Skill 38: Reading Picture and Bar Graphs

Carlos polled his classmates about their favorite animals. He made this picture graph with the results. One animal on the graph means one person.

Our Favorite Animals

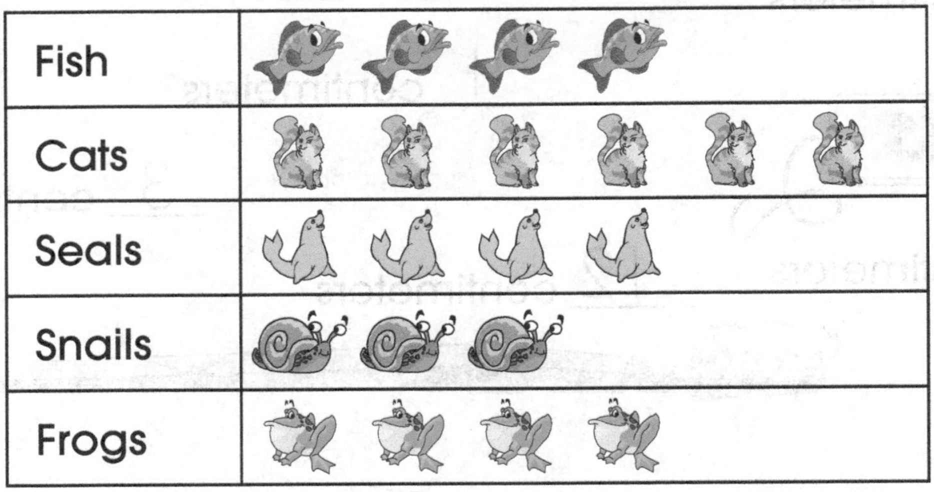

Fish	
Cats	
Seals	
Snails	
Frogs	

Directions: Use the picture graph to answer the questions.

How many classmates chose either seals or cats? ________

How many chose snails or frogs? ________

Which animal did the most classmates choose? ____________

How many classmates did not choose cats? ________

How many more chose fish than chose snails? ________

How many classmates told Carlos their favorite animal?

____

MATH

Skill

38: Reading Picture and Bar Graphs

Keisha asked her classmates about their favorite fruit. She made this bar graph to show the results.

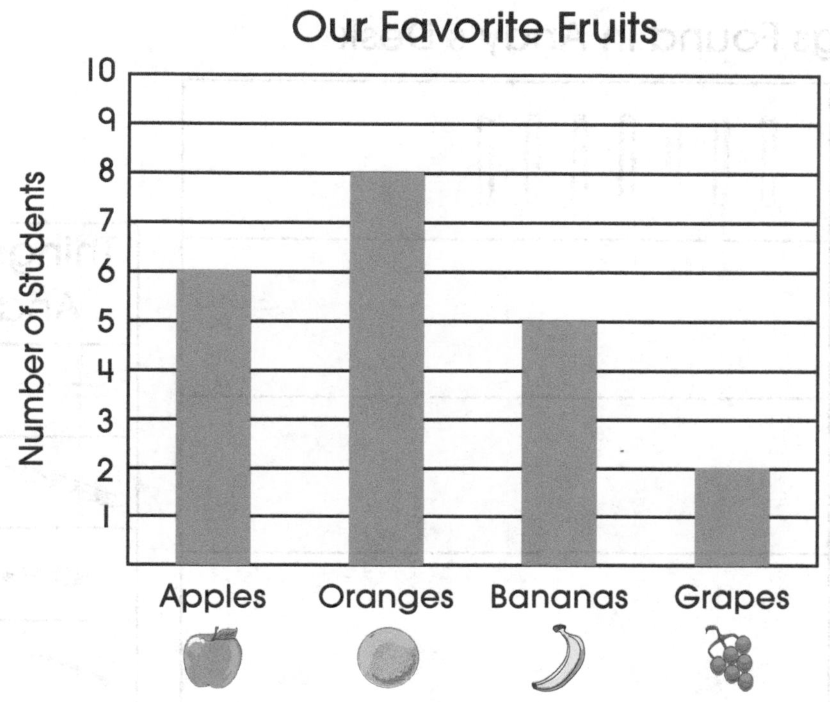

Directions: Use the bar graph to answer the questions.

How many students like apples or oranges best? ________

Which is the most popular fruit? ________________

How many students like either bananas or grapes best? ______

How many students did Keisha talk to? ________

MATH

Skill 39: Creating Picture and Bar Graphs

Directions: Use the information in the tally chart to complete the picture graph.

Things Found in Andy's Desk

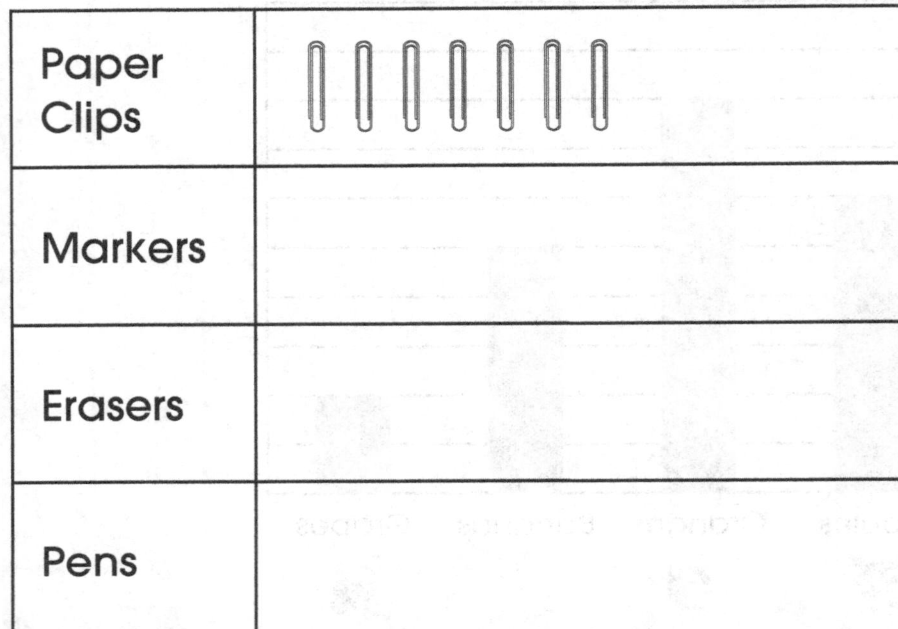

Paper Clips	
Markers	
Erasers	
Pens	

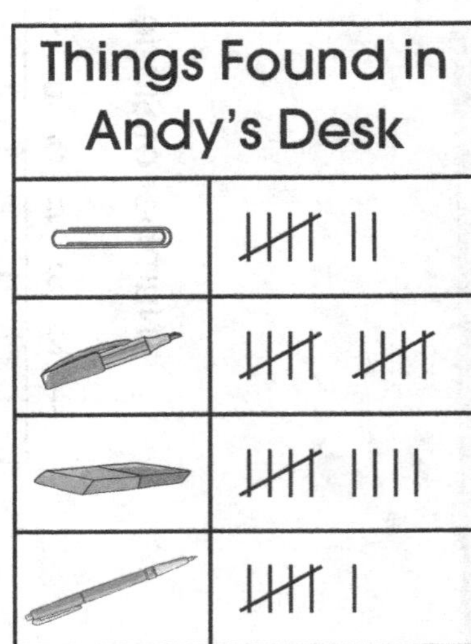

Things Found in Andy's Desk	
	ⵣ卌 II
	卌 卌
	卌 IIII
	卌 I

Directions: Use the picture graph to answer the questions below.

What item is there the most of in Andy's desk? ____________

What item is there the least of in Andy's desk? ____________

How many more markers are there than paper clips? ________

How many more erasers are there than pens? ________

MATH

Skill 39: Creating Picture and Bar Graphs

Directions: Use the information in the tally chart to complete the bar graph.

Points in the Soccer Game

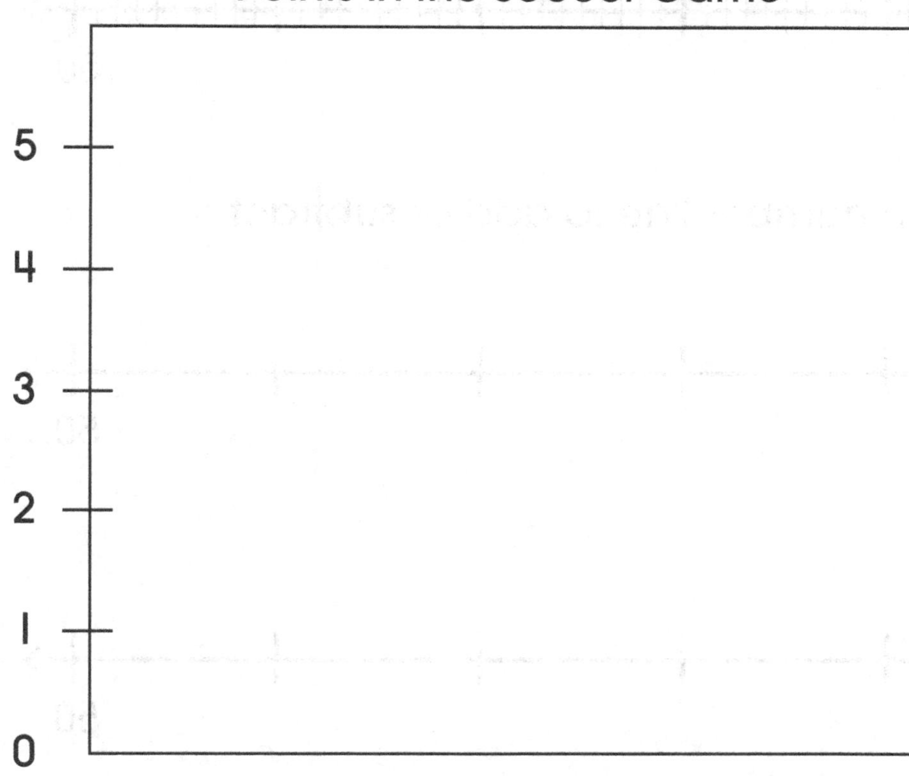

Points in the Soccer Game	
Kevin	|||
Drew	~~||||~~
Kendra	||||
Heather		

Directions: Use the bar graph to answer the questions.

Which student scored the most points? ________________

Which student scored the least points? ________________

How many points were scored altogether in the soccer game? ________

How many more points did Drew score than Heather? ________

Skill 40: Adding and Subtracting on a Number Line

Use the number line to add.

10
+ 30
40

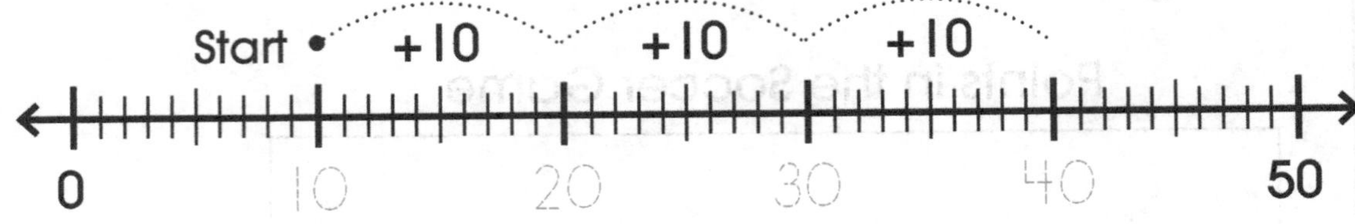

Directions: Use each number line to add or subtract.

40
- 20

30
+ 15

80
- 25

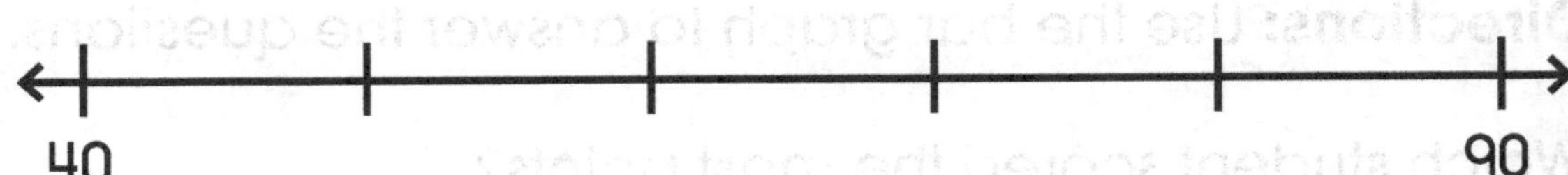

70
+ 13

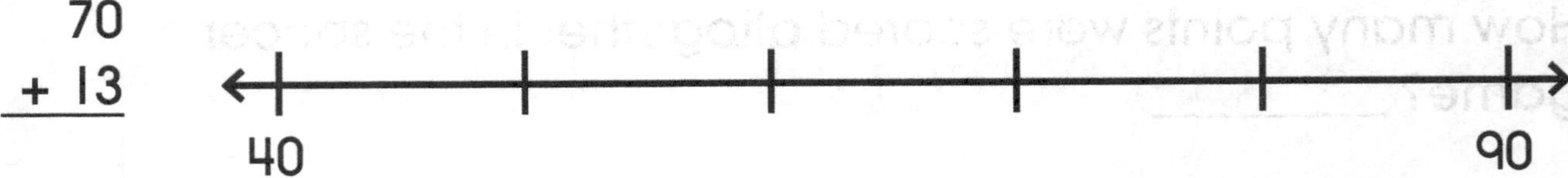

MATH

Skill 40: Adding and Subtracting on a Number Line

Directions: Use each number line to add or subtract.

50
+ 30

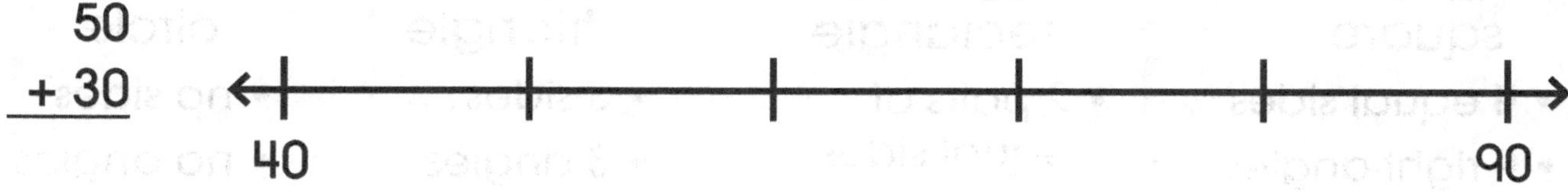

40
- 25

0 ... 50

90
+ 45

90 ... 140

70
- 23

40 ... 90

Skill 41: Plane Shapes

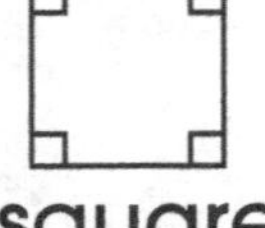

square
- 4 equal sides
- 4 right angles

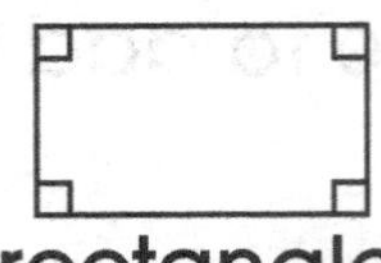

rectangle
- 2 pairs of equal sides
- 4 right angles

triangle
- 3 sides
- 3 angles

circle
- no sides
- no angles

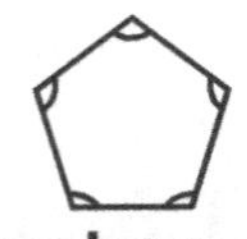

pentagon
- 5 sides
- 5 angles

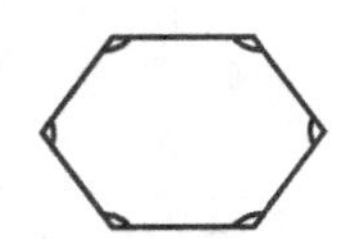

hexagon
- 6 sides
- 6 angles

Directions: Name each shape.

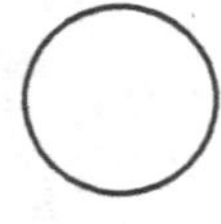

circle

____

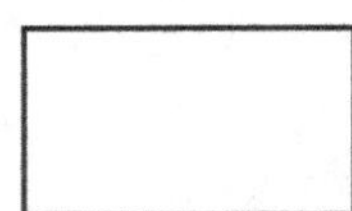

____

____

______________ ______________

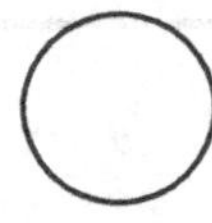

____

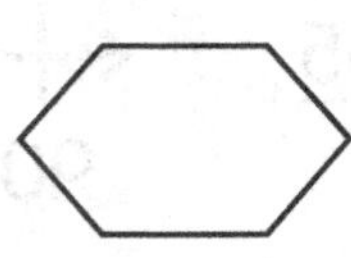

____

Directions: Answer the questions.

Which shape has 6 angles? ______________

Which shape has 4 equal sides? ______________

Which shape has 3 sides? ______________

Which shape has no angles? ______________

MATH

Skill 41: Plane Shapes

Directions: Write the name of the shape next to each item.

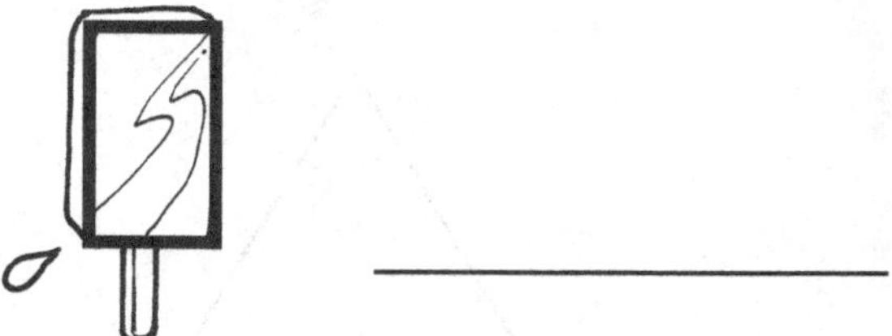

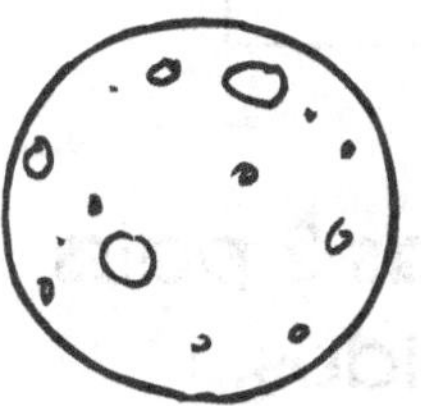

Skill 42: Drawing Plane Shapes

Look at the shape.

Draw your own shape. Color it.

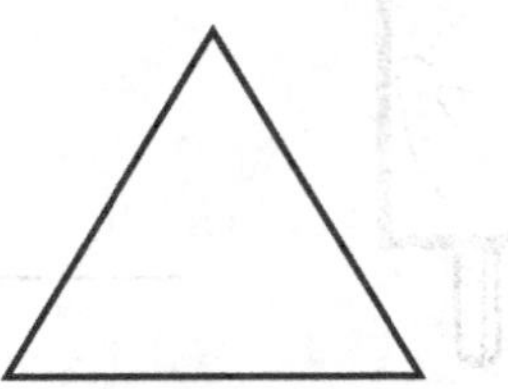

A triangle has 3 sides.

A square has 4 equal sides.

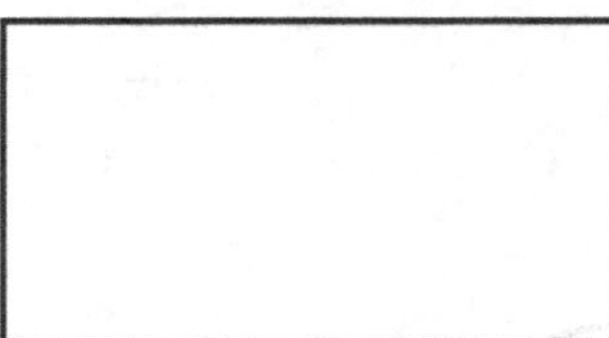

A rectangle has 2 pairs of equal sides.

Skill

42: Drawing Plane Shapes

Look at the shape.	Draw your own shape. Color it.
A circle is perfectly round.	
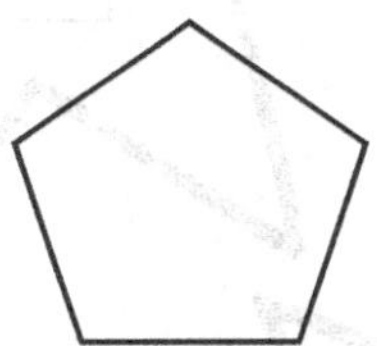 A regular pentagon has 5 equal sides.	
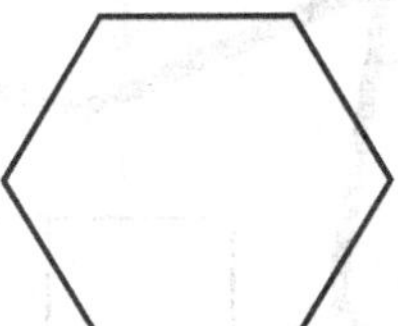 A regular hexagon has 6 equal sides.	

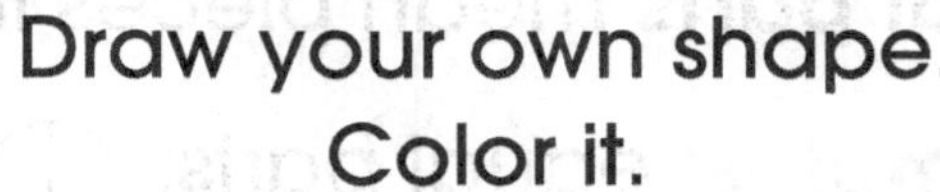

MATH

Skill 43: Equal Parts of Shapes

Equal parts mean pieces that are exactly the same.

Examples: equal parts:

not equal parts:

Directions: Color the stars that show equal parts.

Skill 43: Equal Parts of Shapes

Directions: Circle the shapes that have an equal number of parts shaded.

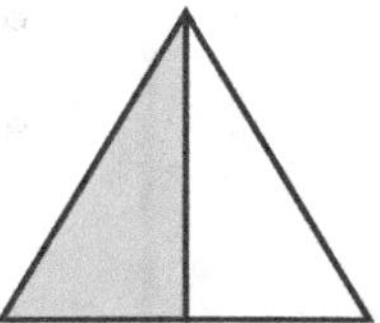

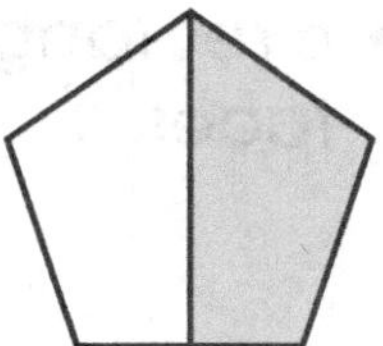

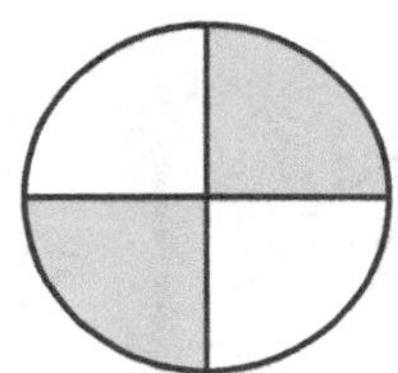

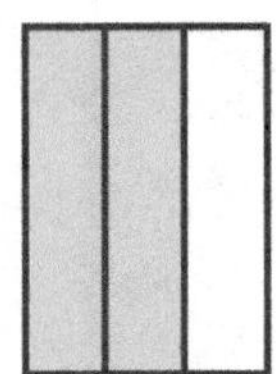

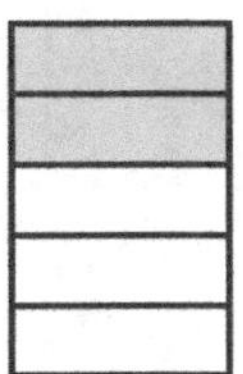

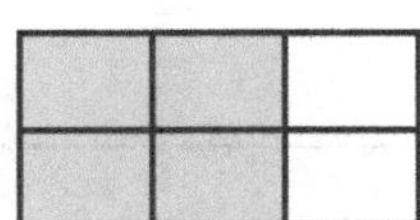

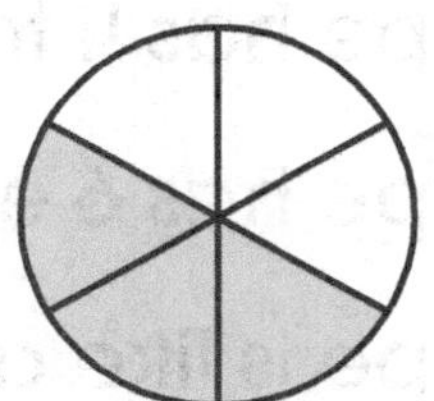

Skill 44: Solid Shapes

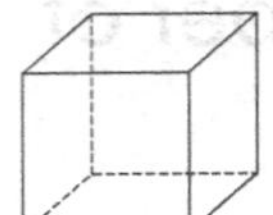

cube
- 6 square faces

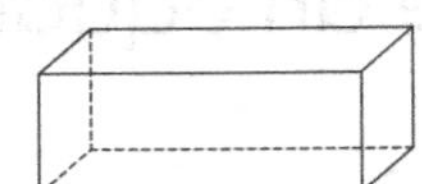

rectangular solid
- 6 rectangular faces

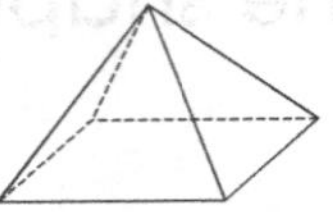

square pyramid
- 4 triangular faces
- 1 square face

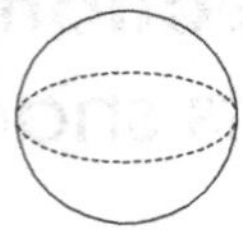

sphere
- no faces
- perfectly round

Directions: Circle the shape named.

rectangular solid 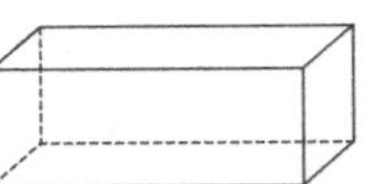 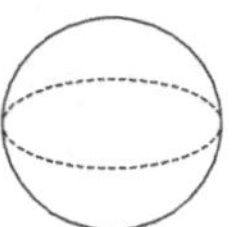 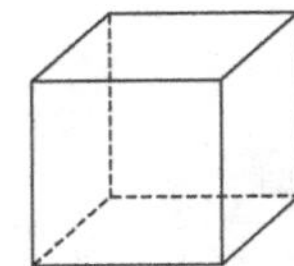

sphere 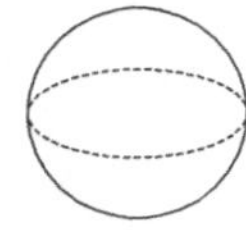 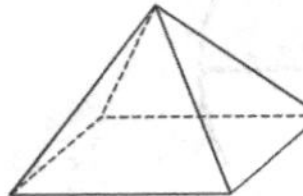 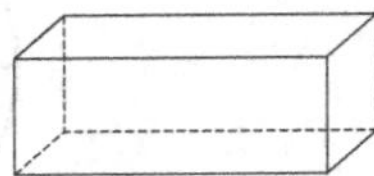

square pyramid 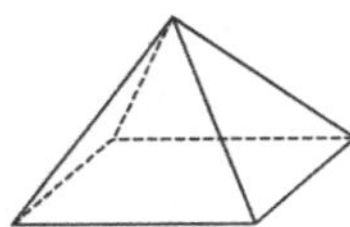 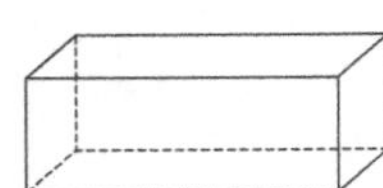 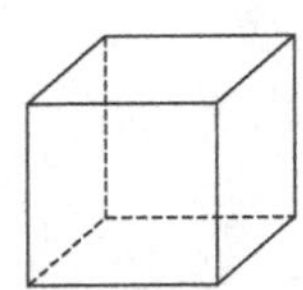

cube 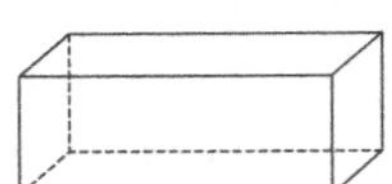 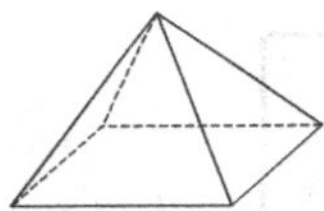 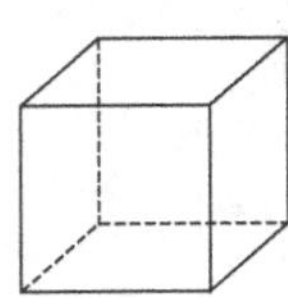

Directions: Answer the questions about the shapes above.

Which shape has 6 rectangular faces? ______________________

Which shape has 4 triangular faces? ______________________

Which shape has 6 equal faces? ______________________

Which shape is like a ball? ______________________

Skill 44: Solid Shapes

Directions: Connect each figure with its name. Then, connect each name with the number of faces it has.

Figure	Name	Number of Faces
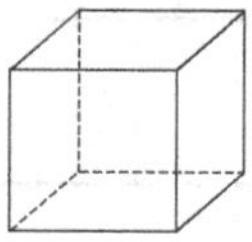	square pyramid	6
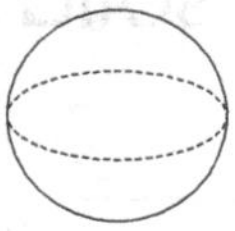	cube	6
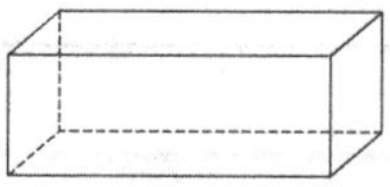	sphere	5
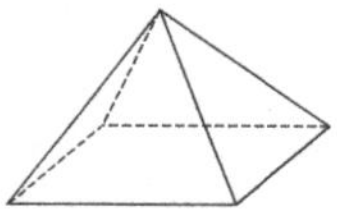	rectangular solid	0

Directions: Classify each item by its shape. Write its name in the chart.

marble

cereal box

block

pyramid

Cube	Rectangular solid
Square Pyramid	**Sphere**

MATH

Skill 45: Drawing Solid Shapes

Directions: Answer the questions.

What two plane shapes make up a square pyramid?

_______________ _______________

What plane shape is most like a sphere? _______________

What two plane shapes can be part of a rectangular solid?

_______________ _______________

What plane shape is used to make a cube? _______________

Look at the shape.	Draw your own shape. Color it.
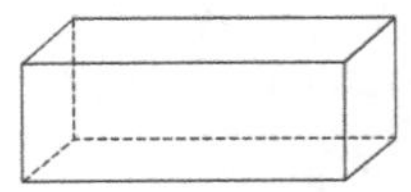 rectangular solid	
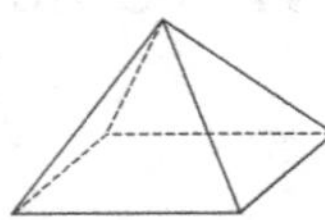 square pyramid	
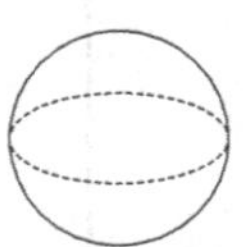 sphere	
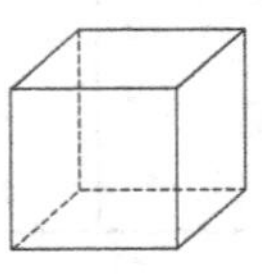 cube	

Skill 45: Drawing Solid Shapes

Directions: Draw an item that is each shape below the pictures.

Sphere

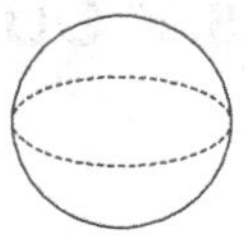

Cube

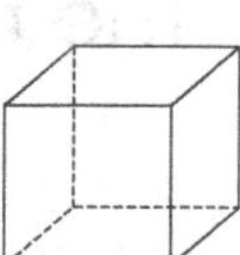

Rectangular Solid

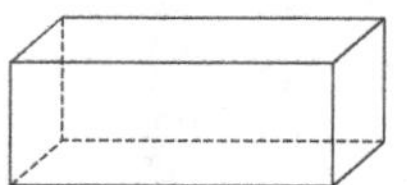

Square Pyramid

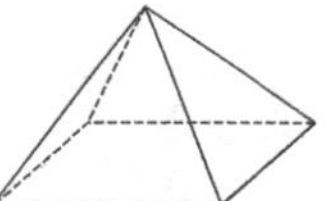

MATH

Skill 46: Parts of Shapes

A shape can be broken into equal parts. These equal parts are called **fractions**.

A **half** is one of two equal parts. Two halves make a whole. The fraction **two-halves** means 2 out of 2 total parts, or $\frac{2}{2}$.

A **third** is one of three equal parts. Three thirds make a whole. The fraction **three-thirds** means 3 out of 3 total parts, or $\frac{3}{3}$.

A **fourth** is one of four equal parts. Four fourths make a whole. The fraction **four-fourths** means 4 out of 4 total parts, or $\frac{4}{4}$.

Directions: Write the fraction shown. Use numbers. Then, use words.

$\frac{\_\_}{\_\_}$ $\frac{\_\_}{\_\_}$

three-thirds __________ __________

MATH

Skill 46: Parts of Shapes

Directions: Write the fraction shown. Use numbers. Then, use words.

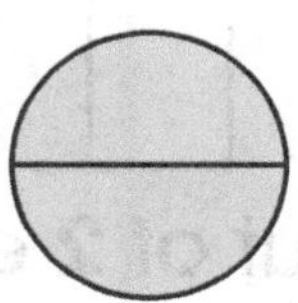

___
___

____

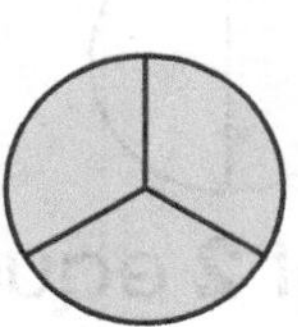

___
___

____

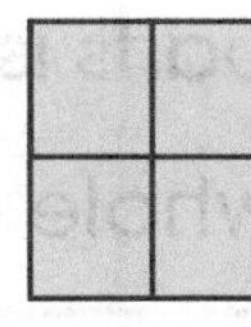

___
___

____

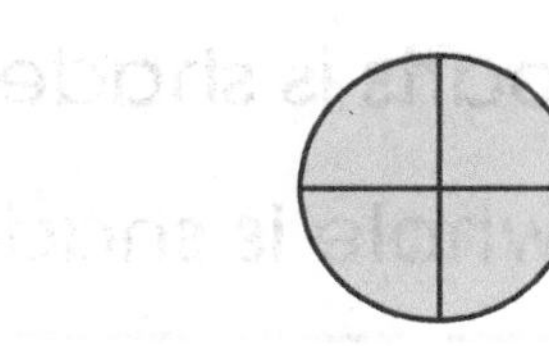

___
___

____

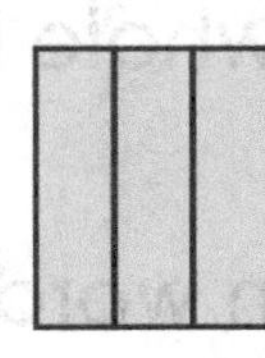

___
___

____

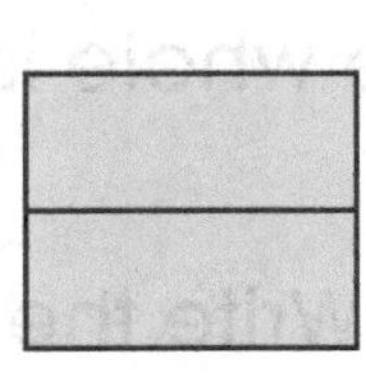

___
___

____

Skill 47: One-Half

One-half of the whole is shaded.

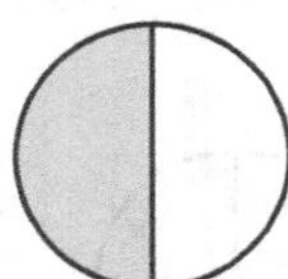

$\frac{1}{2}$ = **1** out of **2** equal parts

One-half of the whole is shaded.

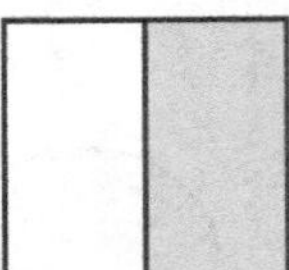

$\frac{1}{2}$ = **1** out of **2** equal parts

Directions: Complete.

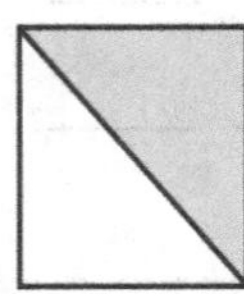

There are __2__ equal parts.

__1__ of the parts is shaded.

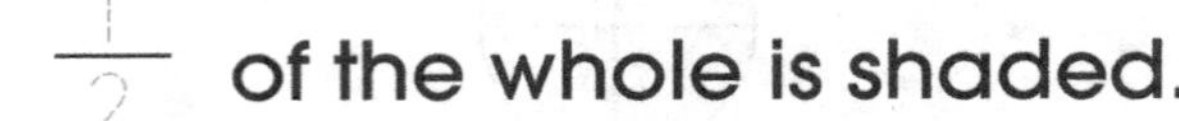

$\frac{1}{2}$ of the whole is shaded.

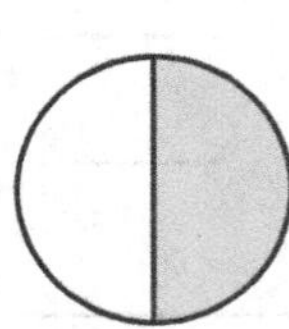

There are __2__ equal parts.

__1__ of the parts is shaded.

$\frac{1}{2}$ of the whole is shaded.

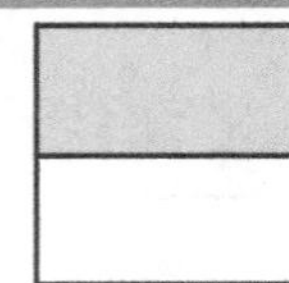

There are _____ equal parts.

_____ of the parts is shaded.

$\frac{\_\_}{\_\_}$ of the whole is shaded.

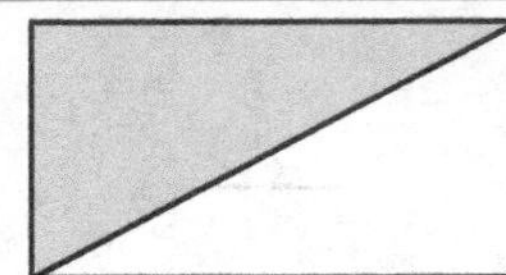

There are _____ equal parts.

_____ of the parts is shaded.

$\frac{\_\_}{\_\_}$ of the whole is shaded.

Directions: Write the fraction that is shaded in words.

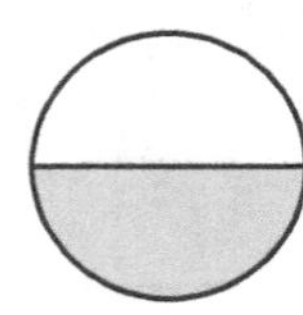

__One-half__ is shaded.

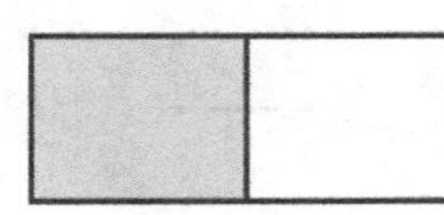

______________ is shaded.

MATH

Skill 47: One-Half

Directions: Decide if each shape is divided in half equally. Circle yes or no.

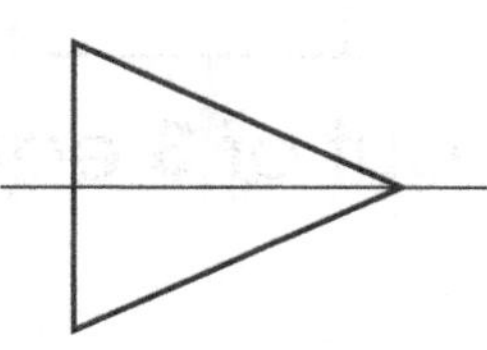

yes **no**

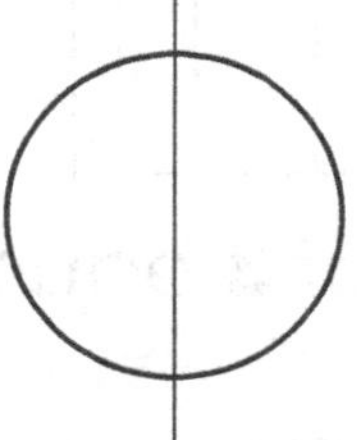

yes **no**

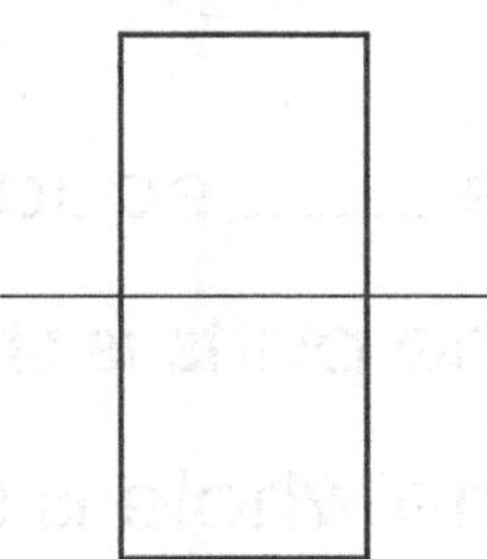

yes **no**

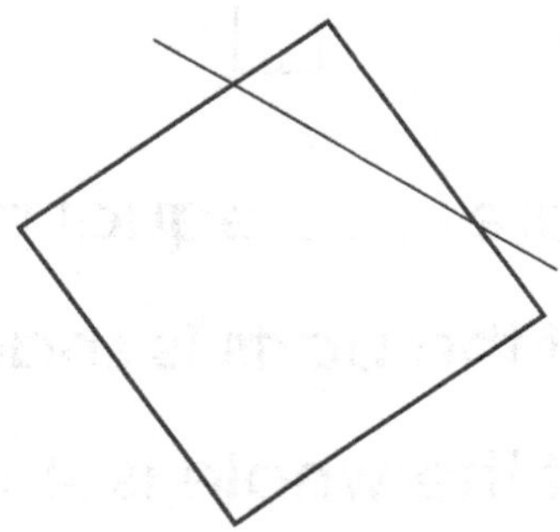

yes **no**

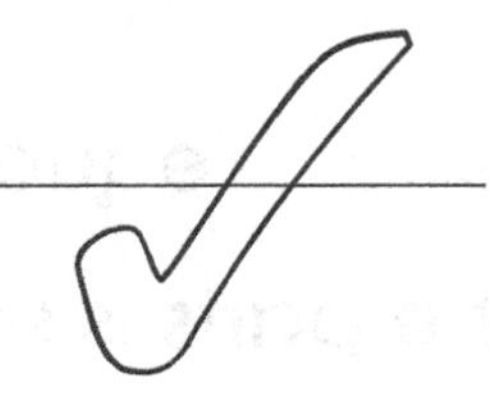

yes **no**

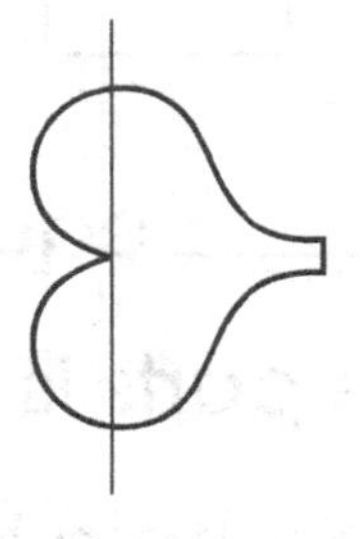

yes **no**

MATH

Skill 48: One-Third

One-third of the whole is shaded.

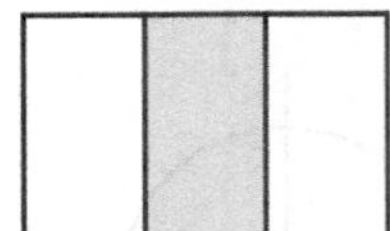

$\frac{1}{3}$ = **1** out of **3** equal parts

One-third of the whole is shaded.

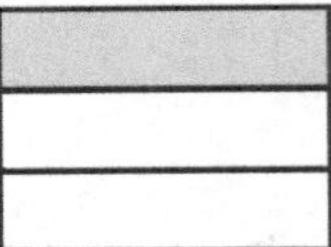

$\frac{1}{3}$ = **1** out of **3** equal parts

Directions: Complete.

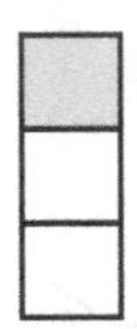

There are __3__ equal parts.

__1__ of the parts is shaded.

$\frac{1}{3}$ of the whole is shaded.

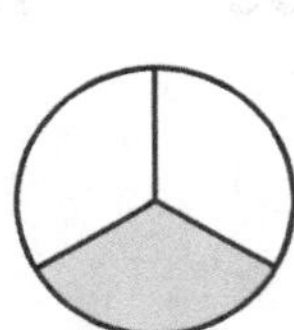

There are __3__ equal parts.

__1__ of the parts is shaded.

$\frac{1}{3}$ of the whole is shaded.

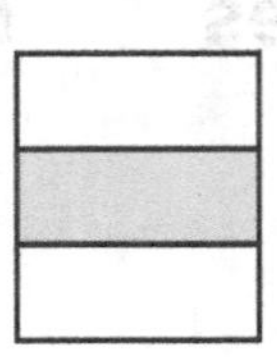

There are ____ equal parts.

____ of the parts is shaded.

$\frac{\_\_}{\_\_}$ of the whole is shaded.

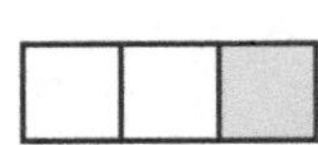

There are ____ equal parts.

____ of the parts is shaded.

$\frac{\_\_}{\_\_}$ of the whole is shaded.

MATH

Skill 48: One-Third

Directions: Write the fraction that is shaded in words.

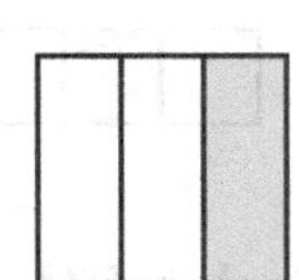

One-third is shaded.

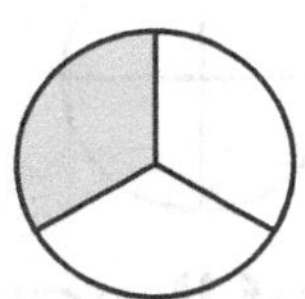

______________ is shaded.

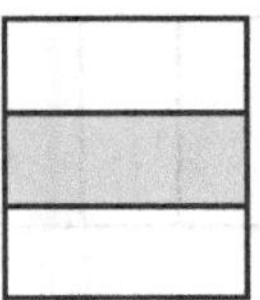

______________ is shaded.

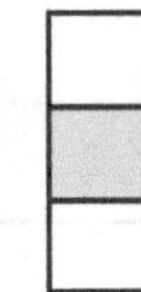

______________ is shaded.

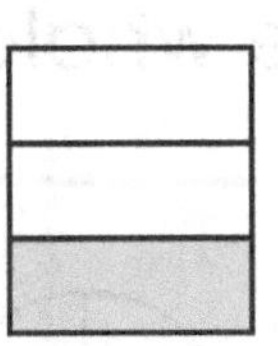

______________ is shaded.

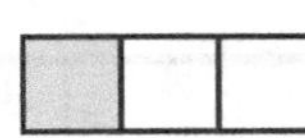

______________ is shaded.

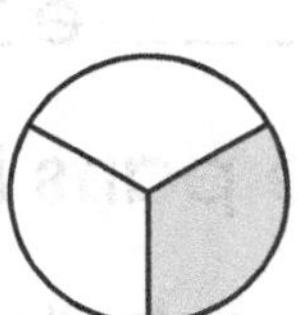

______________ is shaded.

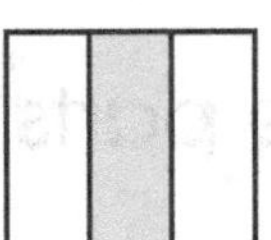

______________ is shaded.

MATH

Skill 49: One-Fourth

One-fourth of the whole is shaded.

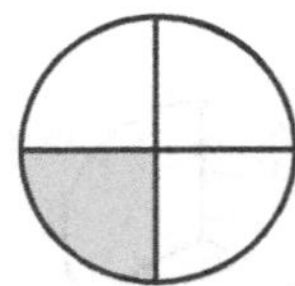

$\frac{1}{4}$ = 1 out of 4 equal parts

One-fourth of the whole is shaded.

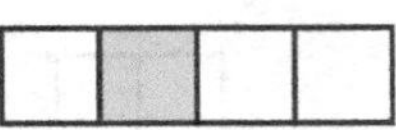

$\frac{1}{4}$ = 1 out of 4 equal parts

Directions: Complete.

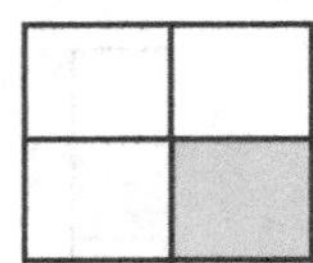

There are ____ equal parts.

____ of the parts is shaded.

$\frac{\_\_}{\_\_}$ of the whole is shaded.

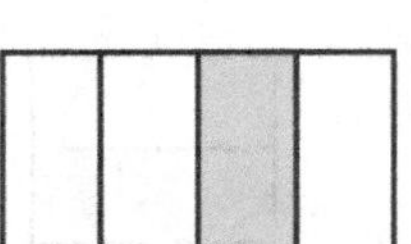

There are ____ equal parts.

____ of the parts is shaded.

$\frac{\_\_}{\_\_}$ of the whole is shaded.

There are ____ equal parts.

____ of the parts is shaded.

$\frac{\_\_}{\_\_}$ of the whole is shaded.

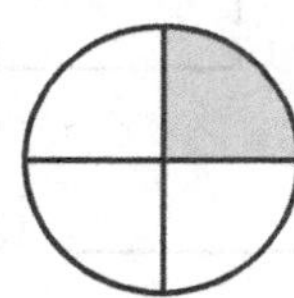

There are ____ equal parts.

____ of the parts is shaded.

$\frac{\_\_}{\_\_}$ of the whole is shaded.

Skill 49: One-Fourth

Directions: Write the fraction that is shaded in words.

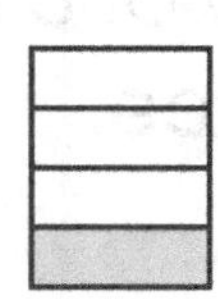

One-fourth is shaded.

_______________ is shaded.

_______________ is shaded.

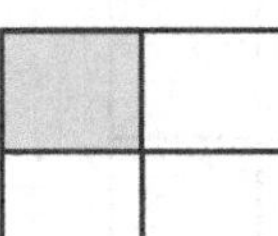

_______________ is shaded.

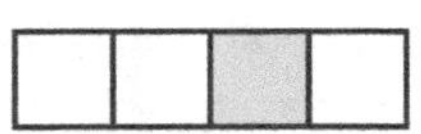

_______________ is shaded.

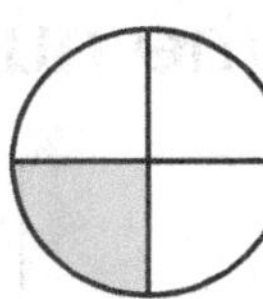

_______________ is shaded.

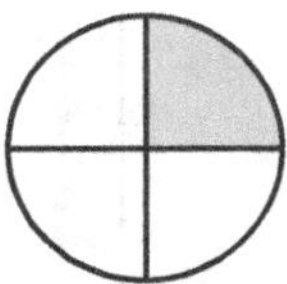

_______________ is shaded.

_______________ is shaded.

MATH

Skill 50: Partitioning Rectangles

Rectangles can be divided up into same-size squares to show how much space they cover.

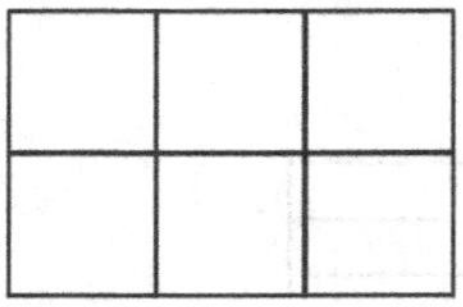

This rectangle is made up of 6 squares. It takes up 6 squares of space.

Directions: Count the squares ☐ that make up each rectangle.

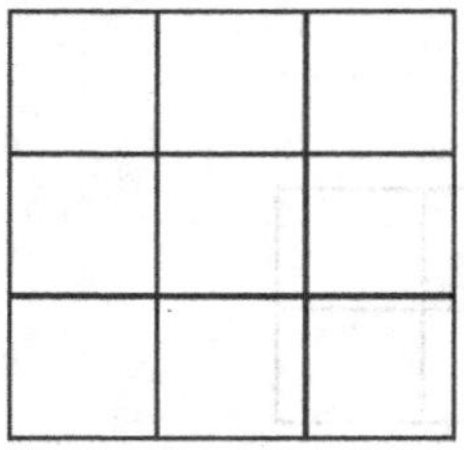

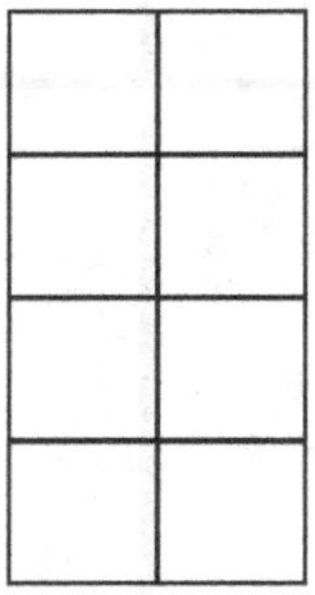

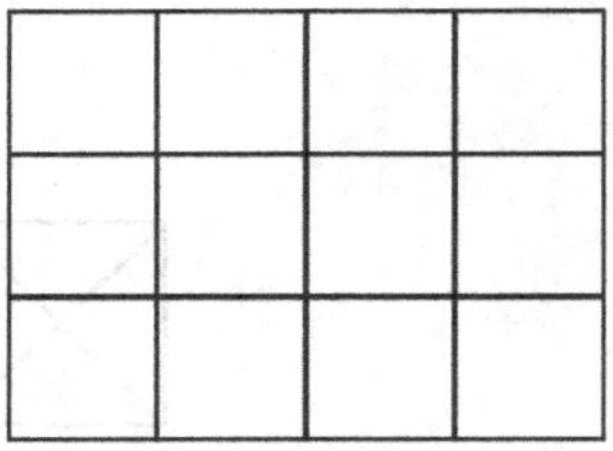

____ equal squares ____ equal squares ____ equal squares

Directions: Draw same-size squares ☐ to fill each rectangle. Then, count the number of squares.

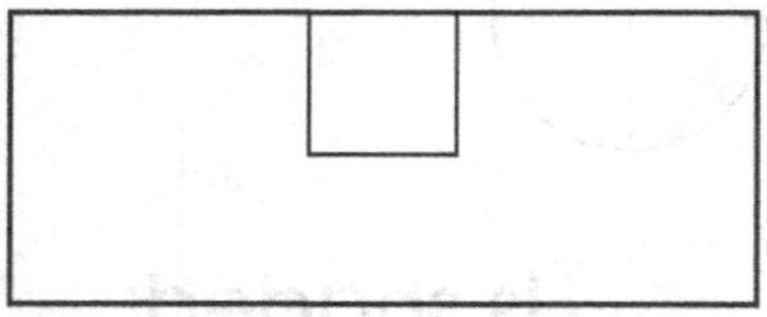

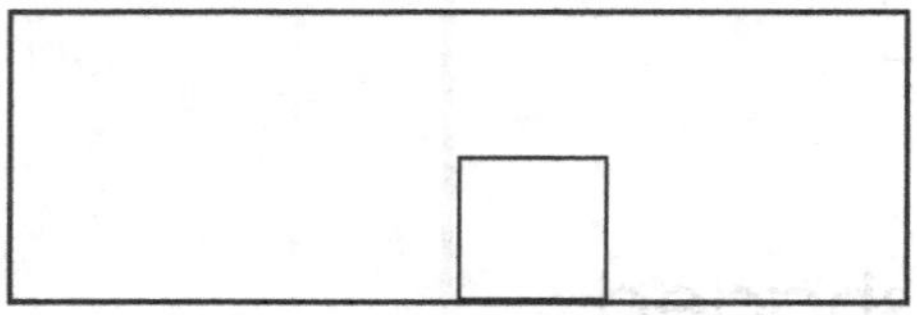

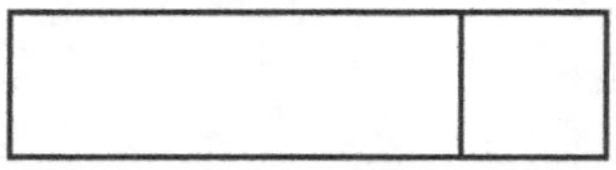

____ square units ____ square units ____ square units

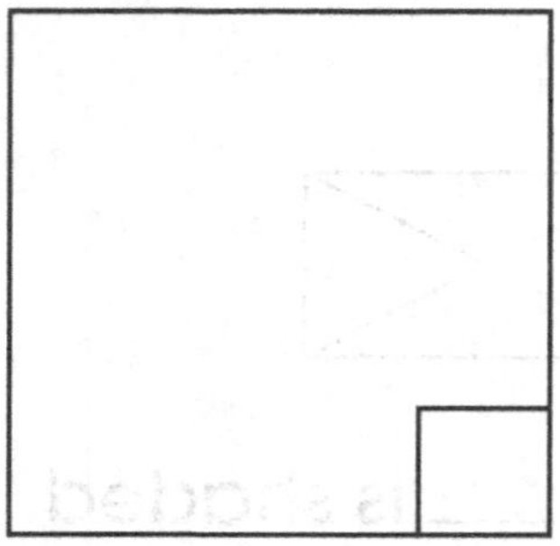

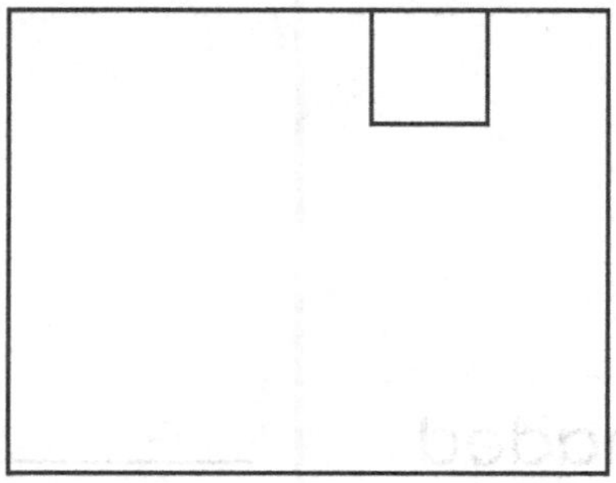

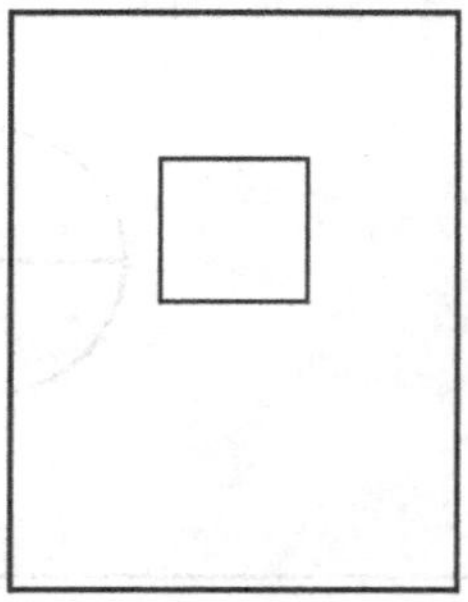

____ square units ____ square units ____ square units

MATH

Skill 50: Partitioning Rectangles

Directions: Count the squares ☐ that make up each rectangle.

____ equal squares ____ equal squares ____ equal squares

Directions: Draw same-size squares ☐ to fill each rectangle. Then, count the number of squares.

____ square units ____ square units ____ square units

____ square units ____ square units ____ square units

50 LANGUAGE ARTS SKILLS

Skill 51: Common Nouns

A **noun** is a word that names a person, a place, or a thing.

Examples: sister (person) school (place) car (thing)

The nouns in the following sentences are in bold.

Examples: The **teacher** gave us **work** to do.
The **school** is next to the **park**.

Directions: Read the paragraph below. Circle each common noun.

I packed my suitcase for the trip. I packed shirts, pants, my bathing suit, and shoes. I added my toothbrush and a comb. My mom said to bring a hat. My dad said to bring a game and a book. I also brought a photo of my cat.

Skill 51: Common Nouns

Directions: Circle all the common nouns. Then, write the common nouns next to the pictures below.

1. We like to go to the playground.

____

2. We like the swings.

____

3. We eat cake for my birthday.

____

4. We drink lemonade.

____

5. Our dog chases a ball.

____

6. Then, we go home.

____

Skill 52: Collective Nouns

A **collective noun** is a word for a group of animals, things, or people.

Examples: a **herd** of horses
a **deck** of cards
a **troupe** of actors

Directions: A collective noun is missing from each sentence below. Fill in each blank with a noun from the box.

fleet	pod
flock	school
litter	team

1. A ________________ of boats left the dock at 5 p.m.

2. Jen's cat gave birth to a ________________ of four kittens.

3. A ________________ of birds landed in the tree.

4. The ________________ won six games in a row.

5. A ________________ of fish swam in the pond.

6. A ________________ of dolphins leaped around the boat.

Skill 52: Collective Nouns

Directions: A collective noun is missing from each sentence below. Fill in each blank with a noun from the box.

school	team	herd

1. The ________________ of soccer players boarded the plane.

2. The whale spotted a ________________ of fish.

3. A ________________ of buffalo roamed the hills.

Directions: Write five sentences about what you would pack if you were going to camp. Each sentence should have two nouns.

____

____

____

____

____

____

____

____

LANGUAGE ARTS

Skill 53: Proper Nouns

Proper nouns are nouns that name specific people, places, and pets. Days of the week and months of the year are also proper nouns. Proper nouns begin with a capital letter.

Directions: Write the proper nouns on the lines below. Use capital letters at the beginning of each word.

boulder, colorado

____

fluffy

____

jessica dobson

____

boston, massachusetts

____

matthew johnson

____

spike

____

Skill 53: Proper Nouns

Directions: Circle the words that are proper nouns. Then, rewrite the proper nouns correctly.

1.	st. patrick's day	leprechaun	__________
2.	city	new york	__________
3.	new year's day	snow	__________
4.	hanukkah	lights	__________
5.	mrs. smith	teacher	__________
6.	pumpkin	halloween	__________
7.	saturday	sister	__________
8.	hearts	february	__________
9.	dog	spot	__________
10.	mr. benham	doctor	__________

LANGUAGE ARTS

Skill 54: Plural Nouns (with s)

Plural nouns name more than one person, place, or thing.

Directions: Circle the correct plural noun in each sentence.

1. The three (school, schools) are on the same street.
2. Two (cat, cats) climbed up the tree.
3. The (crab, crabs) has sharp claws.
4. Many (bush, bushes) have berries on them.
5. There are two (Julio, Julios) in my class.
6. Those (girl, girls) waved at you.
7. Three (doctor, doctors) left for the day.
8. (Flower, Flowers) can have many petals on them.

Skill 54: Plural Nouns (with s)

Directions: Read the words in the box. Write the words in the correct column.

stripes	picture	colors	kittens	cake
moons	glass	book	triangle	stars

Skill 55: Plural Nouns (with es)

If a noun ends in **sh**, **ch**, **s**, or **x**, add **es** to make it plural.

Examples: one ax → two ax**es** one brush → many brush**es**
one pouch → six pouch**es** one bus → seven bus**es**

Directions: Write the sentences with the plural form of the underlined words.

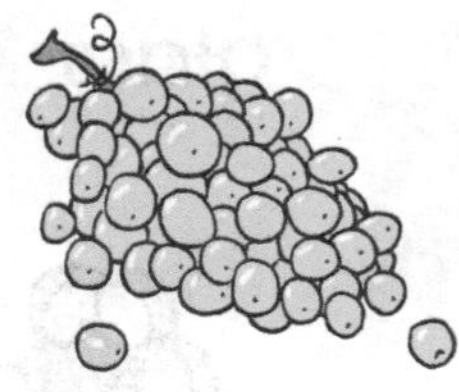
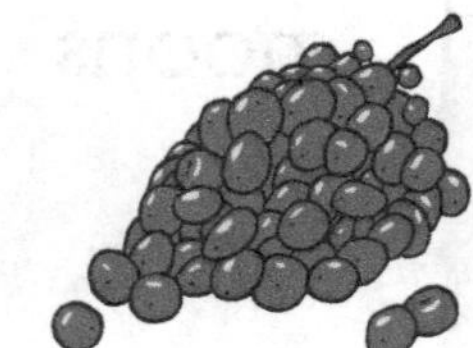

1. Use the box to carry the lemons.

____

2. The peach are on the table.

____

3. There are two bunch of grapes on the table.

____

____

4. Each of the class will get to pick some blueberries.

____

____

5. Put the vegetables in the blue dish.

____

____

Skill 55: Plural Nouns (with es)

Directions: Read the sentences. Write the correct plural word below each underlined word.

1. There were strawberry <u>bush</u> on the farm.

2. We ate our <u>lunch</u> at some picnic tables.

3. The <u>bus</u> picked us up at eight o'clock.

4. Mrs. Jenson gave us <u>glass</u> of lemonade.

5. We waited on the <u>bench</u> outside the library.

6. Mr. Manson gave us some <u>box</u> to use.

7. Many <u>branch</u> were heavy with fruit.

LANGUAGE ARTS

Skill 56: Irregular Plural Nouns

Some plural nouns are formed by changing the whole word.

Examples: one **man** → three **men**
one **goose** → four **geese**
one **woman** → eight **women**
one **foot** → two **feet**
one **child** → a few **children**
one **tooth** → many **teeth**
one **mouse** → fifteen **mice**

Some nouns do not change at all in their plural forms.

Examples: one **deer** → many **deer**
one **moose** → nine **moose**
one **fish** → sixty **fish**
one **sheep** → one hundred **sheep**

Directions: Draw a line to match each phrase to the correct plural form.

one child	nine deer
one tooth	two feet
one foot	seven mice
one man	five teeth
one deer	many children
one mouse	three men
one goose	seven geese

Skill 56: Irregular Plural Nouns

Directions: Look at the following plural words. Write the word that means "one" next to it. Remember, some nouns do not change at all in their plural form.

1. children ____________________
2. moose ____________________
3. people ____________________
4. men ____________________
5. halves ____________________
6. women ____________________
7. sheep ____________________
8. teeth ____________________

LANGUAGE ARTS

Skill 57: Pronouns

Pronouns are words that can be used instead of nouns. **I**, **me**, **you**, **he**, **she**, **him**, **her**, **it**, **we**, **they**, and **them** are pronouns.

Directions: Read each sentence. Then, in the second sentence, use the correct pronoun.

She

He

1. Dan likes funny books.

   ______________ likes funny books.

2. Jack and Sam went to the zoo.

   ______________ went to the zoo.

3. My dog likes to play in the park.

   ______________ likes to play in the park.

4. Sara is a very good swimmer.

   ______________ is a very good swimmer.

5. Meg and Ted are friends.

   ______________ are friends.

6. Todd was born in New York.

   ______________ was born in New York.

Skill 57: Pronouns

Directions: Write a pronoun in each blank. More than one answer may be correct.

1. ______________ went to the school yesterday.

2. ______________ are going to the playground.

3. Is that package for ______________?

4. ______________ are on the same soccer team.

5. ______________ had a great time last year at the museum.

6. Tanya gave ______________ an invitation to the party.

7. ______________ took the subway downtown.

8. Running is good for ______________.

9. ______________ want to go to the movies.

10. ______________ can't wait for my birthday.

Skill 58: Reflexive Pronouns

Reflexive pronouns end in **self** or **selves**. **Myself**, **yourself**, **himself**, **herself**, **itself**, **ourselves**, and **themselves** are reflexive pronouns.

Directions: Circle the pronouns in the following paragraph.

I will never forget the first hockey game I ever saw. Mom, Dad, Irina, and I drove downtown to the stadium. It was so bright compared to the night sky. We were excited to see the Blue Jackets play. The stadium was filled with so many people. They cheered when the players skated onto the rink. Irina and I screamed and clapped ourselves silly. We laughed when the Blue Jackets' mascot did a funny dance. The best part of the game was when the winning goal was scored. It was a night to remember for me.

Directions: Write 3 sentences with reflexive pronouns.

____

____

____

____

____

Skill 58: Reflexive Pronouns

Directions: Fill in each blank below with a reflexive pronoun.

1. The team served __________________ snacks and drinks after practice.

2. Ava cut __________________ when she climbed over the bleachers.

3. Tim blamed __________________ for not checking the stadium better.

4. "You should be proud of __________________ for a great practice!" said Coach.

Directions: Write 3 sentences about your favorite thing to do. Use 3 reflexive pronouns.

____

____

____

____

____

____

____

LANGUAGE ARTS

Skill 59: Adjectives

Adjectives are words that describe nouns. Adjectives can tell number, color, size, shape, or anything that adds detail. A sentence can have more than one adjective.

Example: **Four** tulips are in my **colorful** garden.

Directions: Circle the adjectives in the sentences.

1. Where is the gray bug?
2. Lenny has hot soup and cold milk for lunch.
3. Giant dinosaurs lived many years ago.
4. Eva and Pat used sparkly paint to decorate their pencil boxes.
5. Selma ate a yellow banana and eleven raisins for snack.
6. Jessie is singing a beautiful song.
7. A tired Melina fell asleep on her beach towel.
8. We went to the county zoo on a sunny day.
9. Jacob tried to wash and dry his squirming puppy.

LANGUAGE ARTS

Skill 59: Adjectives

Directions: Circle the adjectives.

heavy	twelve	silly	gold
walked	sneezed	hairy	wiggle
old	dry	blue	new
house	star	school	awful
loose	broken	strong	friend
book	sing	parked	tired
shoe	whale	wrinkled	blink

Directions: Use the above adjectives to finish the sentences. Or, write your own adjectives on the lines.

1. Whitney held the ______________________ snake.
2. Jo broke that ______________________ lamp.
3. Charlie tried to lift the ______________________ lamb.
4. Bailey rode his ______________________ scooter.

LANGUAGE ARTS

Skill 60: Comparative Adjectives

Add **er** to an adjective to show that one thing is more than something else. Add **est** to an adjective to show that it is the most.

Example: Jan is fast.
Jake is fast**er**.
Marcia is fast**est**.

Directions: Read the sentences below. Circle the correct adjective in parentheses.

1. The Nile River is (longest, longer) than the Amazon River.
2. The (tall, tallest) waterfall in the world is Angel Falls in Venezuela.
3. Mount Everest is the (highest, higher) mountain.
4. The Pacific Ocean is (deeper, deep) than the Indian Ocean.
5. It is the world's (deeper, deepest) ocean.
6. That was the (longest, longer) movie I've seen.

Skill 60: Comparative Adjectives

Directions: Fill in the spaces with the missing adjectives.

hard	harder	________
________	faster	fastest
dark	________	darkest
________	younger	________
kind	________	kindest
________	shorter	________
small	________	________
new	________	________

Directions: Write two sentences that compare people or things that are alike in some way.

Example: Naomi is older than Hasaan. Frank is the oldest.

1. ____

____

2. ____

____

LANGUAGE ARTS

Skill 61: Verbs

A **verb** is the action word in a sentence. Verbs tell what something does or that something exists.

Example: **Run**, **sleep**, and **jump** are verbs.

Directions: Circle the verbs in the sentences below.

1. The puppy sniffs the flowers.
2. We play hockey every day.
3. Susan pitches the ball very well.
4. Mike runs faster than everyone.
5. Chris sleeps all morning.
6. Laura hit a home run.
7. We eat a snack when we get home from school.
8. Andrea climbs up the hill.

Skill 61: Verbs

Directions: Write each word in the correct column.

cook	talk	cleans	grass	skip
tree	dances	bird	park	dog

Verbs	**Nouns**
____________________	____________________
____________________	____________________
____________________	____________________
____________________	____________________
____________________	____________________

LANGUAGE ARTS

Skill 62: Subject-Verb Agreement (adding s)

When there is only one person or thing, add **s** to the end of an action verb.

Example: Cameron run**s** to the park.

An action verb does not end with **s** when there is more than one person or thing, or when using **you**.

Example: The balloons float through the air.
You sing the song.

Directions: Read each sentence below. Choose the correct verb form. Then, write it on the line.

1. Wes _______________ a game for the family. (pick, picks)
2. Mrs. Jones _______________ to us every day. (read, reads)
3. Alicia _______________ what the song is. (know, knows)
4. Mom and Dad _______________. (laugh, laughs)
5. Ben _______________ a picture on a big sheet of paper. (draw, draws)
6. She _______________ (raise, raises) her hand.
7. They _______________ a good team. (make, makes)

LANGUAGE ARTS

Skill 62: Subject-Verb Agreement (adding s)

Directions: Read each sentence below. Add an **s** to the end of the verb if needed.

1. She smile__ at her best friend.

2. Lyra choose__ the song.

3. She pick__ her favorite game.

4. Tom roll__ the ball down the hill.

5. Mom take__ the first turn onto Summit Street.

6. He move__ his piece four spaces.

7. Mom roll__ the dice.

8. Jake throw__ his towel into the hamper.

9. Mom never win__ this game!

10. She bike __ to school.

11. Saki dance __ on Fridays.

12. Jackson sing __ in the choir.

Skill 63: Subject-Verb Agreement (adding es)

Sometimes, **es** needs to be added instead of just **s**. Add **es** to verbs that end in **sh**, **ch**, **s**, **x**, and **z**.

Examples: Eve brush**es** her dog every weekend.
Grandma stitch**es** the buttons on the coat.

When there is more than one person or thing, verbs do not end in **s** or **es**.

Directions: Choose the correct verb at the end of each sentence and write it on the line.

1. The bug ________________ when it flies. (buzz, buzzes)

2. Alex and Jesse ________________ all the dishes after dinner. (wash, washes)

3. Jasmine ________________ the ball to Hailey. (toss, tosses)

4. Noelle ________________ for a kitten when she blows out her candles. (wish, wishes)

5. Charles ________________ the batter before he pours it in the pan. (mix, mixes)

6. He ________________ his old neighborhood. (miss, misses)

Skill 63: Subject-Verb Agreement (adding es)

Directions: Circle the verb in each sentence below. If it is not correct, write the correct form.

1. Tina catch the bus each morning. ____________________
2. The cat hisses at the bird. ____________________
3. My parents relaxes on the weekends. ____________________
4. Corey waxes his surfboard on the beach. ____________________
5. The sports car pass the truck. ____________________
6. The plane touches down at noon. ____________________
7. Gail rushes home from school. ____________________
8. The waves crashes on the shore. ____________________
9. Marcia wash her hair every day. ____________________
10. Marco fix the car. ____________________

Skill 64: Irregular Verbs (Am, Is, Are)

Am, **is**, and **are** are special verbs that tell us something is happening now.

Use **am** with **I**. Example: **I am**.
Use **is** to tell about one person or thing. Example: **He is**.
Use **are** to tell about more than one. Example: **We are**.
Use **are** with **you**. Example: **You are**.

Directions: Write **is**, **are**, or **am** in the sentences below.

1. My friends ______________ helping me build a tree house
2. I ______________ happy my birthday is next week.
3. It ______________ in my backyard.
4. You ______________ my friend.
5. We ______________ using hammers, wood, and nails.
6. It ______________ a very hard job.
7. I ______________ lucky to have good friends.
8. The sky ______________ full of stars tonight.

LANGUAGE ARTS

Skill 64: Irregular Verbs (Am, Is, Are)

Directions: Read each sentence below. Choose the correct verb from the parentheses ( ). Write it on the line.

1. You ______________ a great dancer. (are, am)

2. I ______________ tall and strong. (is, am)

3. Blanche and Dante ______________ in second grade. (is, are)

4. This chili ______________ too spicy! (is, are)

5. All the kids in my class ______________ ready. (is, are)

6. I ______________ a niece. (are, am)

7. That skateboard ______________ broken. (are, is)

8. We ______________ in the same class. (are, is)

9. You ______________ lucky you won. (are, is)

10. Everyone ______________ excited for the party. (are, is)

LANGUAGE ARTS

Skill 65: Irregular Verbs (Has, Have, Had)

Use **has** and **have** to tell about now. Use **had** to tell about something that already happened.

Directions: Write **has**, **have**, or **had** in the sentences below.

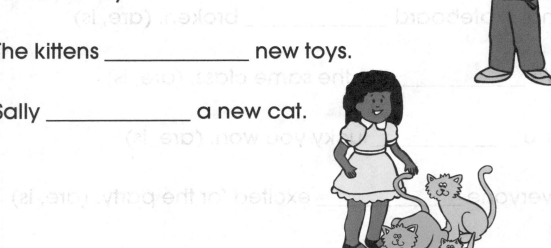

1. We _____________ four cats at home.
2. Gigi _____________ brown fur.
3. Sharon _____________ a book about cats.
4. Bucky and Charlie _____________ gray fur.
5. We _____________ to bring our cat to the vet yesterday.
6. My friend Tom _____________ one cat, but he ran away.
7. The kittens _____________ new toys.
8. Sally _____________ a new cat.

Skill 65: Irregular Verbs (Has, Have, Had)

Directions: Read each sentence below. Then, read the pair of verbs in parentheses. Choose the correct verb form and write it on the line.

1. Maple trees and oak trees ______________ similar leaves. (has, have)

2. A gingko tree ______________ leaves that look like fans. (has, have)

3. We ______________ a large fir tree in the backyard. (has, have)

4. The Nelsons ______________ many trees that bloom in the spring. (has, have)

5. Max ______________ an old maple tree in his front yard. (has, have)

6. An apple tree will ______________ a lot of fruit in the fall. (has, have)

7. He ______________ been gone all night. (has, have)

8. The family ______________ left for the movies. (has, have)

LANGUAGE ARTS

Skill 66: Forming the Past Tense by Adding ed

Verbs in the **past tense** tell about things that already happened. Add **ed** to most verbs to tell about the past.

Examples: Lisa jump**ed** over the log.
Jessica push**ed** the stroller.

If the verb already ends in **e**, just add **d**.

Examples: The class hik**ed** two miles. (hik**e**)
She plac**ed** the plates on the table. (plac**e**)

Directions: The sentences below are missing verbs. Complete each sentence with the past tense of the verb in parentheses ( ).

1. We ________________ to many countries. (travel)
2. She ________________ Mount Shasta in California. (climb)
3. She ________________ to visit Iceland some day. (hope)
4. Jan ________________ a group called the Alpine Club. (start)
5. The class ________________ the volcanoes of South America. (explore)
6. She ________________ hard so she could climb in her spare time. (work)
7. Ann ________________ talking until the end of class. (continue)
8. The boy ________________ the ball. (kick)

Skill 66: Forming the Past Tense by Adding ed

Directions: Rewrite the sentences below in the past tense by changing the underlined verb.

1. The dog pull on his leash.

   ____

2. She live in the house next door.

   ____

3. Bailey show the teacher he could write the report well.

   ____

   ____

4. She want to set records in running.

   ____

5. The girl walk to the store.

   ____

6. Mrs. Samson talk to her students.

   ____

7. The airplane look large.

   ____

8. The band play my favorite songs.

   ____

Skill 67 Past-Tense Verbs (Was, Were)

Was and **were** tell about something that already happened.

Use **was** to tell about one person or thing.

Examples: I **was**, he **was**.

Use **were** to tell about more than one person or thing or when using the word **you**.

Examples: We **were**, you **were**.

Directions: Write **was** or **were** in each sentence.

1. Allison ______________ eight years old on her birthday.
2. Last Saturday, my brother ______________ on TV.
3. Tom and Caleb ______________ happy to be at the party.
4. A news reporter ______________ at the park.
5. Meg ______________ too shy to sing.
6. I ______________ proud of my sister.
7. Ben ______________ sorry he dropped his cupcake.
8. All of the children ______________ happy to be home.

Skill 67: Past-Tense Verbs (Was, Were)

Directions: The sentences below are in the present tense. Rewrite them in the past tense.

Example: The basketball is in the gym.
The basketball was in the gym.

1. Mom is worried we would miss the bus.

____

2. The basketball court is in the gym.

____

3. Mom and Dad are happy to see our good manners.

____

4. We are excited about the interview on TV.

____

5. I am glad Tony wore the hat I gave him.

____

6. You are on vacation.

____

7. Dad is at the pool.

____

8. Lily is writing a report on presidents.

____

LANGUAGE ARTS

Skill 68: Past-Tense Verbs (Went)

The past tense of the verb **go** is **went**.

Present Tense	Past Tense
We **go** to the zoo with our family.	We **went** to the zoo with our family.
Laura **goes** to California.	Laura **went** to California.

Directions: Rewrite each sentence in the past tense.

1. We go to class.

____

2. He goes to his music lesson on Wednesday.

____

3. The nurse goes home at lunch.

____

4. We go skiing with David and Luke.

____

5. Who goes to pick up the pizza?

____

6. The family goes to the movies.

____

LANGUAGE ARTS

Skill

68: Past-Tense Verbs (Went)

Directions: Write the correct past-tense verb for the underlined verb on the lines below.

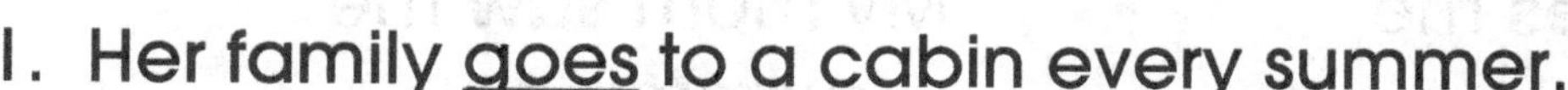

1. Her family goes to a cabin every summer.

2. Everyone goes swimming in the lake.

3. Sam goes on long bike rides.

4. Grandma and Grandpa go for walks.

5. They go to a big family party on the lake.

6. We go to visit the new bookstore.

7. We go to see Dr. Benson.

8. Maria goes to visit her grandparents.

LANGUAGE ARTS

Skill 69: Past-Tense Verbs (Saw)

The past tense of the verb **see** is **saw**.

Present Tense	Past Tense
My mom **sees** me swimming.	My mom **saw** me swimming.
Franco and Ana **see** the puppy every day.	Franco and Ana **saw** the puppy every day.

Directions: Rewrite each sentence in the past tense.

1. We see clouds in the sky.

____

2. The bear sees the girl climbing the mountain.

____

3. Dad sees better when he put on his glasses.

____

4. The deer see their mother.

____

5. Emily sees that movie three times.

____

6. Dylan sees the hot air balloon.

____

Skill 69: Past-Tense Verbs (Saw)

Directions: Write the correct past-tense verb for each underlined verb.

1. We see many interesting things on our visit.

   ____

2. My sister sees seals playing in the water.

   ____

3. Nate sees many strange and amazing things there.

   ____

   ____

4. We see so many animals at the zoo.

   ____

5. What is the first thing you see in the morning?

   ____

6. The family sees many movies

   ____

7. The class sees many animals at the zoo.

   ____

8. Pedro sees the stars from his window.

   ____

LANGUAGE ARTS

Skill 70: Adverbs

Adverbs are words that tell more about verbs. They tell how, where, or when something happens. Adverbs often end with *ly*.

Directions: What does each adverb tell about the verb? Write ***how***, ***where***, or ***when*** on each line.

1. Ben walked **near** the beehive. ______________
2. Rita whispered **quietly** in my ear. ______________
3. Lucy yelled **loudly** at the game. ______________
4. Mrs. Holmes exercises **daily**. ______________
5. Jared arrived at the movie **early**. ______________
6. Adrian's boots are **here**. ______________
7. Darla pedaled her bike **quickly**. ______________
8. Hannah **often** reads books about animals. ______________
9. Drew found the toy **inside** the cereal box. ______________

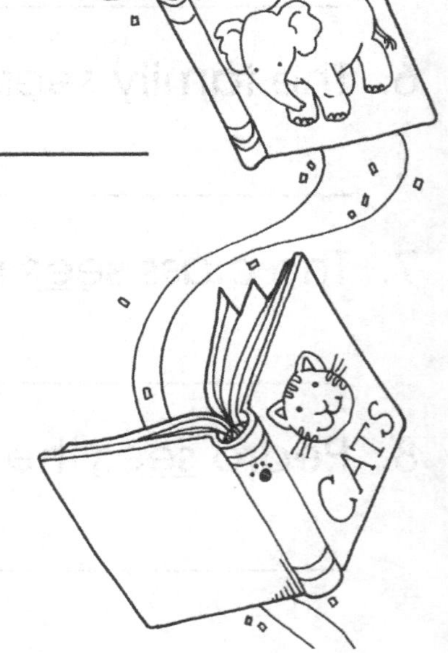

Skill

70: Adverbs

Directions: Use the adverbs to finish the sentences.

quickly	quietly	easily	softly
sadly	too	fast	well
slowly	carefully	loudly	gracefully

1. Jenny ran ______________________ and finished first.

2. Did Sal ride ______________________?

3. My friend speaks so ______________________, I can't hear her.

4. Will you work ______________________?

5. Check your homework ______________________.

6. Rianne and Bert danced ______________________.

7. The turtle moved ______________________ across the yard.

8. We heard Marlene blow her whistle ______________________.

LANGUAGE ARTS

Skill 71: Statements

A **statement** is a sentence that begins with a capital letter and ends with a period. A statement tells the reader something.

Example: My brother and I fly kites when we go to the beach.

Directions: Rewrite the following sentences. Each statement should begin with a capital letter and end with a period.

1. people have flown kites for thousands of years

___

2. early kites were made in China

___

3. they were covered in silk

___

4. some kites are shaped like dragons or fish

___

5. some kites are tiny

___

6. other kites are as long as one hundred feet

___

7. flying kites is a fun thing to do

___

Skill 71: Statements

Directions: Rewrite the following sentences. Each statement should begin with a capital letter and end with a period.

1. we like to ride our bikes

   ____

2. we ride by the beach and in the mountains

   ____

3. we go down the hill very fast

   ____

4. bikes are fun to bring camping

   ____

5. we keep our bikes shiny and clean

   ____

6. we know how to change the tires

   ____

7. i'd like to be in a bike race

   ____

8. it would be fun to meet other bikers

   ____

LANGUAGE ARTS

Skill 72: Questions

Questions are sentences that ask something. They begin with a capital letter and end with a question mark.

Directions: Write the questions on the lines below. Begin each sentence with a capital letter and end it with a question mark.

1. are you in my class

   ____

2. what is your name

   ____

3. how old are you

   ____

4. do you like to play any sports

   ____

5. where are your toys

   ____

6. did you put the dishes away

   ____

LANGUAGE ARTS

Skill 72: Questions

Directions: If a sentence is a statement, add a period on the line. If a sentence is a question, add a question mark on the line.

1. Taylor and her family drove to New York__
2. What city do you want to visit__
3. They drove for five days__
4. Liz has two cats__
5. What did you do during the long plane ride__
6. Can you guess what I found on the beach__
7. Beth is going to join the drama club__
8. Where will they go on vacation next year__

LANGUAGE ARTS

Skill 73: Exclamations

Exclamations are sentences that are said with great feeling and end with an exclamation point. An exclamation may be only one or two words showing fear, surprise, or pain.

Example: Oh, no!

Directions: Put a period at the end of the sentences that tell something. Put an exclamation point at the end of the sentences that show a strong feeling. Put a question mark at the end of the sentences that ask a question.

1. How fast can the deer run__
2. Wow__
3. Look at that cheetah go__
4. What a great day__
5. Hurray__
6. I ran upstairs to find my dad__

7. What fun__
8. Where did you leave your book__

Skill 73: Exclamations

Directions: Put a period at the end of the sentences that tell something. Put an exclamation point at the end of the sentences that tell a strong feeling. Put a question mark at the end of the sentences that ask a question.

1. Should we run together__
2. I brought the mail into the house__
3. Do you want to see the movie__
4. It is almost time to leave__
5. The snow began to fall__
6. Hurry__
7. Get your sled__
8. Do you want to make a snowman__

LANGUAGE ARTS

Skill 74: Commands

Commands tell someone to do something.

Example: "Be careful."

It can also be written as "Be careful!" if it tells a strong feeling.

Directions: Put a period at the end of the command sentences. Use an exclamation point if the sentence tells a strong feeling. Then, write your own commands on the lines below.

1. Clean your room__
2. Now__
3. Be careful when your stove is hot__
4. Watch out__
5. Read the recipe__

____

____

____

____

Skill 74: Commands

Directions: Put a period at the end of the command sentences. Use an exclamation point if the sentence tells a strong feeling.

1. Do not forget your lunch__
2. Look inside the envelope__
3. Wait__
4. Wash your hands before you cook__
5. Look out__
6. Share your toys with your brother__
7. Close the door__
8. Walk to school__
9. Don't be late__
10. Watch your step__

Skill 75: Combining Sentences (Nouns)

Sometimes, sentences can be combined if they tell about the same thing.

Example: Bats eat bugs.   Birds eat bugs.

Both sentences tell about things that eat bugs. These two sentences can be combined into one by using the word **and**.

Example: Bats **and** birds eat bugs.

Directions: Read each pair of sentences below. If the sentences can be joined with the word **and**, make a check mark (✓) on the line. If not, leave the line blank.

1. _____ Hummingbirds visit my birdfeeder. Doves visit my birdfeeder.

2. _____ Parrots live in warm places. Penguins live in cold places.

3. _____ Hawks build nests on ledges. Eagles build nests on ledges.

4. _____ Hummingbirds like flowers. Bees like flowers.

5. _____ Geese fly south for the winter. Owls do not fly south in the winter.

Skill 75: Combining Sentences (Nouns)

Directions: Combine each pair of sentences below into one sentence. Write the new sentence.

1. David played the drums. Rick played the drums.

   ____

2. Cardinals eat seeds. Finches eat seeds.

   ____

3. Cats like to be pet. Dogs like to be pet.

   ____

4. The dogs were hungry. The birds were hungry.

   ____

5. The sky was cloudy. The sky was gray.

   ____

6. We went to dinner. We went to the concert.

   ____

7. Seth buys ice cream. Seth buys soda.

   ____

8. Mom went to the beach. Dad went to the beach.

   ____

LANGUAGE ARTS

Skill 76: Combining Sentences (Verbs)

Sometimes sentences can be combined.

Example: Penny cooks on Sunday afternoon.
Penny writes on Sunday afternoon.

Both sentences tell what Penny does on Sunday afternoon. These two sentences can be joined using the word **and**.

Example: Penny cooks **and** writes on Sunday afternoon.

Directions: Read the sentences below. Write the missing word or words.

1. Dad carried out the sandwiches. Dad placed them on the table. ______________ carried out the sandwiches ______________ placed them on the table.

2. Kate took a deep breath. Kate blew out the candles. ______________ took a deep breath ______________ blew out the candles.

3. Mom flies a kite. Mom unpacks the lunch basket. ______________ flies a kite ______________ unpacks the lunch basket.

LANGUAGE ARTS

Skill 76: Combining Sentences (Verbs)

Directions: Combine each pair of sentences below into one sentence.

1. We are throwing a party. We are buying decorations.

   ____

2. I went to the library. I chose many books.

   ____

3. Travis drove to the store. Travis bought groceries.

   ____

4. My cat likes to sleep. My cat likes to eat her food.

   ____

Directions: Write two sentences that tell about things you do at school. Use a different verb in each sentence.

____

____

Directions: Now, combine the two sentences you wrote using the word **and**.

____

____

LANGUAGE ARTS

Skill 77: Combining Sentences (Adjectives)

Sometimes sentences can be combined.

Example: The car was black. The car was shiny.

The adjectives **black** and **shiny** both describe **car**. These two sentences can be combined into one by using the word **and**.

Example: The car was black **and** shiny.

Directions: Read each pair of sentences below. If the adjectives in both sentences describe the same person or thing, the sentences can be combined. Make a check mark (✓) on the line if the two sentences can be combined.

1. _____ Jayna's drawing is bright. Jayna's drawing is cheerful.

2. _____ Jayna painted the forest. The forest was colorful.

3. _____ Jayna's paintbrush is soft. Jayna's paints are new.

4. _____ The couch is small. The couch is yellow.

5. _____ The roses are red. The bushes are big.

6. _____ The otter is gray. The whale is gray.

LANGUAGE ARTS

Skill 77: Combining Sentences (Adjectives)

Directions: Combine each pair of sentences below into one sentence.

1. The ring is shiny. The ring is silver.

   ____

2. The night is cold. The night is dark.

   ____

3. Lori's paintings are beautiful. Lori's paintings are popular.

   ____

4. Jake's bike is new. Jake's bike is red.

   ____

Directions: Write two sentences that describe your clothes. Use a different adjective in each sentence.

____

____

Directions: Now, combine the two sentences you wrote using the word **and**.

____

____

Skill 78: Capitalizing the First Word in a Sentence

The first word in a sentence begins with a capital letter.

Directions: Read each sentence. Underline with three short lines the first letter of each word. Rewrite the word correctly.

1. Today today is the first day of school.
2. ________ sam takes the bus to school.
3. ________ the children play soccer.
4. ________ everyone has fun reading.
5. ________ when will we do a science experiment?
6. ________ lunch is served.
7. ________ our principal came to visit.
8. ________ students should be on time.
9. ________ the teacher gives us homework.
10. ________ clean your desk.
11. ________ have a great day.

LANGUAGE ARTS

Skill 78: Capitalizing the First Word in a Sentence

Directions: Rewrite each sentence below. Make sure your sentences begin with a capital letter.

1. heather likes to bake.

   ____

2. her grandma likes to help her.

   ____

3. they make delicious chocolate cookies.

   ____

4. grandma teaches her how to make bread.

   ____

5. would you like to learn how to bake?

   ____

Directions: Write a sentence about something new. Be sure to start your sentence with a capital letter.

____

Directions: Write a sentence that explains one reason you like autumn. Be sure to start your sentence with a capital letter.

____

LANGUAGE ARTS

Skill 79: Capitalizing Names

The **name of a person**, **pet**, or **product** always begins with a capital letter.

Example: Ⓐndrew is Ⓑrian's brother.
The baby polar bear's name is Ⓔllie.

Directions: Complete each sentence below. Write each name in parentheses ( ). Remember to capitalize the names of people, pets, and products.

1. ________________ (ken's) favorite food is corn on the cob.

2. ________________ (ollie) loves pickles and crackers.

3. ________________ (jan's) pet kitten, ________________ (zorro), eats ________________________ (pet food plus) food.

4. ____ (tom's banana brand crunch) is ________________ (amy's) favorite cereal.

5. ________________ (donna's) bunny, ________________ (jake), eats lettuce.

6. ________________ (alyssa) and ________________ (vicki) like ____ (tito's tasty tacos).

LANGUAGE ARTS

Skill 79: Capitalizing Names

Directions: Complete each sentence below. Write each name in parentheses ( ). Remember to capitalize the names of people, pets, and products.

1. My brother named his pet lizard ________________ (izzy).

2. ________________ (finn's) favorite pizza is ________________ (denny's deep dish).

3. ________________ (samantha) dances after school.

4. We named the kittens ________________ (phantom) and ________________ (shadow).

5. ________________ (joyce's) birthday is in December.

6. ________________ (hal) and ________________ (eddie) went camping.

7. ________________ (kim) wrote a report on Thomas Jefferson.

8. Mom bought ________________ (creamy's) ice cream for ________________ (tanya's) party.

Skill 80: Capitalizing Titles

A **title** is a word that comes before a person's name. A title gives more information about who a person is. Titles that come before a name begin with a capital letter.

Examples: Grandma Stella Cousin Holly Doctor Johnson

Titles of respect also begin with a capital letter. Here are some titles of respect: **Mr.**, **Mrs.**, **Ms.**, and **Miss**.

Examples: Mr. Garcia Miss Billo Ms. Ramirez Mrs. Chang

Directions: Cross out the titles that should be capitalized and write the correct capitalized titles above them.

1. Last night, I went to a play with aunt Stacy and uncle Brian.
2. I sat next to cousin Daniel and cousin Mia.
3. The play was about ms. Amelia Earhart, the first woman to fly across the Atlantic Ocean alone.
4. ms. Earhart led an eventful life.
5. She even met president Roosevelt.
6. After the play, I met aunt Stacy's friend, mrs. Simpson.
7. She played the role of ms. Earhart.
8. I also met mr. Davis.
9. He played the role of president Roosevelt.

LANGUAGE ARTS

Skill 80: Capitalizing Titles

Directions: Rewrite each of the following sentences. Remember, titles begin with a capital letter.

1. dr. Donovan has been my doctor since I was a baby.

2. judge Millan recently went on vacation.

3. grandpa Emil gave aunt Bea the book.

4. grandma Helen read it last year.

5. She read a book about president George Washington.

6. mrs. Ritter brought her class to the zoo.

LANGUAGE ARTS

Skill 81: Capitalizing Place Names

The **names of specific places** always begin with a capital letter.

Examples: Rockwell Elementary School
Orlando, Florida
Mars

Directions: Complete each sentence with the correct capitalized word in parentheses ( ).

1. My family left San Diego, ______________________________ (california), yesterday morning.

2. We waved good-bye to our house on ____________________ ____________________ (marzo avenue).

3. We passed ____ (mountain view library).

4. Then, we crossed ______________________________ (coronado bridge).

5. We were on our way across the ________________________ (united states)!

LANGUAGE ARTS

Skill 81: Capitalizing Place Names

Directions: Cross out the words that should be capitalized and write the correct capitalized words above them.

1. I want to visit seattle, washington.

2. My family is in colorado.

3. Today, we went to the denver children's museum.

4. Tomorrow, we will head to mt. evans.

5. Next week, we'll be in new york.

6. We will visit columbia university, where my parents went to college.

7. Then, we will head northeast through new hampshire.

8. I can't wait to see portland, maine.

Skill 82: Capitalizing Days, Months, and Holidays

The **days of the week** each begin with a capital letter.

Examples: Tuesday, Thursday, Saturday

The **months of the year** are also capitalized.

Examples: January, May, October

The **names of holidays** begin with a capital letter.

Examples: Christmas, Thanksgiving, Kwanzaa

Directions: Cross out the words that should be capitalized and write the correct capitalized words above them.

1. I have to go to the dentist on wednesday.

2. Soccer practice starts on monday afternoon.

3. Sara's favorite holiday is valentine's day.

4. There is no school on presidents' day.

5. Winter starts in december.

6. We will go to the pet store on saturday morning.

7. Grandma will visit in july.

LANGUAGE ARTS

Skill 82: Capitalizing Days, Months, and Holidays

Directions: Read the list of holidays and dates. Rewrite the holiday or date correctly.

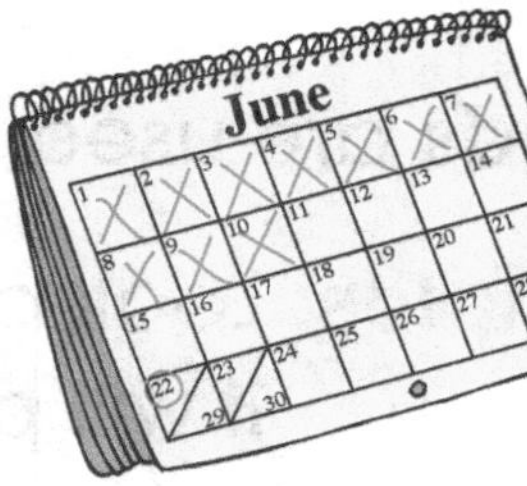

1. Jamie's birthday march 20 ____________________
2. valentine's Day February 14 ____________________
3. Simon's party april 2 ____________________
4. Kati's first birthday august 22 ____________________
5. the Nelsons' trip october 4 ____________________
6. thanksgiving November 23 ____________________
7. Jackson's birthday december 29 ____________________
8. new year's day January 1 ____________________
9. softball practice every tuesday ____________________
10. first day of school september 3 ____________________

LANGUAGE ARTS

Skill 83: Periods

Periods are used at the end of statements and commands.

Examples: Look at that big yard.
It will probably snow tomorrow.

Directions: Add the missing periods at the end of the sentences.

1. Most people do not like spiders__
2. That elm tree is tall__
3. Some mosquitoes like birds or flowers__
4. Every Saturday we go for a hike__
5. Today we will clean the house__
6. Bike up the trail__
7. Ray made a cake for the party__
8. Come help me in the kitchen__

Skill 83: Periods

Directions: Rewrite the following sentences. Each one should end with a period.

1. There are many types of flowers

____

2. Mrs. Samuel left us snacks

____

3. Go ask Mr. Glenson to come see the new pool

____

4. The family watched the fireworks

____

5. Bug spray can protect you from mosquito bites

____

6. Look at the plane

____

LANGUAGE ARTS

Skill 84: Question Marks

Use a **question mark** to end a sentence that asks a question.

Examples: Where did you park the car**?**
Did you go skating**?**

Directions: Read each answer below. Then, write the question that goes with the answer.

Example: **Q:** What color is the coat?
A: The coat is green.

1. **Q:** ______________________
   A: The book is about a dragon.

2. **Q:** ______________________
   A: Ashley is eight years old.

3. **Q:** ______________________
   A: Keiko went to the library.

4. **Q:** ______________________
   A: My skateboard is in the garage.

5. **Q:** ______________________
   A: Mr. Arnold lives in Seattle.

6. **Q:** ______________________
   A: I ate tacos for dinner.

Skill 84: Question Marks

Directions: Add question marks to the sentences that need them. Cross out the incorrect end marks.

1. What do you like about being a runner.
2. I love to tell stories.
3. Where do you get your ideas.
4. He used to be a teacher.
5. When do you sleep.
6. I camp about two weeks a year.
7. Do you have any brothers or sisters.
8. Do you like to ski or snowboard.
9. What time do you want to leave.
10. Are you finished with your book.

Skill 85: Exclamation Points

An **exclamation point** is used to end a sentence that is exciting. Sometimes, exclamation points are used to show surprise.

Examples: Look at the sunset! Wow!

Directions: Add exclamation points and periods where needed.

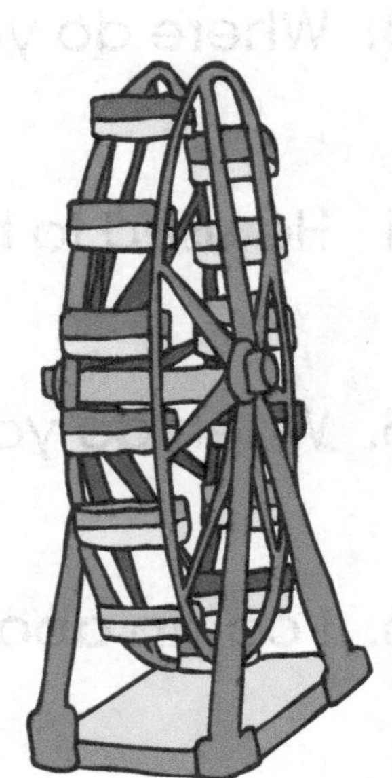

1. The fair is coming to town in September__
2. Win great prizes__
3. Hurry__
4. You can sample many foods__
5. There are new rides this year__

6. Admission is $10.00 for adults and $8.00 for kids under twelve__
7. The fair opens September 6 and closes September 12__
8. Don't miss all the fun__

Skill 85: Exclamation Points

Directions: Add exclamation points and periods where needed.

1. I went to the Crestview Fair__

2. I played a game called Catch the Ball__

3. I had the best time__

4. I won four stuffed animals__

5. I ate a snow cone and some popcorn__

6. All the goats escaped from their pen__

7. It did not take the farmers long to catch them, though__

8. Cotton candy got stuck in my hair__

9. My brother's favorite game was Spin the Wheel__

10. I can't wait to go again next year__

LANGUAGE ARTS

Skill 86: Periods in Abbreviations

An **abbreviation** is a short way of writing something. Most abbreviations are followed by a period.

The **days of the week** can be abbreviated.

Examples: Mon. Tues. Wed.

The **months of the year** can be abbreviated. **May, June**, and **July** are not abbreviated because their names are so short.

Examples: Jan. Feb. Mar.

People's titles are almost always abbreviated.

Examples: Mr. = mister Dr. = doctor

Types of streets are abbreviated in addresses.

Examples: St. = street Ave. = avenue

Directions: Read each underlined word in the first column. Find the matching abbreviation in the second column. Write the letter of the abbreviation on the line.

1. _____ 182 Summit <u>Street</u>	**a.** Thurs.
2. _____ <u>Doctor</u> Westin	**b.** Jan.
3. _____ <u>Thursday</u> morning	**c.** Dr.
4. _____ <u>October</u> 31, 2015	**d.** Ln.
5. _____ 92 Nookview <u>Lane</u>	**e.** St.
6. _____ <u>January</u> 1, 2017	**f.** Oct.

Skill 86: Periods in Abbreviations

Directions: Read each word in parentheses ( ). Write the abbreviation.

Example: Sunday, ___Nov.___ (November) 12

1. 167 Millway ____________ (Street)

2. ____________ (February) 10, 2006

3. ____________ (April) 4, 2014

4. ____________ (Mister) Fortega

5. Pacific ____________ (Drive)

6. ____________ (Wednesday) morning

Directions: Write your street address using an abbreviation.

____

Directions: Write today's date using abbreviations for the day of the week and month.

____

Skill 87: Commas With Dates, Cities, and States

Commas are used in dates. They are used in between the day of the month and the year.

Examples: October 8, 2002

Commas are also used in between the names of cities and states.

Examples: Portland, Oregon

When the names of cities and states are in the middle of a sentence, a comma goes after the name of the state, too.

Examples: After we left Orlando, Florida, we headed north.

Directions: Add commas where they are needed.

1. Seth was born on September 26 2009.

2. He lives in Austin Texas.

3. Her cousin was born on November 3 2008.

4. Glen's grandparents live in Cleveland Ohio.

5. It is a long drive from Denver Colorado to Taos New Mexico.

6. The last time my grandparents visited was December 20 2014.

LANGUAGE ARTS

Skill 87: Commas With Dates, Cities, and States

Directions: Rewrite each item, adding commas where they are needed.

1. March 5 1984

______

2. Butte Montana

______

3. July 24 1974

______

4. The plane stopped in St. Louis Missouri to get more passengers.

______

______

5. It snowed nine inches in Portland Maine.

______

6. November 4 2015

______

7. Columbus Ohio is where my grandma lives.

______

8. My birthday is December 8 2008.

______

LANGUAGE ARTS

Skill 88: Commas in Series and in Letters

A **series** is a list of words. Use a comma after each word in the series except the last word.

Example: Mom bought fruit, vegetables, and bread.

In a letter, a comma follows **the greeting** and **the closing**.

Example: Dear Mr. Chang, Your friend,

Directions: Rewrite the sentences below. Use commas where needed.

1. Lily packed forks knives spoons and napkins.

___

___

2. Mom got out the picnic basket the plates and the cups.

___

___

3. Dad made sandwiches a salad and brownies.

___

___

4. Amelia brought bananas chocolate and apples.

___

___

LANGUAGE ARTS

Skill 88: Commas in Series and in Letters

Directions: Add commas where they are needed.

Dear Aiden

Yesterday, we went to the park. Owen Sam and Mom put down the picnic blanket. Dad carried the basket the drinks and the basketball from the car. We all ate tacos apples and cookies.

Pedro Maria and Mendo were at the park with their family, too. We played ball and fed the birds. Later, we shared our cookies with the Gomez family. I wish you could have been there!

Love

Nate

Directions: What three things would you bring to a picnic? Remember to separate the things in your list with commas.

____

____

Skill 89: Commas in Compound Sentences

A **compound sentence** is made up of two shorter sentences. The sentences are joined by a comma and the word **and** or **but**.

Example: Michelle went to the store.
She bought some markers.
Michelle went to the store**, and** she bought some markers.

Directions: Read the sentences below. Combine them using a comma and the word **and** or **but**.

1. The black cat is beautiful. The orange cat is friendly.

____

____

2. Raul is quick. Sophie is more graceful.

____

3. Anita rode her bike. Tony rode his scooter.

____

____

4. My new house is big. My old house was cozy.

____

____

Skill 89: Commas in Compound Sentences

Directions: Add commas where they are needed.

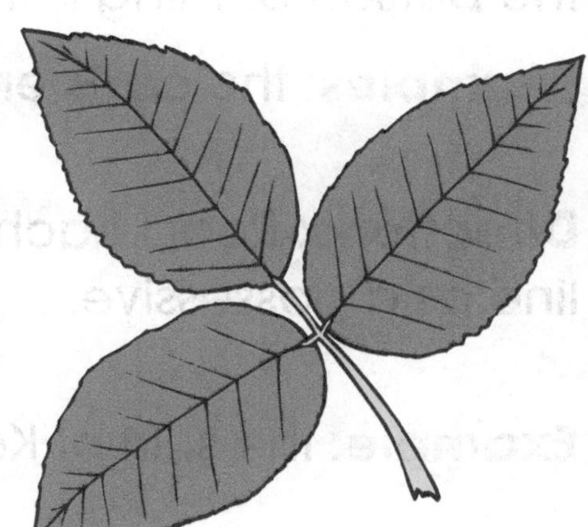

1. The leaves of the poison ivy plant are shaped like almonds and they come in groups of three.
2. Poison ivy can cause a rash and it can make you itch.
3. The leaves of the plant contain oil and it can cause a rash.
4. Some people can touch the plant but they will not get a rash.
5. The oil can stick to your clothes and is hard to remove.
6. Washing with soap and water can get rid of the oil and it can keep the rash from spreading.
7. You should be careful when hiking and you should know what poison ivy looks like.

Skill 90: Apostrophes in Possessives

When something belongs to a person or thing, they own it. An apostrophe and the letter **s** ('s) at the end of a word show that the person or thing is the owner.

Examples: the car**'s** engine Stacy**'s** eyes

Directions: Read each phrase below. Then, rewrite it on the line as a possessive.

Example: the shirt of Kali Kali's shirt

1. the roar of the lion ____________________
2. the lens of the camera ____________________
3. the bike of Jenna ____________________
4. the stripes of the tiger ____________________
5. the roof of the house ____________________
6. the hat of Tamika ____________________

Skill 90: Apostrophes in Possessives

Directions: Read the words below. Then, read the answer choices. Write the letter of your answer on the line.

1. _____ the trunk of the elephant
   a. the elephant's trunk **b.** the trunk's elephant

2. _____ the animals of Africa
   a. the animal's of Africa **b.** Africa's animals

3. _____ the books of Jake
   a. Jake book's **b.** Jake's books

4. _____ the leader of the band
   a. the band's leader **b.** the leader band's

5. _____ the favorite animal of Dawn
   a. Dawn favorite animal's **b.** Dawn's favorite animal

6. _____ the baby of the hippo
   a. the baby's hippo **b.** the hippo's baby

7. _____ the tent of Andy
   a. Andy's tent **b.** Andy tent

Skill 91: Quotation Marks in Dialogue

Quotation marks are used around the exact words a person says. One set of quotation marks is used before the first word the person says. Another set is used at the end of the person's words.

Example: Jorge said, **"**I am going to play in the band on Saturday.**"**

Remember to put the second pair of quotation marks after the punctuation mark that ends the sentence.

Directions: Read each sentence below. Underline the speaker's exact words. Then, add a set of quotation marks before and after the speaker's words.

Example: Kate shouted, "<u>Catch the ball, Randy!</u>"

1. Would you like to go to skiing this afternoon? asked Dad.

2. Angel asked, Where will we go?

3. Mom said, Salem Mountain is not too far away.

4. Can I bring a friend? asked Zane.

5. Mom said, You can each bring along one friend.

6. Angel said, Riley will be so excited!

Skill 91: Quotation Marks in Dialogue

Directions: Read each sentence below. Write the sentence again. Add quotation marks where they are needed.

1. Have you ever been sledding? Zach asked his friend.

2. Jacob said, No, but it sounds like fun.

3. Tamara said, My grandpa taught me how to ski.

4. She added, He lives near the mountains in New York.

5. Mr. Jones said, I have a meeting at noon.

6. I want to go to the mountains on vacation, said Katrina.

LANGUAGE ARTS

Skill 92: Titles of Books and Movies

The **titles of books and movies** are underlined in text. This lets the reader know that the underlined words are part of a title.

Examples: Shel Silverstein is the author of <u>Where the Sidewalk Ends</u>.

I have seen the movie <u>Aladdin</u> four times.

Directions: Read the sentences below. Rewrite each sentence and underline the title of each movie.

1. In the movie Shrek, Cameron Diaz was the voice of Princess Fiona.

   ____

   ____

2. Harriet the Spy is the name of a book and a movie.

   ____

3. Tom Hanks was the voice of Woody in the movie Toy Story.

   ____

4. The movie Fly Away Home is based on a true story.

   ____

5. Jude is sleeping over tonight, and we are going to watch Star Wars.

   ____

   ____

Skill 92: Titles of Books and Movies

Directions: Underline the book titles in each sentence.

1. My mom's favorite book when she was young was Tales of a Fourth Grade Nothing.

2. Jon Scieszka is best known for his book The Stinky Cheese Man and Other Fairly Stupid Tales.

3. Dr. Seuss's famous book Green Eggs and Ham made my class laugh.

4. The book Science Verse is popular.

Directions: Write the title of the last movie you saw. Remember to underline it.

____

____

Directions: Write the title of your favorite book. Remember to underline it.

____

____

LANGUAGE ARTS

Skill

93: Contractions With Not

A **contraction** is two words that are put together to make one word. Some of the letters drop out of the second word when the words are joined. An apostrophe takes the place of the dropped letters. Many contractions are formed with the word **not**. The apostrophe takes the place of the letter **o** in **not**.

Example: *did + not = didn't*

Directions: Draw lines to match the word pairs with their contractions.

are not	couldn't
were not	isn't
could not	aren't
did not	haven't
do not	wasn't
have not	don't
is not	didn't
was not	weren't

Skill 93: Contractions With Not

Directions: Write a contraction on the line to finish each sentence.

1. We ________________ going to the circus tonight.
   are not

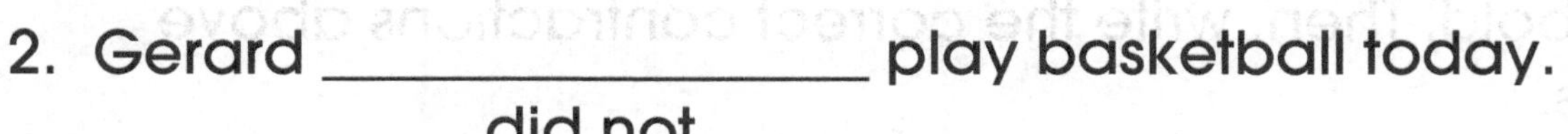

2. Gerard ________________ play basketball today.
   did not

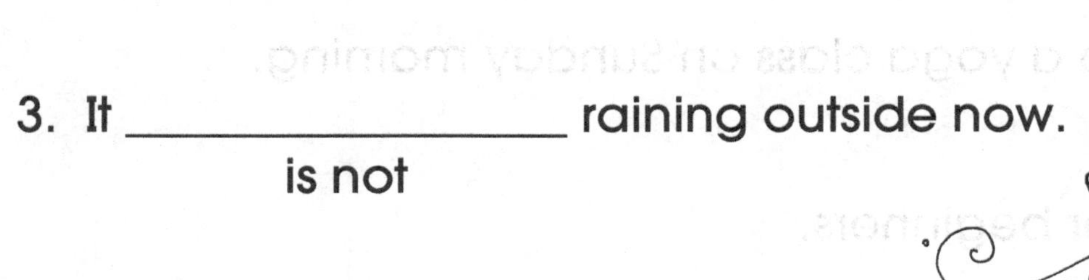

3. It ________________ raining outside now.
   is not

4. You ________________ need a jacket.
   do not

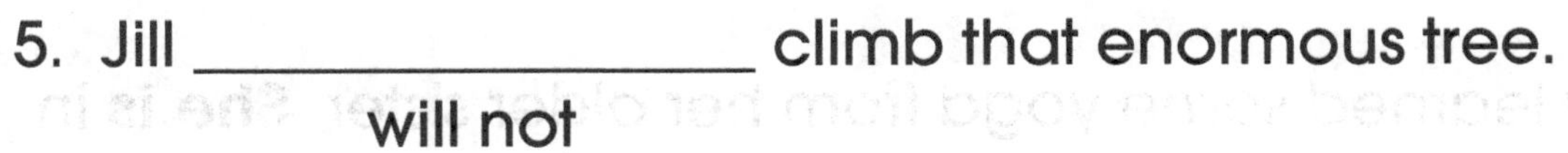

5. Jill ________________ climb that enormous tree.
   will not

6. That ________________ the fourth bell.
   was not

7. I ________________ seen that movie.
   have not

Skill 94: Contractions With Am, Is, Are

Some contractions are formed with the words **am**, **is**, and **are**. The apostrophe takes the place of the letter **a** in **am**. It takes the place of **i** in **is**. It takes the place of **a** in **are**.

Examples: I am = I'm   we are = we're   it is = it's

Directions: Read the sentences. Draw a line through the words in bold. Then, write the correct contractions above the words.

1. **I am** going to a yoga class on Sunday morning.

2. **It is** a class for beginners.

3. Mandy and Shelia are taking yoga too. **They are** in my class.

4. Mandy learned some yoga from her older sister. **She is** in a different class.

5. Max knows how to do more moves than anyone else. I think **he is** the best student.

6. Molly is our karate teacher. **She is** 39 years old.

Skill 94: Contractions With Am, Is, Are

Directions: Fill in the blanks below with a contraction from the box.

It's	You're	He's
We're	She's	They're

1. I think Mark is a great teacher. ________________ patient and funny.

2. Jill's mom comes to every class. ________________ interested in what we learn.

3. Marco, Paco, and I will get our yellow belts next month.

   ________________ excited to move up a level.

4. Marco and Paco are cousins. ________________ both part of the Tarrano family.

5. I like karate class a lot. ________________ a good way to exercise and make friends.

6. Do you think you would like to try karate? ________________ welcome to come watch one of our classes.

LANGUAGE ARTS

Skill 95: Contractions With Will

Many contractions are formed with pronouns and the verb **will**. An apostrophe (') takes the place of the letters **wi** in **will**.

Examples: I will = I'll, you will = you'll, she will = she'll, he will = he'll, it will = it'll, we will = we'll, they will = they'll

Directions: Match each pair of underlined words with its contraction. Write the letter of the contraction in the space.

1. _____ I will travel to Iceland one day.
2. _____ A plane will take me there. It will move very fast.
3. _____ You will be my travel partner.
4. _____ My sister, Eva, can come along, too. She will help plan the trip.
5. _____ We will see many beautiful things.
6. _____ Our families can have a party when we return. They will be excited to hear about our trip.

a. She'll
b. We'll
c. I'll
d. They'll
e. You'll
f. It'll

LANGUAGE ARTS

Skill 95: Contractions With Will

Directions: Draw lines to match the word pairs with their contractions.

he will	she'll
I will	it'll
she will	they'll
it will	I'll
they will	we'll
we will	he'll

Directions: Write a sentence using the contraction for **he will**.

____

____

Directions: Write a sentence using the contraction for **I will**.

____

____

Skill 96: Synonyms

Synonyms are words that have the same, or almost the same, meanings.

Examples: little, tiny, small   easy, simple

Directions: Match each word in the first column with its synonym in the second column. Write the letter of the synonym on the line.

1. ____ beautiful	**a.** enjoy
2. ____ windy	**b.** toss
3. ____ like	**c.** happy
4. ____ tired	**d.** breezy
5. ____ funny	**e.** frightening
6. ____ glad	**f.** sleepy
7. ____ scary	**g.** pretty
8. ____ throw	**h.** silly

Skill 96: Synonyms

Directions: Read the story below. Decide which word in the word box has almost the same meaning as each underlined word in the story. Write your answers on the lines.

pick	large	tidy	box	hop
small	vacation	crying	just	states

Our New Kittens

Over spring break[1], our cat had kittens. They were tiny[2], and they made squeaking[3] sounds instead of meows. Our cat licked their faces to keep them clean[4]. They stayed in a basket[5] until they were big[6] enough to jump[7] out. Mom says[8] that we can keep only[9] one. It is hard to decide[10] which one!

1. ______________________
2. ______________________
3. ______________________
4. ______________________
5. ______________________
6. ______________________
7. ______________________
8. ______________________
9. ______________________
10. ______________________

LANGUAGE ARTS

Skill 97: Antonyms

An **antonym** is a word that means the opposite of another word.

Examples: big, little old, young

Directions: Circle the pair of antonyms in each sentence.

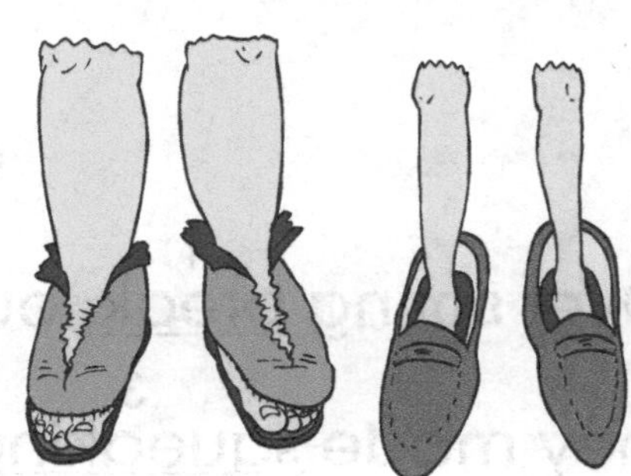

1. One pair of shoes is too tight, and one pair is too loose.
2. Jack wore his new shirt with his favorite pair of old jeans.
3. It is cold outside, but it will be hot tomorrow.
4. Did Mindy smile or frown when she saw you?
5. The tall bottle is next to the short can.
6. Open the cupboard, take out the pasta, and close the door.
7. I thought the report would be hard, but it was easy.
8. Would you rather go in the morning or night?

Skill

97: Antonyms

Directions: Write an antonym for each word below.

1. love ____________________

2. pull ____________________

3. yes ____________________

4. win ____________________

5. empty ____________________

6. yell ____________________

7. over ____________________

8. down ____________________

9. soft ____________________

10. loud ____________________

Skill 98: Homophones

Homophones are words that sound the same but are spelled differently and have different meanings. Sometimes a group of homophones can be more than two words.

Examples: **Pear** and **pair** are homophones.
To, **too**, and **two** are three homophones.

to,
too,
two

Directions: Draw a line from each word on the left to its homophone on the right.

bye	bee
beet	too
night	buy
write	see
hi	meet
sun	son
meat	knight
sea	high
be	beat
two	right

LANGUAGE ARTS

Skill

98: Homophones

Directions: Match each word with its homophone.

red	blew
buy	whole
pail	ate
eight	pale
our	read
blue	by
hole	hour

Directions: Choose 2 homophone pairs and write sentences using them.

1. ______________________________

____

2. ______________________________

____

LANGUAGE ARTS

Skill 99: Multiple-Meaning Words

Multiple-meaning words are words that are spelled the same but have different meanings.

Example: There are swings and a slide at the **park**. (an open, grassy area for relaxing)
Park next to the bakery. (to stop and leave a car)

Directions: Read this dictionary entry. It shows two different meanings for the same word. Each meaning is a different part of speech. Use the dictionary entry to answer the questions below.

cold *adj.* having a low temperature; cool, chilly, or icy; not warm; *noun* an illness that often includes a cough, a sore throat, and a runny nose

1. Dante caught a cold from his brother.

   Which definition of **cold** is used in this sentence? _____
   a. the first definition **b.** the second definition

2. It will be cold but sunny on Friday.

   Which definition of **cold** is used in this sentence? _____
   a. the first definition **b.** the second definition

Skill 99: Multiple-Meaning Words

Directions: Look at the definitions of each underlined word. Choose the definition that matches the way the word is used. Write the letter of that definition on the line.

1. _____ May I pet your cat?
   a. an animal that lives with people
   b. to touch lightly or stroke

2. _____ The leaves were red, gold, and brown.
   a. parts of a tree or a plant
   b. goes away

3. _____ Airplanes fly at amazing speeds.
   a. a small insect with two wings
   b. to move through the air

4. _____ Keely will train her puppy to roll over.
   a. to teach something by doing it over and over
   b. a long line of cars that run on a track

5. _____ The Carsons did not watch the entire movie.
   a. view or look at
   b. a small clock worn on the wrist

6. _____ Carla got a baseball bat for her birthday.
   a. a wooden stick used in baseball
   b. a small, flying mammal

LANGUAGE ARTS

Skill 100: Compound Words

Sometimes two words can be put together to make a new word with its own meaning. This new word is called a **compound word**.

Example: *farm + house = farmhouse*

Directions: Write each word pair as a compound word.

1. sun + light = ___________________________
2. birth + day = ___________________________
3. every + one = ___________________________
4. rain + bow = ___________________________
5. water + melon = ___________________________
6. bare + foot = ___________________________
7. home + work = ___________________________
8. mid + night = ___________________________
9. rail + road = ___________________________

Skill 100: Compound Words

Directions: Write each word pair as a compound word.

1. after + noon = ______________________
2. back + yard = ______________________
3. class + mate = ______________________
4. break + fast = ______________________
5. flash + light = ______________________
6. oat + meal = ______________________
7. pop + corn = ______________________

Directions: Use a compound word from above to finish each sentence.

8. Nate saw fireflies in his ______________________.
9. Ricky will need a ______________________ when he camps outside.
10. Claire likes to eat ______________________ at the movies with her grandmother.

Directions: Underline the other compound words used in the sentences above.

Answer Key

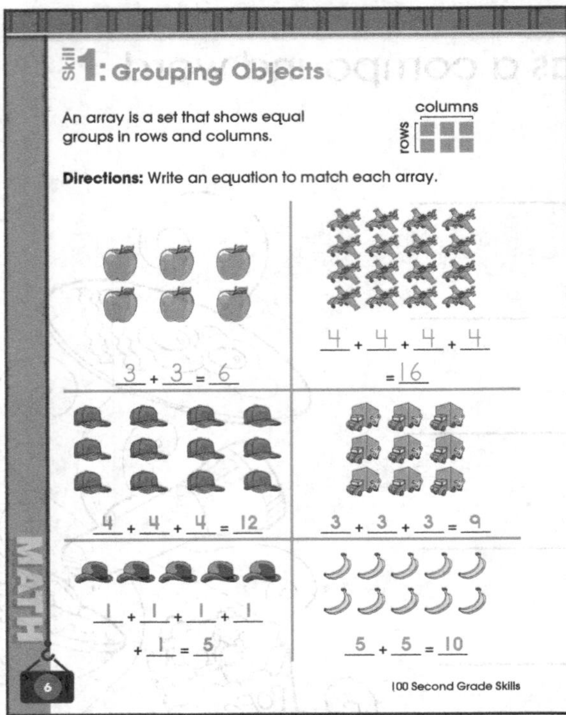

Skill **1: Grouping Objects**

An array is a set that shows equal groups in rows and columns.

columns

rows

Directions: Write an equation to match each array.

3 + 3 = 6

4 + 4 + 4 + 4 = 16

4 + 4 + 4 = 12

3 + 3 + 3 = 9

1 + 1 + 1 + 1 + 1 = 5

5 + 5 = 10

MATH

6

100 Second Grade Skills

Page 6

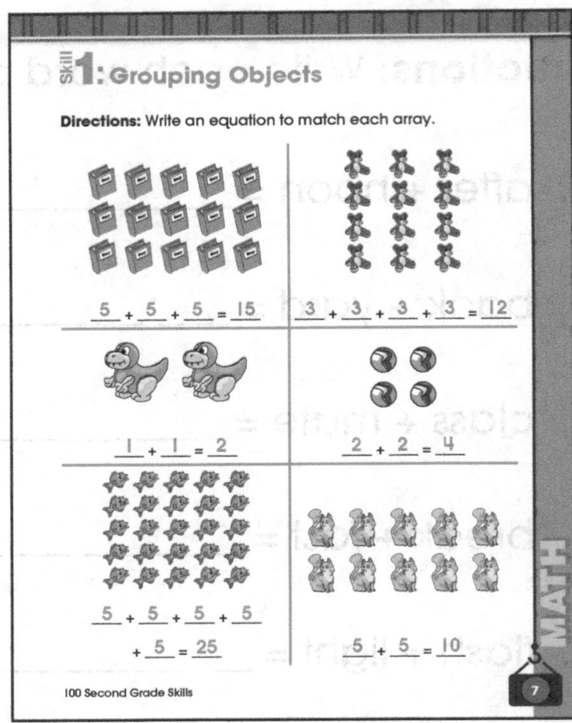

Skill **1: Grouping Objects**

Directions: Write an equation to match each array.

5 + 5 + 5 = 15

3 + 3 + 3 + 3 = 12

1 + 1 = 2

2 + 2 = 4

5 + 5 + 5 + 5 + 5 = 25

5 + 5 = 10

100 Second Grade Skills

MATH

7

Page 7

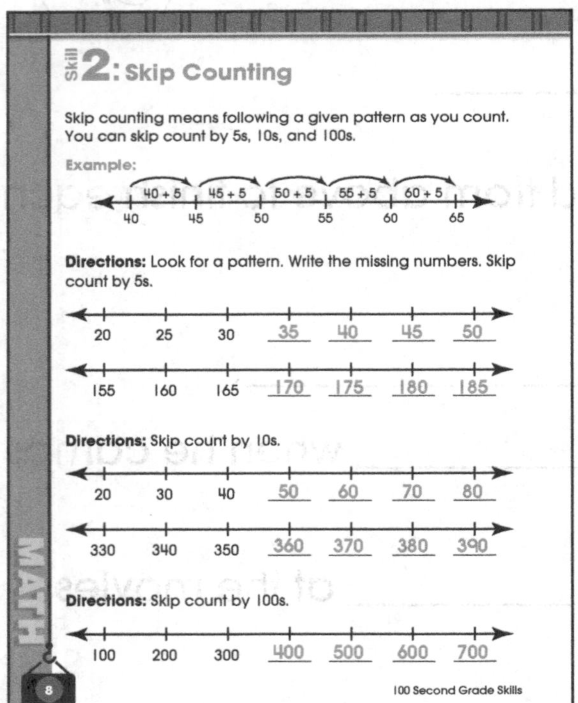

Skill **2: Skip Counting**

Skip counting means following a given pattern as you count. You can skip count by 5s, 10s, and 100s.

Example:

40 + 5, 45 + 5, 50 + 5, 55 + 5, 60 + 5

40, 45, 50, 55, 60, 65

Directions: Look for a pattern. Write the missing numbers. Skip count by 5s.

20, 25, 30, 35, 40, 45, 50

155, 160, 165, 170, 175, 180, 185

Directions: Skip count by 10s.

20, 30, 40, 50, 60, 70, 80

330, 340, 350, 360, 370, 380, 390

Directions: Skip count by 100s.

100, 200, 300, 400, 500, 600, 700

MATH

8

100 Second Grade Skills

Page 8

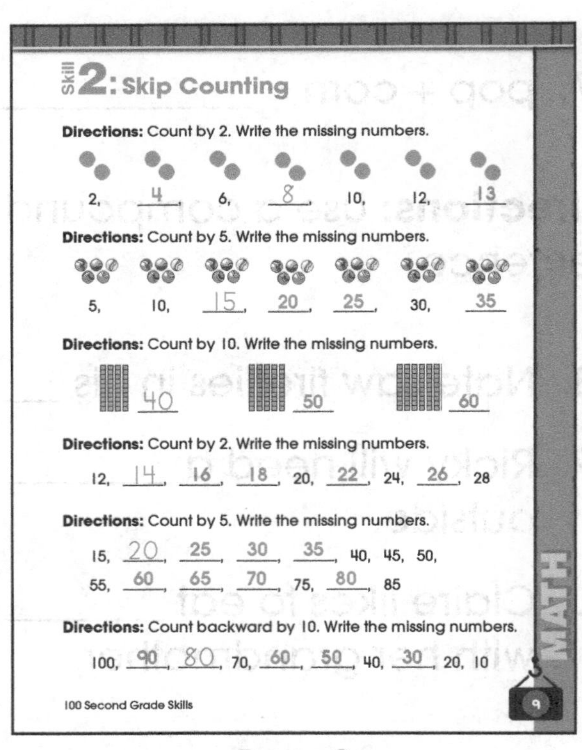

Skill **2: Skip Counting**

Directions: Count by 2. Write the missing numbers.

2, 4, 6, 8, 10, 12, 13

Directions: Count by 5. Write the missing numbers.

5, 10, 15, 20, 25, 30, 35

Directions: Count by 10. Write the missing numbers.

40 50 60

Directions: Count by 2. Write the missing numbers.

12, 14, 16, 18, 20, 22, 24, 26, 28

Directions: Count by 5. Write the missing numbers.

15, 20, 25, 30, 35, 40, 45, 50,

55, 60, 65, 70, 75, 80, 85

Directions: Count backward by 10. Write the missing numbers.

100, 90, 80, 70, 60, 50, 40, 30, 20, 10

100 Second Grade Skills

MATH

9

Page 9

Answer Key

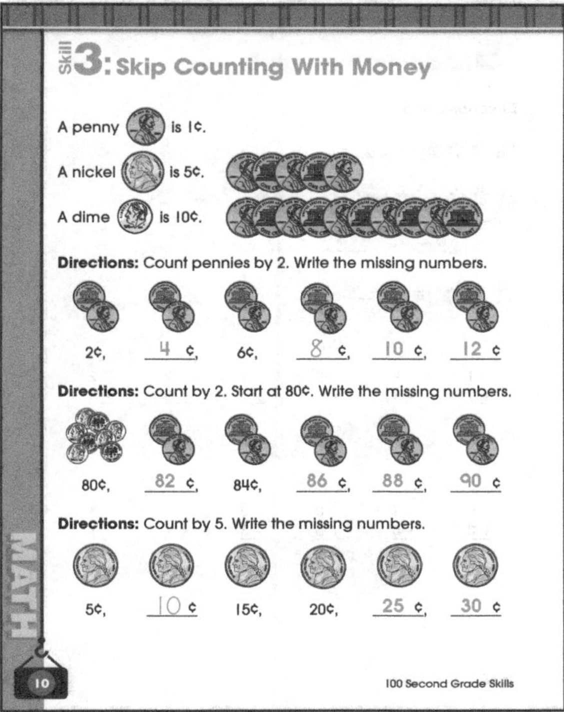

Skill **3: Skip Counting With Money**

A penny is 1¢.
A nickel is 5¢.
A dime is 10¢.

Directions: Count pennies by 2. Write the missing numbers.

2¢, 4 ¢, 6¢, 8 ¢, 10 ¢, 12 ¢

Directions: Count by 2. Start at 80¢. Write the missing numbers.

80¢, 82 ¢, 84¢, 86 ¢, 88 ¢, 90 ¢

Directions: Count by 5. Write the missing numbers.

5¢, 10 ¢, 15¢, 20¢, 25 ¢, 30 ¢

MATH

10

100 Second Grade Skills

Page 10

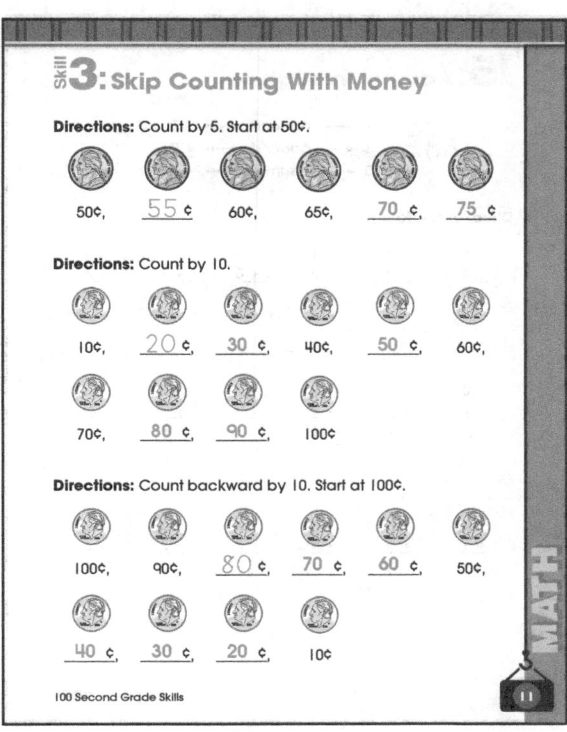

Skill **3: Skip Counting With Money**

Directions: Count by 5. Start at 50¢.

50¢, 55 ¢, 60¢, 65¢, 70 ¢, 75 ¢

Directions: Count by 10.

10¢, 20 ¢, 30 ¢, 40¢, 50 ¢, 60¢,

70¢, 80 ¢, 90 ¢, 100¢

Directions: Count backward by 10. Start at 100¢.

100¢, 90¢, 80 ¢, 70 ¢, 60 ¢, 50¢,

40 ¢, 30 ¢, 20 ¢, 10¢

100 Second Grade Skills

MATH

11

Page 11

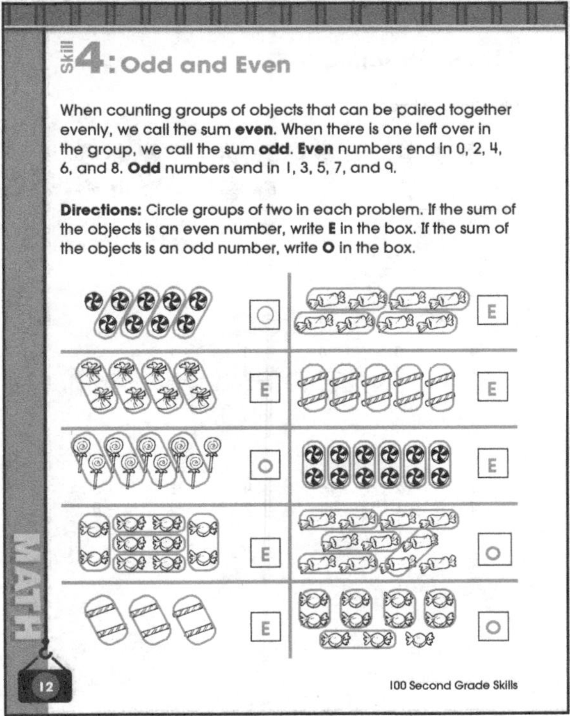

Skill **4: Odd and Even**

When counting groups of objects that can be paired together evenly, we call the sum **even**. When there is one left over in the group, we call the sum **odd**. **Even** numbers end in 0, 2, 4, 6, and 8. **Odd** numbers end in 1, 3, 5, 7, and 9.

Directions: Circle groups of two in each problem. If the sum of the objects is an even number, write **E** in the box. If the sum of the objects is an odd number, write **O** in the box.

O	E
E	E
O	E
E	O
E	O

MATH

12

100 Second Grade Skills

Page 12

Skill **4: Odd and Even**

Even numbers end in 0, 2, 4, 6, and 8.
Odd numbers end in 1, 3, 5, 7, and 9.

Directions: Count the candles on each cake. Write the number on the cake. Color each cake that has an even number.

10, 5, 8, 14

6, 12, 4, 11

9, 13, 7, 15

Draw candles on the cake to show how old you are. Answers will vary.
Is your age even or odd? vary.

100 Second Grade Skills

MATH

13

Page 13

Answer Key

Skill 5: Adding Through 5

2 ← addend → 2
+ 3 ← addend → + 0
5 ← sum → 2

Directions: Add.

2 + 3 = 5	5 + 0 = 5	1 + 2 = 3	4 + 0 = 4	0 + 1 = 1	1 + 3 = 4
0 + 2 = 2	3 + 1 = 4	2 + 2 = 4	1 + 4 = 5	2 + 1 = 3	3 + 0 = 3
1 + 1 = 2	0 + 0 = 0	0 + 4 = 4	3 + 2 = 5	2 + 2 = 4	0 + 2 = 2

MATH

14 100 Second Grade Skills

Page 14

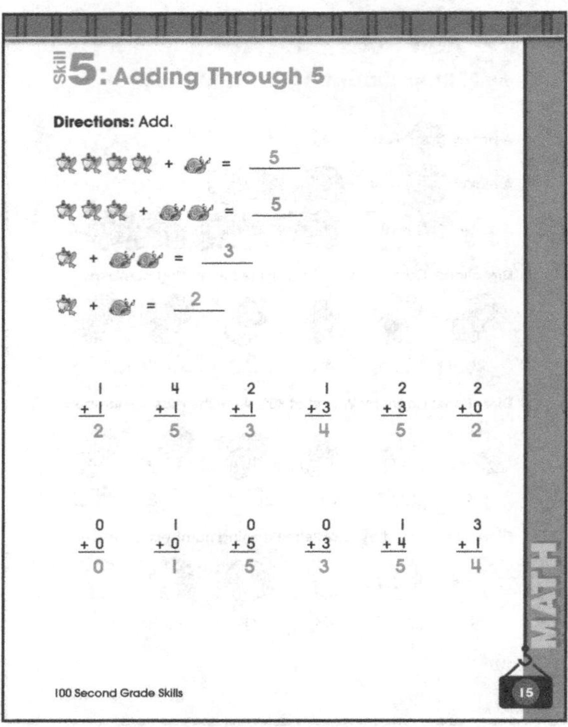

Skill 5: Adding Through 5

Directions: Add.

+ = 5
+ = 5
+ = 3
+ = 2

1 + 1 = 2	4 + 1 = 5	2 + 1 = 3	1 + 3 = 4	2 + 3 = 5	2 + 0 = 2
0 + 0 = 0	1 + 0 = 1	0 + 5 = 5	0 + 3 = 3	1 + 4 = 5	3 + 1 = 4

MATH

100 Second Grade Skills 15

Page 15

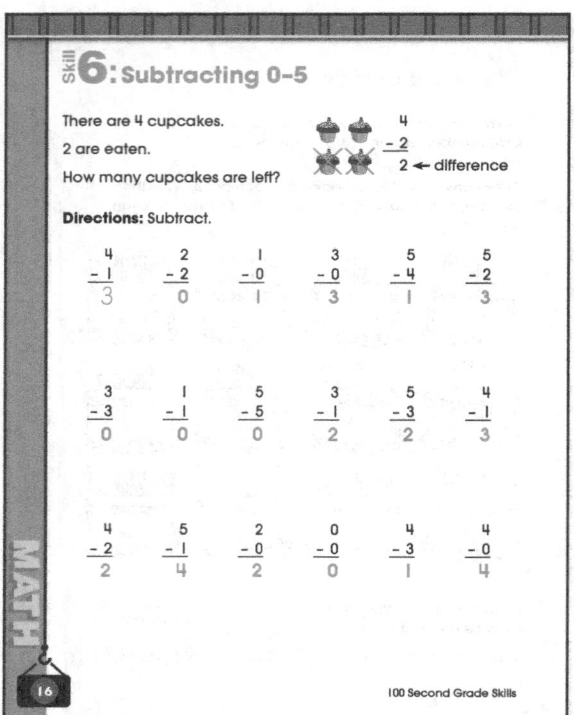

Skill 6: Subtracting 0–5

There are 4 cupcakes.
2 are eaten.
How many cupcakes are left?

4
− 2
2 ← difference

Directions: Subtract.

4 − 1 = 3	2 − 2 = 0	1 − 0 = 1	3 − 0 = 3	5 − 4 = 1	5 − 2 = 3
3 − 3 = 0	1 − 1 = 0	5 − 5 = 0	3 − 1 = 2	5 − 3 = 2	4 − 1 = 3
4 − 2 = 2	5 − 1 = 4	2 − 0 = 2	0 − 0 = 0	4 − 3 = 1	4 − 0 = 4

MATH

16 100 Second Grade Skills

Page 16

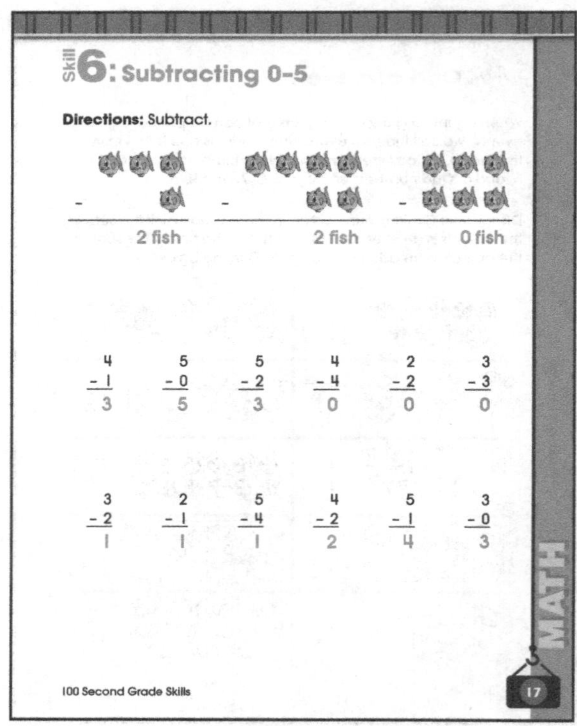

Skill 6: Subtracting 0–5

Directions: Subtract.

− 2 fish — − 2 fish — − 0 fish

4 − 1 = 3	5 − 0 = 5	5 − 2 = 3	4 − 4 = 0	2 − 2 = 0	3 − 3 = 0
3 − 2 = 1	2 − 1 = 1	5 − 4 = 1	4 − 2 = 2	5 − 1 = 4	3 − 0 = 3

MATH

100 Second Grade Skills 17

Page 17

Answer Key

Skill 7: Adding 6–8

1 + 6 = 7 ← sum → 5 + 3 = 8

Directions: Add.

0 + 6 = 6	2 + 5 = 7	1 + 6 = 7	3 + 3 = 6	6 + 2 = 8	5 + 3 = 8
3 + 4 = 7	5 + 1 = 6	7 + 0 = 7	2 + 4 = 6	5 + 3 = 8	7 + 1 = 8
4 + 3 = 7	4 + 4 = 8	1 + 7 = 8	6 + 1 = 7	6 + 0 = 6	4 + 2 = 6
3 + 4 = 7	8 + 0 = 8	5 + 2 = 7	1 + 5 = 6	2 + 6 = 8	0 + 7 = 7
3 + 5 = 8	4 + 4 = 8	0 + 8 = 8	2 + 4 = 6	3 + 3 = 6	1 + 6 = 7

MATH 18 100 Second Grade Skills

Page 18

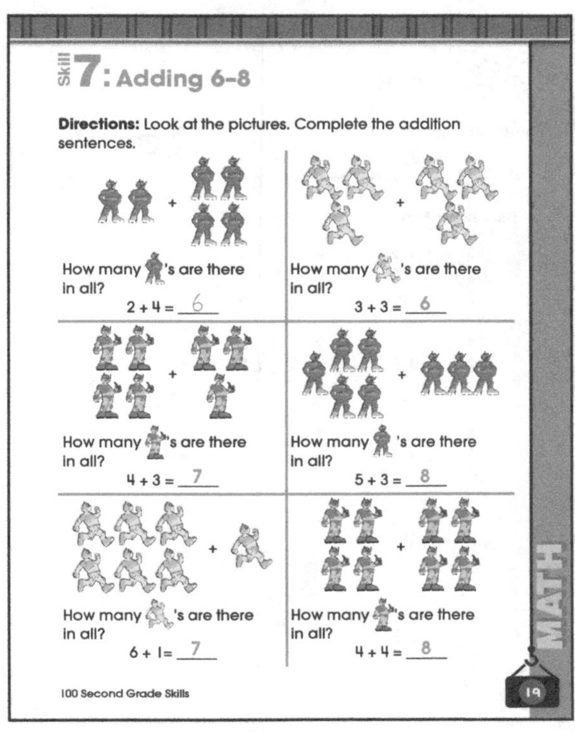

Skill 7: Adding 6–8

Directions: Look at the pictures. Complete the addition sentences.

How many 's are there in all? 2 + 4 = 6

How many 's are there in all? 3 + 3 = 6

How many 's are there in all? 4 + 3 = 7

How many 's are there in all? 5 + 3 = 8

How many 's are there in all? 6 + 1 = 7

How many 's are there in all? 4 + 4 = 8

100 Second Grade Skills MATH 19

Page 19

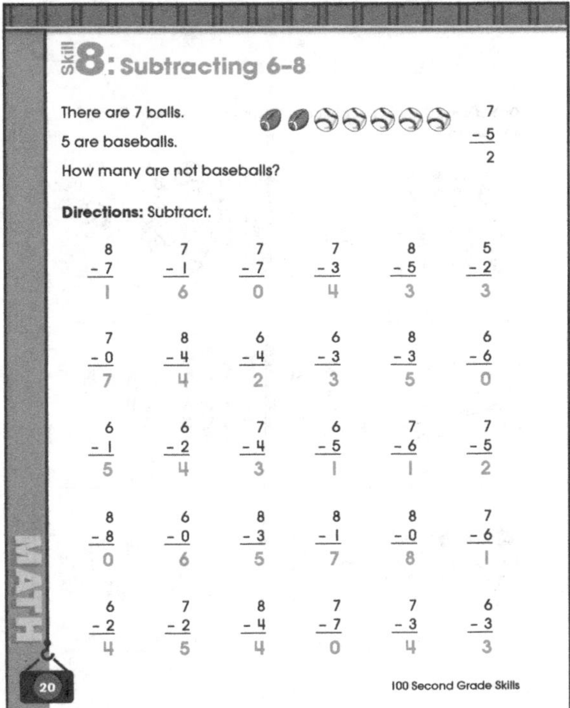

Skill 8: Subtracting 6–8

There are 7 balls.
5 are baseballs.
How many are not baseballs?

7 − 5 = 2

Directions: Subtract.

8 − 7 = 1	7 − 1 = 6	7 − 7 = 0	7 − 3 = 4	8 − 5 = 3	5 − 2 = 3
7 − 0 = 7	8 − 4 = 4	6 − 4 = 2	6 − 3 = 3	8 − 3 = 5	6 − 6 = 0
6 − 1 = 5	6 − 2 = 4	7 − 4 = 3	6 − 5 = 1	7 − 6 = 1	7 − 5 = 2
8 − 8 = 0	6 − 0 = 6	8 − 3 = 5	8 − 1 = 7	8 − 0 = 8	7 − 6 = 1
6 − 2 = 4	7 − 2 = 5	8 − 4 = 4	7 − 7 = 0	7 − 3 = 4	6 − 3 = 3

MATH 20 100 Second Grade Skills

Page 20

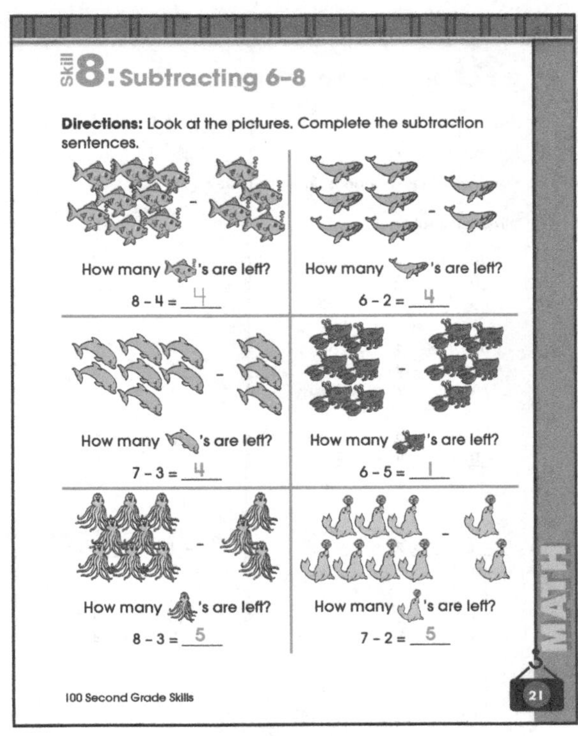

Skill 8: Subtracting 6–8

Directions: Look at the pictures. Complete the subtraction sentences.

How many 's are left? 8 − 4 = 4

How many 's are left? 6 − 2 = 4

How many 's are left? 7 − 3 = 4

How many 's are left? 6 − 5 = 1

How many 's are left? 8 − 3 = 5

How many 's are left? 7 − 2 = 5

100 Second Grade Skills MATH 21

Page 21

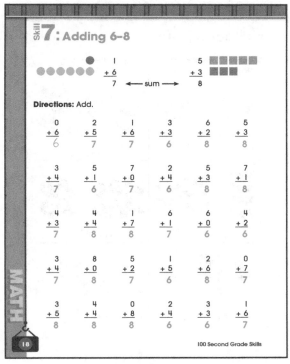

Answer Key

Skill 9: Adding 9–10

5 + 3 = 8 ⟵ sum ⟶ 5 + 5 = 10

Directions: Add.

7 + 1 8	2 + 8 10	4 + 6 10	3 + 6 9	5 + 4 9	7 + 3 10
7 + 2 9	9 + 0 9	7 + 2 9	5 + 5 10	9 + 1 10	0 + 9 9
6 + 3 9	1 + 8 9	3 + 6 9	4 + 5 9	1 + 7 8	6 + 4 10
1 + 9 10	5 + 4 9	7 + 3 10	0 + 9 9	3 + 7 10	8 + 1 9
7 + 2 9	5 + 5 10	6 + 4 10	9 + 1 10	2 + 8 10	4 + 5 9

MATH

22 100 Second Grade Skills

Page 22

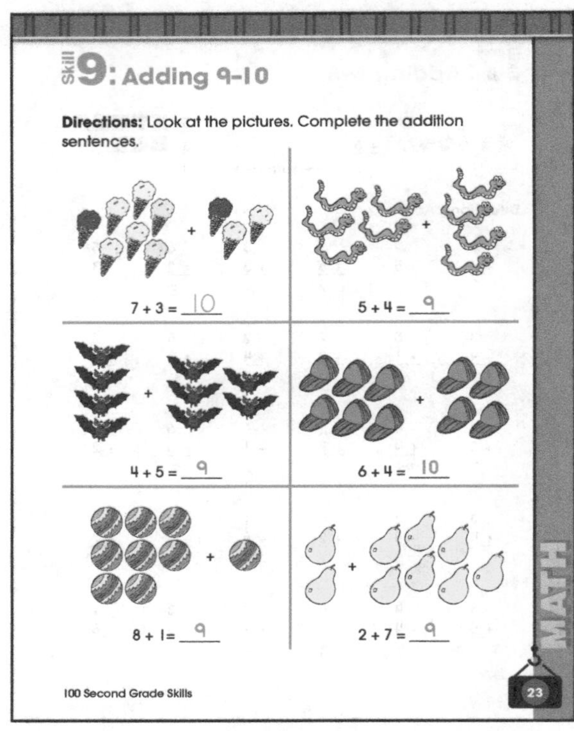

Skill 9: Adding 9–10

Directions: Look at the pictures. Complete the addition sentences.

7 + 3 = 10

5 + 4 = 9

4 + 5 = 9

6 + 4 = 10

8 + 1 = 9

2 + 7 = 9

MATH

100 Second Grade Skills 23

Page 23

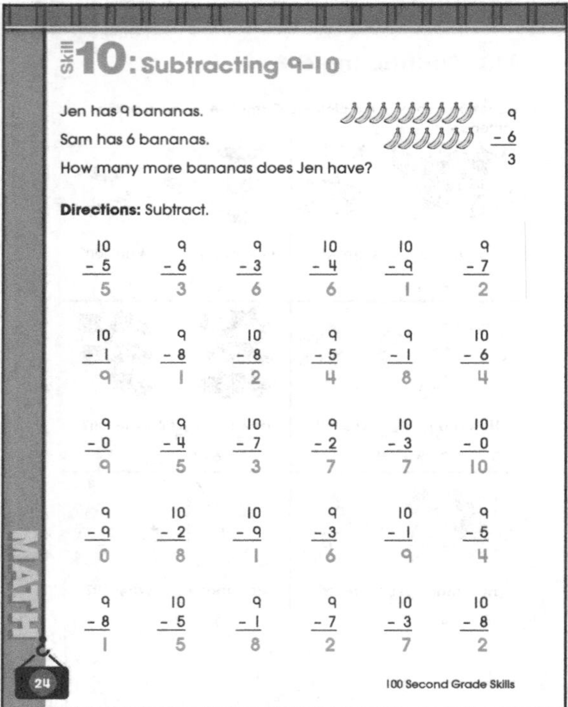

Skill 10: Subtracting 9–10

Jen has 9 bananas.
Sam has 6 bananas.
How many more bananas does Jen have?

9 − 6 = 3

Directions: Subtract.

10 − 5 5	9 − 6 3	9 − 3 6	10 − 4 6	10 − 9 1	9 − 7 2
10 − 1 9	9 − 8 1	10 − 8 2	9 − 5 4	9 − 1 8	10 − 6 4
9 − 0 9	9 − 4 5	10 − 7 3	9 − 2 7	10 − 3 7	10 − 0 10
9 − 9 0	10 − 2 8	10 − 9 1	9 − 3 6	10 − 1 9	9 − 5 4
9 − 8 1	10 − 5 5	9 − 1 8	9 − 7 2	10 − 3 7	10 − 8 2

MATH

24 100 Second Grade Skills

Page 24

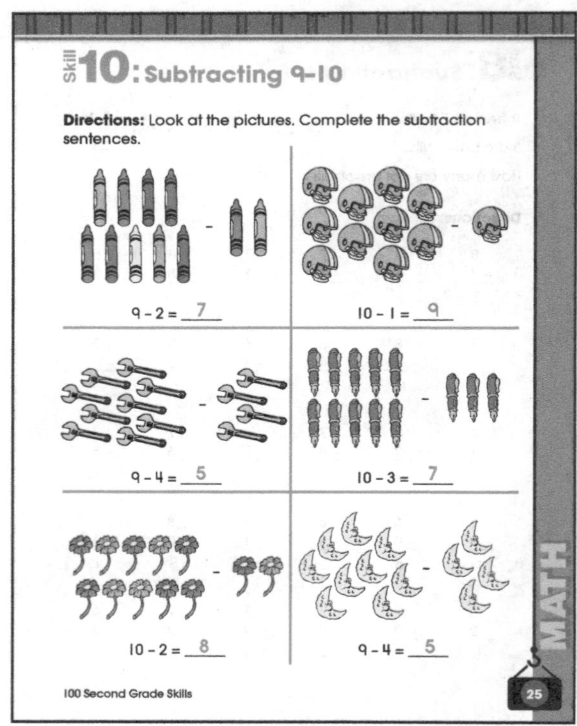

Skill 10: Subtracting 9–10

Directions: Look at the pictures. Complete the subtraction sentences.

9 − 2 = 7

10 − 1 = 9

9 − 4 = 5

10 − 3 = 7

10 − 2 = 8

9 − 4 = 5

MATH

100 Second Grade Skills 25

Page 25

Answer Key

Skill 11: Adding 11-15

6 + 7 = 10 + 3 = 13

8 + 4 = 10 + 2 = 12

Directions: Add.

4 + 7 11	5 + 9 14	7 + 6 13	9 + 2 11	6 + 5 11	9 + 6 15
6 + 5 11	9 + 4 13	7 + 7 14	6 + 6 12	7 + 4 11	7 + 8 15
9 + 6 15	8 + 4 12	9 + 2 11	6 + 7 13	4 + 9 13	2 + 9 11
8 + 5 13	8 + 6 14	7 + 5 12	9 + 3 12	7 + 8 15	6 + 6 12
3 + 8 11	5 + 7 12	9 + 3 12	5 + 8 13	9 + 4 13	6 + 9 15

MATH

26 100 Second Grade Skills

Page 26

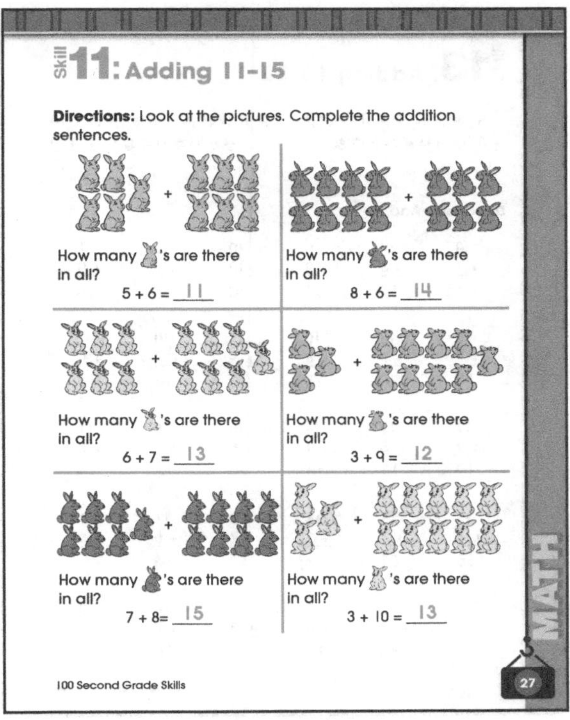
Skill 11: Adding 11-15

Directions: Look at the pictures. Complete the addition sentences.

How many 's are there in all? 5 + 6 = 11

How many 's are there in all? 8 + 6 = 14

How many 's are there in all? 6 + 7 = 13

How many 's are there in all? 3 + 9 = 12

How many 's are there in all? 7 + 8= 15

How many 's are there in all? 3 + 10 = 13

MATH

100 Second Grade Skills 27

Page 27

Skill 12: Subtracting 11-15

12 = 1 ten 2 ones

Cross out to solve.

12
− 7
5

13 = 1 ten 3 ones

Cross out to solve.

13
− 5
8

Directions: Subtract.

13 − 6 7	13 − 9 4	11 − 9 2	12 − 8 4	15 − 4 11	11 − 7 4
15 − 8 7	12 − 4 8	13 − 8 5	11 − 3 8	14 − 5 9	12 − 6 6
13 − 4 9	11 − 6 5	12 − 9 3	14 − 4 10	11 − 3 8	13 − 7 6
14 − 11 3	15 − 5 10	12 − 5 7	11 − 5 6	11 − 4 7	13 − 9 4
12 − 3 9	13 − 6 7	12 − 3 9	11 − 8 3	12 − 7 5	15 − 6 9

MATH

28 100 Second Grade Skills

Page 28

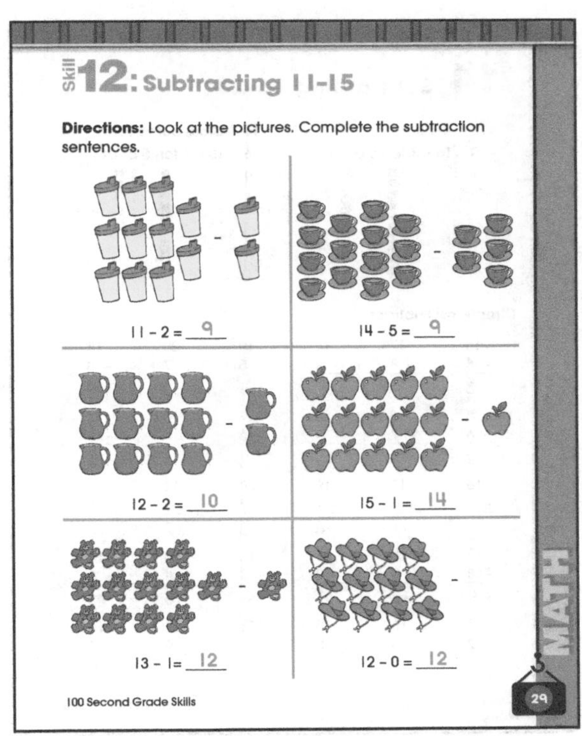
Skill 12: Subtracting 11-15

Directions: Look at the pictures. Complete the subtraction sentences.

11 − 2 = 9

14 − 5 = 9

12 − 2 = 10

15 − 1 = 14

13 − 1 = 12

12 − 0 = 12

MATH

100 Second Grade Skills 29

Page 29

Answer Key

Skill 13: Adding 16–20

9 + 8 = 17 10 + 9 = 19

Directions: Add.

9 + 7 = 16	14 + 3 = 17	9 + 9 = 18	10 + 10 = 20	15 + 2 = 17	7 + 9 = 16
12 + 7 = 19	13 + 7 = 20	10 + 8 = 18	11 + 9 = 20	14 + 3 = 17	7 + 9 = 16
17 + 2 = 19	12 + 5 = 17	14 + 4 = 18	15 + 5 = 20	8 + 8 = 16	11 + 8 = 19
12 + 6 = 18	13 + 3 = 16	16 + 1 = 17	12 + 7 = 19	11 + 5 = 16	11 + 8 = 19
15 + 2 = 17	11 + 9 = 20	12 + 6 = 18	16 + 3 = 19	14 + 2 = 16	12 + 8 = 20

MATH

30 100 Second Grade Skills

Page 30

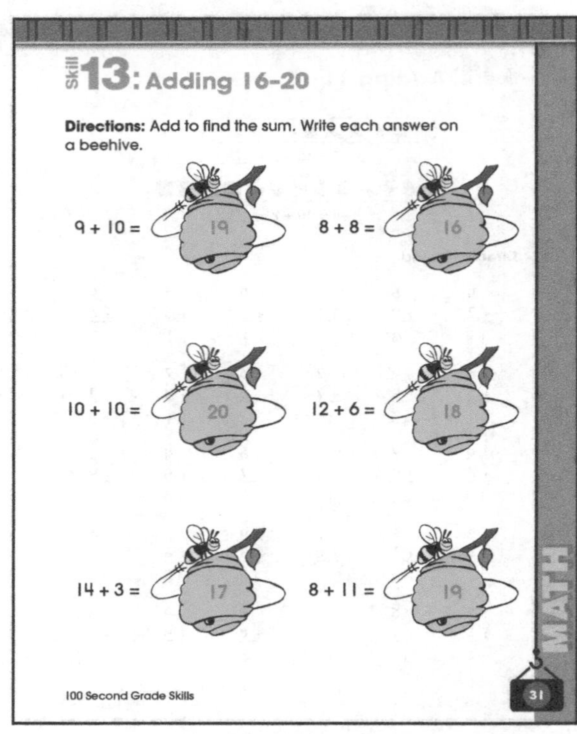

Skill 13: Adding 16–20

Directions: Add to find the sum. Write each answer on a beehive.

9 + 10 = 19

8 + 8 = 16

10 + 10 = 20

12 + 6 = 18

14 + 3 = 17

8 + 11 = 19

MATH

100 Second Grade Skills 31

Page 31

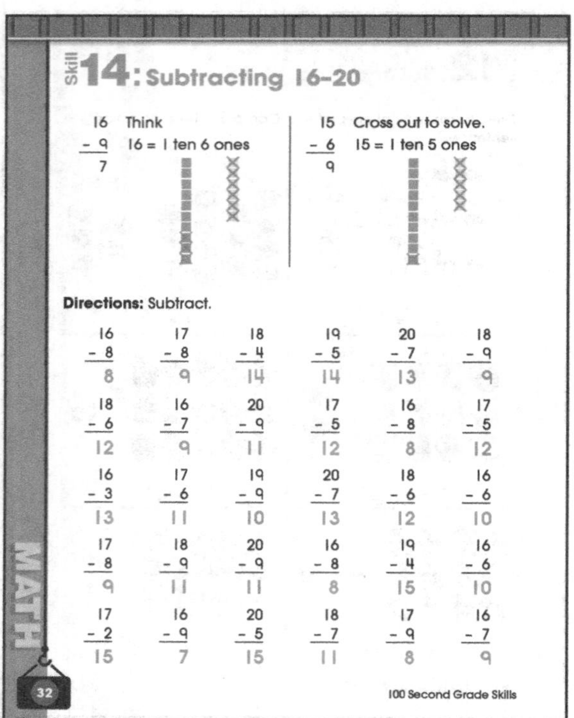

Skill 14: Subtracting 16–20

16 − 9 = 7 Think 16 = 1 ten 6 ones

15 − 6 = 9 Cross out to solve. 15 = 1 ten 5 ones

Directions: Subtract.

16 − 8 = 8	17 − 8 = 9	18 − 4 = 14	19 − 5 = 14	20 − 7 = 13	18 − 9 = 9
18 − 6 = 12	16 − 7 = 9	20 − 9 = 11	17 − 5 = 12	16 − 8 = 8	17 − 5 = 12
16 − 3 = 13	17 − 6 = 11	19 − 9 = 10	20 − 7 = 13	18 − 6 = 12	16 − 6 = 10
17 − 8 = 9	18 − 9 = 11	20 − 9 = 11	16 − 8 = 8	19 − 4 = 15	16 − 6 = 10
17 − 2 = 15	16 − 9 = 7	20 − 5 = 15	18 − 7 = 11	17 − 9 = 8	16 − 7 = 9

MATH

32 100 Second Grade Skills

Page 32

Skill 14: Subtracting 16–20

Directions: Subtract. Write each answer on a cloud.

18 − 5 = 13

20 − 9 = 11

17 − 8 = 9

17 − 3 = 14

20 − 6 = 14

20 − 11 = 9

16 − 7 = 9

19 − 6 = 13

18 − 12 = 6

16 − 9 = 7

MATH

100 Second Grade Skills 33

Page 33

Answer Key

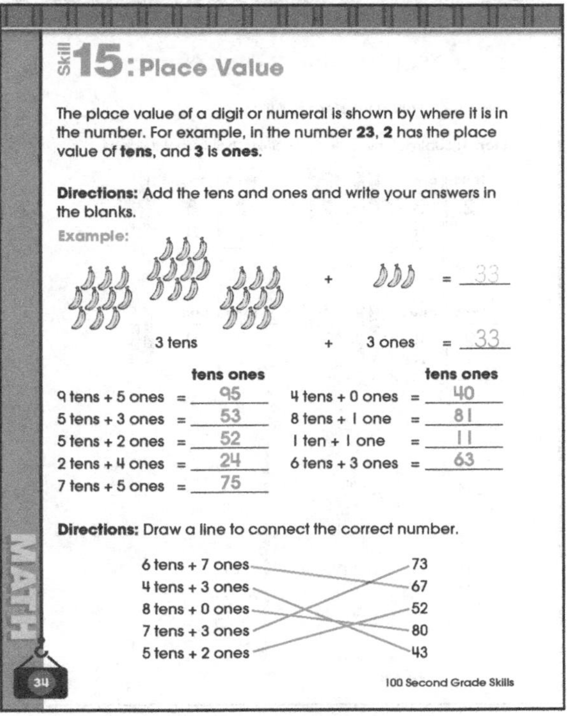

Skill **15: Place Value**

The place value of a digit or numeral is shown by where it is in the number. For example, in the number **23**, **2** has the place value of **tens**, and **3** is **ones**.

Directions: Add the tens and ones and write your answers in the blanks.

Example:

+ = 33

3 tens + 3 ones = 33

tens ones		tens ones	
9 tens + 5 ones =	95	4 tens + 0 ones =	40
5 tens + 3 ones =	53	8 tens + 1 one =	81
5 tens + 2 ones =	52	1 ten + 1 one =	11
2 tens + 4 ones =	24	6 tens + 3 ones =	63
7 tens + 5 ones =	75		

Directions: Draw a line to connect the correct number.

6 tens + 7 ones — 73
4 tens + 3 ones — 67
8 tens + 0 ones — 52
7 tens + 3 ones — 80
5 tens + 2 ones — 43

MATH

34 100 Second Grade Skills

Page 34

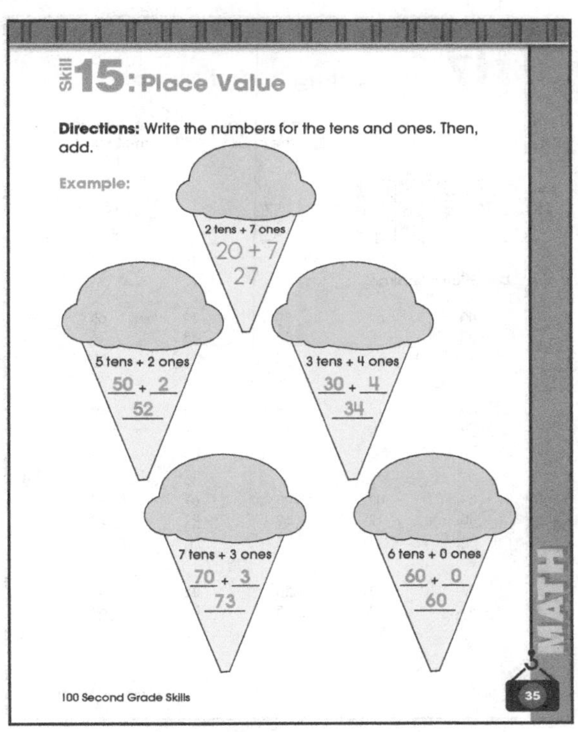

Skill **15: Place Value**

Directions: Write the numbers for the tens and ones. Then, add.

Example:

2 tens + 7 ones
20 + 7
27

5 tens + 2 ones
50 + 2
52

3 tens + 4 ones
30 + 4
34

7 tens + 3 ones
70 + 3
73

6 tens + 0 ones
60 + 0
60

MATH

100 Second Grade Skills 35

Page 35

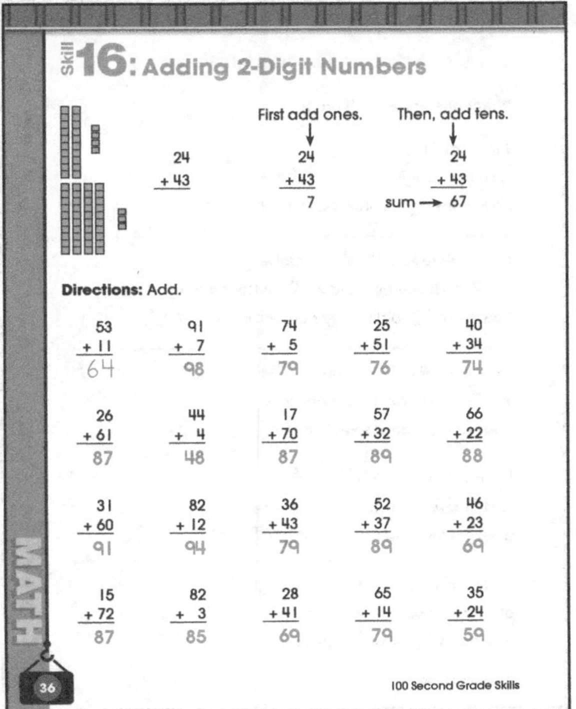

Skill **16: Adding 2-Digit Numbers**

First add ones. Then, add tens.

24 + 43

24 + 43 = 7

24 + 43 sum → 67

Directions: Add.

53 + 11 = 64 | 91 + 7 = 98 | 74 + 5 = 79 | 25 + 51 = 76 | 40 + 34 = 74

26 + 61 = 87 | 44 + 4 = 48 | 17 + 70 = 87 | 57 + 32 = 89 | 66 + 22 = 88

31 + 60 = 91 | 82 + 12 = 94 | 36 + 43 = 79 | 52 + 37 = 89 | 46 + 23 = 69

15 + 72 = 87 | 82 + 3 = 85 | 28 + 41 = 69 | 65 + 14 = 79 | 35 + 24 = 59

MATH

36 100 Second Grade Skills

Page 36

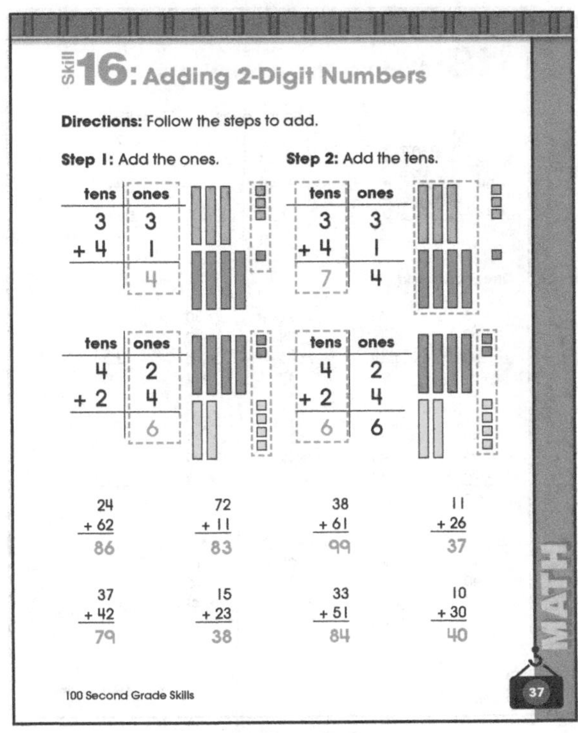

Skill **16: Adding 2-Digit Numbers**

Directions: Follow the steps to add.

Step 1: Add the ones. **Step 2:** Add the tens.

tens	ones
3	3
+ 4	1
	4

tens	ones
3	3
+ 4	1
7	4

tens	ones
4	2
+ 2	4
	6

tens	ones
4	2
+ 2	4
6	6

24 + 62 = 86 | 72 + 11 = 83 | 38 + 61 = 99 | 11 + 26 = 37

37 + 42 = 79 | 15 + 23 = 38 | 33 + 51 = 84 | 10 + 30 = 40

MATH

100 Second Grade Skills 37

Page 37

Answer Key

Skill 17: Subtracting 2-Digit Numbers

77 - 26	First, subtract the ones. 77 - 26 1	Then, subtract the tens. 77 - 26 51

Directions: Subtract.

49 - 39 10	87 - 6 81	79 - 63 16	59 - 38 21	68 - 16 52
36 - 24 12	78 - 25 53	28 - 14 14	19 - 7 12	26 - 11 15
54 - 40 14	42 - 12 30	95 - 62 33	67 - 41 26	74 - 50 24
92 - 81 11	77 - 17 60	35 - 5 30	82 - 51 31	86 - 64 22

MATH

38 100 Second Grade Skills

Page 38

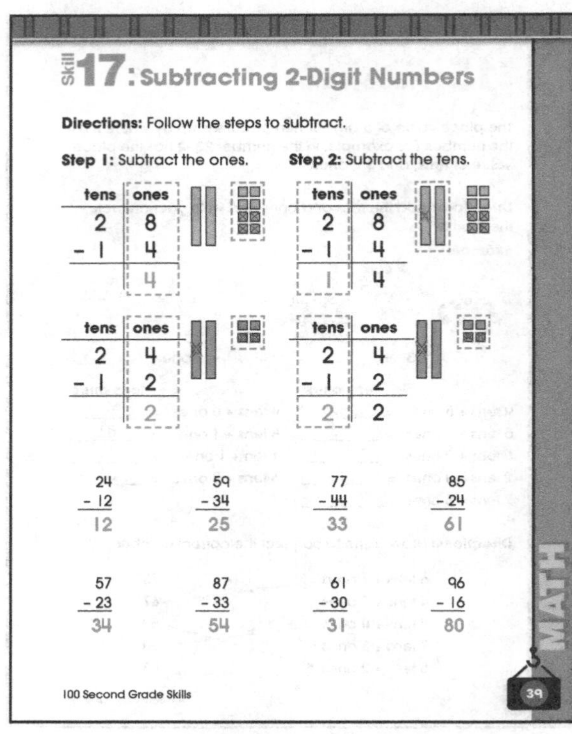

Skill 17: Subtracting 2-Digit Numbers

Directions: Follow the steps to subtract.

Step 1: Subtract the ones. **Step 2:** Subtract the tens.

tens	ones
2	8
- 1	4
	4

tens	ones
2	8
- 1	4
1	4

tens	ones
2	4
- 1	2
	2

tens	ones
2	4
- 1	2
2	2

24 - 12 12	59 - 34 25	77 - 44 33	85 - 24 61
57 - 23 34	87 - 33 54	61 - 30 31	96 - 16 80

MATH

100 Second Grade Skills 39

Page 39

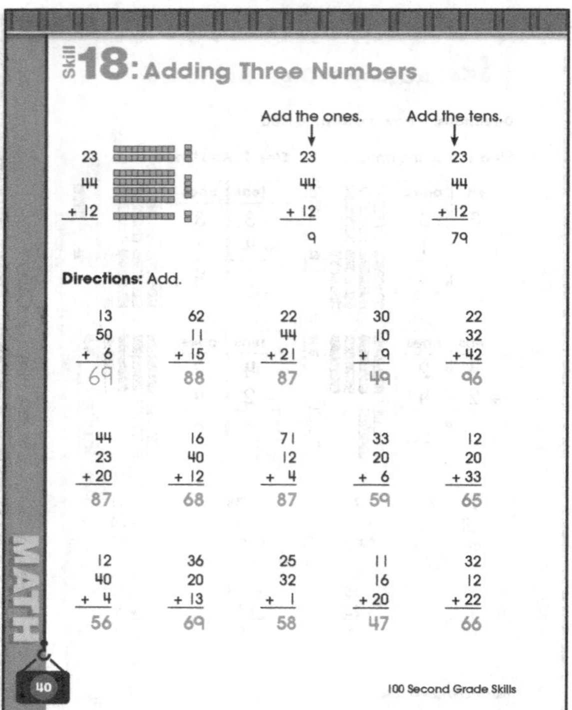

Skill 18: Adding Three Numbers

23 44 + 12	Add the ones. 23 44 + 12 9	Add the tens. 23 44 + 12 79

Directions: Add.

13 50 + 6 69	62 11 + 15 88	22 44 + 21 87	30 10 + 9 49	22 32 + 42 96
44 23 + 20 87	16 40 + 12 68	71 12 + 4 87	33 20 + 6 59	12 20 + 33 65
12 40 + 4 56	36 20 + 13 69	25 32 + 1 58	11 16 + 20 47	32 12 + 22 66

MATH

40 100 Second Grade Skills

Page 40

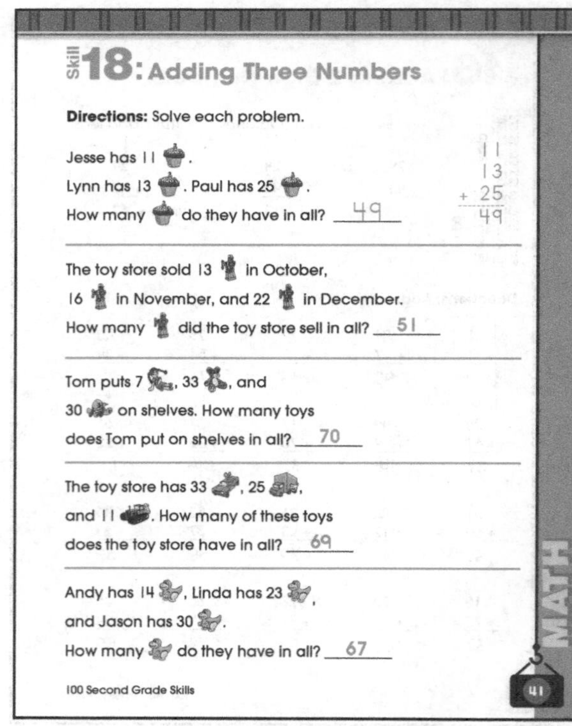

Skill 18: Adding Three Numbers

Directions: Solve each problem.

Jesse has 11 .
Lynn has 13 . Paul has 25 .
How many do they have in all? 49

11
13
+ 25
49

The toy store sold 13 in October,
16 in November, and 22 in December.
How many did the toy store sell in all? 51

Tom puts 7 , 33 , and
30 on shelves. How many toys
does Tom put on shelves in all? 70

The toy store has 33 , 25 ,
and 11 . How many of these toys
does the toy store have in all? 69

Andy has 14 , Linda has 23 ,
and Jason has 30 .
How many do they have in all? 67

MATH

100 Second Grade Skills 41

Page 41

Answer Key

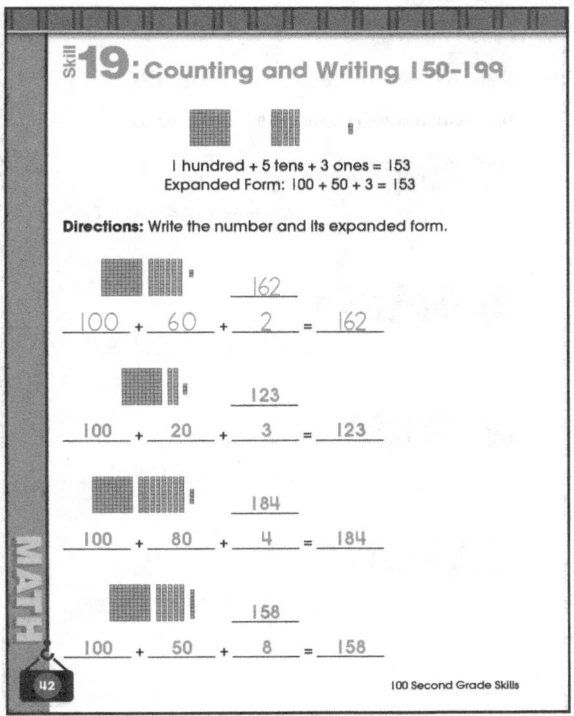

Skill **19: Counting and Writing 150–199**

1 hundred + 5 tens + 3 ones = 153
Expanded Form: 100 + 50 + 3 = 153

Directions: Write the number and its expanded form.

162
100 + 60 + 2 = 162

123
100 + 20 + 3 = 123

184
100 + 80 + 4 = 184

158
100 + 50 + 8 = 158

42 100 Second Grade Skills

Page 42

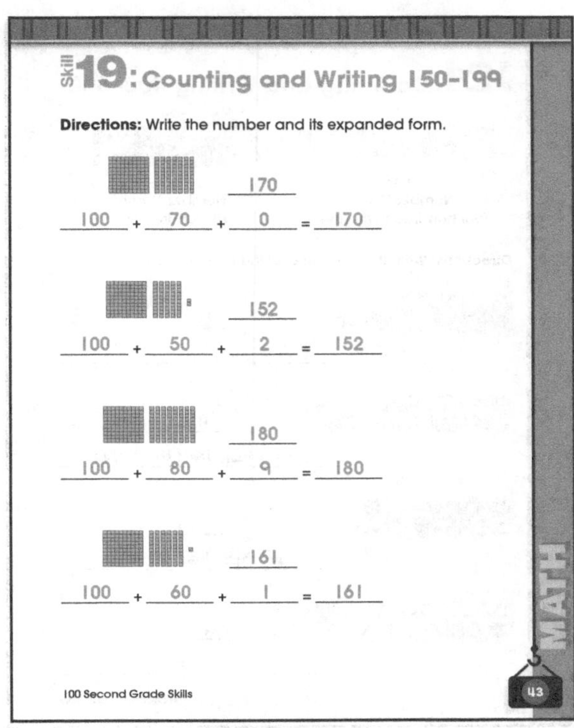

Skill **19: Counting and Writing 150–199**

Directions: Write the number and its expanded form.

170
100 + 70 + 0 = 170

152
100 + 50 + 2 = 152

180
100 + 80 + 9 = 180

161
100 + 60 + 1 = 161

100 Second Grade Skills 43

Page 43

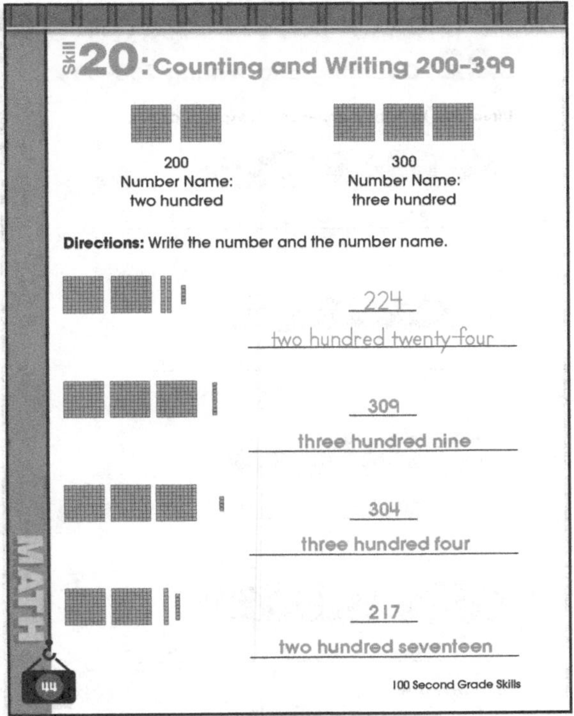

Skill **20: Counting and Writing 200–399**

200
Number Name:
two hundred

300
Number Name:
three hundred

Directions: Write the number and the number name.

224
two hundred twenty-four

309
three hundred nine

304
three hundred four

217
two hundred seventeen

44 100 Second Grade Skills

Page 44

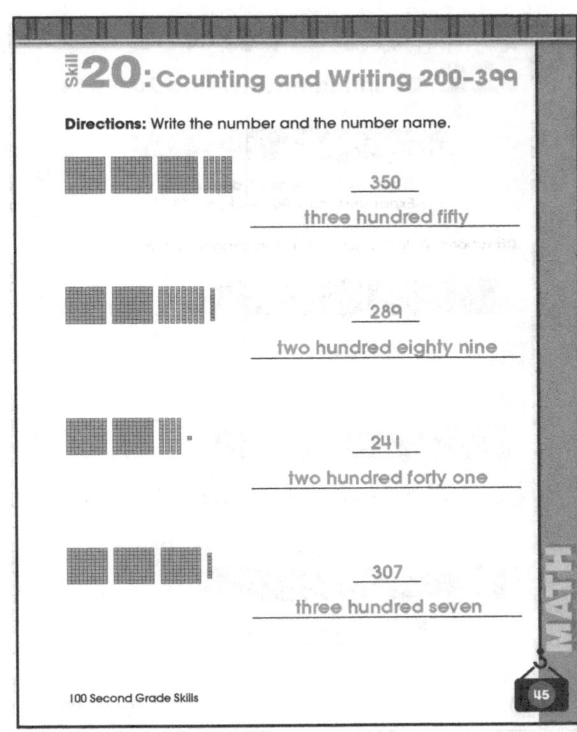

Skill **20: Counting and Writing 200–399**

Directions: Write the number and the number name.

350
three hundred fifty

289
two hundred eighty nine

241
two hundred forty one

307
three hundred seven

100 Second Grade Skills 45

Page 45

Answer Key

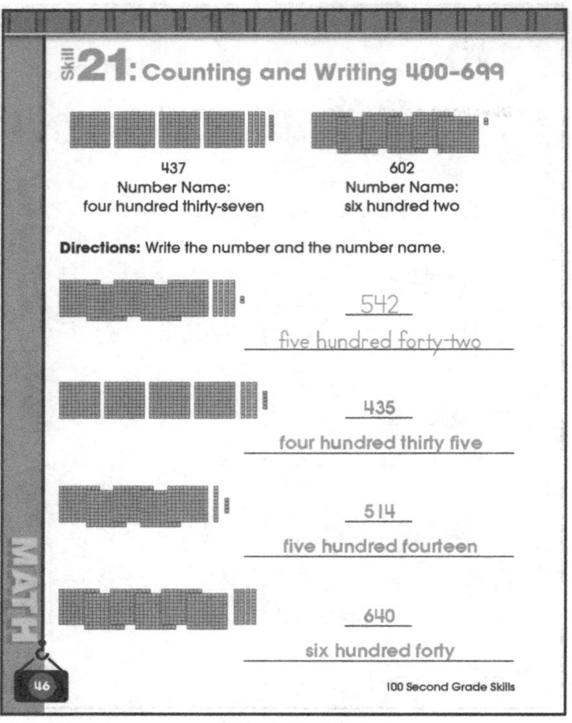

Skill 21: Counting and Writing 400-699

437
Number Name:
four hundred thirty-seven

602
Number Name:
six hundred two

Directions: Write the number and the number name.

542
five hundred forty-two

435
four hundred thirty five

514
five hundred fourteen

640
six hundred forty

MATH

46

100 Second Grade Skills

Page 46

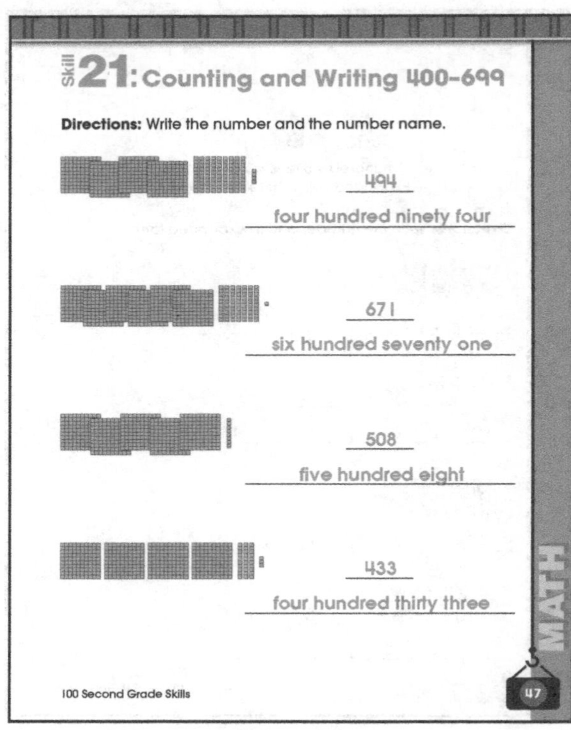

Skill 21: Counting and Writing 400-699

Directions: Write the number and the number name.

494
four hundred ninety four

671
six hundred seventy one

508
five hundred eight

433
four hundred thirty three

MATH

100 Second Grade Skills

47

Page 47

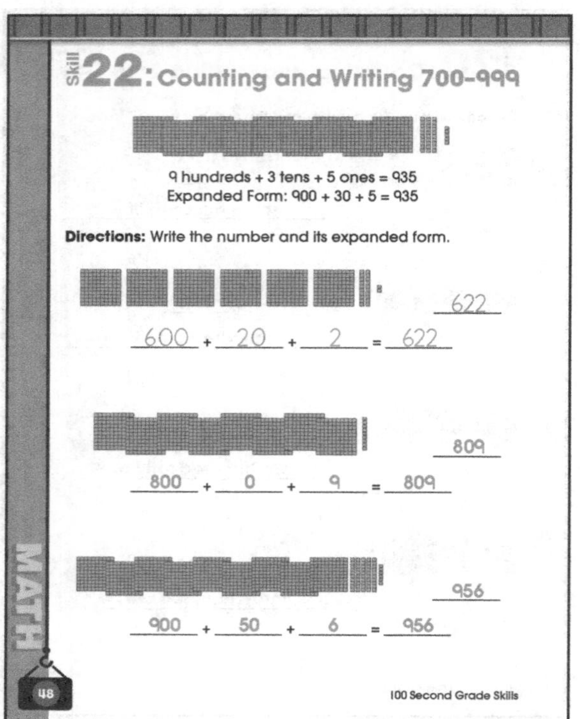

Skill 22: Counting and Writing 700-999

9 hundreds + 3 tens + 5 ones = 935
Expanded Form: 900 + 30 + 5 = 935

Directions: Write the number and its expanded form.

622
600 + 20 + 2 = 622

809
800 + 0 + 9 = 809

956
900 + 50 + 6 = 956

MATH

48

100 Second Grade Skills

Page 48

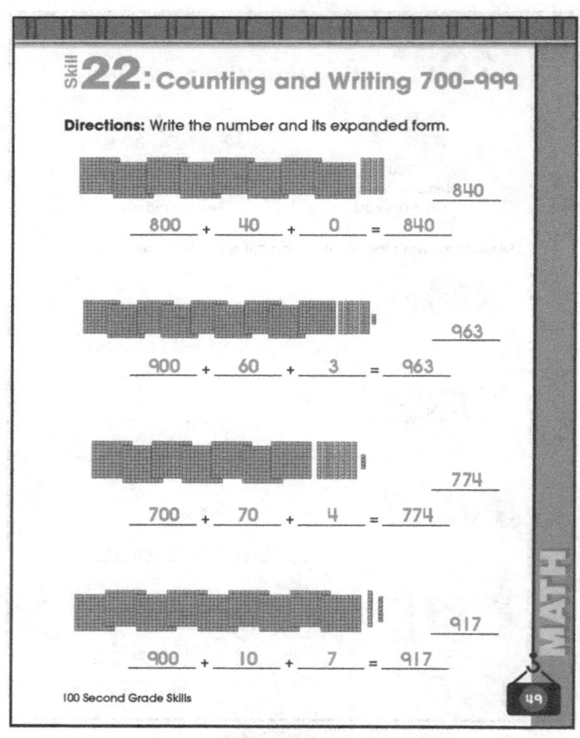

Skill 22: Counting and Writing 700-999

Directions: Write the number and its expanded form.

840
800 + 40 + 0 = 840

963
900 + 60 + 3 = 963

774
700 + 70 + 4 = 774

917
900 + 10 + 7 = 917

MATH

100 Second Grade Skills

49

Page 49

Answer Key

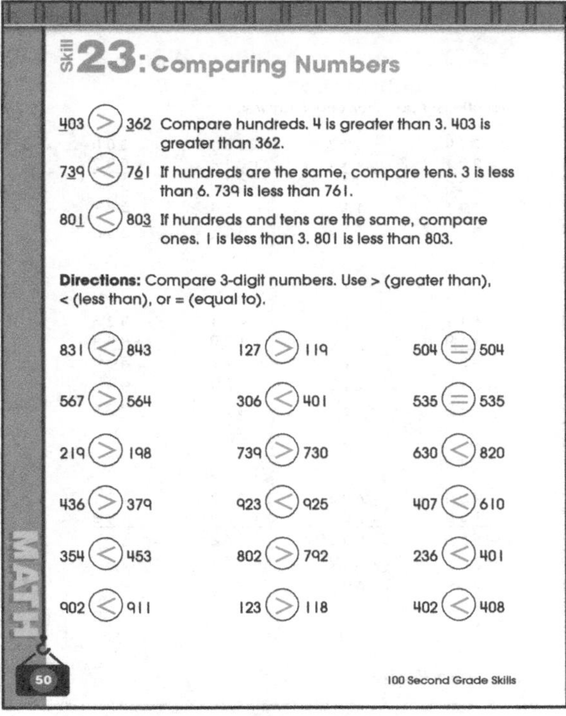

Skill 23: Comparing Numbers

403 > 362 Compare hundreds. 4 is greater than 3. 403 is greater than 362.

739 < 761 If hundreds are the same, compare tens. 3 is less than 6. 739 is less than 761.

801 < 803 If hundreds and tens are the same, compare ones. 1 is less than 3. 801 is less than 803.

Directions: Compare 3-digit numbers. Use > (greater than), < (less than), or = (equal to).

831 < 843	127 > 119	504 = 504
567 > 564	306 < 401	535 = 535
219 > 198	739 > 730	630 < 820
436 > 379	923 < 925	407 < 610
354 < 453	802 > 792	236 < 401
902 < 911	123 > 118	402 < 408

MATH

50 100 Second Grade Skills

Page 50

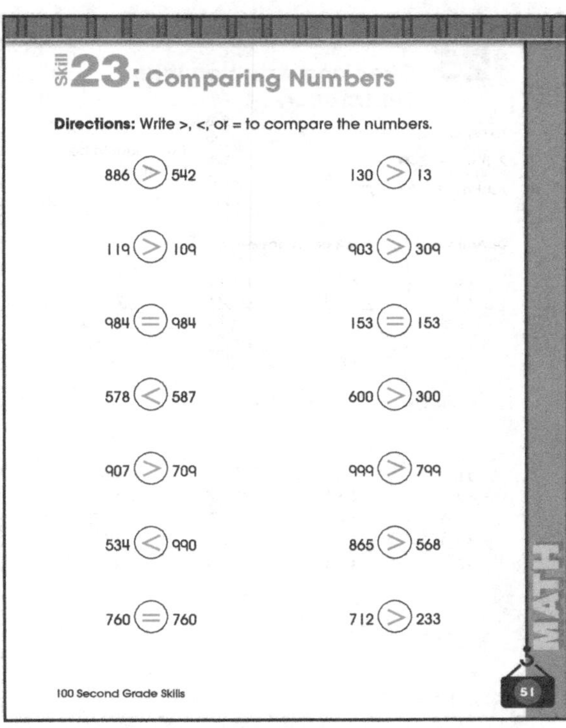

Skill 23: Comparing Numbers

Directions: Write >, <, or = to compare the numbers.

886 > 542	130 > 13
119 > 109	903 > 309
984 = 984	153 = 153
578 < 587	600 > 300
907 > 709	999 > 799
534 < 990	865 > 568
760 = 760	712 > 233

MATH

100 Second Grade Skills 51

Page 51

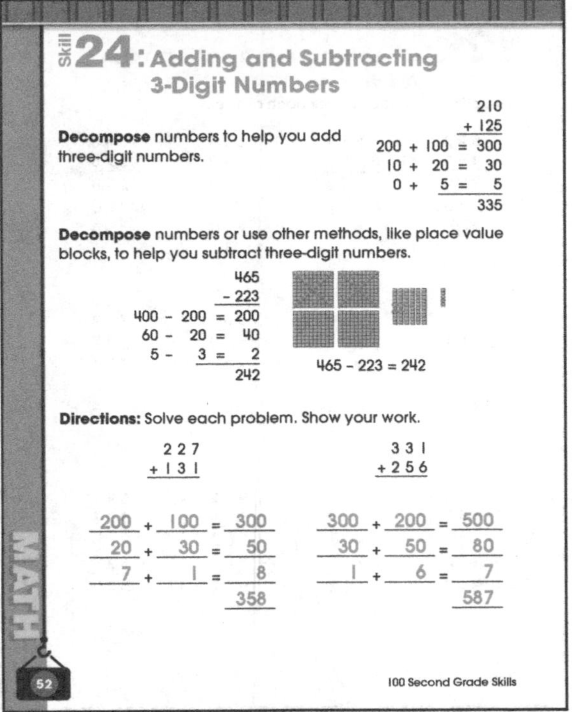

Skill 24: Adding and Subtracting 3-Digit Numbers

Decompose numbers to help you add three-digit numbers.

```
            210
          + 125
200 + 100 = 300
 10 +  20 =  30
  0 +   5 =   5
            335
```

Decompose numbers or use other methods, like place value blocks, to help you subtract three-digit numbers.

```
            465
          - 223
400 - 200 = 200
 60 -  20 =  40
  5 -   3 =   2
            242
```

465 - 223 = 242

Directions: Solve each problem. Show your work.

```
  227                       331
+ 131                     + 256

200 + 100 = 300           300 + 200 = 500
 20 +  30 =  50            30 +  50 =  80
  7 +   1 =   8             1 +   6 =   7
            358                       587
```

MATH

52 100 Second Grade Skills

Page 52

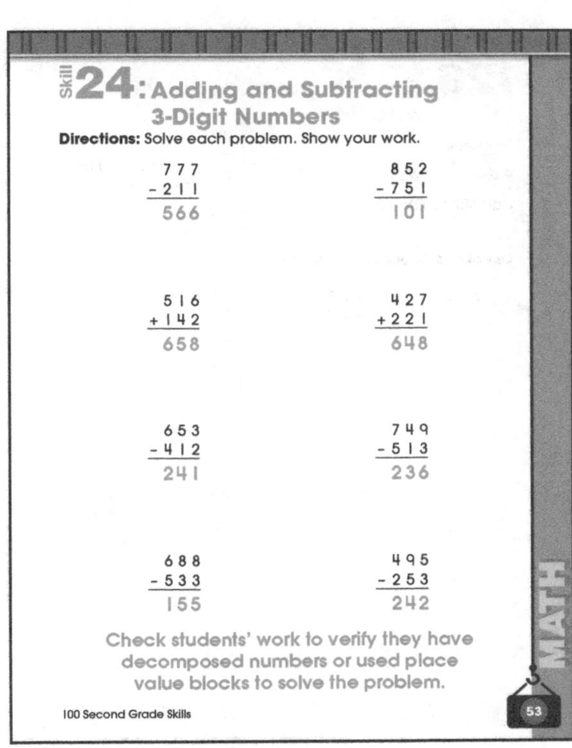

Skill 24: Adding and Subtracting 3-Digit Numbers

Directions: Solve each problem. Show your work.

```
  777        852
- 211      - 751
  566        101

  516        427
+ 142      + 221
  658        648

  653        749
- 412      - 513
  241        236

  688        495
- 533      - 253
  155        242
```

Check students' work to verify they have decomposed numbers or used place value blocks to solve the problem.

MATH

100 Second Grade Skills 53

Page 53

Answer Key

Skill 25: Checking Addition With Subtraction

To check 215 + 109 = 324, subtract 109 from 324.

215
+ 109
324
− 109
215

These should be the same.

Directions: Add. Check each answer.

157	625	312	710
+ 212	+ 111	+ 105	+ 225
369	736	417	935
− 212	− 111	− 105	− 225
157	625	312	710

301	461	712	351
+ 215	+ 218	+ 263	+ 611
516	679	975	962
− 215	− 218	− 263	− 611
301	461	712	351

MATH

54

100 Second Grade Skills

Page 54

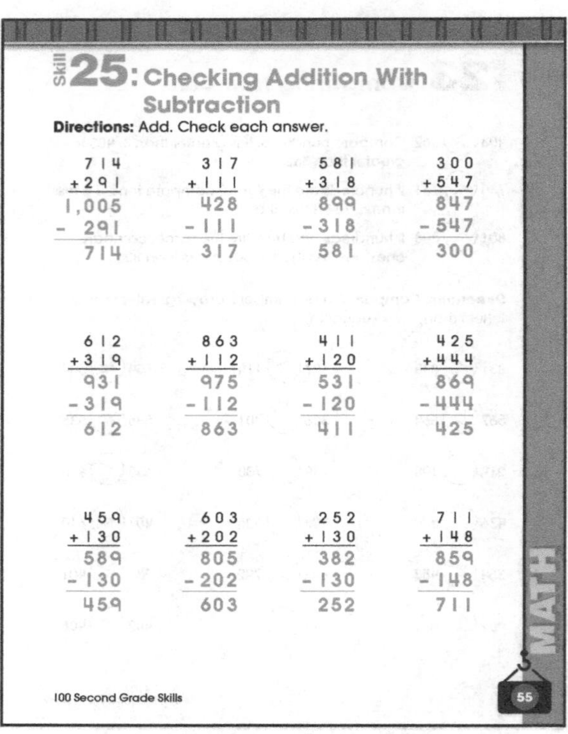

Skill 25: Checking Addition With Subtraction

Directions: Add. Check each answer.

714	317	581	300
+ 291	+ 111	+ 318	+ 547
1,005	428	899	847
− 291	− 111	− 318	− 547
714	317	581	300

612	863	411	425
+ 319	+ 112	+ 120	+ 444
931	975	531	869
− 319	− 112	− 120	− 444
612	863	411	425

459	603	252	711
+ 130	+ 202	+ 130	+ 148
589	805	382	859
− 130	− 202	− 130	− 148
459	603	252	711

MATH

100 Second Grade Skills

55

Page 55

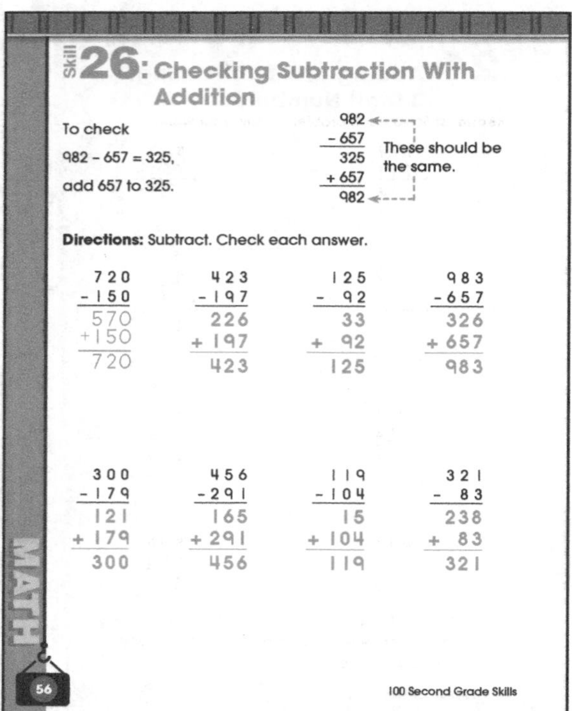

Skill 26: Checking Subtraction With Addition

To check 982 − 657 = 325, add 657 to 325.

982
− 657
325
+ 657
982

These should be the same.

Directions: Subtract. Check each answer.

720	423	125	983
− 150	− 197	− 92	− 657
570	226	33	326
+ 150	+ 197	+ 92	+ 657
720	423	125	983

300	456	119	321
− 179	− 291	− 104	− 83
121	165	15	238
+ 179	+ 291	+ 104	+ 83
300	456	119	321

MATH

56

100 Second Grade Skills

Page 56

Skill 26: Checking Subtraction With Addition

Directions: Subtract. Check each answer.

592	259	519	540
− 463	− 147	− 120	− 320
129	112	399	220
+ 463	+ 147	+ 120	+ 320
592	259	519	540

192	710	683	719
− 86	− 447	− 419	− 532
106	263	264	187
+ 86	+ 447	+ 419	+ 532
192	710	683	719

919	687	912	542
− 457	− 250	− 609	− 327
462	437	303	215
+ 457	+ 250	+ 609	+ 327
919	687	912	542

MATH

100 Second Grade Skills

57

Page 57

Answer Key

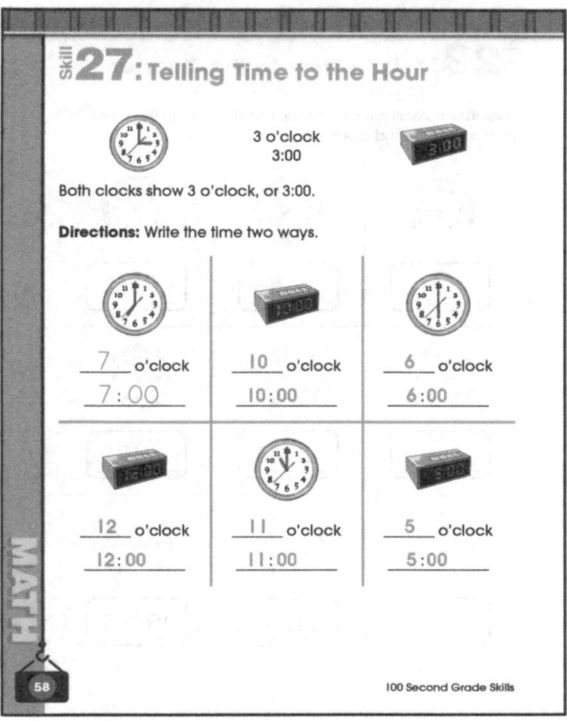

Skill 27: Telling Time to the Hour

3 o'clock
3:00

Both clocks show 3 o'clock, or 3:00.

Directions: Write the time two ways.

7 o'clock 7:00	10 o'clock 10:00	6 o'clock 6:00
12 o'clock 12:00	11 o'clock 11:00	5 o'clock 5:00

58 100 Second Grade Skills

Page 58

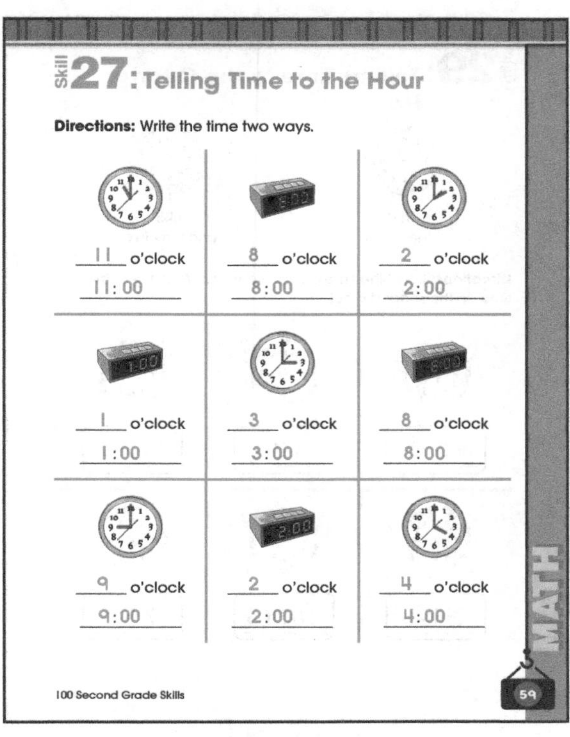

Skill 27: Telling Time to the Hour

Directions: Write the time two ways.

11 o'clock 11:00	8 o'clock 8:00	2 o'clock 2:00
1 o'clock 1:00	3 o'clock 3:00	8 o'clock 8:00
9 o'clock 9:00	2 o'clock 2:00	4 o'clock 4:00

100 Second Grade Skills 59

Page 59

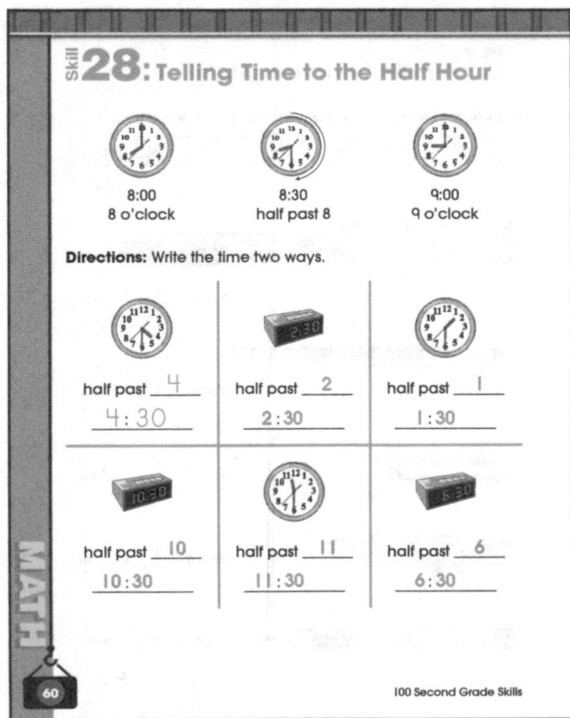

Skill 28: Telling Time to the Half Hour

8:00
8 o'clock

8:30
half past 8

9:00
9 o'clock

Directions: Write the time two ways.

half past 4 4:30	half past 2 2:30	half past 1 1:30
half past 10 10:30	half past 11 11:30	half past 6 6:30

60 100 Second Grade Skills

Page 60

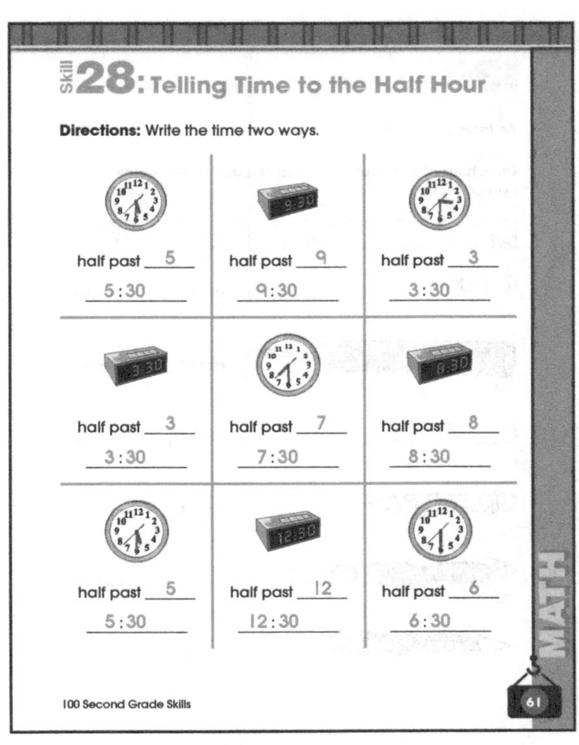

Skill 28: Telling Time to the Half Hour

Directions: Write the time two ways.

half past 5 5:30	half past 9 9:30	half past 3 3:30
half past 3 3:30	half past 7 7:30	half past 8 8:30
half past 5 5:30	half past 12 12:30	half past 6 6:30

100 Second Grade Skills 61

Page 61

Answer Key

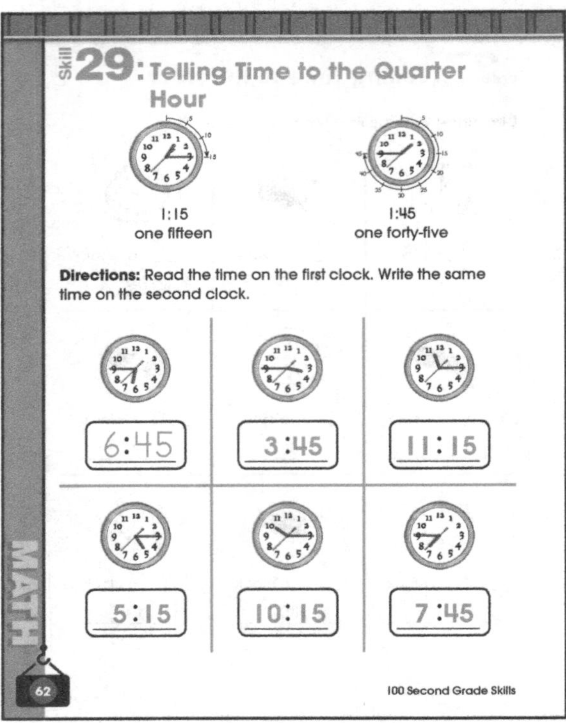

Skill **29**: Telling Time to the Quarter Hour

1:15
one fifteen

1:45
one forty-five

Directions: Read the time on the first clock. Write the same time on the second clock.

6:45	3:45	11:15
5:15	10:15	7:45

MATH

62 100 Second Grade Skills

Page 62

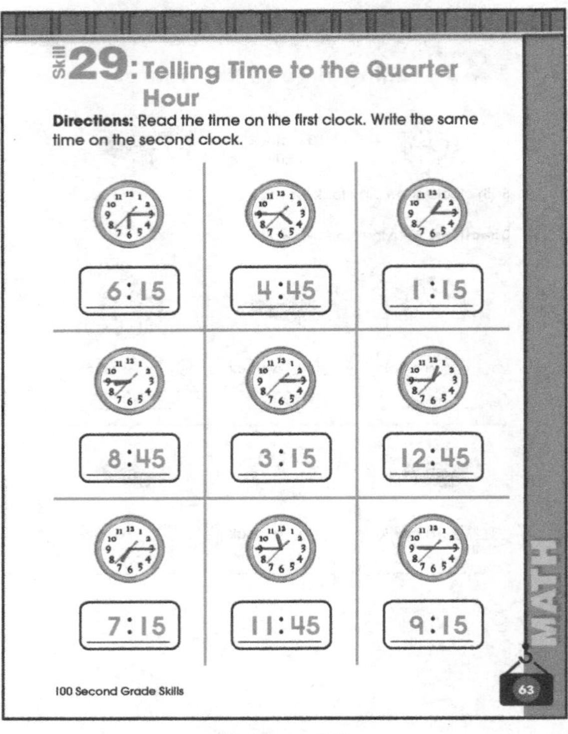

Skill **29**: Telling Time to the Quarter Hour

Directions: Read the time on the first clock. Write the same time on the second clock.

6:15	4:45	1:15
8:45	3:15	12:45
7:15	11:45	9:15

MATH

100 Second Grade Skills 63

Page 63

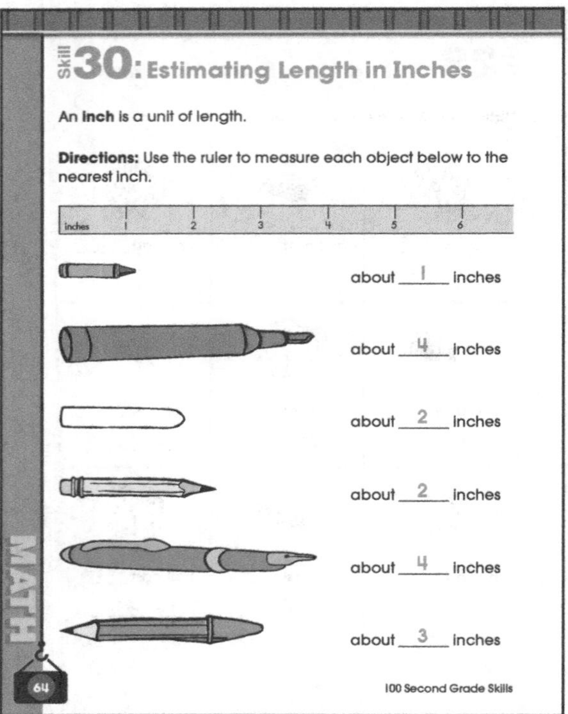

Skill **30**: Estimating Length in Inches

An **inch** is a unit of length.

Directions: Use the ruler to measure each object below to the nearest inch.

inches 1 2 3 4 5 6

about 1 inches

about 4 inches

about 2 inches

about 2 inches

about 4 inches

about 3 inches

MATH

64 100 Second Grade Skills

Page 64

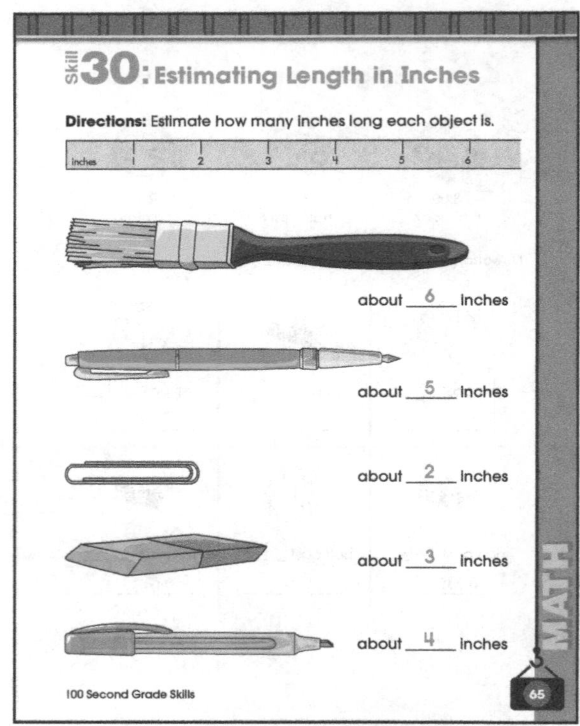

Skill **30**: Estimating Length in Inches

Directions: Estimate how many inches long each object is.

inches 1 2 3 4 5 6

about 6 inches

about 5 inches

about 2 inches

about 3 inches

about 4 inches

MATH

100 Second Grade Skills 65

Page 65

Answer Key

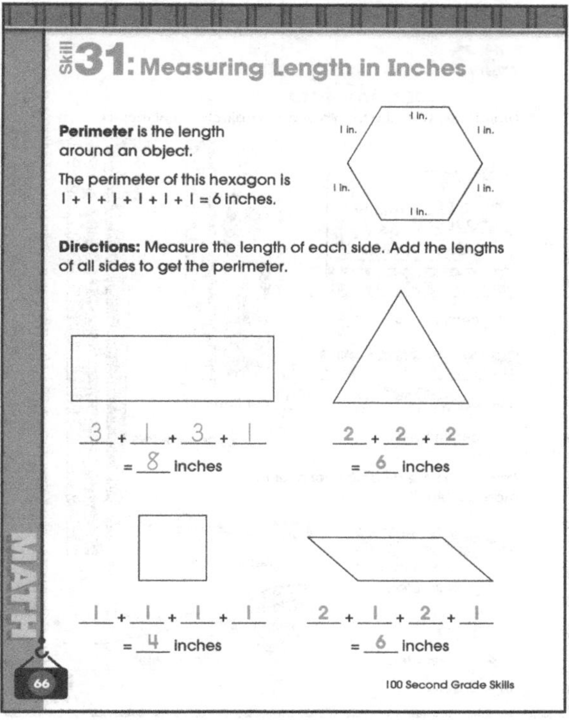

Page 66

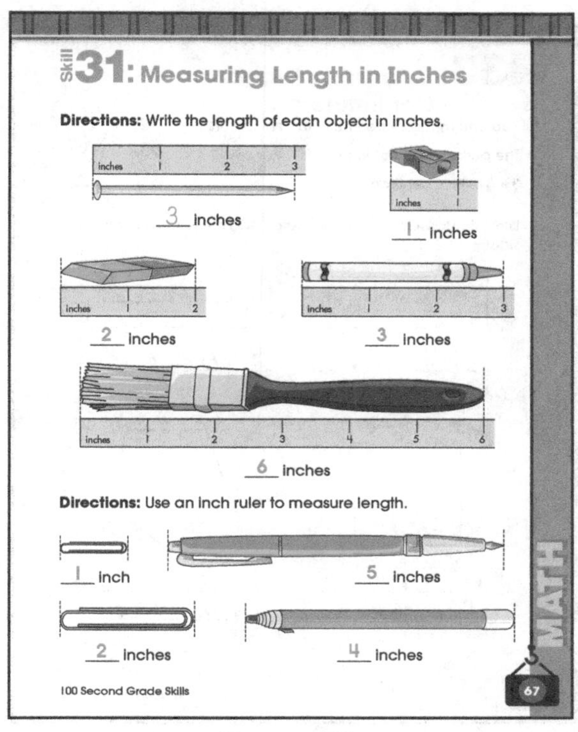

Skill 31: Measuring Length in Inches
Directions: Write the length of each object in inches.
3 inches
1 inches
2 inches
3 inches
6 inches
Directions: Use an inch ruler to measure length.
1 inch
5 inches
2 inches
4 inches
100 Second Grade Skills
67
MATH

Page 67

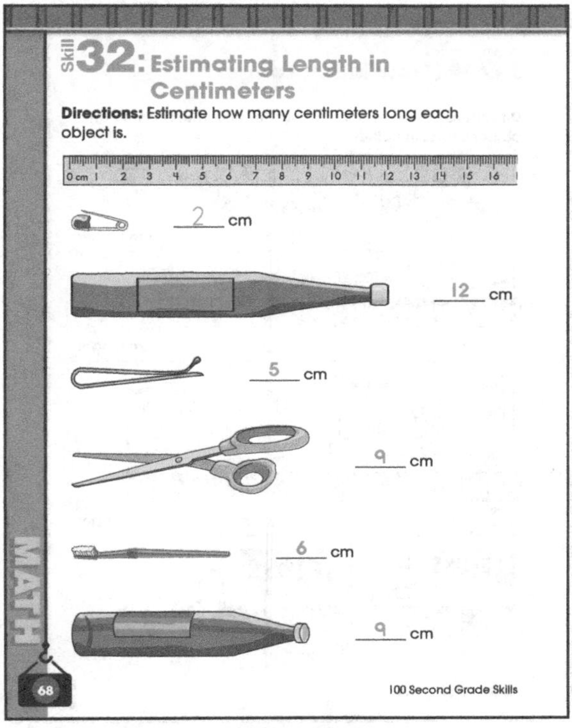

Skill 32: Estimating Length in Centimeters
Directions: Estimate how many centimeters long each object is.
2 cm
12 cm
5 cm
9 cm
6 cm
9 cm
MATH
68
100 Second Grade Skills

Page 68

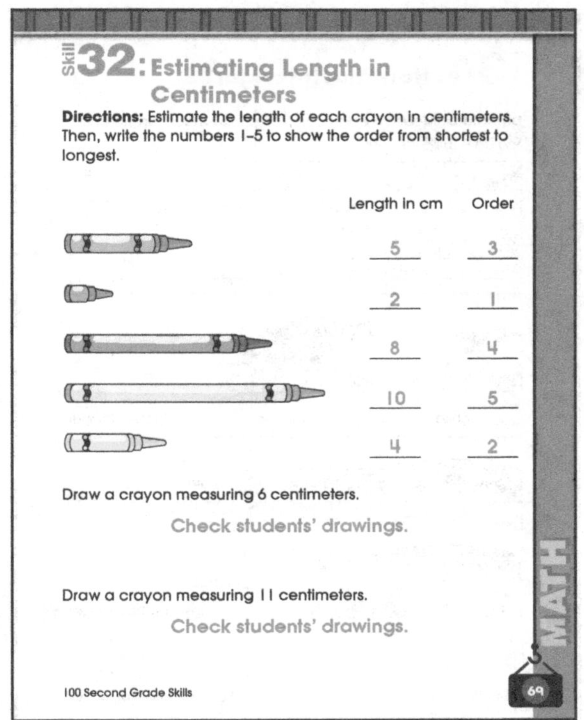

Skill 32: Estimating Length in Centimeters
Directions: Estimate the length of each crayon in centimeters. Then, write the numbers 1-5 to show the order from shortest to longest.
Length in cm Order
5 3
2 1
8 4
10 5
4 2
Draw a crayon measuring 6 centimeters.
Check students' drawings.
Draw a crayon measuring 11 centimeters.
Check students' drawings.
100 Second Grade Skills
69
MATH

Page 69

Answer Key

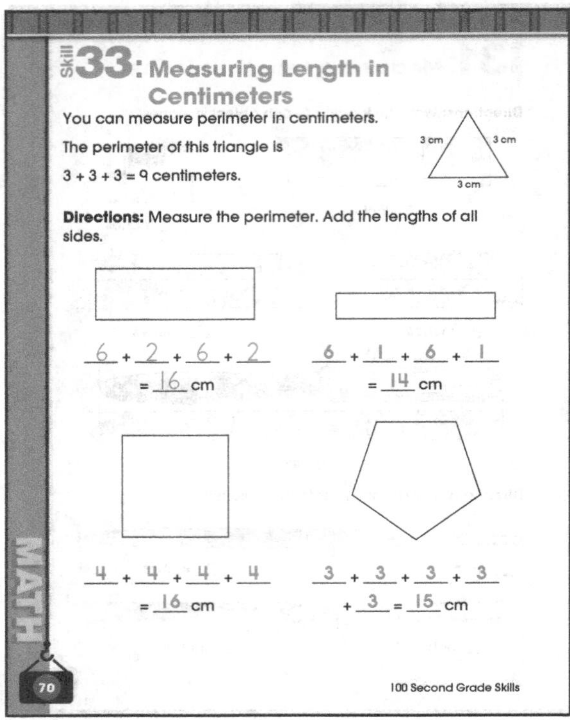

Skill 33: Measuring Length in Centimeters
You can measure perimeter in centimeters.
The perimeter of this triangle is
3 + 3 + 3 = 9 centimeters.
3 cm
3 cm
3 cm
Directions: Measure the perimeter. Add the lengths of all sides.
6 + 2 + 6 + 2
= 16 cm
6 + 1 + 6 + 1
= 14 cm
4 + 4 + 4 + 4
= 16 cm
3 + 3 + 3 + 3
+ 3 = 15 cm
MATH
70
100 Second Grade Skills

Page 70

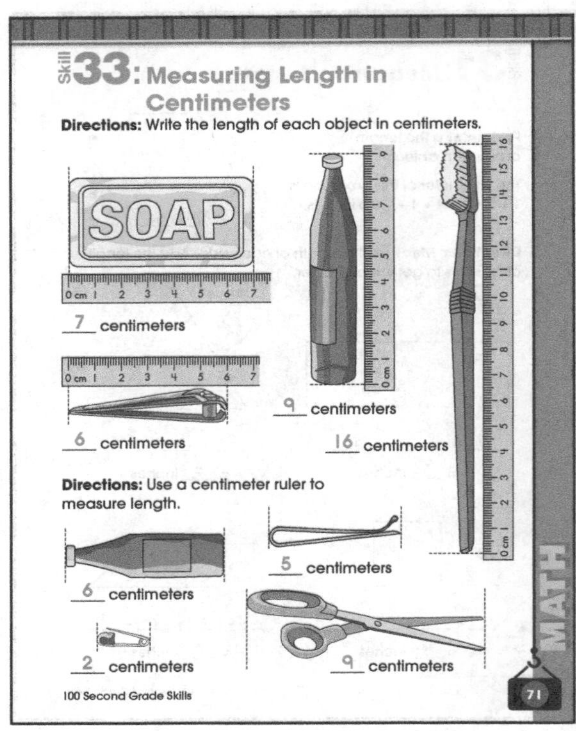

Skill 33: Measuring Length in Centimeters
Directions: Write the length of each object in centimeters.
SOAP
7 centimeters
6 centimeters
9 centimeters
16 centimeters
Directions: Use a centimeter ruler to measure length.
5 centimeters
6 centimeters
2 centimeters
9 centimeters
100 Second Grade Skills
MATH
71

Page 71

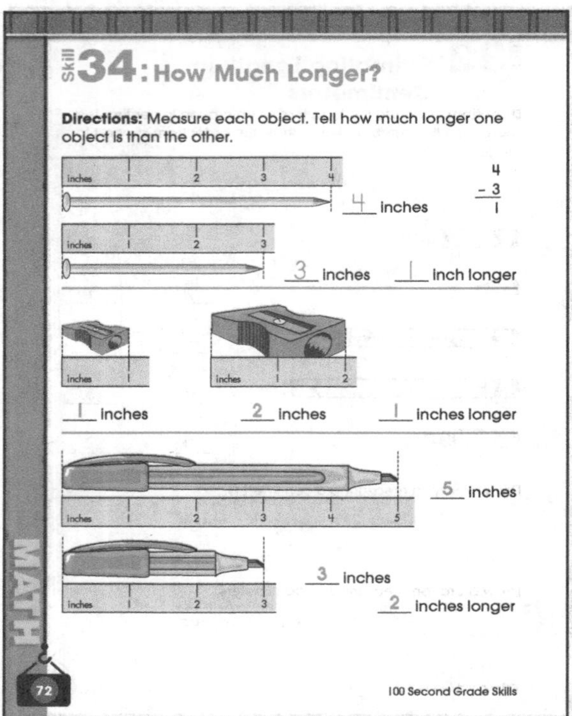

Page 72

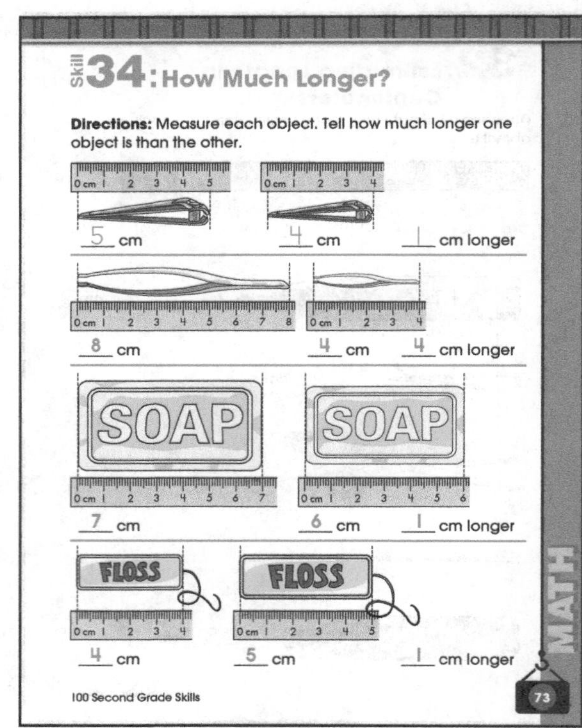

Skill 34: How Much Longer?
Directions: Measure each object. Tell how much longer one object is than the other.
5 cm
4 cm
1 cm longer
8 cm
4 cm
4 cm longer
SOAP
SOAP
7 cm
6 cm
1 cm longer
FLOSS
FLOSS
4 cm
5 cm
1 cm longer
100 Second Grade Skills
MATH
73

Page 73

Answer Key

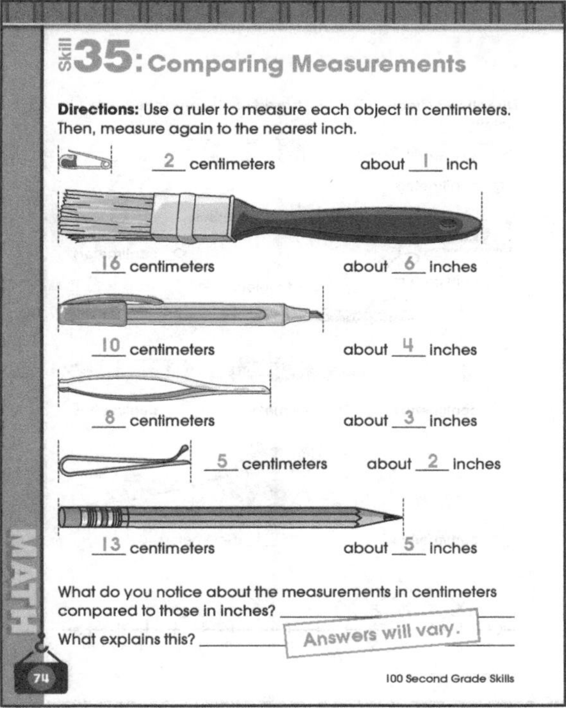

Skill 35: Comparing Measurements

Directions: Use a ruler to measure each object in centimeters. Then, measure again to the nearest inch.

2 centimeters — about 1 inch

16 centimeters — about 6 inches

10 centimeters — about 4 inches

8 centimeters — about 3 inches

5 centimeters — about 2 inches

13 centimeters — about 5 inches

What do you notice about the measurements in centimeters compared to those in inches?

What explains this?

Answers will vary.

74 — 100 Second Grade Skills

Page 74

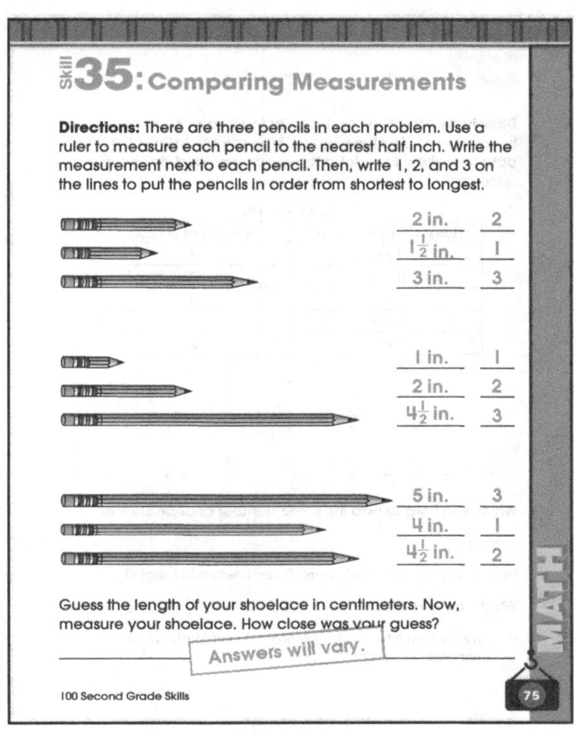

Skill 35: Comparing Measurements

Directions: There are three pencils in each problem. Use a ruler to measure each pencil to the nearest half inch. Write the measurement next to each pencil. Then, write 1, 2, and 3 on the lines to put the pencils in order from shortest to longest.

2 in.	2
$1\frac{1}{2}$ in.	1
3 in.	3

1 in.	1
2 in.	2
$4\frac{1}{2}$ in.	3

5 in.	3
4 in.	1
$4\frac{1}{2}$ in.	2

Guess the length of your shoelace in centimeters. Now, measure your shoelace. How close was your guess?

Answers will vary.

100 Second Grade Skills — 75

Page 75

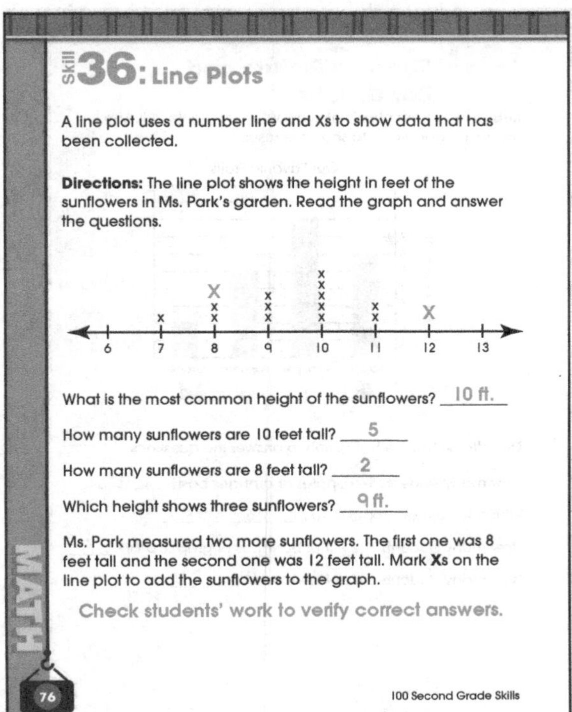

Skill 36: Line Plots

A line plot uses a number line and Xs to show data that has been collected.

Directions: The line plot shows the height in feet of the sunflowers in Ms. Park's garden. Read the graph and answer the questions.

What is the most common height of the sunflowers? 10 ft.

How many sunflowers are 10 feet tall? 5

How many sunflowers are 8 feet tall? 2

Which height shows three sunflowers? 9 ft.

Ms. Park measured two more sunflowers. The first one was 8 feet tall and the second one was 12 feet tall. Mark **X**s on the line plot to add the sunflowers to the graph.

Check students' work to verify correct answers.

76 — 100 Second Grade Skills

Page 76

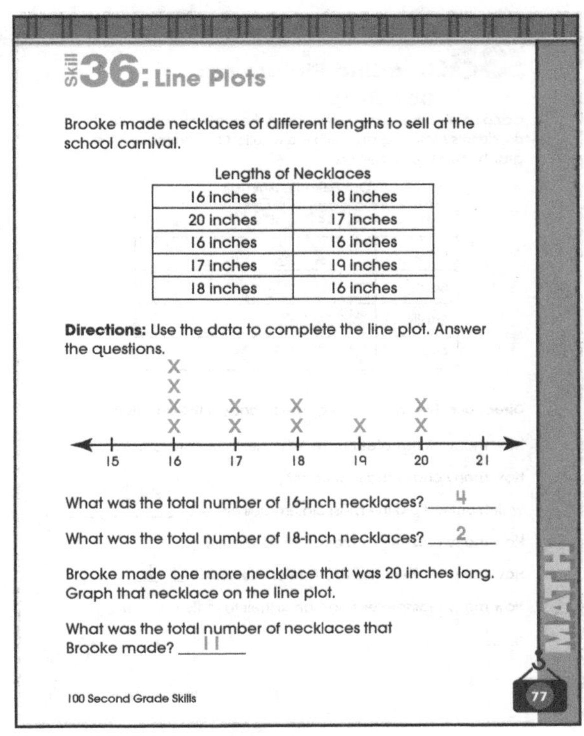

Skill 36: Line Plots

Brooke made necklaces of different lengths to sell at the school carnival.

Lengths of Necklaces

16 inches	18 inches
20 inches	17 inches
16 inches	16 inches
17 inches	19 inches
18 inches	16 inches

Directions: Use the data to complete the line plot. Answer the questions.

What was the total number of 16-inch necklaces? 4

What was the total number of 18-inch necklaces? 2

Brooke made one more necklace that was 20 inches long. Graph that necklace on the line plot.

What was the total number of necklaces that Brooke made? 11

100 Second Grade Skills — 77

Page 77

Answer Key

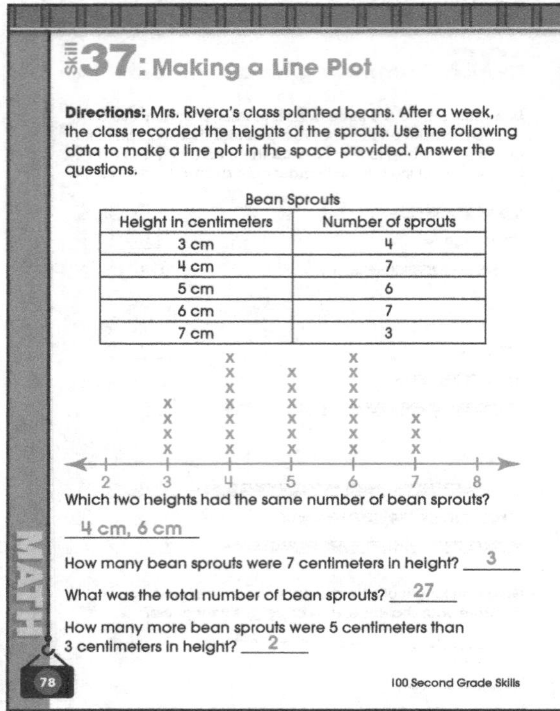

Skill 37: Making a Line Plot

Directions: Mrs. Rivera's class planted beans. After a week, the class recorded the heights of the sprouts. Use the following data to make a line plot in the space provided. Answer the questions.

Bean Sprouts

Height in centimeters	Number of sprouts
3 cm	4
4 cm	7
5 cm	6
6 cm	7
7 cm	3

Which two heights had the same number of bean sprouts? 4 cm, 6 cm

How many bean sprouts were 7 centimeters in height? 3

What was the total number of bean sprouts? 27

How many more bean sprouts were 5 centimeters than 3 centimeters in height? 2

78 100 Second Grade Skills

Page 78

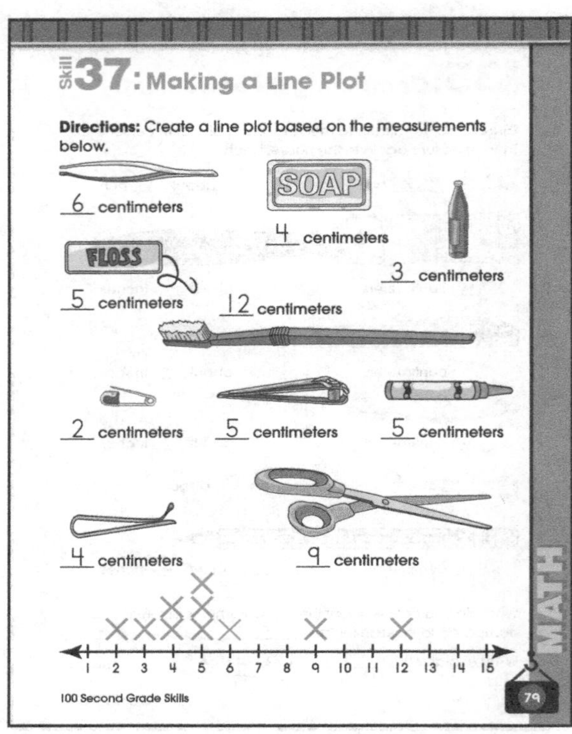

Skill 37: Making a Line Plot

Directions: Create a line plot based on the measurements below.

6 centimeters

4 centimeters

5 centimeters

12 centimeters

3 centimeters

2 centimeters

5 centimeters

5 centimeters

4 centimeters

9 centimeters

100 Second Grade Skills 79

Page 79

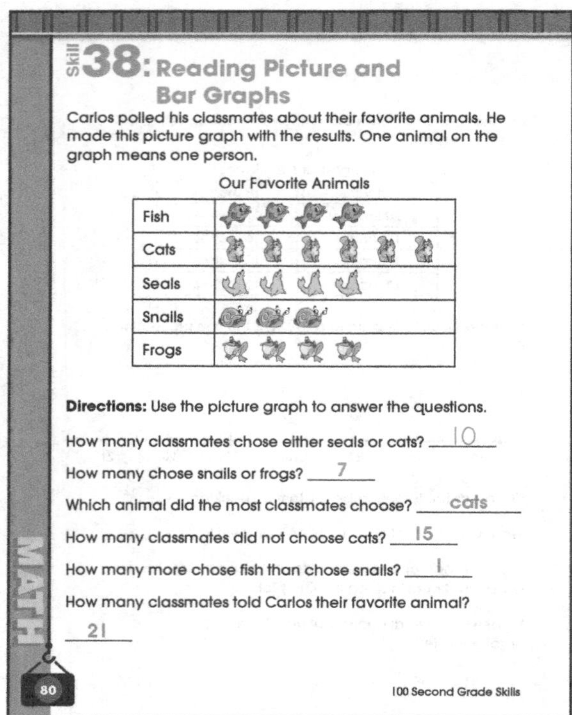

Skill 38: Reading Picture and Bar Graphs

Carlos polled his classmates about their favorite animals. He made this picture graph with the results. One animal on the graph means one person.

Our Favorite Animals

Fish

Cats

Seals

Snails

Frogs

Directions: Use the picture graph to answer the questions.

How many classmates chose either seals or cats? 10

How many chose snails or frogs? 7

Which animal did the most classmates choose? cats

How many classmates did not choose cats? 15

How many more chose fish than chose snails? 1

How many classmates told Carlos their favorite animal? 21

80 100 Second Grade Skills

Page 80

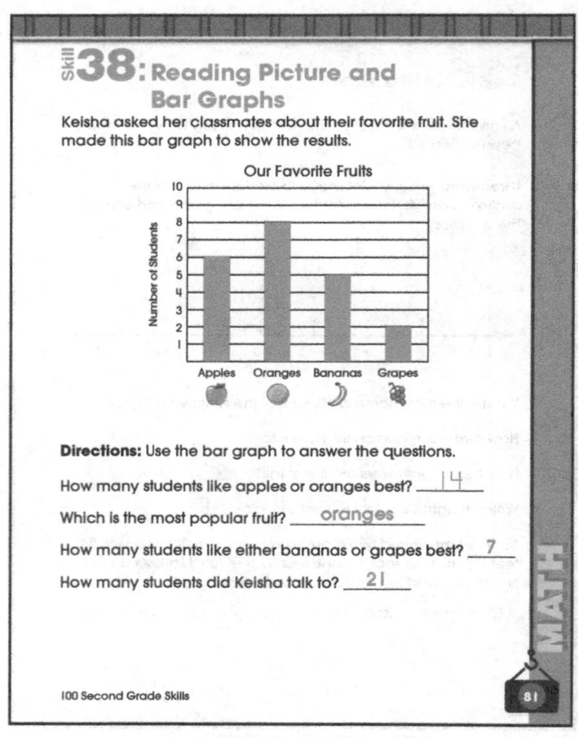

Skill 38: Reading Picture and Bar Graphs

Keisha asked her classmates about their favorite fruit. She made this bar graph to show the results.

Directions: Use the bar graph to answer the questions.

How many students like apples or oranges best? 14

Which is the most popular fruit? oranges

How many students like either bananas or grapes best? 7

How many students did Keisha talk to? 21

100 Second Grade Skills 81

Page 81

Answer Key

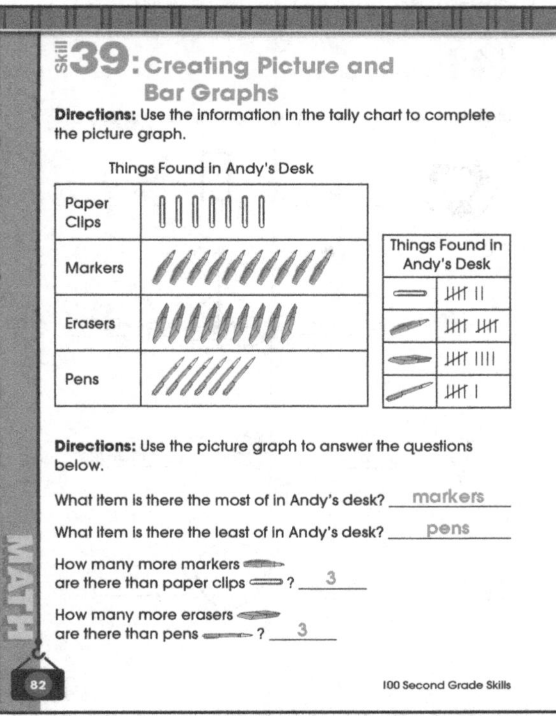

Skill 39: Creating Picture and Bar Graphs

Directions: Use the information in the tally chart to complete the picture graph.

Things Found in Andy's Desk

Paper Clips	
Markers	
Erasers	
Pens	

Things Found in Andy's Desk	
	卌 II
	卌 卌
	卌 IIII
	卌 I

Directions: Use the picture graph to answer the questions below.

What item is there the most of in Andy's desk? markers

What item is there the least of in Andy's desk? pens

How many more markers are there than paper clips? 3

How many more erasers are there than pens? 3

MATH

82 100 Second Grade Skills

Page 82

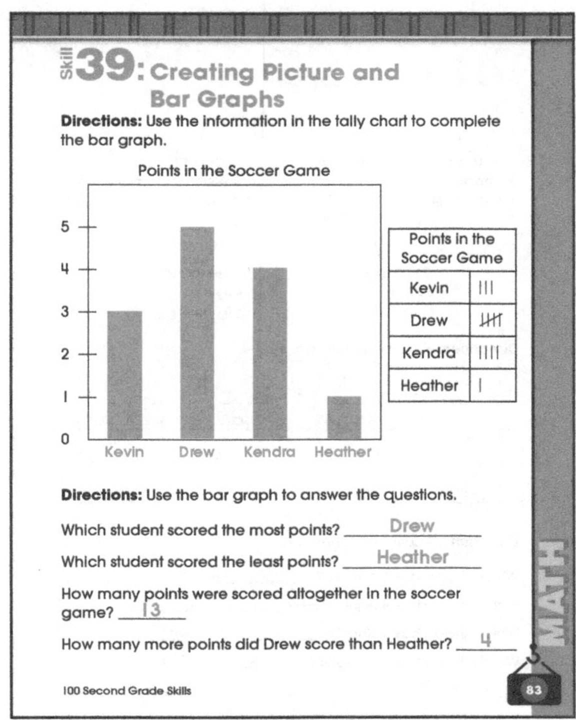

Skill 39: Creating Picture and Bar Graphs

Directions: Use the information in the tally chart to complete the bar graph.

Points in the Soccer Game	
Kevin	III
Drew	卌
Kendra	IIII
Heather	I

Directions: Use the bar graph to answer the questions.

Which student scored the most points? Drew

Which student scored the least points? Heather

How many points were scored altogether in the soccer game? 13

How many more points did Drew score than Heather? 4

100 Second Grade Skills MATH 83

Page 83

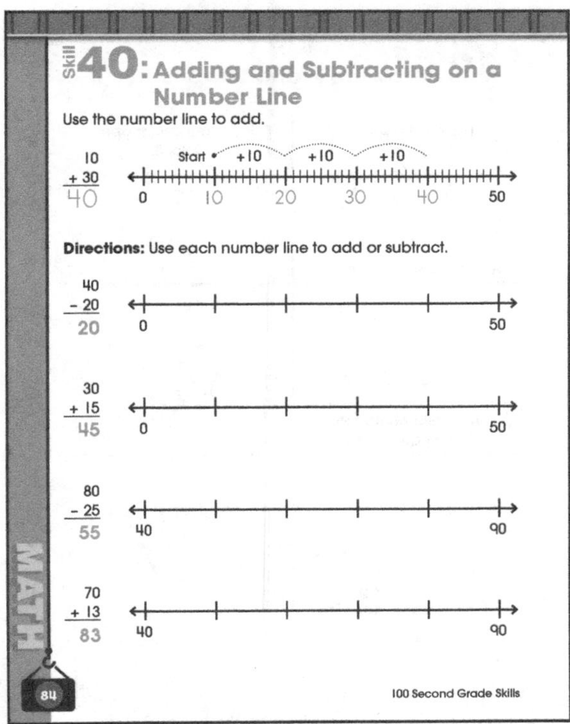

Skill 40: Adding and Subtracting on a Number Line

Use the number line to add.

10 + 30 = 40

Directions: Use each number line to add or subtract.

40 − 20 = 20 (0 to 50)

30 + 15 = 45 (0 to 50)

80 − 25 = 55 (40 to 90)

70 + 13 = 83 (40 to 90)

MATH

84 100 Second Grade Skills

Page 84

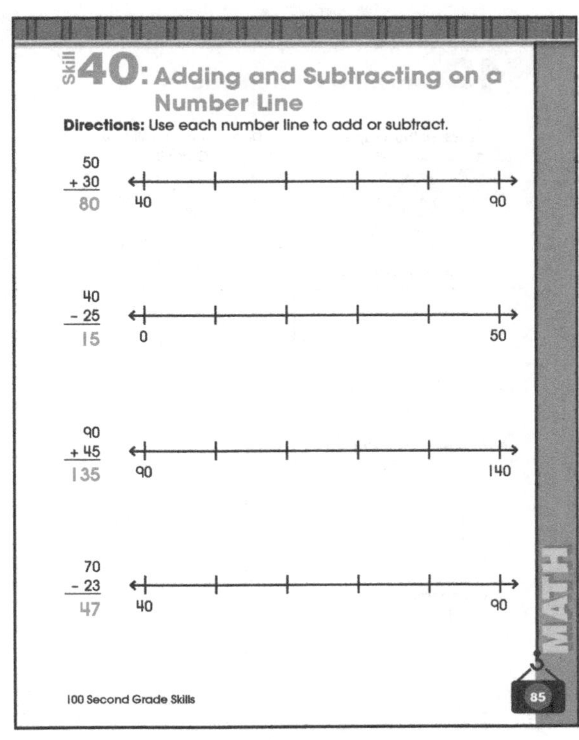

Skill 40: Adding and Subtracting on a Number Line

Directions: Use each number line to add or subtract.

50 + 30 = 80 (40 to 90)

40 − 25 = 15 (0 to 50)

90 + 45 = 135 (90 to 140)

70 − 23 = 47 (40 to 90)

100 Second Grade Skills MATH 85

Page 85

Answer Key

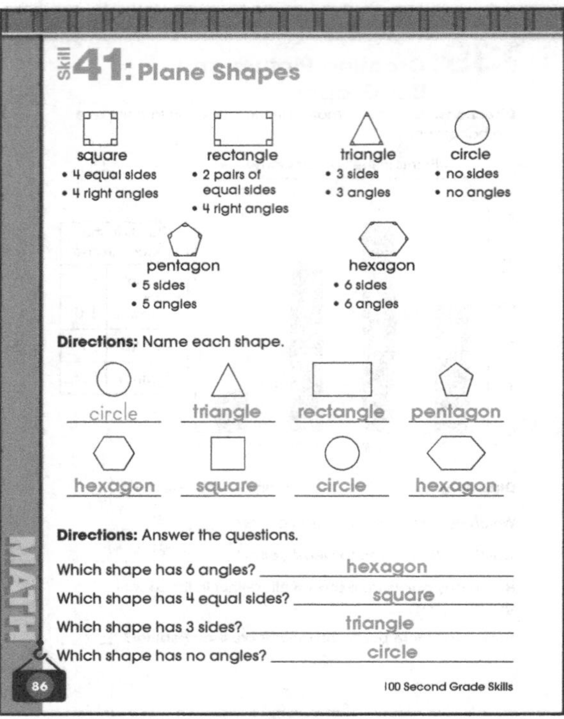

Skill **41: Plane Shapes**

square
- 4 equal sides
- 4 right angles

rectangle
- 2 pairs of equal sides
- 4 right angles

triangle
- 3 sides
- 3 angles

circle
- no sides
- no angles

pentagon
- 5 sides
- 5 angles

hexagon
- 6 sides
- 6 angles

Directions: Name each shape.

circle, triangle, rectangle, pentagon

hexagon, square, circle, hexagon

Directions: Answer the questions.

Which shape has 6 angles? hexagon

Which shape has 4 equal sides? square

Which shape has 3 sides? triangle

Which shape has no angles? circle

MATH

86

100 Second Grade Skills

Page 86

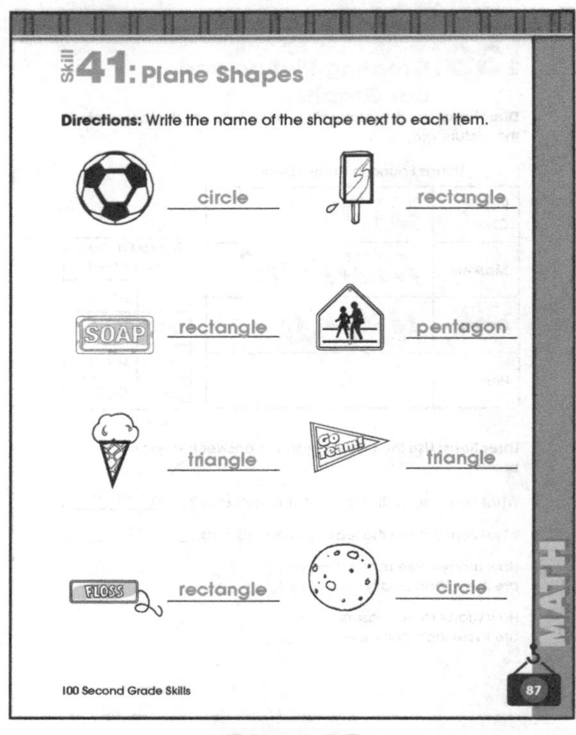

Skill **41: Plane Shapes**

Directions: Write the name of the shape next to each item.

circle

rectangle

SOAP rectangle

pentagon

triangle

Go Team! triangle

FLOSS rectangle

circle

100 Second Grade Skills

MATH

87

Page 87

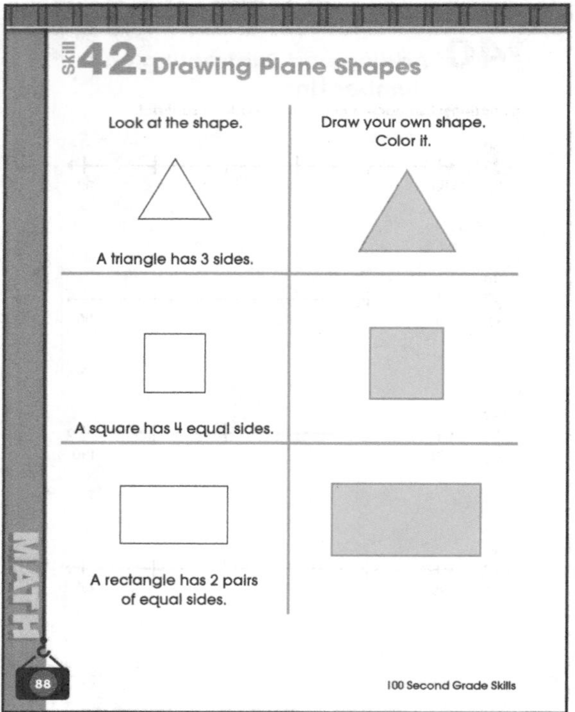

Skill **42: Drawing Plane Shapes**

Look at the shape.	Draw your own shape. Color it.
A triangle has 3 sides.	
A square has 4 equal sides.	
A rectangle has 2 pairs of equal sides.	

MATH

88

100 Second Grade Skills

Page 88

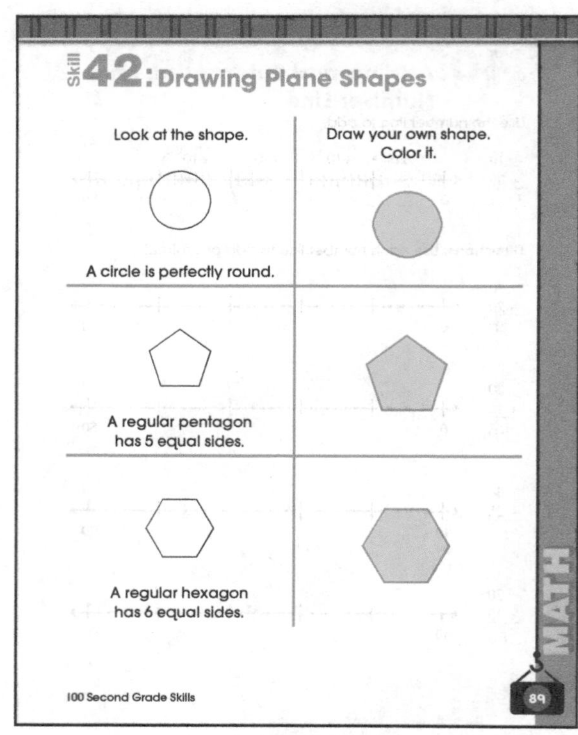

Skill **42: Drawing Plane Shapes**

Look at the shape.	Draw your own shape. Color it.
A circle is perfectly round.	
A regular pentagon has 5 equal sides.	
A regular hexagon has 6 equal sides.	

100 Second Grade Skills

MATH

89

Page 89

Answer Key

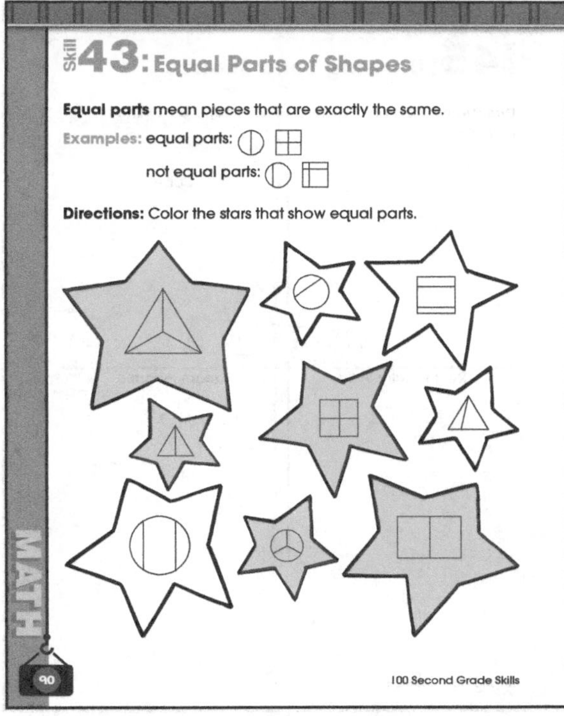
Skill **43: Equal Parts of Shapes**

Equal parts mean pieces that are exactly the same.

Examples: equal parts:

not equal parts:

Directions: Color the stars that show equal parts.

MATH

90

100 Second Grade Skills

Page 90

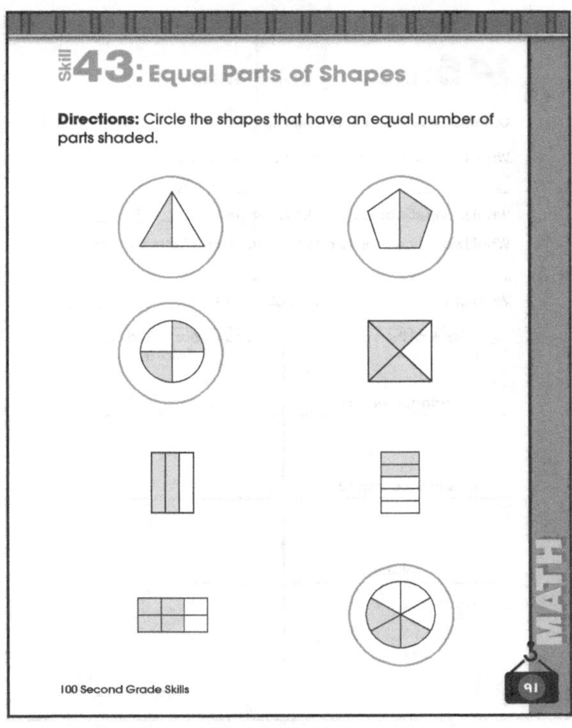
Skill **43: Equal Parts of Shapes**

Directions: Circle the shapes that have an equal number of parts shaded.

MATH

100 Second Grade Skills

91

Page 91

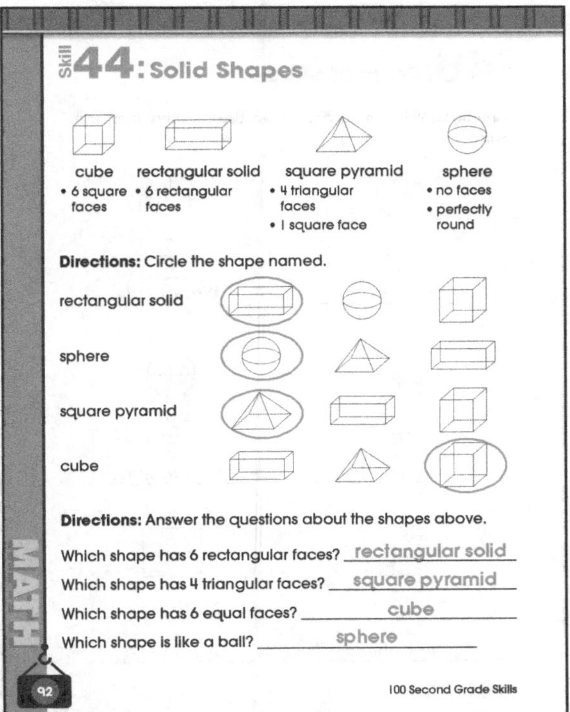
Skill **44: Solid Shapes**

cube	rectangular solid	square pyramid	sphere
• 6 square faces	• 6 rectangular faces	• 4 triangular faces • 1 square face	• no faces • perfectly round

Directions: Circle the shape named.

rectangular solid

sphere

square pyramid

cube

Directions: Answer the questions about the shapes above.

Which shape has 6 rectangular faces? rectangular solid

Which shape has 4 triangular faces? square pyramid

Which shape has 6 equal faces? cube

Which shape is like a ball? sphere

MATH

92

100 Second Grade Skills

Page 92

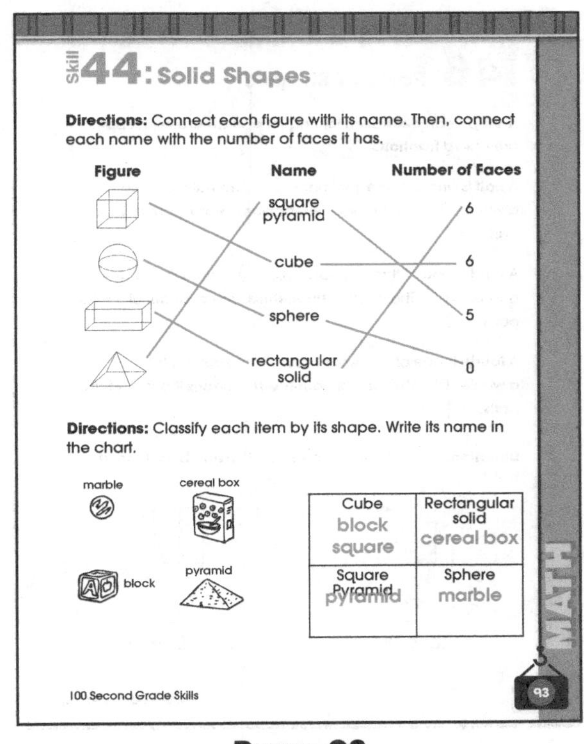
Skill **44: Solid Shapes**

Directions: Connect each figure with its name. Then, connect each name with the number of faces it has.

Figure	Name	Number of Faces
	square pyramid	6
	cube	6
	sphere	5
	rectangular solid	0

Directions: Classify each item by its shape. Write its name in the chart.

marble

cereal box

block

pyramid

Cube	Rectangular solid
block square	cereal box
Square Pyramid	**Sphere**
pyramid	marble

MATH

100 Second Grade Skills

93

Page 93

Answer Key

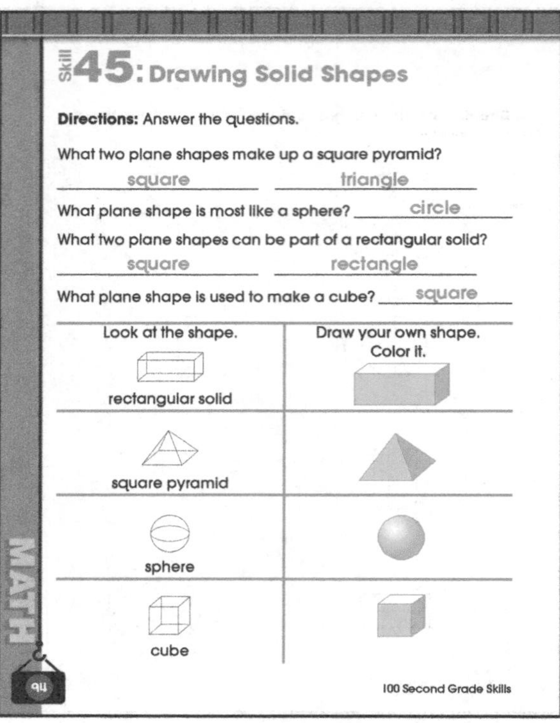

Skill 45: Drawing Solid Shapes

Directions: Answer the questions.

What two plane shapes make up a square pyramid? square triangle

What plane shape is most like a sphere? circle

What two plane shapes can be part of a rectangular solid? square rectangle

What plane shape is used to make a cube? square

Look at the shape.	Draw your own shape. Color it.
rectangular solid	
square pyramid	
sphere	
cube	

94 100 Second Grade Skills

Page 94

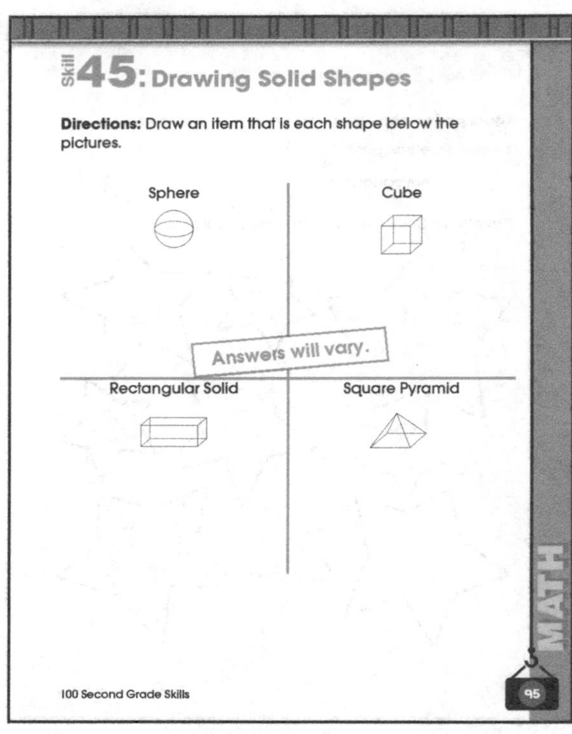

Skill 45: Drawing Solid Shapes

Directions: Draw an item that is each shape below the pictures.

Sphere

Cube

Answers will vary.

Rectangular Solid

Square Pyramid

100 Second Grade Skills 95

Page 95

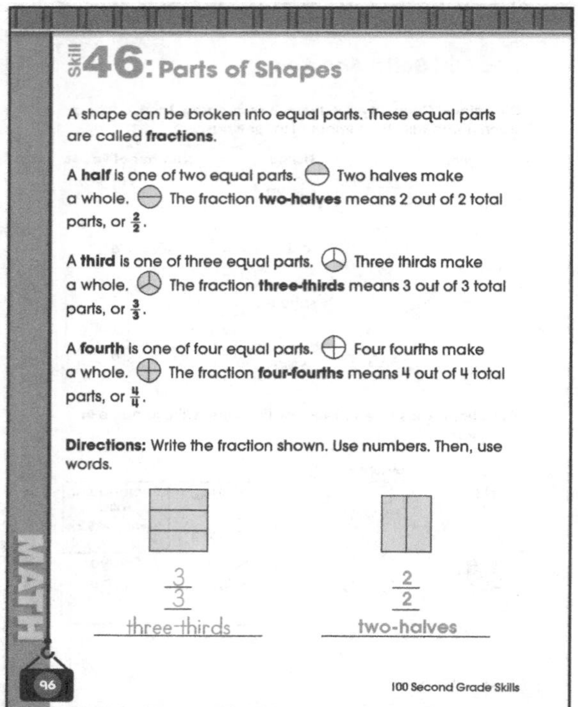

Skill 46: Parts of Shapes

A shape can be broken into equal parts. These equal parts are called **fractions**.

A **half** is one of two equal parts. Two halves make a whole. The fraction **two-halves** means 2 out of 2 total parts, or $\frac{2}{2}$.

A **third** is one of three equal parts. Three thirds make a whole. The fraction **three-thirds** means 3 out of 3 total parts, or $\frac{3}{3}$.

A **fourth** is one of four equal parts. Four fourths make a whole. The fraction **four-fourths** means 4 out of 4 total parts, or $\frac{4}{4}$.

Directions: Write the fraction shown. Use numbers. Then, use words.

$\frac{3}{3}$ three-thirds

$\frac{2}{2}$ two-halves

96 100 Second Grade Skills

Page 96

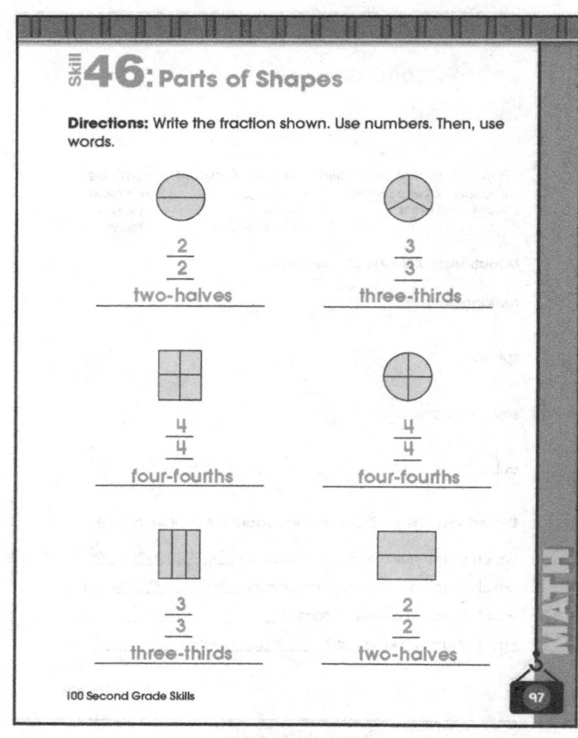

Skill 46: Parts of Shapes

Directions: Write the fraction shown. Use numbers. Then, use words.

$\frac{2}{2}$ two-halves

$\frac{3}{3}$ three-thirds

$\frac{4}{4}$ four-fourths

$\frac{4}{4}$ four-fourths

$\frac{3}{3}$ three-thirds

$\frac{2}{2}$ two-halves

100 Second Grade Skills 97

Page 97

Answer Key

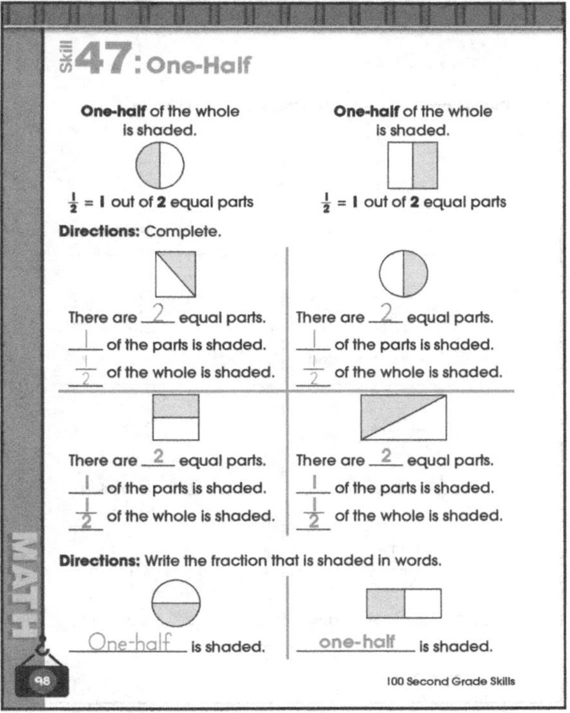

Skill 47: One-Half

One-half of the whole is shaded.

$\frac{1}{2}$ = 1 out of 2 equal parts

One-half of the whole is shaded.

$\frac{1}{2}$ = 1 out of 2 equal parts

Directions: Complete.

There are 2 equal parts.
1 of the parts is shaded.
$\frac{1}{2}$ of the whole is shaded.

There are 2 equal parts.
1 of the parts is shaded.
$\frac{1}{2}$ of the whole is shaded.

There are 2 equal parts.
1 of the parts is shaded.
$\frac{1}{2}$ of the whole is shaded.

There are 2 equal parts.
1 of the parts is shaded.
$\frac{1}{2}$ of the whole is shaded.

Directions: Write the fraction that is shaded in words.

One-half is shaded.

one-half is shaded.

MATH

98 100 Second Grade Skills

Page 98

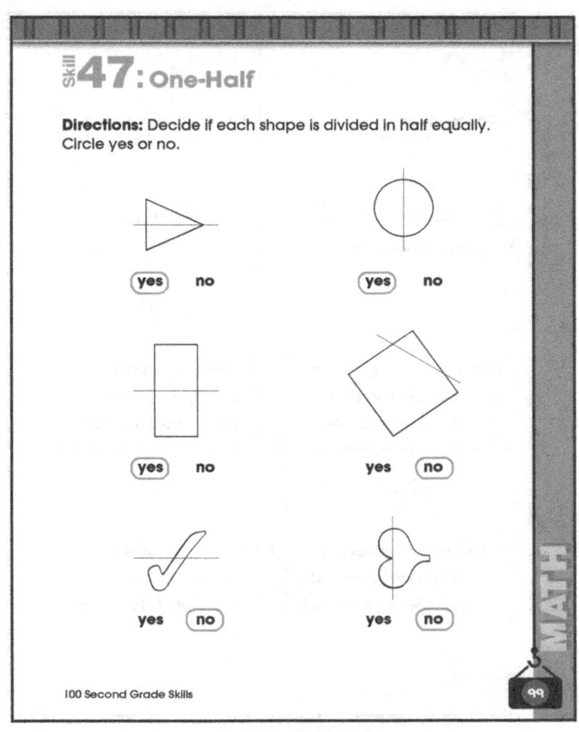

Skill 47: One-Half

Directions: Decide if each shape is divided in half equally. Circle yes or no.

yes no (yes circled)

yes no (yes circled)

yes no (yes circled)

yes no (no circled)

yes no (no circled)

yes no (no circled)

100 Second Grade Skills 99

MATH

Page 99

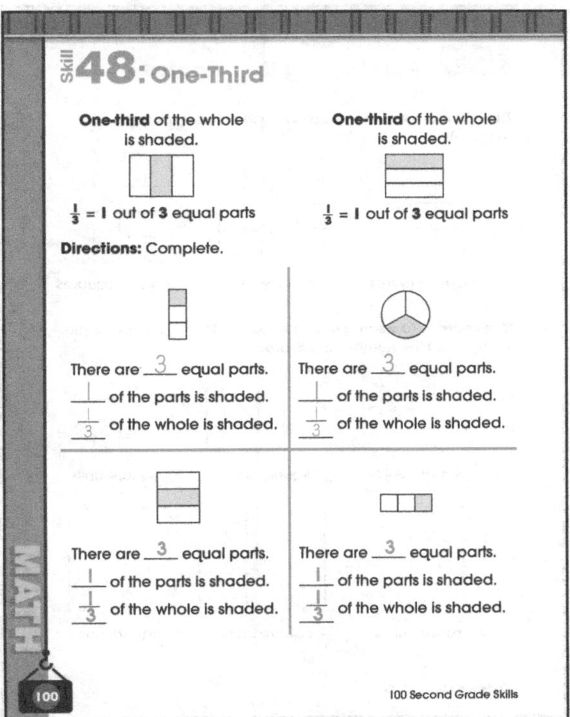

Skill 48: One-Third

One-third of the whole is shaded.

$\frac{1}{3}$ = 1 out of 3 equal parts

One-third of the whole is shaded.

$\frac{1}{3}$ = 1 out of 3 equal parts

Directions: Complete.

There are 3 equal parts.
1 of the parts is shaded.
$\frac{1}{3}$ of the whole is shaded.

There are 3 equal parts.
1 of the parts is shaded.
$\frac{1}{3}$ of the whole is shaded.

There are 3 equal parts.
1 of the parts is shaded.
$\frac{1}{3}$ of the whole is shaded.

There are 3 equal parts.
1 of the parts is shaded.
$\frac{1}{3}$ of the whole is shaded.

MATH

100 100 Second Grade Skills

Page 100

Skill 48: One-Third

Directions: Write the fraction that is shaded in words.

One-third is shaded.

one-third is shaded.

one-third is shaded.

one-third is shaded.

one-third is shaded.

one-third is shaded.

one-third is shaded.

one-third is shaded.

100 Second Grade Skills 101

MATH

Page 101

Answer Key

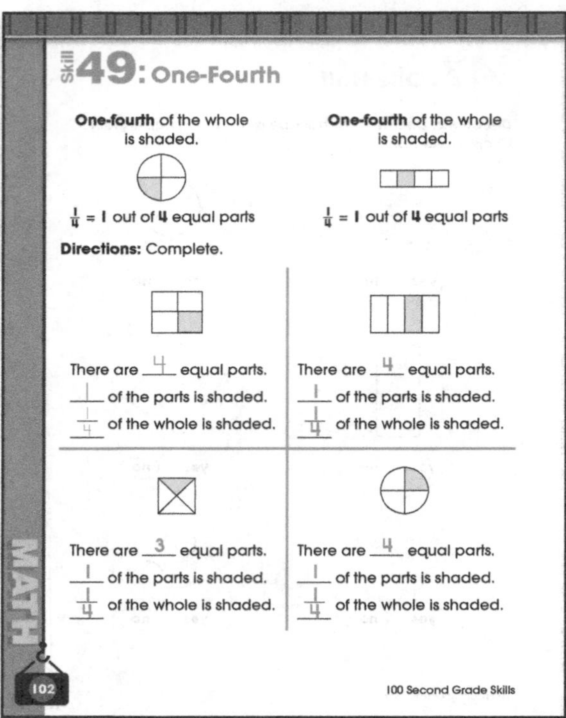

Skill **49: One-Fourth**

One-fourth of the whole is shaded.

$\frac{1}{4}$ = 1 out of 4 equal parts

One-fourth of the whole is shaded.

$\frac{1}{4}$ = 1 out of 4 equal parts

Directions: Complete.

There are 4 equal parts.
1 of the parts is shaded.
$\frac{1}{4}$ of the whole is shaded.

There are 4 equal parts.
1 of the parts is shaded.
$\frac{1}{4}$ of the whole is shaded.

There are 3 equal parts.
1 of the parts is shaded.
$\frac{1}{4}$ of the whole is shaded.

There are 4 equal parts.
1 of the parts is shaded.
$\frac{1}{4}$ of the whole is shaded.

MATH

102 100 Second Grade Skills

Page 102

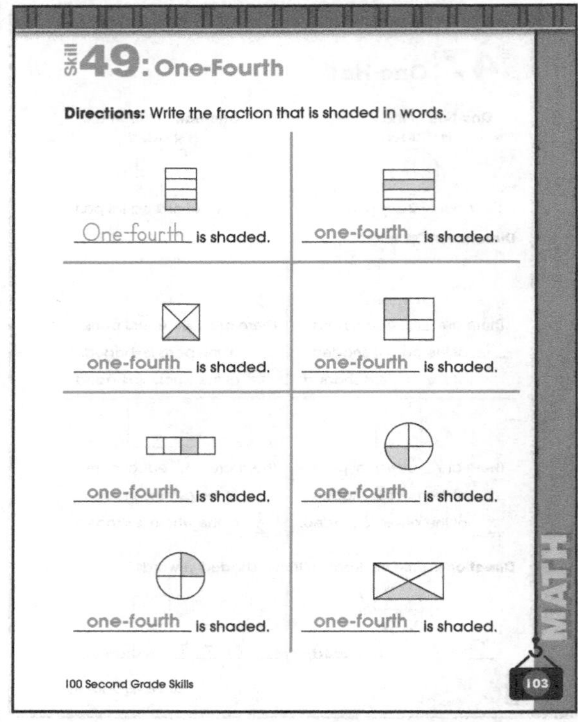

Skill **49: One-Fourth**

Directions: Write the fraction that is shaded in words.

One-fourth is shaded. one-fourth is shaded.

one-fourth is shaded. one-fourth is shaded.

one-fourth is shaded. one-fourth is shaded.

one-fourth is shaded. one-fourth is shaded.

100 Second Grade Skills 103

MATH

Page 103

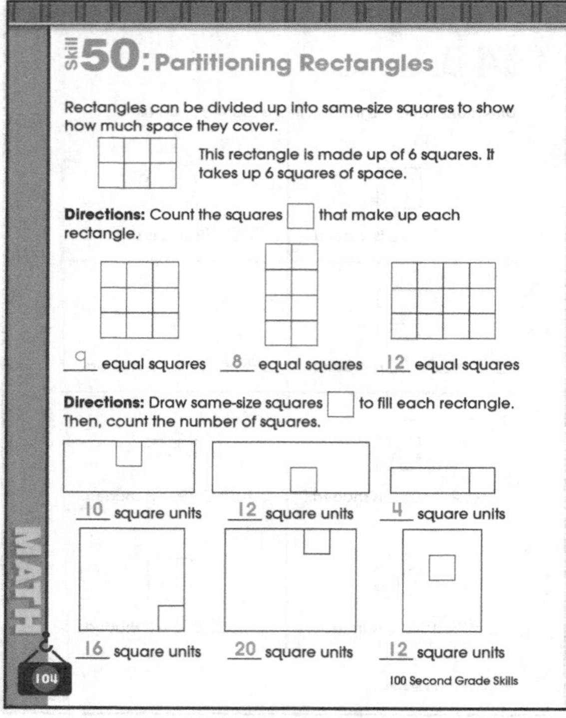

Skill **50: Partitioning Rectangles**

Rectangles can be divided up into same-size squares to show how much space they cover.

This rectangle is made up of 6 squares. It takes up 6 squares of space.

Directions: Count the squares ☐ that make up each rectangle.

9 equal squares 8 equal squares 12 equal squares

Directions: Draw same-size squares ☐ to fill each rectangle. Then, count the number of squares.

10 square units 12 square units 4 square units

16 square units 20 square units 12 square units

MATH

104 100 Second Grade Skills

Page 104

Skill **50: Partitioning Rectangles**

Directions: Count the squares ☐ that make up each rectangle.

6 equal squares 15 equal squares 12 equal squares

Directions: Draw same-size squares ☐ to fill each rectangle. Then, count the number of squares.

15 square units 18 square units 6 square units

8 square units 12 square units 20 square units

MATH

100 Second Grade Skills 105

Page 105

Answer Key

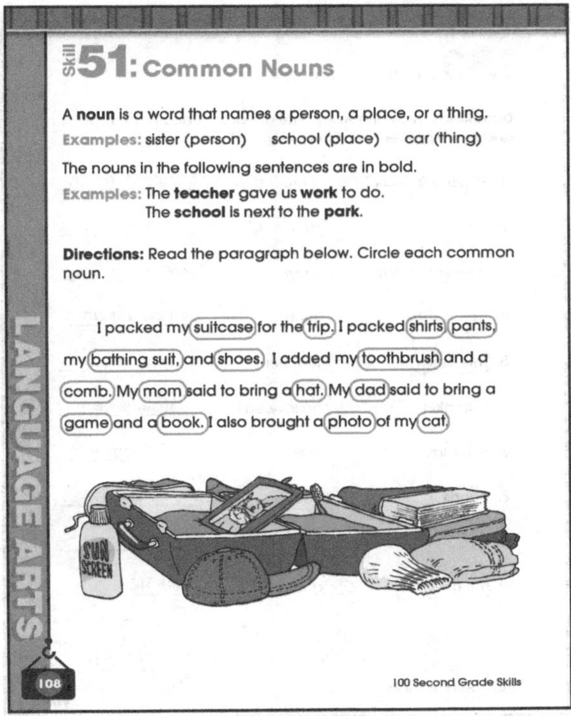

Skill 51: Common Nouns

A **noun** is a word that names a person, a place, or a thing.

Examples: sister (person) school (place) car (thing)

The nouns in the following sentences are in bold.

Examples: The **teacher** gave us **work** to do.
The **school** is next to the **park**.

Directions: Read the paragraph below. Circle each common noun.

I packed my (suitcase) for the (trip.) I packed (shirts) (pants,) my (bathing suit,) and (shoes.) I added my (toothbrush) and a (comb.) My (mom) said to bring a (hat.) My (dad) said to bring a (game) and a (book.) I also brought a (photo) of my (cat.)

LANGUAGE ARTS

108 100 Second Grade Skills

Page 108

Skill 51: Common Nouns

Directions: Circle all the common nouns. Then, write the common nouns next to the pictures below.

1. We like to go to the (playground) — playground
2. We like the (swings.) — swings
3. We eat (cake) for my (birthday.) — cake, birthday
4. We drink (lemonade.) — lemonade
5. Our (dog) chases a (ball.) — dog, ball
6. Then, we go (home.) — home

LANGUAGE ARTS

100 Second Grade Skills 109

Page 109

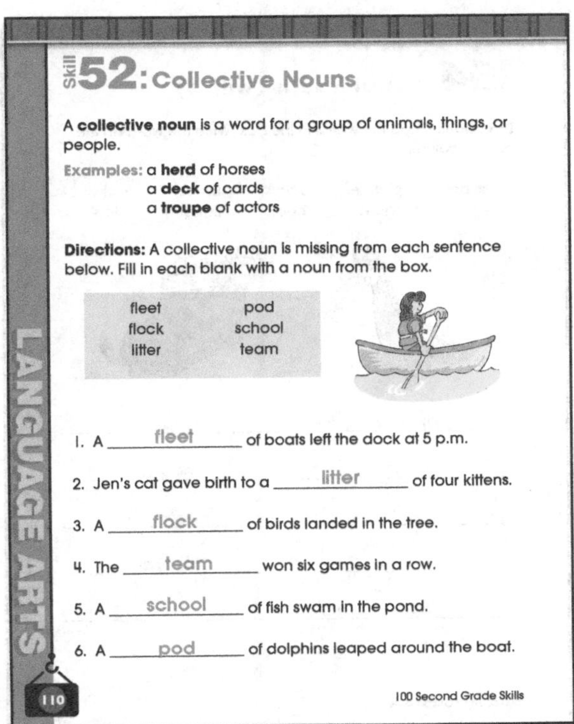

Skill 52: Collective Nouns

A **collective noun** is a word for a group of animals, things, or people.

Examples: a **herd** of horses
a **deck** of cards
a **troupe** of actors

Directions: A collective noun is missing from each sentence below. Fill in each blank with a noun from the box.

fleet	pod
flock	school
litter	team

1. A ___fleet___ of boats left the dock at 5 p.m.
2. Jen's cat gave birth to a ___litter___ of four kittens.
3. A ___flock___ of birds landed in the tree.
4. The ___team___ won six games in a row.
5. A ___school___ of fish swam in the pond.
6. A ___pod___ of dolphins leaped around the boat.

LANGUAGE ARTS

110 100 Second Grade Skills

Page 110

Skill 52: Collective Nouns

Directions: A collective noun is missing from each sentence below. Fill in each blank with a noun from the box.

school	team	herd

1. The ___team___ of soccer players boarded the plane.
2. The whale spotted a ___school___ of fish.
3. A ___herd___ of buffalo roamed the hills.

Directions: Write five sentences about what you would pack if you were going to camp. Each sentence should have two nouns.

Answers will vary.

LANGUAGE ARTS

100 Second Grade Skills 111

Page 111

Answer Key

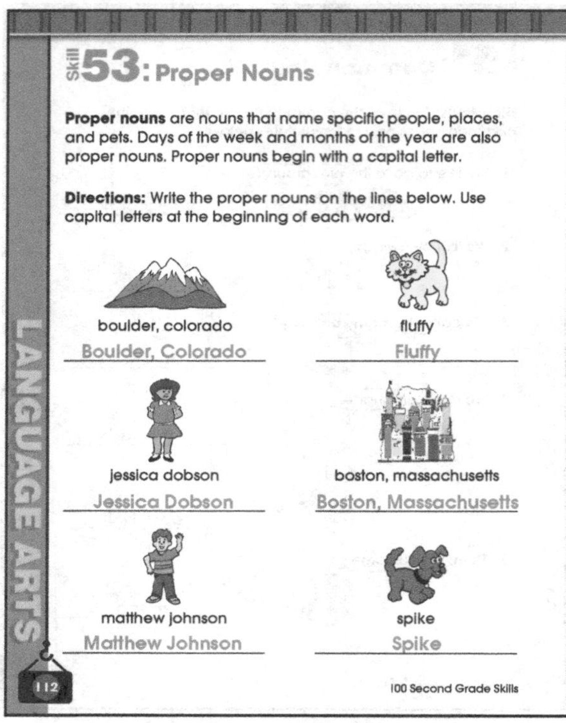

Page 112

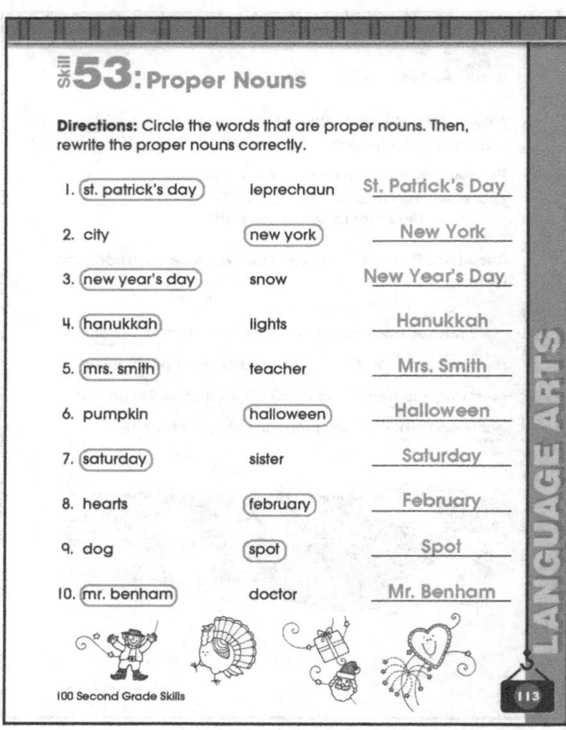

Skill 53: Proper Nouns
Directions: Circle the words that are proper nouns. Then, rewrite the proper nouns correctly.
1. st. patrick's day leprechaun St. Patrick's Day
2. city new york New York
3. new year's day snow New Year's Day
4. hanukkah lights Hanukkah
5. mrs. smith teacher Mrs. Smith
6. pumpkin halloween Halloween
7. saturday sister Saturday
8. hearts february February
9. dog spot Spot
10. mr. benham doctor Mr. Benham
100 Second Grade Skills
LANGUAGE ARTS
113

Page 113

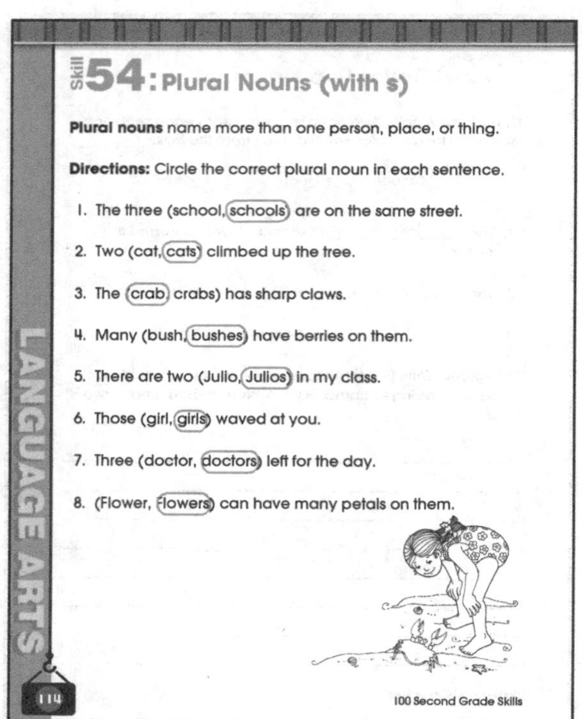

Page 114

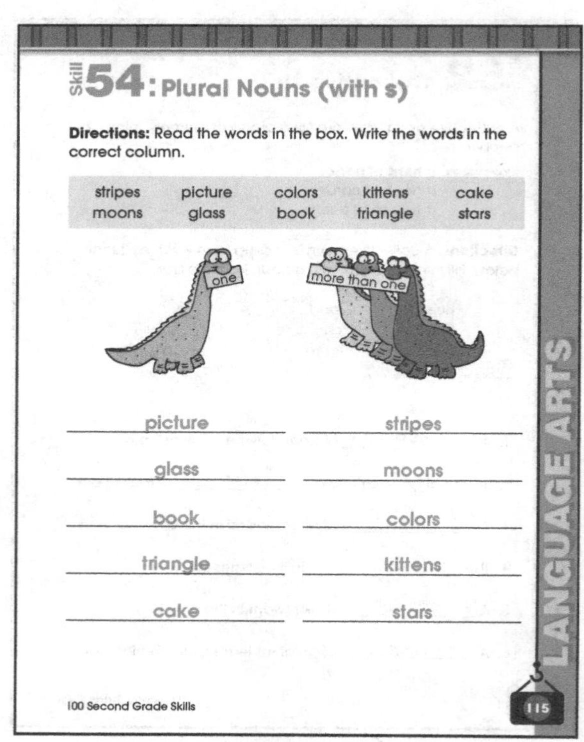

Skill 54: Plural Nouns (with s)
Directions: Read the words in the box. Write the words in the correct column.
stripes picture colors kittens cake
moons glass book triangle stars
one
more than one
picture stripes
glass moons
book colors
triangle kittens
cake stars
100 Second Grade Skills
LANGUAGE ARTS
115

Page 115

Answer Key

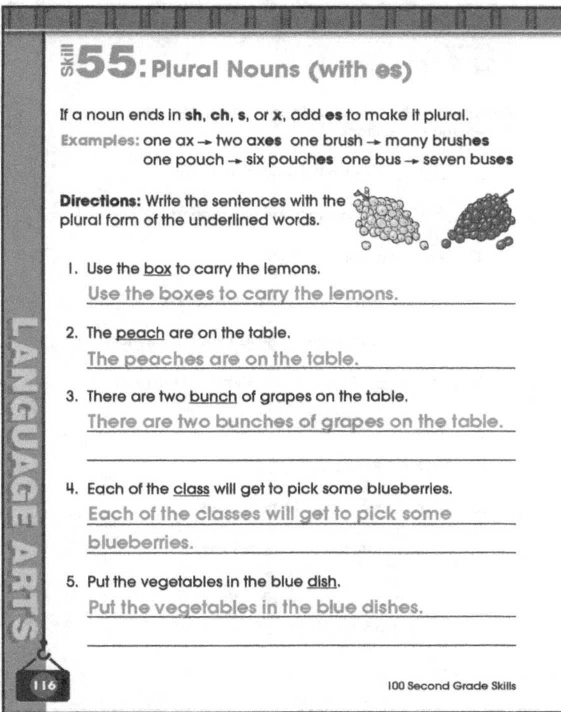

Skill **55: Plural Nouns (with es)**

If a noun ends in **sh**, **ch**, **s**, or **x**, add **es** to make it plural.

Examples: one ax → two ax**es** one brush → many brush**es**
one pouch → six pouch**es** one bus → seven bus**es**

Directions: Write the sentences with the plural form of the underlined words.

1. Use the box to carry the lemons.
   Use the boxes to carry the lemons.
2. The peach are on the table.
   The peaches are on the table.
3. There are two bunch of grapes on the table.
   There are two bunches of grapes on the table.
4. Each of the class will get to pick some blueberries.
   Each of the classes will get to pick some blueberries.
5. Put the vegetables in the blue dish.
   Put the vegetables in the blue dishes.

LANGUAGE ARTS

116 100 Second Grade Skills

Page 116

Skill **55: Plural Nouns (with es)**

Directions: Read the sentences. Write the correct plural word below each underlined word.

1. There were strawberry bush on the farm.
   bushes
2. We ate our lunch at some picnic tables.
   lunches
3. The bus picked us up at eight o'clock.
   buses
4. Mrs. Jenson gave us glass of lemonade.
   glasses
5. We waited on the bench outside the library.
   benches
6. Mr. Manson gave us some box to use.
   boxes
7. Many branch were heavy with fruit.
   branches

LANGUAGE ARTS

100 Second Grade Skills 117

Page 117

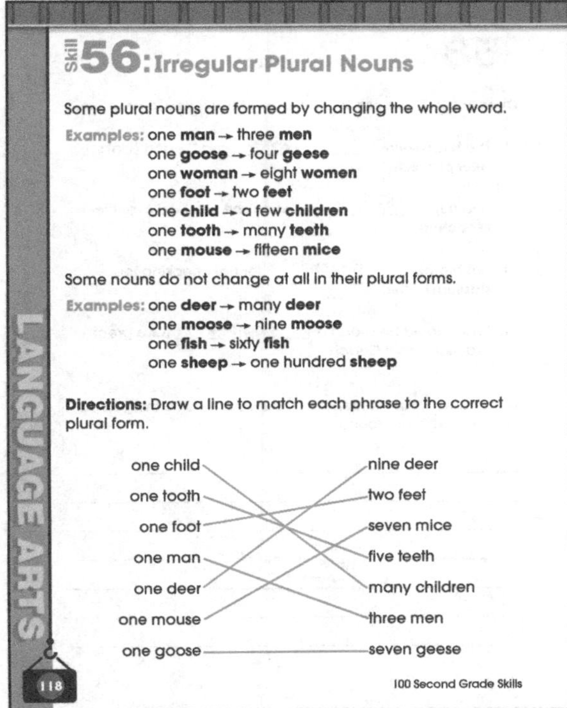

Skill **56: Irregular Plural Nouns**

Some plural nouns are formed by changing the whole word.

Examples: one **man** → three **men**
one **goose** → four **geese**
one **woman** → eight **women**
one **foot** → two **feet**
one **child** → a few **children**
one **tooth** → many **teeth**
one **mouse** → fifteen **mice**

Some nouns do not change at all in their plural forms.

Examples: one **deer** → many **deer**
one **moose** → nine **moose**
one **fish** → sixty **fish**
one **sheep** → one hundred **sheep**

Directions: Draw a line to match each phrase to the correct plural form.

one child	nine deer
one tooth	two feet
one foot	seven mice
one man	five teeth
one deer	many children
one mouse	three men
one goose	seven geese

LANGUAGE ARTS

118 100 Second Grade Skills

Page 118

Skill **56: Irregular Plural Nouns**

Directions: Look at the following plural words. Write the word that means "one" next to it. Remember, some nouns do not change at all in their plural form.

1. children child
2. moose moose
3. people person
4. men man
5. halves half
6. women woman
7. sheep sheep
8. teeth tooth

LANGUAGE ARTS

100 Second Grade Skills 119

Page 119

Answer Key

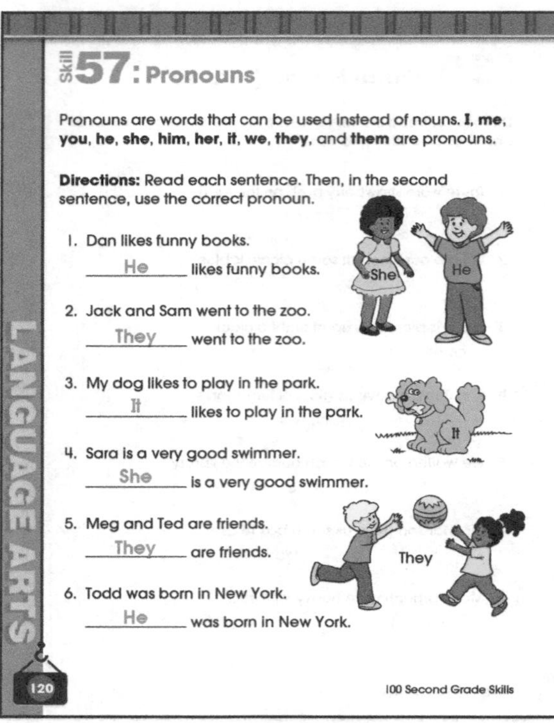

Skill 57: Pronouns

Pronouns are words that can be used instead of nouns. **I, me, you, he, she, him, her, it, we, they,** and **them** are pronouns.

Directions: Read each sentence. Then, in the second sentence, use the correct pronoun.

1. Dan likes funny books.
   He likes funny books.
2. Jack and Sam went to the zoo.
   They went to the zoo.
3. My dog likes to play in the park.
   It likes to play in the park.
4. Sara is a very good swimmer.
   She is a very good swimmer.
5. Meg and Ted are friends.
   They are friends.
6. Todd was born in New York.
   He was born in New York.

LANGUAGE ARTS

120 100 Second Grade Skills

Page 120

Skill 57: Pronouns

Directions: Write a pronoun in each blank. More than one answer may be correct.

1. I went to the school yesterday.
2. We are going to the playground.
3. Is that package for me?
4. They are on the same soccer team.
5. He had a great time last year at the museum.
6. Tanya gave me an invitation to the party.
7. She took the subway downtown.
8. Running is good for you.
9. They want to go to the movies.
10. He can't wait for my birthday.

Answers may vary.
Sample answers shown.

100 Second Grade Skills 121

LANGUAGE ARTS

Page 121

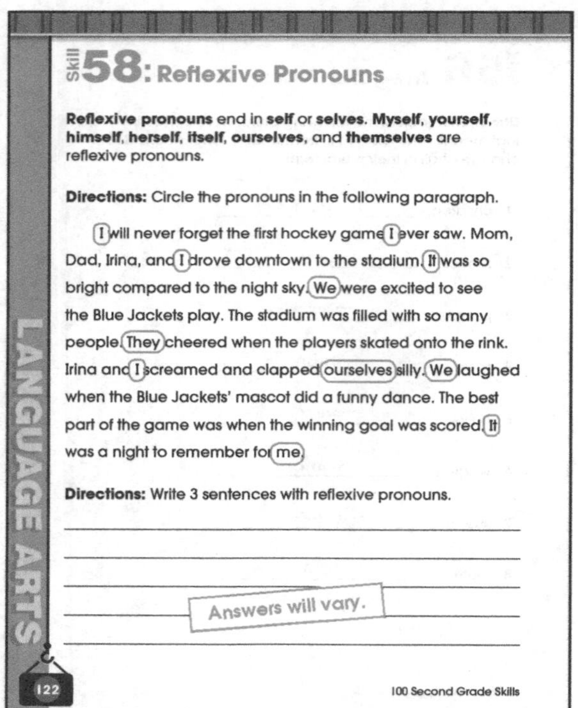

Skill 58: Reflexive Pronouns

Reflexive pronouns end in **self** or **selves. Myself, yourself, himself, herself, itself, ourselves,** and **themselves** are reflexive pronouns.

Directions: Circle the pronouns in the following paragraph.

I will never forget the first hockey game I ever saw. Mom, Dad, Irina, and I drove downtown to the stadium. It was so bright compared to the night sky. We were excited to see the Blue Jackets play. The stadium was filled with so many people. They cheered when the players skated onto the rink. Irina and I screamed and clapped ourselves silly. We laughed when the Blue Jackets' mascot did a funny dance. The best part of the game was when the winning goal was scored. It was a night to remember for me.

Directions: Write 3 sentences with reflexive pronouns.

Answers will vary.

LANGUAGE ARTS

122 100 Second Grade Skills

Page 122

Skill 58: Reflexive Pronouns

Directions: Fill in each blank below with a reflexive pronoun.

1. The team served themselves snacks and drinks after practice.
2. Ava cut herself when she climbed over the bleachers.
3. Tim blamed himself for not checking the stadium better.
4. "You should be proud of yourself for a great practice!" said Coach.

Directions: Write 3 sentences about your favorite thing to do. Use 3 reflexive pronouns.

Answers will vary.

100 Second Grade Skills 123

LANGUAGE ARTS

Page 123

Answer Key

Skill 59: Adjectives

Adjectives are words that describe nouns. Adjectives can tell number, color, size, shape, or anything that adds detail. A sentence can have more than one adjective.

Example: **Four** tulips are in my **colorful** garden.

Directions: Circle the adjectives in the sentences.

1. Where is the (gray) bug?
2. Lenny has (hot) soup and (cold) milk for lunch.
3. (Giant) dinosaurs lived (many) years ago.
4. Eva and Pat used (sparkly) paint to decorate their (pencil) boxes.
5. Selma ate a (yellow) banana and (eleven) raisins for snack.
6. Jessie is singing a (beautiful) song.
7. A (tired) Melina fell asleep on her (beach) towel.
8. We went to the (county) zoo on a (sunny) day.
9. Jacob tried to wash and dry his (squirming) puppy.

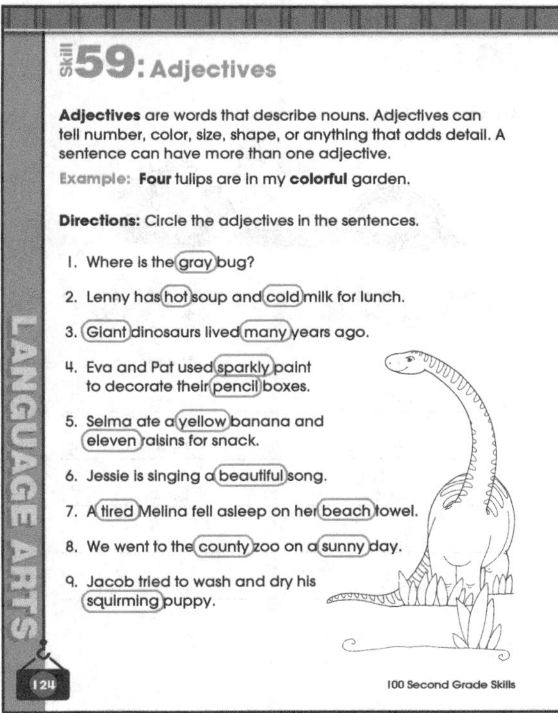

LANGUAGE ARTS

124 100 Second Grade Skills

Page 124

Skill 59: Adjectives

Directions: Circle the adjectives.

(heavy)	(twelve)	(silly)	(gold)
walked	sneezed	(hairy)	wiggle
(old)	(dry)	(blue)	(new)
house	star	school	(awful)
(loose)	(broken)	(strong)	friend
book	sing	parked	(tired)
shoe	whale	(wrinkled)	blink

Directions: Use the above adjectives to finish the sentences. Or, write your own adjectives on the lines.

1. Whitney held the ______________ snake.
2. Jo broke that ______________ lamp.
3. Charlie tried to ______________ lamb.
4. Bailey rode his ______________ scooter.

Answers will vary.

LANGUAGE ARTS

100 Second Grade Skills 125

Page 125

Skill 60: Comparative Adjectives

Add **er** to an adjective to show that one thing is more than something else. Add **est** to an adjective to show that it is the most.

Example: Jan is fast.
Jake is fast**er**.
Marcia is fast**est**.

Directions: Read the sentences below. Circle the correct adjective in parentheses.

1. The Nile River is (longest, (longer)) than the Amazon River.
2. The (tall, (tallest)) waterfall in the world is Angel Falls in Venezuela.
3. Mount Everest is the ((highest,) higher) mountain.
4. The Pacific Ocean is ((deeper,) deep) than the Indian Ocean.
5. It is the world's (deeper, (deepest)) ocean.
6. That was the ((longest,) longer) movie I've seen.

LANGUAGE ARTS

126 100 Second Grade Skills

Page 126

Skill 60: Comparative Adjectives

Directions: Fill in the spaces with the missing adjectives.

hard	harder	hardest
fast	faster	fastest
dark	darker	darkest
young	younger	youngest
kind	kinder	kindest
short	shorter	shortest
small	smaller	smallest
new	newer	newest

Directions: Write two sentences that compare people or things that are alike in some way.

Example: Naomi is older than Hasaan. Frank is the oldest.

1. ______________________________
2. ______________________________

Answers will vary.

LANGUAGE ARTS

100 Second Grade Skills 127

Page 127

Answer Key

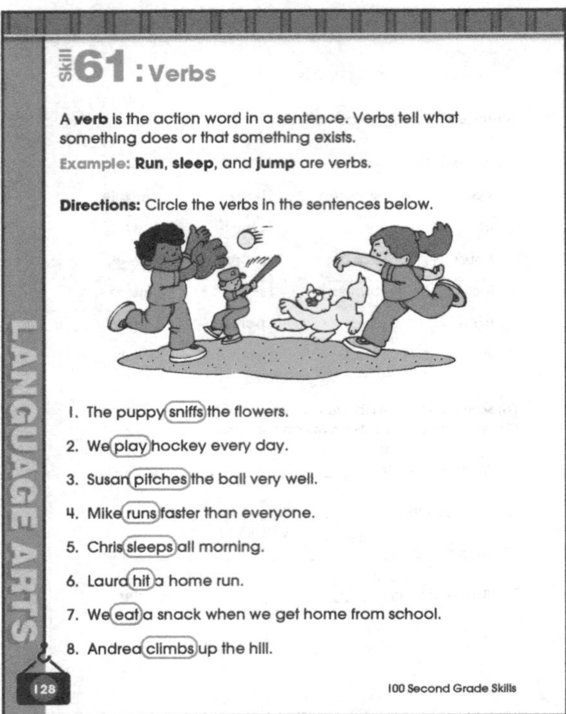

Skill 61: Verbs

A **verb** is the action word in a sentence. Verbs tell what something does or that something exists.

Example: **Run**, **sleep**, and **jump** are verbs.

Directions: Circle the verbs in the sentences below.

1. The puppy (sniffs) the flowers.
2. We (play) hockey every day.
3. Susan (pitches) the ball very well.
4. Mike (runs) faster than everyone.
5. Chris (sleeps) all morning.
6. Laura (hit) a home run.
7. We (eat) a snack when we get home from school.
8. Andrea (climbs) up the hill.

LANGUAGE ARTS

128 100 Second Grade Skills

Page 128

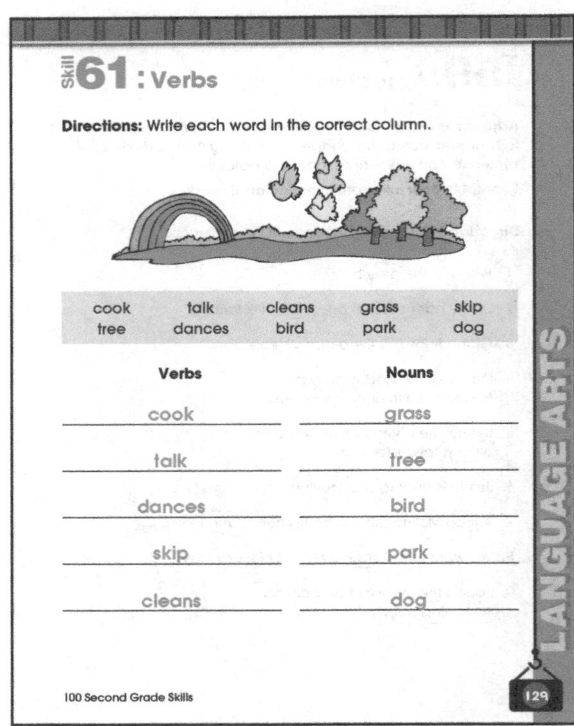

Skill 61: Verbs

Directions: Write each word in the correct column.

cook	talk	cleans	grass	skip
tree	dances	bird	park	dog

Verbs	Nouns
cook	grass
talk	tree
dances	bird
skip	park
cleans	dog

LANGUAGE ARTS

100 Second Grade Skills 129

Page 129

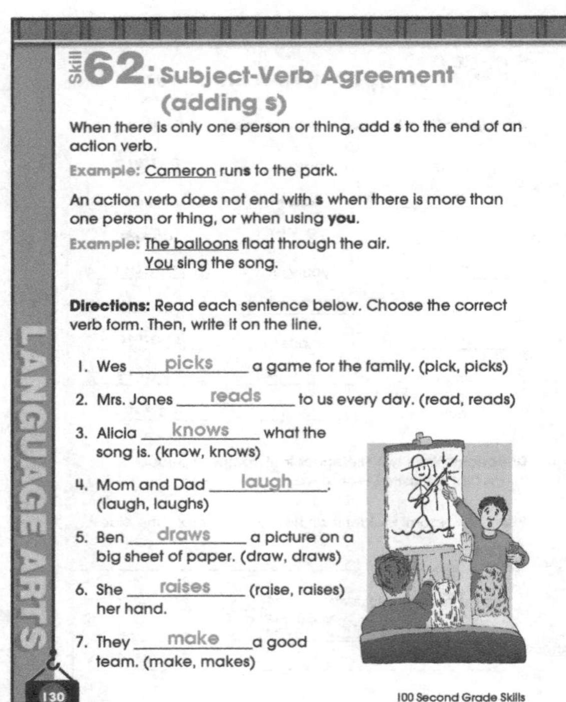

Skill 62: Subject-Verb Agreement (adding s)

When there is only one person or thing, add **s** to the end of an action verb.

Example: Cameron runs to the park.

An action verb does not end with **s** when there is more than one person or thing, or when using **you**.

Example: The balloons float through the air.
You sing the song.

Directions: Read each sentence below. Choose the correct verb form. Then, write it on the line.

1. Wes __picks__ a game for the family. (pick, picks)
2. Mrs. Jones __reads__ to us every day. (read, reads)
3. Alicia __knows__ what the song is. (know, knows)
4. Mom and Dad __laugh__. (laugh, laughs)
5. Ben __draws__ a picture on a big sheet of paper. (draw, draws)
6. She __raises__ (raise, raises) her hand.
7. They __make__ a good team. (make, makes)

LANGUAGE ARTS

130 100 Second Grade Skills

Page 130

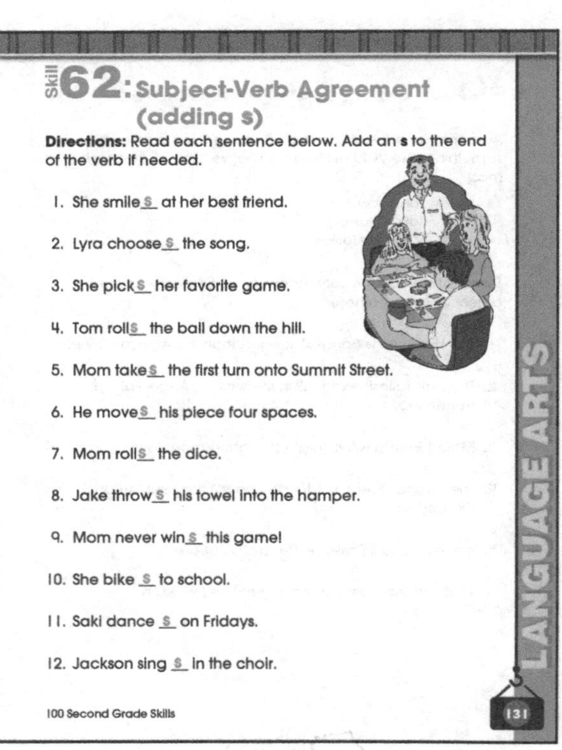

Skill 62: Subject-Verb Agreement (adding s)

Directions: Read each sentence below. Add an **s** to the end of the verb if needed.

1. She smile_s_ at her best friend.
2. Lyra choose_s_ the song.
3. She pick_s_ her favorite game.
4. Tom roll_s_ the ball down the hill.
5. Mom take_s_ the first turn onto Summit Street.
6. He move_s_ his piece four spaces.
7. Mom roll_s_ the dice.
8. Jake throw_s_ his towel into the hamper.
9. Mom never win_s_ this game!
10. She bike _s_ to school.
11. Saki dance _s_ on Fridays.
12. Jackson sing _s_ in the choir.

LANGUAGE ARTS

100 Second Grade Skills 131

Page 131

Answer Key

Skill 63: Subject-Verb Agreement (adding es)

Sometimes, **es** needs to be added instead of just **s**. Add **es** to verbs that end in **sh**, **ch**, **s**, **x**, and **z**.

Examples: Eve brush**es** her dog every weekend.
Grandma stitch**es** the buttons on the coat.

When there is more than one person or thing, verbs do not end in **s** or **es**.

Directions: Choose the correct verb at the end of each sentence and write it on the line.

1. The bug buzzes when it flies. (buzz, buzzes)
2. Alex and Jesse wash all the dishes after dinner. (wash, washes)
3. Jasmine tosses the ball to Hailey. (toss, tosses)
4. Noelle wishes for a kitten when she blows out her candles. (wish, wishes)
5. Charles mixes the batter before he pours it in the pan. (mix, mixes)
6. He misses his old neighborhood. (miss, misses)

LANGUAGE ARTS

132 100 Second Grade Skills

Page 132

Skill 63: Subject-Verb Agreement (adding es)

Directions: Circle the verb in each sentence below. If it is not correct, write the correct form.

1. Tina (catch) the bus each morning. catches
2. The cat (hisses) at the bird. _____
3. My parents (relaxes) on the weekends. relax
4. Corey (waxes) his surfboard on the beach. _____
5. The sports car (pass) the truck. passes
6. The plane (touches) down at noon. _____
7. Gail (rushes) home from school. _____
8. The waves (crashes) on the shore. crash
9. Marcia (wash) her hair every day. washes
10. Marco (fix) the car. fixes

100 Second Grade Skills 133

LANGUAGE ARTS

Page 133

Skill 64: Irregular Verbs (Am, Is, Are)

Am, **is**, and **are** are special verbs that tell us something is happening now.

Use **am** with **I**. Example: **I am.**
Use **is** to tell about one person or thing. Example: **He is.**
Use **are** to tell about more than one. Example: **We are.**
Use **are** with **you**. Example: **You are.**

Directions: Write **is**, **are**, or **am** in the sentences below.

1. My friends are helping me build a tree house
2. I am happy my birthday is next week.
3. It is in my backyard.
4. You are my friend.
5. We are using hammers, wood, and nails.
6. It is a very hard job.
7. I am lucky to have good friends.
8. The sky is full of stars tonight.

LANGUAGE ARTS

134 100 Second Grade Skills

Page 134

Skill 64: Irregular Verbs (Am, Is, Are)

Directions: Read each sentence below. Choose the correct verb from the parentheses ( ). Write it on the line.

1. You are a great dancer. (are, am)
2. I am tall and strong. (is, am)
3. Blanche and Dante are in second grade. (is, are)
4. This chili is too spicy! (is, are)
5. All the kids in my class are ready. (is, are)
6. I am a niece. (are, am)
7. That skateboard is broken. (are, is)
8. We are in the same class. (are, is)
9. You are lucky you won. (are, is)
10. Everyone is excited for the party. (are, is)

100 Second Grade Skills 135

LANGUAGE ARTS

Page 135

Answer Key

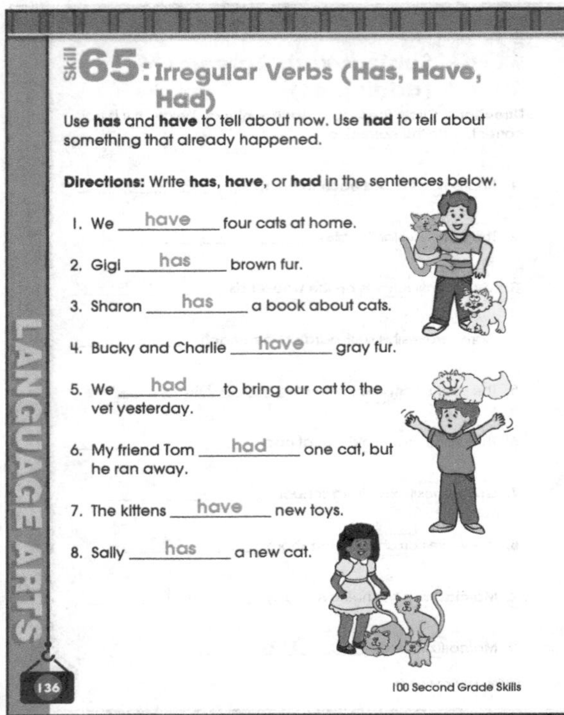

Skill **65: Irregular Verbs (Has, Have, Had)**

Use **has** and **have** to tell about now. Use **had** to tell about something that already happened.

Directions: Write **has, have,** or **had** in the sentences below.

1. We ____have____ four cats at home.
2. Gigi ____has____ brown fur.
3. Sharon ____has____ a book about cats.
4. Bucky and Charlie ____have____ gray fur.
5. We ____had____ to bring our cat to the vet yesterday.
6. My friend Tom ____had____ one cat, but he ran away.
7. The kittens ____have____ new toys.
8. Sally ____has____ a new cat.

LANGUAGE ARTS

136 100 Second Grade Skills

Page 136

Skill **65: Irregular Verbs (Has, Have, Had)**

Directions: Read each sentence below. Then, read the pair of verbs in parentheses. Choose the correct verb form and write it on the line.

1. Maple trees and oak trees ____have____ similar leaves. (has, have)
2. A gingko tree ____has____ leaves that look like fans. (has, have)
3. We ____have____ a large fir tree in the backyard. (has, have)
4. The Nelsons ____have____ many trees that bloom in the spring. (has, have)
5. Max ____has____ an old maple tree in his front yard. (has, have)
6. An apple tree will ____have____ a lot of fruit in the fall. (has, have)
7. He ____has____ been gone all night. (has, have)
8. The family ____has____ left for the movies. (has, have)

LANGUAGE ARTS

100 Second Grade Skills 137

Page 137

Skill **66: Forming the Past Tense by Adding ed**

Verbs in the **past tense** tell about things that already happened. Add **ed** to most verbs to tell about the past.

Examples: Lisa jump**ed** over the log.
Jessica push**ed** the stroller.

If the verb already ends in **e**, just add **d**.

Examples: The class hik**ed** two miles. (hik**e**)
She plac**ed** the plates on the table. (plac**e**)

Directions: The sentences below are missing verbs. Complete each sentence with the past tense of the verb in parentheses ( ).

1. We ____traveled____ to many countries. (travel)
2. She ____climbed____ Mount Shasta in California. (climb)
3. She ____hoped____ to visit Iceland some day. (hope)
4. Jan ____started____ a group called the Alpine Club. (start)
5. The class ____explored____ the volcanoes of South America. (explore)
6. She ____worked____ hard so she could climb in her spare time. (work)
7. Ann ____continued____ talking until the end of class. (continue)
8. The boy ____kicked____ the ball. (kick)

LANGUAGE ARTS

138 100 Second Grade Skills

Page 138

Skill **66: Forming the Past Tense by Adding ed**

Directions: Rewrite the sentences below in the past tense by changing the underlined verb.

1. The dog <u>pull</u> on his leash.
   The dog pulled on his leash.
2. She <u>live</u> in the house next door.
   She lived in the house next door.
3. Bailey <u>show</u> the teacher he could write the report well.
   Bailey showed the teacher he could write the report well.
4. She <u>want</u> to set records in running.
   She wanted to set records in running.
5. The girl <u>walk</u> to the store.
   The girl walked to the store.
6. Mrs. Samson <u>talk</u> to her students.
   Mrs. Samson talked to her students.
7. The airplane <u>look</u> large.
   The airplane looked large.
8. The band <u>play</u> my favorite songs.
   The band played my favorite songs.

LANGUAGE ARTS

100 Second Grade Skills 139

Page 139

Answer Key

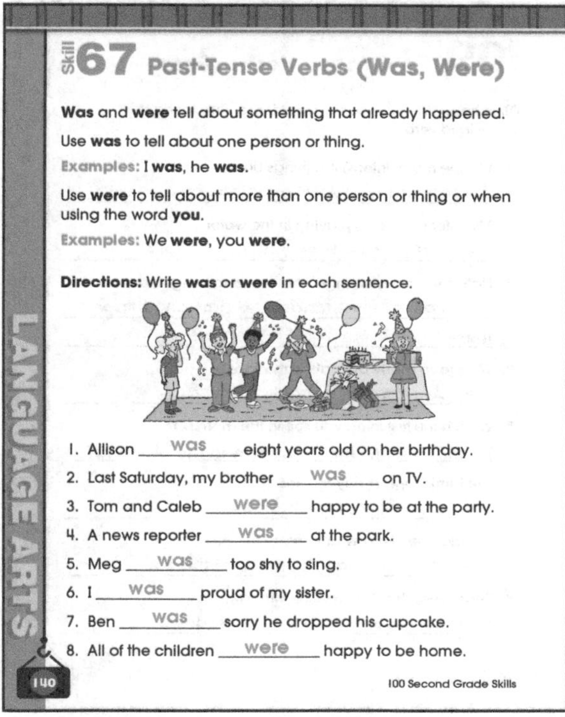

Skill 67 Past-Tense Verbs (Was, Were)

Was and **were** tell about something that already happened.

Use **was** to tell about one person or thing.

Examples: I **was**, he **was**.

Use **were** to tell about more than one person or thing or when using the word **you**.

Examples: We **were**, you **were**.

Directions: Write **was** or **were** in each sentence.

1. Allison __was__ eight years old on her birthday.
2. Last Saturday, my brother __was__ on TV.
3. Tom and Caleb __were__ happy to be at the party.
4. A news reporter __was__ at the park.
5. Meg __was__ too shy to sing.
6. I __was__ proud of my sister.
7. Ben __was__ sorry he dropped his cupcake.
8. All of the children __were__ happy to be home.

LANGUAGE ARTS

140 100 Second Grade Skills

Page 140

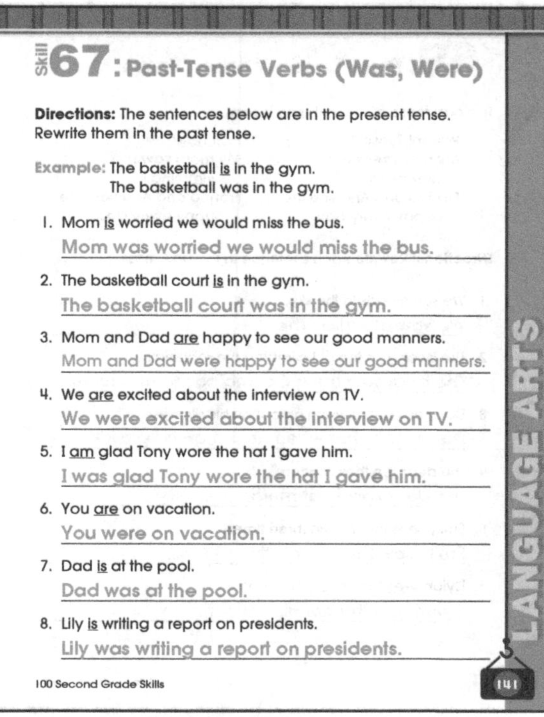

Skill 67: Past-Tense Verbs (Was, Were)

Directions: The sentences below are in the present tense. Rewrite them in the past tense.

Example: The basketball is in the gym.
The basketball was in the gym.

1. Mom is worried we would miss the bus.
   Mom was worried we would miss the bus.
2. The basketball court is in the gym.
   The basketball court was in the gym.
3. Mom and Dad are happy to see our good manners.
   Mom and Dad were happy to see our good manners.
4. We are excited about the interview on TV.
   We were excited about the interview on TV.
5. I am glad Tony wore the hat I gave him.
   I was glad Tony wore the hat I gave him.
6. You are on vacation.
   You were on vacation.
7. Dad is at the pool.
   Dad was at the pool.
8. Lily is writing a report on presidents.
   Lily was writing a report on presidents.

LANGUAGE ARTS

100 Second Grade Skills 141

Page 141

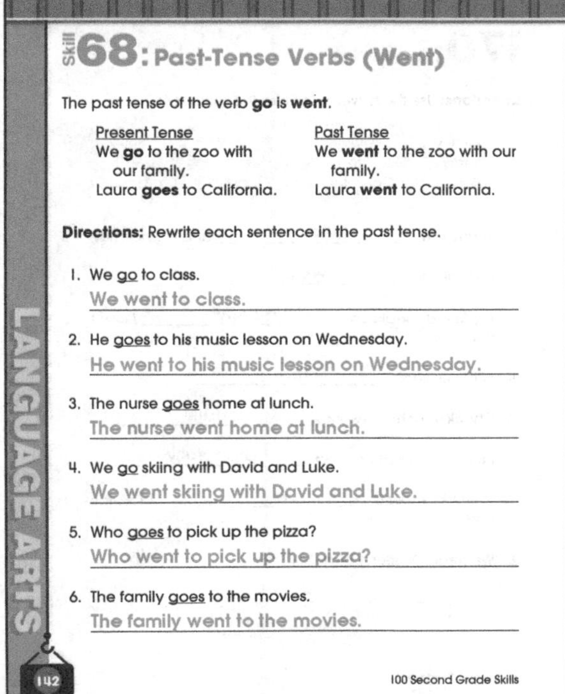

Skill 68: Past-Tense Verbs (Went)

The past tense of the verb **go** is **went**.

Present Tense	Past Tense
We **go** to the zoo with our family.	We **went** to the zoo with our family.
Laura **goes** to California.	Laura **went** to California.

Directions: Rewrite each sentence in the past tense.

1. We go to class.
   We went to class.
2. He goes to his music lesson on Wednesday.
   He went to his music lesson on Wednesday.
3. The nurse goes home at lunch.
   The nurse went home at lunch.
4. We go skiing with David and Luke.
   We went skiing with David and Luke.
5. Who goes to pick up the pizza?
   Who went to pick up the pizza?
6. The family goes to the movies.
   The family went to the movies.

LANGUAGE ARTS

142 100 Second Grade Skills

Page 142

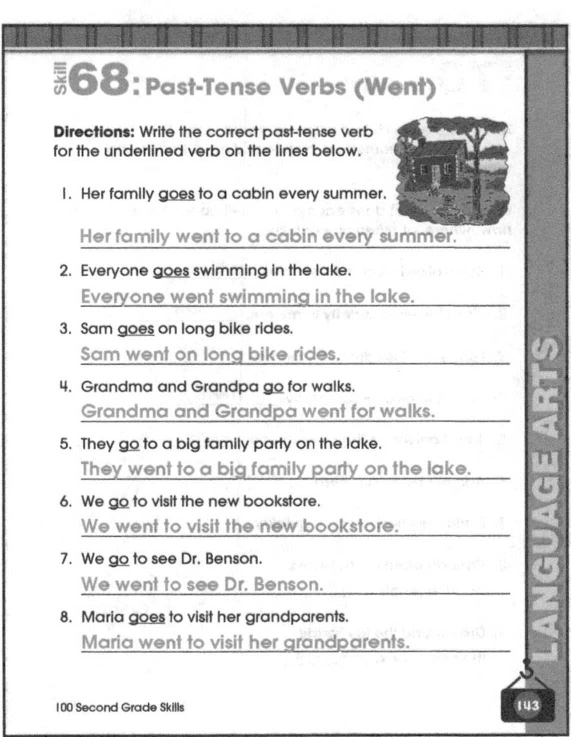

Skill 68: Past-Tense Verbs (Went)

Directions: Write the correct past-tense verb for the underlined verb on the lines below.

1. Her family goes to a cabin every summer.
   Her family went to a cabin every summer.
2. Everyone goes swimming in the lake.
   Everyone went swimming in the lake.
3. Sam goes on long bike rides.
   Sam went on long bike rides.
4. Grandma and Grandpa go for walks.
   Grandma and Grandpa went for walks.
5. They go to a big family party on the lake.
   They went to a big family party on the lake.
6. We go to visit the new bookstore.
   We went to visit the new bookstore.
7. We go to see Dr. Benson.
   We went to see Dr. Benson.
8. Maria goes to visit her grandparents.
   Maria went to visit her grandparents.

LANGUAGE ARTS

100 Second Grade Skills 143

Page 143

Answer Key

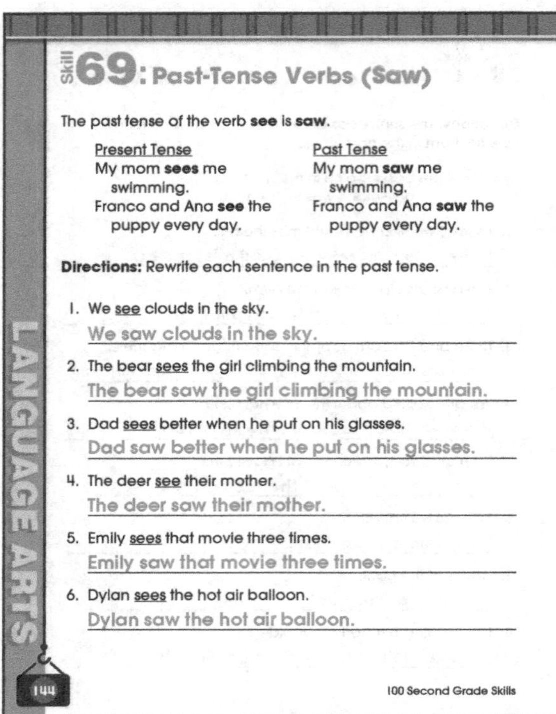

Skill 69: Past-Tense Verbs (Saw)

The past tense of the verb **see** is **saw**.

Present Tense	Past Tense
My mom **sees** me swimming.	My mom **saw** me swimming.
Franco and Ana **see** the puppy every day.	Franco and Ana **saw** the puppy every day.

Directions: Rewrite each sentence in the past tense.

1. We see clouds in the sky.
   We saw clouds in the sky.
2. The bear sees the girl climbing the mountain.
   The bear saw the girl climbing the mountain.
3. Dad sees better when he put on his glasses.
   Dad saw better when he put on his glasses.
4. The deer see their mother.
   The deer saw their mother.
5. Emily sees that movie three times.
   Emily saw that movie three times.
6. Dylan sees the hot air balloon.
   Dylan saw the hot air balloon.

LANGUAGE ARTS

144 100 Second Grade Skills

Page 144

Skill 69: Past-Tense Verbs (Saw)

Directions: Write the correct past-tense verb for each underlined verb.

1. We see many interesting things on our visit.
   We saw many interesting things on our visit.
2. My sister sees seals playing in the water.
   My sister saw seals playing in the water.
3. Nate sees many strange and amazing things there.
   Nate saw many strange and amazing things there.
4. We see so many animals at the zoo.
   We saw so many animals at the zoo.
5. What is the first thing you see in the morning?
   What is the first thing you saw in the morning?
6. The family sees many movies
   The family saw many movies.
7. The class sees many animals at the zoo.
   The class saw many animals at the zoo.
8. Pedro sees the stars from his window.
   Pedro saw the stars from his window.

100 Second Grade Skills 145

LANGUAGE ARTS

Page 145

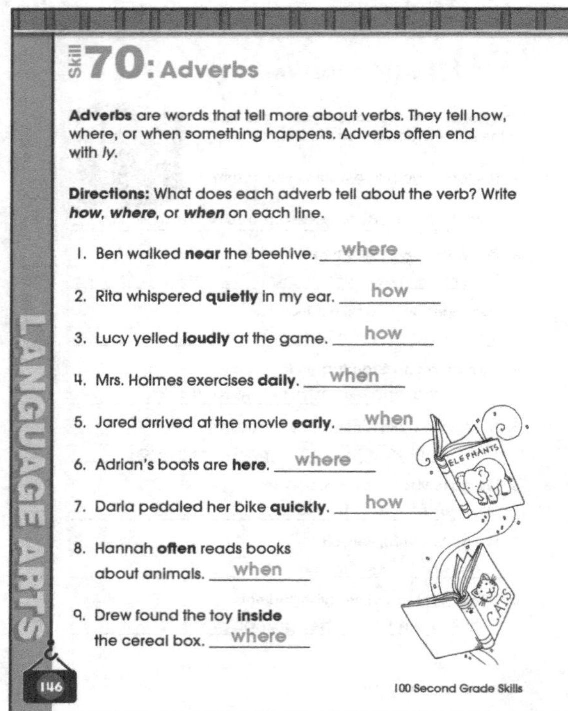

Skill 70: Adverbs

Adverbs are words that tell more about verbs. They tell how, where, or when something happens. Adverbs often end with *ly*.

Directions: What does each adverb tell about the verb? Write ***how***, ***where***, or ***when*** on each line.

1. Ben walked **near** the beehive. where
2. Rita whispered **quietly** in my ear. how
3. Lucy yelled **loudly** at the game. how
4. Mrs. Holmes exercises **daily**. when
5. Jared arrived at the movie **early**. when
6. Adrian's boots are **here**. where
7. Darla pedaled her bike **quickly**. how
8. Hannah **often** reads books about animals. when
9. Drew found the toy **inside** the cereal box. where

LANGUAGE ARTS

146 100 Second Grade Skills

Page 146

Skill 70: Adverbs

Directions: Use the adverbs to finish the sentences.

quickly	quietly	easily	softly
sadly	too	fast	well
slowly	carefully	loudly	gracefully

1. Jenny ran quickly and finished first.
2. Did Sal ride well?
3. My friend speaks so quietly, I can't hear her.
4. Will you work too?
5. Check your homework carefully.
6. Rianne and Bert danced gracefully.
7. The turtle moved slowly across the yard.
8. We heard Marlene blow her whistle loudly.

Answers may vary. Sample answers shown.

100 Second Grade Skills 147

LANGUAGE ARTS

Page 147

Answer Key

Skill 71: Statements

LANGUAGE ARTS

A **statement** is a sentence that begins with a capital letter and ends with a period. A statement tells the reader something.

Example: My brother and I fly kites when we go to the beach.

Directions: Rewrite the following sentences. Each statement should begin with a capital letter and end with a period.

1. people have flown kites for thousands of years
   People have flown kites for thousands of years.
2. early kites were made in China
   Early kites were made in China.
3. they were covered in silk
   They were covered in silk.
4. some kites are shaped like dragons or fish
   Some kites are shaped like dragons or fish.
5. some kites are tiny
   Some kites are tiny.
6. other kites are as long as one hundred feet
   Other kites are as long as one hundred feet.
7. flying kites is a fun thing to do
   Flying kites is a fun thing to do.

148 100 Second Grade Skills

Page 148

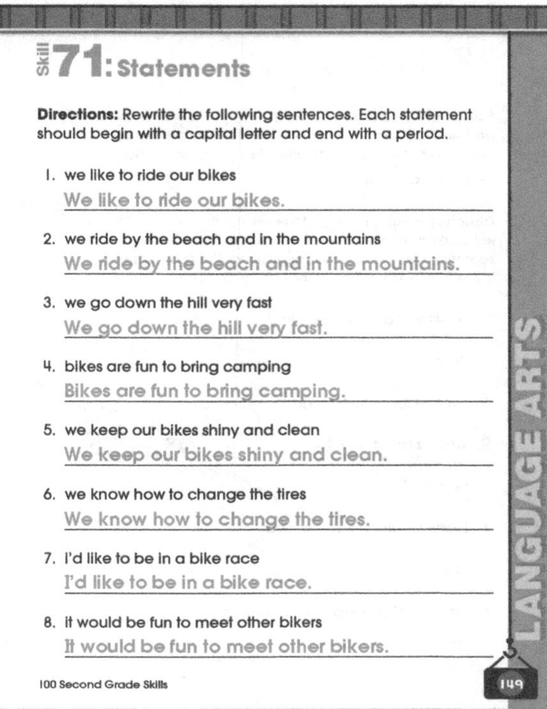

Skill 71: Statements

Directions: Rewrite the following sentences. Each statement should begin with a capital letter and end with a period.

1. we like to ride our bikes
   We like to ride our bikes.
2. we ride by the beach and in the mountains
   We ride by the beach and in the mountains.
3. we go down the hill very fast
   We go down the hill very fast.
4. bikes are fun to bring camping
   Bikes are fun to bring camping.
5. we keep our bikes shiny and clean
   We keep our bikes shiny and clean.
6. we know how to change the tires
   We know how to change the tires.
7. I'd like to be in a bike race
   I'd like to be in a bike race.
8. it would be fun to meet other bikers
   It would be fun to meet other bikers.

LANGUAGE ARTS

100 Second Grade Skills 149

Page 149

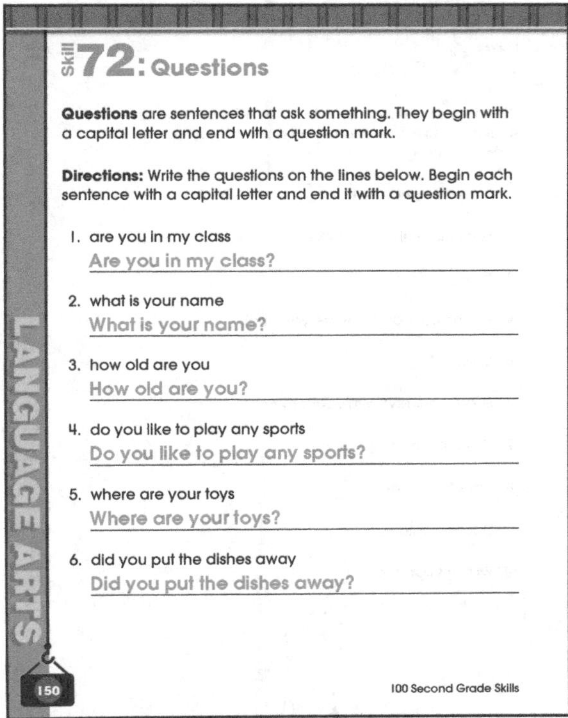

Skill 72: Questions

LANGUAGE ARTS

Questions are sentences that ask something. They begin with a capital letter and end with a question mark.

Directions: Write the questions on the lines below. Begin each sentence with a capital letter and end it with a question mark.

1. are you in my class
   Are you in my class?
2. what is your name
   What is your name?
3. how old are you
   How old are you?
4. do you like to play any sports
   Do you like to play any sports?
5. where are your toys
   Where are your toys?
6. did you put the dishes away
   Did you put the dishes away?

150 100 Second Grade Skills

Page 150

Skill 72: Questions

Directions: If a sentence is a statement, add a period on the line. If a sentence is a question, add a question mark on the line.

1. Taylor and her family drove to New York .
2. What city do you want to visit ?
3. They drove for five days .
4. Liz has two cats .
5. What did you do during the long plane ride ?
6. Can you guess what I found on the beach ?
7. Beth is going to join the drama club .
8. Where will they go on vacation next year ?

LANGUAGE ARTS

100 Second Grade Skills 151

Page 151

Answer Key

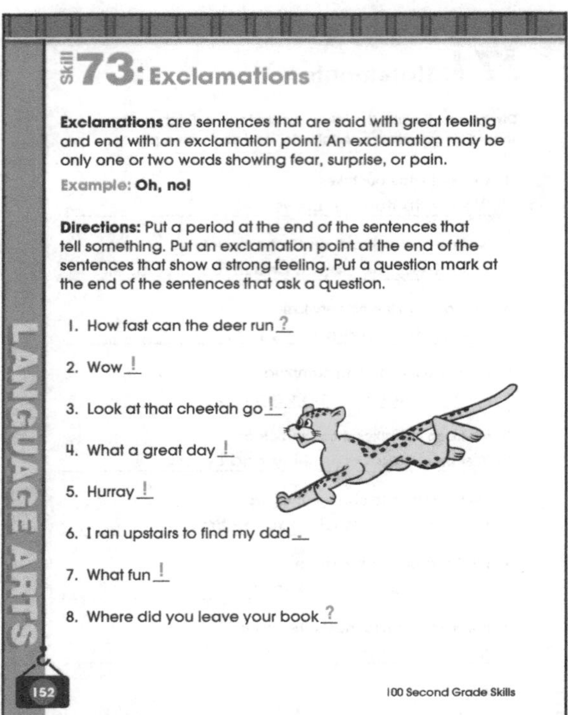

Skill 73: Exclamations

Exclamations are sentences that are said with great feeling and end with an exclamation point. An exclamation may be only one or two words showing fear, surprise, or pain.

Example: **Oh, no!**

Directions: Put a period at the end of the sentences that tell something. Put an exclamation point at the end of the sentences that show a strong feeling. Put a question mark at the end of the sentences that ask a question.

1. How fast can the deer run ?
2. Wow !
3. Look at that cheetah go !
4. What a great day !
5. Hurray !
6. I ran upstairs to find my dad .
7. What fun !
8. Where did you leave your book ?

LANGUAGE ARTS

152 100 Second Grade Skills

Page 152

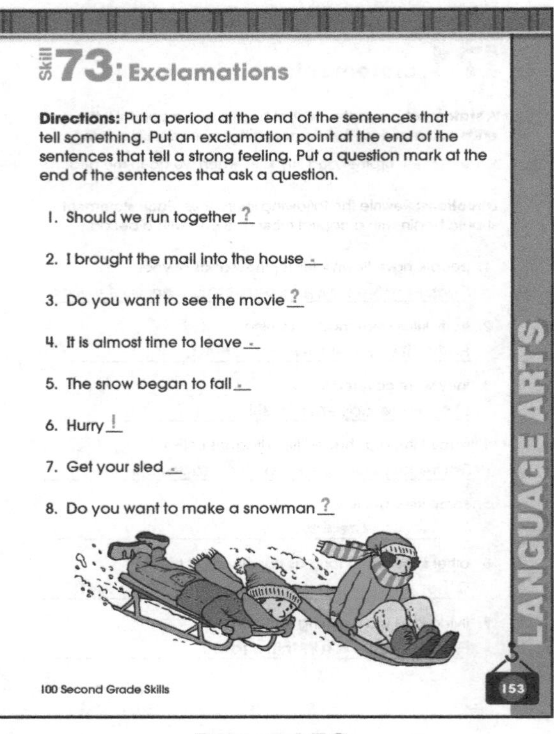

Skill 73: Exclamations

Directions: Put a period at the end of the sentences that tell something. Put an exclamation point at the end of the sentences that tell a strong feeling. Put a question mark at the end of the sentences that ask a question.

1. Should we run together ?
2. I brought the mail into the house .
3. Do you want to see the movie ?
4. It is almost time to leave .
5. The snow began to fall .
6. Hurry !
7. Get your sled .
8. Do you want to make a snowman ?

LANGUAGE ARTS

100 Second Grade Skills 153

Page 153

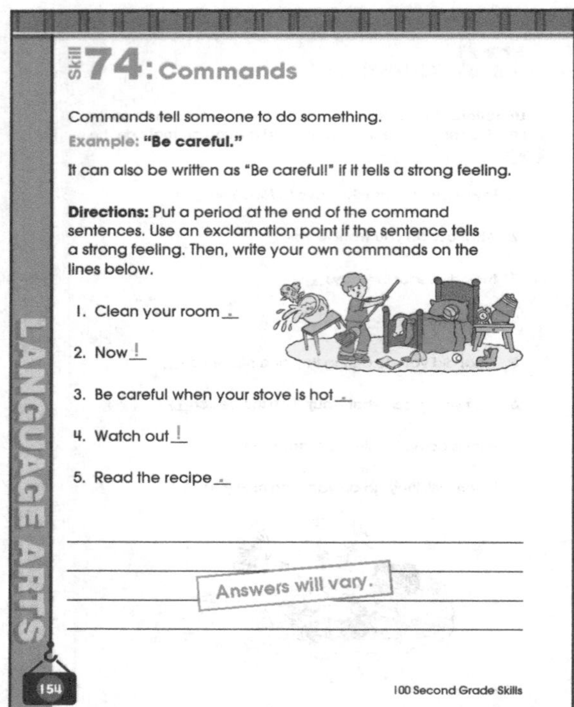

Skill 74: Commands

Commands tell someone to do something.

Example: **"Be careful."**

It can also be written as "Be careful!" if it tells a strong feeling.

Directions: Put a period at the end of the command sentences. Use an exclamation point if the sentence tells a strong feeling. Then, write your own commands on the lines below.

1. Clean your room .
2. Now !
3. Be careful when your stove is hot .
4. Watch out !
5. Read the recipe .

Answers will vary.

LANGUAGE ARTS

154 100 Second Grade Skills

Page 154

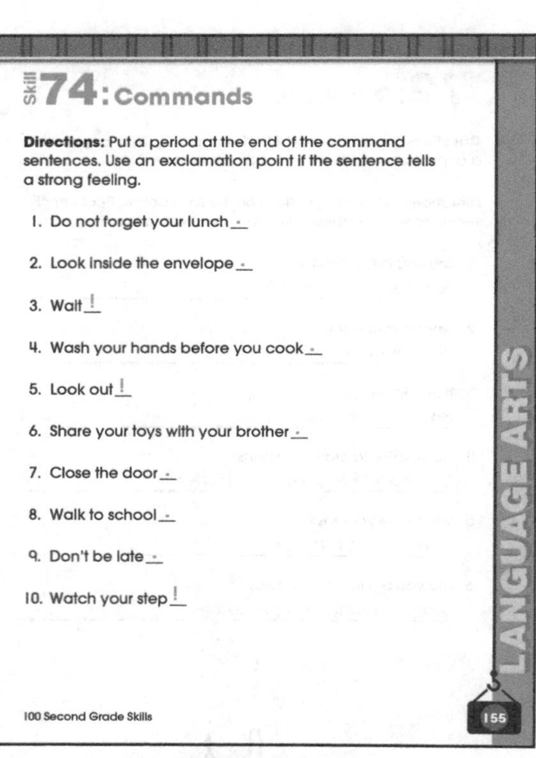

Skill 74: Commands

Directions: Put a period at the end of the command sentences. Use an exclamation point if the sentence tells a strong feeling.

1. Do not forget your lunch .
2. Look inside the envelope .
3. Wait !
4. Wash your hands before you cook .
5. Look out !
6. Share your toys with your brother .
7. Close the door .
8. Walk to school .
9. Don't be late .
10. Watch your step !

LANGUAGE ARTS

100 Second Grade Skills 155

Page 155

Answer Key

Skill 75: Combining Sentences (Nouns)

Sometimes, sentences can be combined if they tell about the same thing.

Example: Bats eat bugs. Birds eat bugs.

Both sentences tell about things that eat bugs. These two sentences can be combined into one by using the word **and**.

Example: Bats **and** birds eat bugs.

Directions: Read each pair of sentences below. If the sentences can be joined with the word **and**, make a check mark (✓) on the line. If not, leave the line blank.

1. ✓ Hummingbirds visit my birdfeeder. Doves visit my birdfeeder.
2. ____ Parrots live in warm places. Penguins live in cold places.
3. ✓ Hawks build nests on ledges. Eagles build nests on ledges.
4. ✓ Hummingbirds like flowers. Bees like flowers.
5. ____ Geese fly south for the winter. Owls do not fly south in the winter.

LANGUAGE ARTS

156 100 Second Grade Skills

Page 156

Skill 75: Combining Senten

Directions: Combine each pair of sentences b
sentence. Write the new sentence.

1. David played the drums. Rick played the drum
   David and Rick played the drums.
2. Cardinals eat seeds. Finches eat seeds.
   Cardinals and finches eat seeds.
3. Cats like to be pet. Dogs like to be pet.
   Cats and dogs like to be pet.
4. The dogs were hungry. The birds were hungry.
   The dogs and birds were hungry.
5. The sky was cloudy. The sky was gray.
   The sky was cloudy and gray.
6. We went to dinner. We went to the concert.
   We went to dinner and the concert.
7. Seth buys ice cream. Seth buys soda.
   Seth buys ice cream and soda.
8. Mom went to the beach. Dad went to the beach.
   Mom and Dad went to the beach.

LANGUAG

100 Second Grade Skills 157

Page 157

Skill 76: Combining Sentences (Verbs)

Sometimes sentences can be combined.

Example: Penny cooks on Sunday afternoon.
Penny writes on Sunday afternoon.

Both sentences tell what Penny does on Sunday afternoon. These two sentences can be joined using the word **and**.

Example: Penny cooks **and** writes on Sunday afternoon.

Directions: Read the sentences below. Write the missing word or words.

1. Dad carried out the sandwiches. Dad placed them on the table. Dad carried out the sandwiches and placed them on the table.
2. Kate took a deep breath. Kate blew out the candles. Kate took a deep breath and blew out the candles.
3. Mom flies a kite. Mom unpacks the lunch basket. Mom flies a kite and unpacks the lunch basket.

LANGUAGE ARTS

158 100 Second Grade Skills

Page 158

Skill 76: Combining Sentences (Verbs)

Directions: Combine each pair of sentences below into one sentence.

1. We are throwing a party. We are buying decorations.
   We are throwing a party and buying decorations.
2. I went to the library. I chose many books.
   I went to the library and chose many books.
3. Travis drove to the store. Travis bought groceries.
   Travis drove to the store and bought groceries.
4. My cat likes to sleep. My cat likes to eat her food.
   My cat likes to sleep and eat her food.

Directions: Write two sentences that tell about things you do at school. Use a different verb in each sentence.

Answers will vary.

Directions: Now, combine the two sentences you wrote using the word **and**.

Answers will vary.

LANGUAGE ARTS

100 Second Grade Skills 159

Page 159

Answer Key

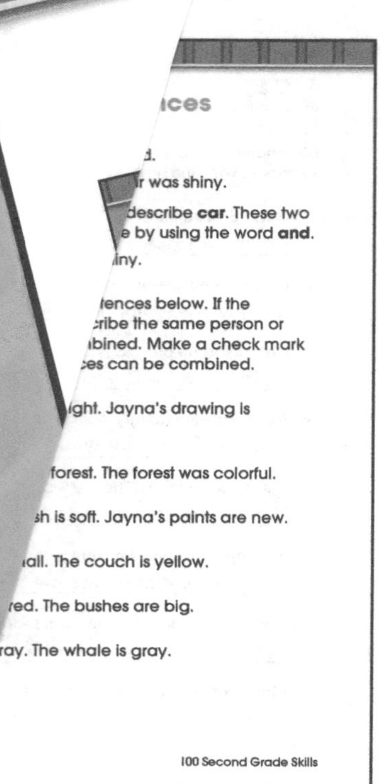

ces

d.

r was shiny.

describe **car**. These two
e by using the word **and**.

iny.

tences below. If the
cribe the same person or
bined. Make a check mark
es can be combined.

ight. Jayna's drawing is

forest. The forest was colorful.

sh is soft. Jayna's paints are new.

all. The couch is yellow.

red. The bushes are big.

gray. The whale is gray.

100 Second Grade Skills

Page 160

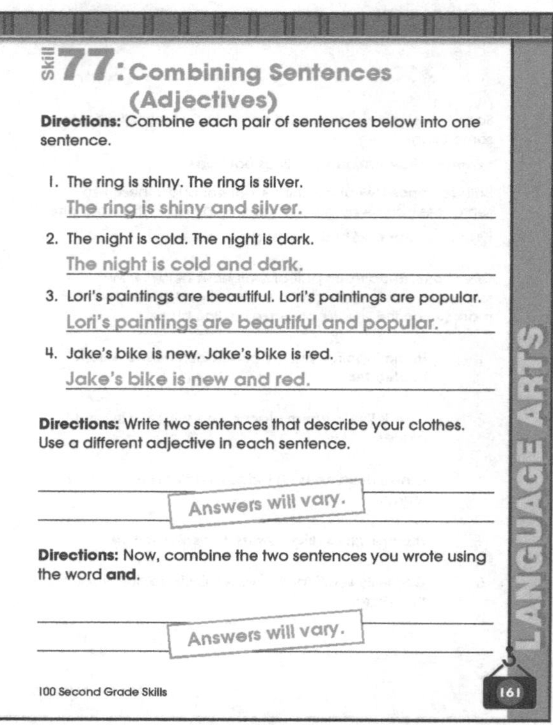

Skill 77: Combining Sentences (Adjectives)

Directions: Combine each pair of sentences below into one sentence.

1. The ring is shiny. The ring is silver.
   The ring is shiny and silver.
2. The night is cold. The night is dark.
   The night is cold and dark.
3. Lori's paintings are beautiful. Lori's paintings are popular.
   Lori's paintings are beautiful and popular.
4. Jake's bike is new. Jake's bike is red.
   Jake's bike is new and red.

Directions: Write two sentences that describe your clothes. Use a different adjective in each sentence.

Answers will vary.

Directions: Now, combine the two sentences you wrote using the word **and**.

Answers will vary.

100 Second Grade Skills

LANGUAGE ARTS

161

Page 161

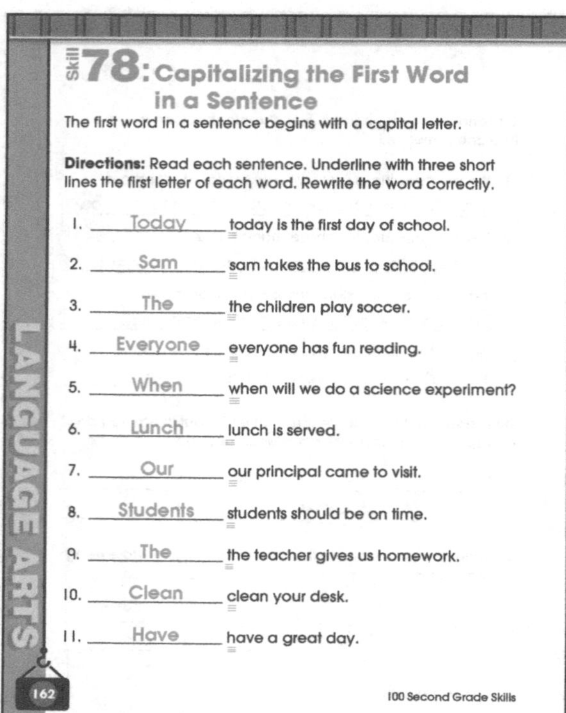

Skill 78: Capitalizing the First Word in a Sentence

The first word in a sentence begins with a capital letter.

Directions: Read each sentence. Underline with three short lines the first letter of each word. Rewrite the word correctly.

1. Today — today is the first day of school.
2. Sam — sam takes the bus to school.
3. The — the children play soccer.
4. Everyone — everyone has fun reading.
5. When — when will we do a science experiment?
6. Lunch — lunch is served.
7. Our — our principal came to visit.
8. Students — students should be on time.
9. The — the teacher gives us homework.
10. Clean — clean your desk.
11. Have — have a great day.

LANGUAGE ARTS

162

100 Second Grade Skills

Page 162

Skill 78: Capitalizing the First Word in a Sentence

Directions: Rewrite each sentence below. Make sure your sentences begin with a capital letter.

1. heather likes to bake.
   Heather likes to bake.
2. her grandma likes to help her.
   Her grandma likes to help her.
3. they make delicious chocolate cookies.
   They make delicious chocolate cookies.
4. grandma teaches her how to make bread.
   Grandma teaches her how to make bread.
5. would you like to learn how to bake?
   Would you like to learn how to bake?

Directions: Write a sentence about something new. Be sure to start your sentence with a capital letter.

Answers will vary.

Directions: Write a sentence that explains one reason you like autumn. Be sure to start your sentence with a capital letter.

Answers will vary.

100 Second Grade Skills

LANGUAGE ARTS

163

Page 163

Answer Key

Skill 79: Capitalizing Names

The **name of a person**, **pet**, or **product** always begins with a capital letter.

Example: Andrew is Brian's brother.
The baby polar bear's name is Ellie.

Directions: Complete each sentence below. Write each name in parentheses ( ). Remember to capitalize the names of people, pets, and products.

1. Ken's (ken's) favorite food is corn on the cob.
2. Ollie (ollie) loves pickles and crackers.
3. Jan's (jan's) pet kitten, Zorro (zorro), eats Pet Food Plus (pet food plus) food.
4. Tom's Banana Brand Crunch (tom's banana brand crunch) is Amy's (amy's) favorite cereal.
5. Donna's (donna's) bunny, Jake (jake), eats lettuce.
6. Alyssa (alyssa) and Vicki (vicki) like Tito's Tasty Tacos (tito's tasty tacos).

LANGUAGE ARTS 164 100 Second Grade Skills

Page 164

Skill 79: Capitalizin

Directions: Complete each sen name in parentheses ( ). Rememi of people, pets, and products.

1. My brother named his pet lizard
2. Finn's (finn's) favorite pizz (denny's deep dish).
3. Samantha (samantha) dances aft
4. We named the kittens Phantom (pha Shadow (shadow).
5. Joyce's (joyce's) birthday is in Decem
6. Hal (hal) and Eddie (eddie camping.
7. Kim (kim) wrote a report on Thomas Jeffe
8. Mom bought Creamy's (creamy's) ice cream for Tanya's (tanya's) party.

100 Second Grade Skills

Page 165

Skill 80: Capitalizing Titles

A **title** is a word that comes before a person's name. A title gives more information about who a person is. Titles that come before a name begin with a capital letter.

Examples: Grandma Stella Cousin Holly Doctor Johnson

Titles of respect also begin with a capital letter. Here are some titles of respect: **Mr.**, **Mrs.**, **Ms.**, and **Miss**.

Examples: Mr. Garcia Miss Billo Ms. Ramirez Mrs. Chang

Directions: Cross out the titles that should be capitalized and write the correct capitalized titles above them.

1. Last night, I went to a play with ~~aunt~~ Aunt Stacy and ~~uncle~~ Uncle Brian.
2. I sat next to ~~cousin~~ Cousin Daniel and ~~cousin~~ Cousin Mia.
3. The play was about ~~ms.~~ Ms. Amelia Earhart, the first woman to fly across the Atlantic Ocean alone.
4. ~~ms.~~ Ms. Earhart led an eventful life.
5. She even met ~~president~~ President Roosevelt.
6. After the play, I met ~~aunt~~ Aunt Stacy's friend, ~~mrs.~~ Mrs Simpson.
7. She played the role of ~~ms.~~ Ms. Earhart.
8. I also met ~~mr.~~ Mr. Davis.
9. He played the role of ~~president~~ President Roosevelt.

LANGUAGE ARTS 166 100 Second Grade Skills

Page 166

Skill 80: Capitalizing Titles

Directions: Rewrite each of the following sentences. Remember, titles begin with a capital letter.

1. dr. Donovan has been my doctor since I was a baby.
Dr. Donovan has been my doctor since I was a baby.
2. judge Millan recently went on vacation.
Judge Millan recently went on vacation.
3. grandpa Emil gave aunt Bea the book.
Grandpa Emil gave Aunt Bea the book.
4. grandma Helen read it last year.
Grandma Helen read it last year.
5. She read a book about president George Washington.
She read a book about President George Washington.
6. mrs. Ritter brought her class to the zoo.
Mrs. Ritter brought her class to the zoo.

100 Second Grade Skills LANGUAGE ARTS 167

Page 167

Answer Key

Page 168

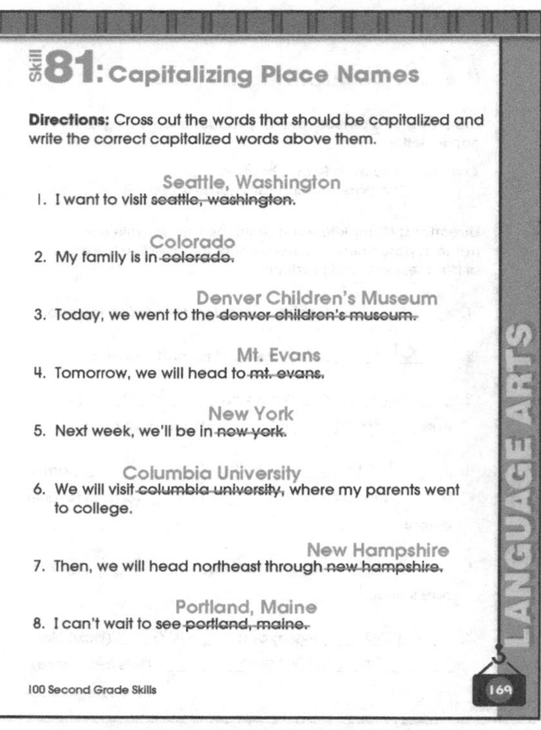

Page 169

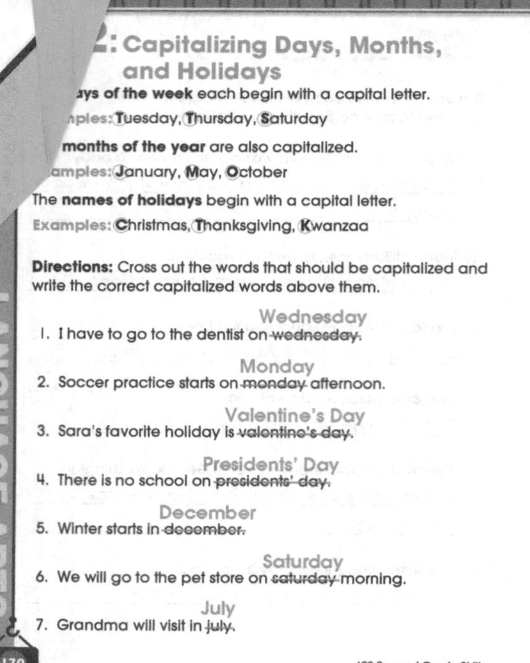

Page 170

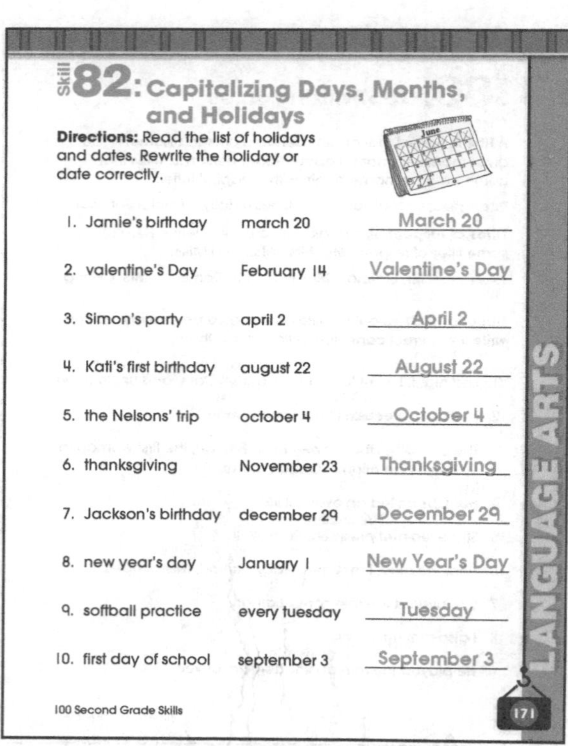

Page 171

Answer Key

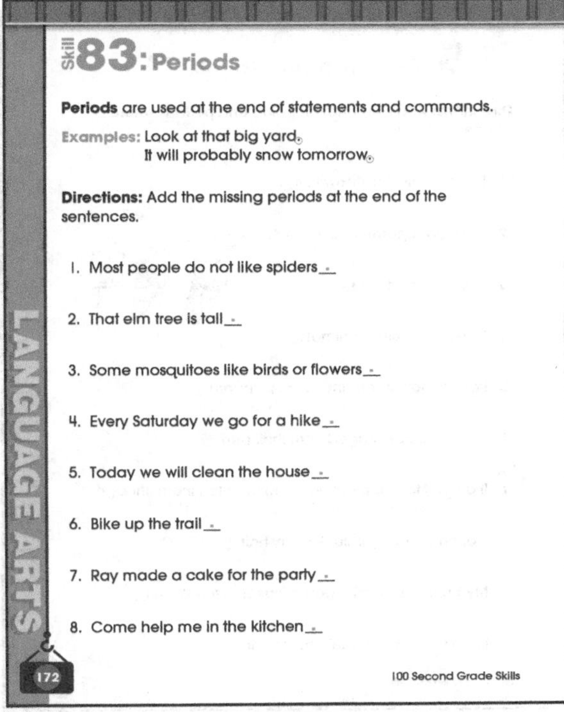
Skill 83: Periods

Periods are used at the end of statements and commands.

Examples: Look at that big yard.
It will probably snow tomorrow.

Directions: Add the missing periods at the end of the sentences.

1. Most people do not like spiders.
2. That elm tree is tall.
3. Some mosquitoes like birds or flowers.
4. Every Saturday we go for a hike.
5. Today we will clean the house.
6. Bike up the trail.
7. Ray made a cake for the party.
8. Come help me in the kitchen.

LANGUAGE ARTS

172 100 Second Grade Skills

Page 172

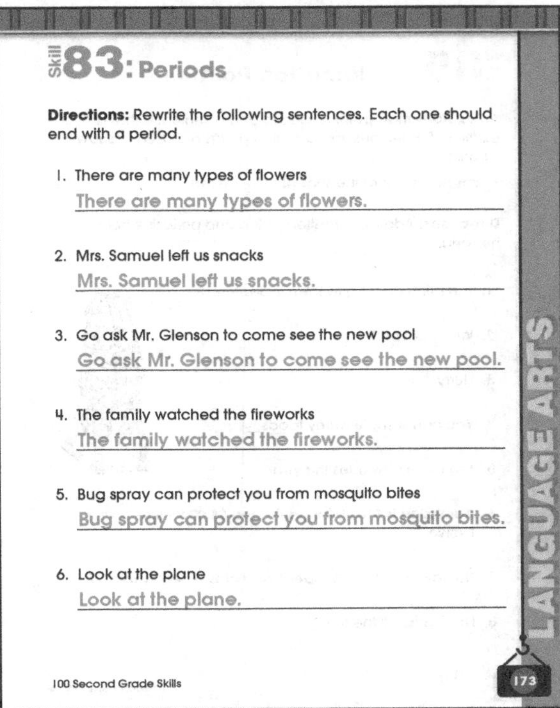
Skill 83: Periods

Directions: Rewrite the following sentences. Each one should end with a period.

1. There are many types of flowers
There are many types of flowers.
2. Mrs. Samuel left us snacks
Mrs. Samuel left us snacks.
3. Go ask Mr. Glenson to come see the new pool
Go ask Mr. Glenson to come see the new pool.
4. The family watched the fireworks
The family watched the fireworks.
5. Bug spray can protect you from mosquito bites
Bug spray can protect you from mosquito bites.
6. Look at the plane
Look at the plane.

LANGUAGE ARTS

100 Second Grade Skills 173

Page 173

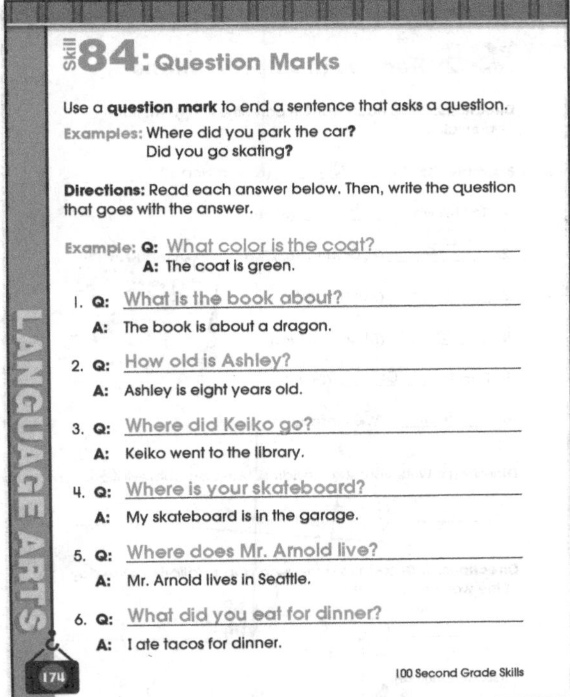
Skill 84: Question Marks

Use a question mark to end a sentence that asks a question.

Examples: Where did you park the car?
Did you go skating?

Directions: Read each answer below. Then, write the question that goes with the answer.

Example: Q: What color is the coat?
A: The coat is green.

1. Q: What is the book about?
A: The book is about a dragon.
2. Q: How old is Ashley?
A: Ashley is eight years old.
3. Q: Where did Keiko go?
A: Keiko went to the library.
4. Q: Where is your skateboard?
A: My skateboard is in the garage.
5. Q: Where does Mr. Arnold live?
A: Mr. Arnold lives in Seattle.
6. Q: What did you eat for dinner?
A: I ate tacos for dinner.

LANGUAGE ARTS

174 100 Second Grade Skills

Page 174

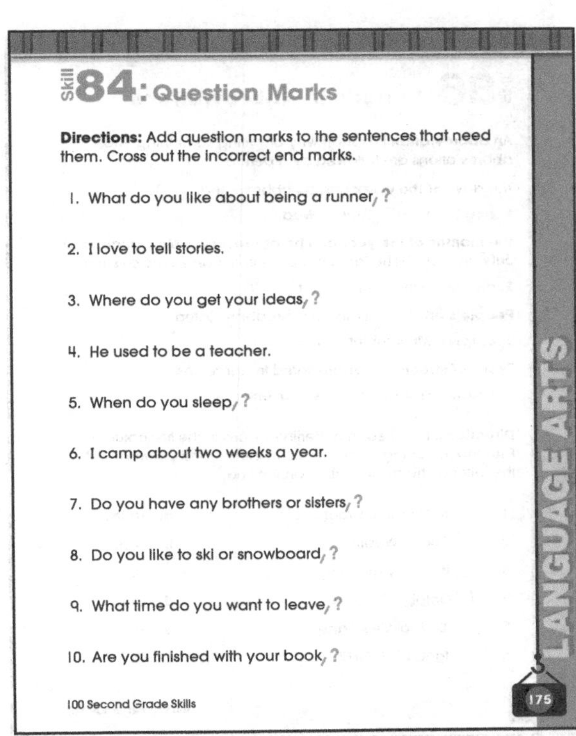
Skill 84: Question Marks

Directions: Add question marks to the sentences that need them. Cross out the incorrect end marks.

1. What do you like about being a runner. ?
2. I love to tell stories.
3. Where do you get your ideas. ?
4. He used to be a teacher.
5. When do you sleep. ?
6. I camp about two weeks a year.
7. Do you have any brothers or sisters. ?
8. Do you like to ski or snowboard. ?
9. What time do you want to leave. ?
10. Are you finished with your book. ?

LANGUAGE ARTS

100 Second Grade Skills 175

Page 175

Answer Key

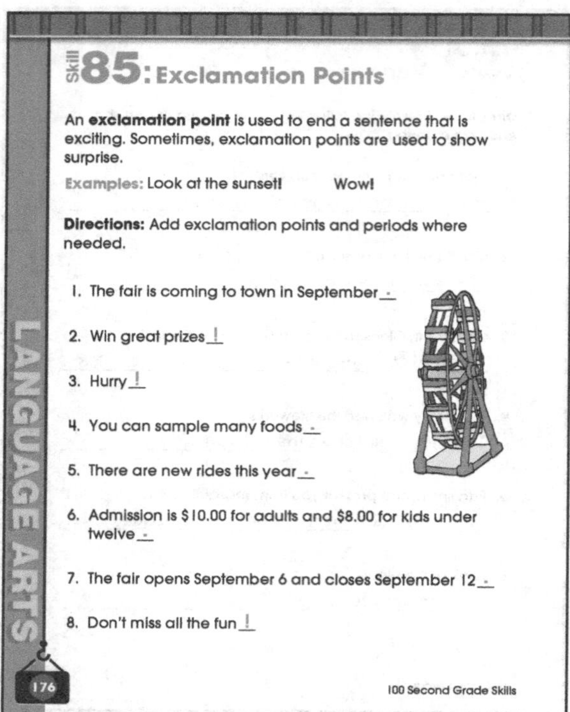

Skill 85: Exclamation Points

An **exclamation point** is used to end a sentence that is exciting. Sometimes, exclamation points are used to show surprise.

Examples: Look at the sunset! Wow!

Directions: Add exclamation points and periods where needed.

1. The fair is coming to town in September .
2. Win great prizes !
3. Hurry !
4. You can sample many foods .
5. There are new rides this year .
6. Admission is $10.00 for adults and $8.00 for kids under twelve .
7. The fair opens September 6 and closes September 12 .
8. Don't miss all the fun !

LANGUAGE ARTS

176 100 Second Grade Skills

Page 176

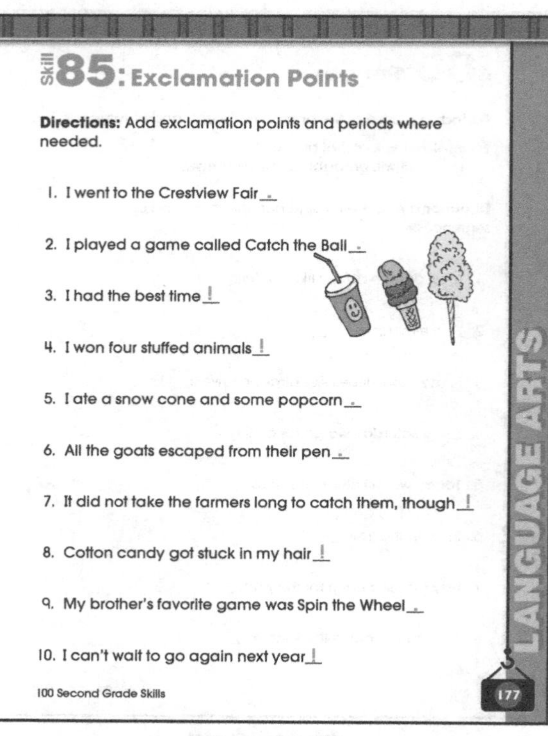

Skill 85: Exclamation Points

Directions: Add exclamation points and periods where needed.

1. I went to the Crestview Fair .
2. I played a game called Catch the Ball .
3. I had the best time !
4. I won four stuffed animals !
5. I ate a snow cone and some popcorn .
6. All the goats escaped from their pen .
7. It did not take the farmers long to catch them, though !
8. Cotton candy got stuck in my hair !
9. My brother's favorite game was Spin the Wheel .
10. I can't wait to go again next year !

LANGUAGE ARTS

100 Second Grade Skills 177

Page 177

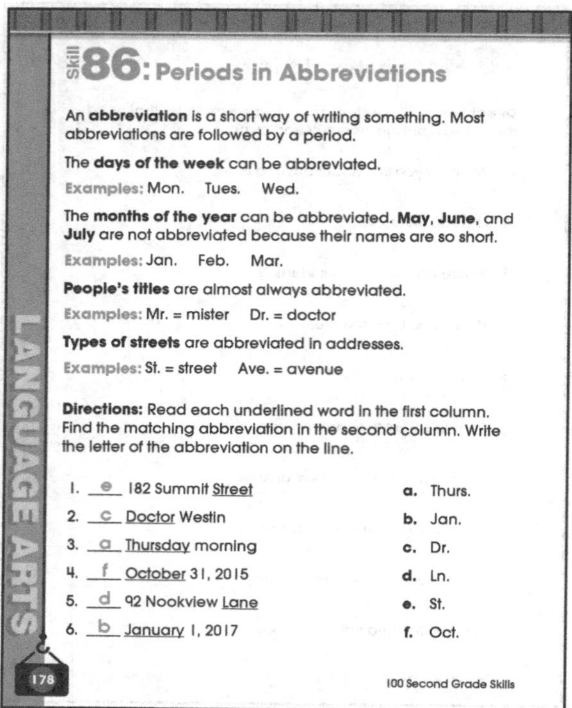

Skill 86: Periods in Abbreviations

An **abbreviation** is a short way of writing something. Most abbreviations are followed by a period.

The **days of the week** can be abbreviated.

Examples: Mon. Tues. Wed.

The **months of the year** can be abbreviated. **May, June,** and **July** are not abbreviated because their names are so short.

Examples: Jan. Feb. Mar.

People's titles are almost always abbreviated.

Examples: Mr. = mister Dr. = doctor

Types of streets are abbreviated in addresses.

Examples: St. = street Ave. = avenue

Directions: Read each underlined word in the first column. Find the matching abbreviation in the second column. Write the letter of the abbreviation on the line.

1. e 182 Summit Street	a. Thurs.
2. c Doctor Westin	b. Jan.
3. a Thursday morning	c. Dr.
4. f October 31, 2015	d. Ln.
5. d 92 Nookview Lane	e. St.
6. b January 1, 2017	f. Oct.

LANGUAGE ARTS

178 100 Second Grade Skills

Page 178

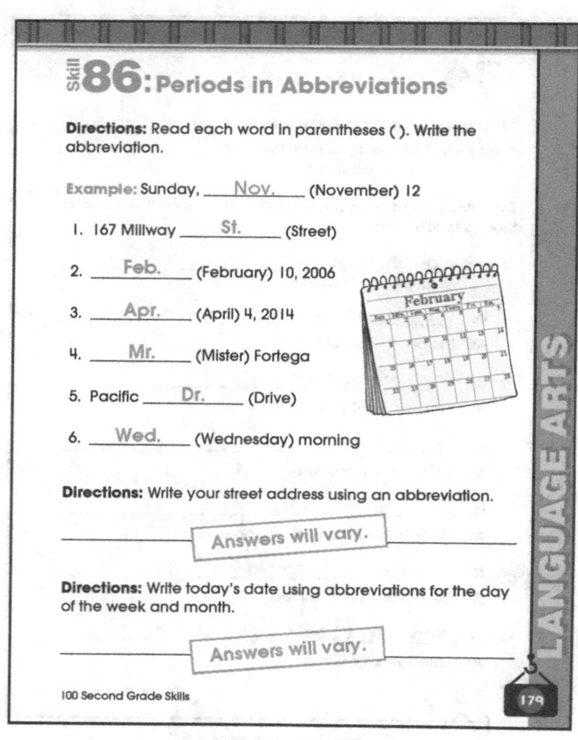

Skill 86: Periods in Abbreviations

Directions: Read each word in parentheses ( ). Write the abbreviation.

Example: Sunday, Nov. (November) 12

1. 167 Millway St. (Street)
2. Feb. (February) 10, 2006
3. Apr. (April) 4, 2014
4. Mr. (Mister) Fortega
5. Pacific Dr. (Drive)
6. Wed. (Wednesday) morning

Directions: Write your street address using an abbreviation.

Answers will vary.

Directions: Write today's date using abbreviations for the day of the week and month.

Answers will vary.

LANGUAGE ARTS

100 Second Grade Skills 179

Page 179

Answer Key

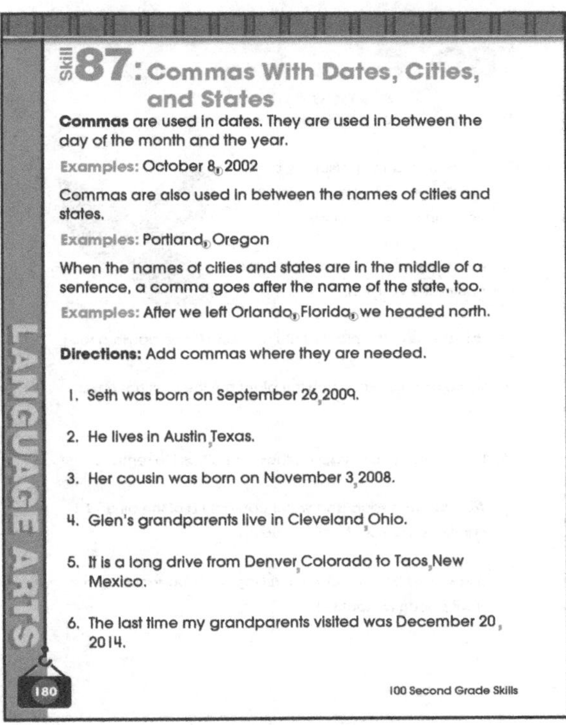
Skill 87: Commas With Dates, Cities, and States

Commas are used in dates. They are used in between the day of the month and the year.

Examples: October 8, 2002

Commas are also used in between the names of cities and states.

Examples: Portland, Oregon

When the names of cities and states are in the middle of a sentence, a comma goes after the name of the state, too.

Examples: After we left Orlando, Florida, we headed north.

Directions: Add commas where they are needed.

1. Seth was born on September 26, 2009.
2. He lives in Austin, Texas.
3. Her cousin was born on November 3, 2008.
4. Glen's grandparents live in Cleveland, Ohio.
5. It is a long drive from Denver, Colorado to Taos, New Mexico.
6. The last time my grandparents visited was December 20, 2014.

LANGUAGE ARTS

180 100 Second Grade Skills

Page 180

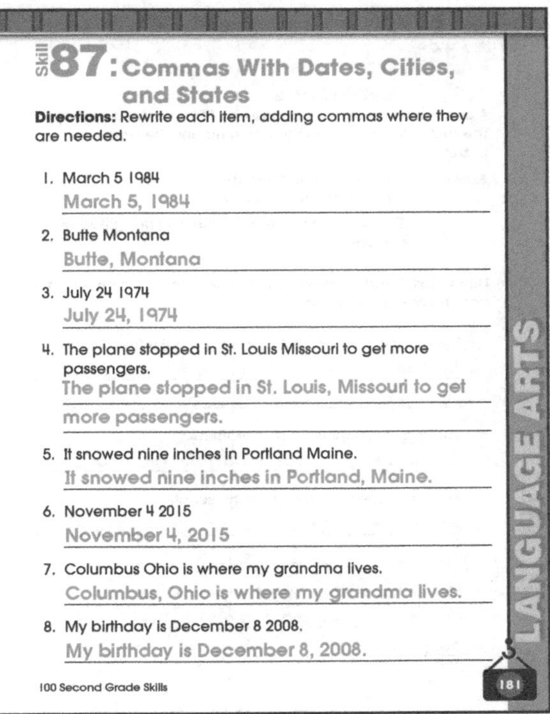
Skill 87: Commas With Dates, Cities, and States

Directions: Rewrite each item, adding commas where they are needed.

1. March 5 1984
   March 5, 1984
2. Butte Montana
   Butte, Montana
3. July 24 1974
   July 24, 1974
4. The plane stopped in St. Louis Missouri to get more passengers.
   The plane stopped in St. Louis, Missouri to get more passengers.
5. It snowed nine inches in Portland Maine.
   It snowed nine inches in Portland, Maine.
6. November 4 2015
   November 4, 2015
7. Columbus Ohio is where my grandma lives.
   Columbus, Ohio is where my grandma lives.
8. My birthday is December 8 2008.
   My birthday is December 8, 2008.

LANGUAGE ARTS

100 Second Grade Skills 181

Page 181

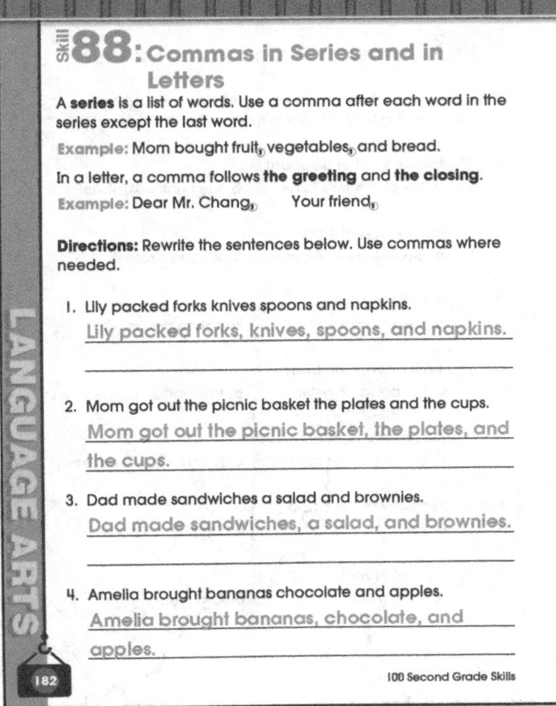
Skill 88: Commas in Series and in Letters

A **series** is a list of words. Use a comma after each word in the series except the last word.

Example: Mom bought fruit, vegetables, and bread.

In a letter, a comma follows **the greeting** and **the closing**.

Example: Dear Mr. Chang, Your friend,

Directions: Rewrite the sentences below. Use commas where needed.

1. Lily packed forks knives spoons and napkins.
   Lily packed forks, knives, spoons, and napkins.
2. Mom got out the picnic basket the plates and the cups.
   Mom got out the picnic basket, the plates, and the cups.
3. Dad made sandwiches a salad and brownies.
   Dad made sandwiches, a salad, and brownies.
4. Amelia brought bananas chocolate and apples.
   Amelia brought bananas, chocolate, and apples.

LANGUAGE ARTS

182 100 Second Grade Skills

Page 182

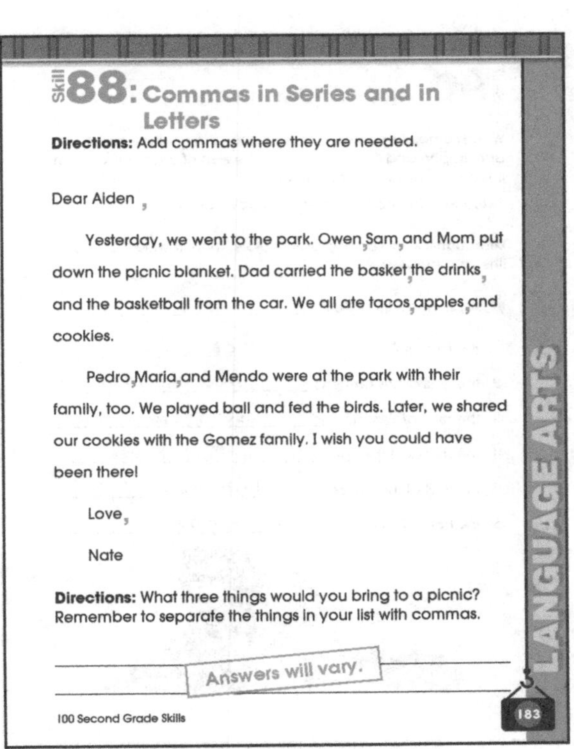
Skill 88: Commas in Series and in Letters

Directions: Add commas where they are needed.

Dear Aiden,

Yesterday, we went to the park. Owen, Sam, and Mom put down the picnic blanket. Dad carried the basket, the drinks, and the basketball from the car. We all ate tacos, apples, and cookies.

Pedro, Maria, and Mendo were at the park with their family, too. We played ball and fed the birds. Later, we shared our cookies with the Gomez family. I wish you could have been there!

Love,

Nate

Directions: What three things would you bring to a picnic? Remember to separate the things in your list with commas.

Answers will vary.

LANGUAGE ARTS

100 Second Grade Skills 183

Page 183

Answer Key

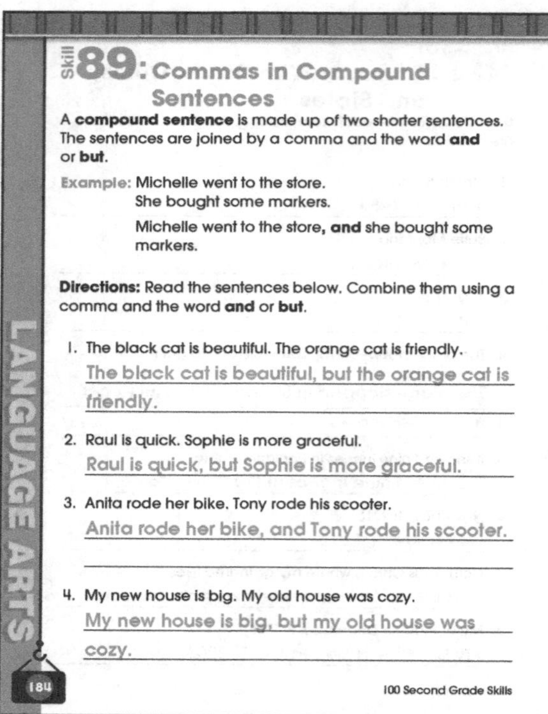

Skill 89: Commas in Compound Sentences

A **compound sentence** is made up of two shorter sentences. The sentences are joined by a comma and the word **and** or **but**.

Example: Michelle went to the store.
She bought some markers.

Michelle went to the store**, and** she bought some markers.

Directions: Read the sentences below. Combine them using a comma and the word **and** or **but**.

1. The black cat is beautiful. The orange cat is friendly.
The black cat is beautiful, but the orange cat is friendly.
2. Raul is quick. Sophie is more graceful.
Raul is quick, but Sophie is more graceful.
3. Anita rode her bike. Tony rode his scooter.
Anita rode her bike, and Tony rode his scooter.
4. My new house is big. My old house was cozy.
My new house is big, but my old house was cozy.

LANGUAGE ARTS

184 100 Second Grade Skills

Page 184

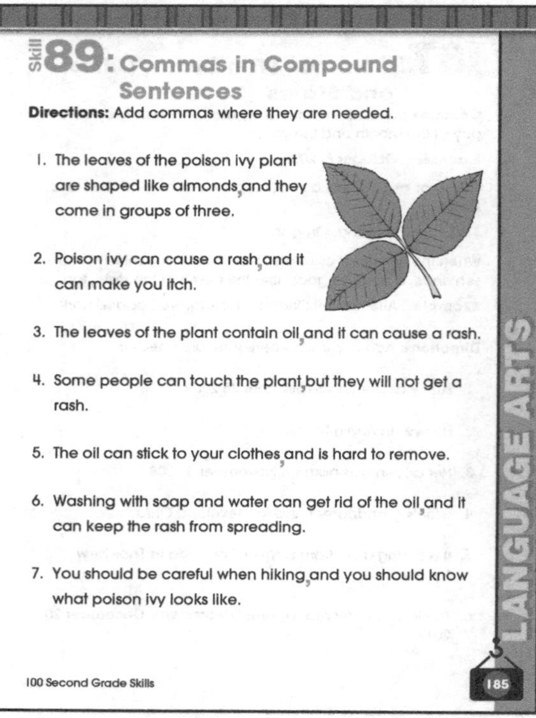

Skill 89: Commas in Compound Sentences

Directions: Add commas where they are needed.

1. The leaves of the poison ivy plant are shaped like almonds, and they come in groups of three.
2. Poison ivy can cause a rash, and it can make you itch.
3. The leaves of the plant contain oil, and it can cause a rash.
4. Some people can touch the plant, but they will not get a rash.
5. The oil can stick to your clothes, and is hard to remove.
6. Washing with soap and water can get rid of the oil, and it can keep the rash from spreading.
7. You should be careful when hiking, and you should know what poison ivy looks like.

LANGUAGE ARTS

100 Second Grade Skills 185

Page 185

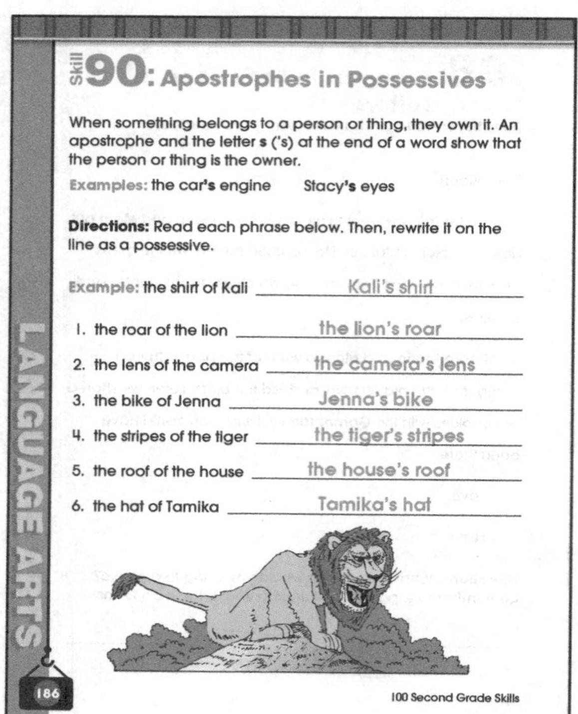

Skill 90: Apostrophes in Possessives

When something belongs to a person or thing, they own it. An apostrophe and the letter **s** (**'s**) at the end of a word show that the person or thing is the owner.

Examples: the car's engine Stacy**'s** eyes

Directions: Read each phrase below. Then, rewrite it on the line as a possessive.

Example: the shirt of Kali Kali's shirt

1. the roar of the lion the lion's roar
2. the lens of the camera the camera's lens
3. the bike of Jenna Jenna's bike
4. the stripes of the tiger the tiger's stripes
5. the roof of the house the house's roof
6. the hat of Tamika Tamika's hat

LANGUAGE ARTS

186 100 Second Grade Skills

Page 186

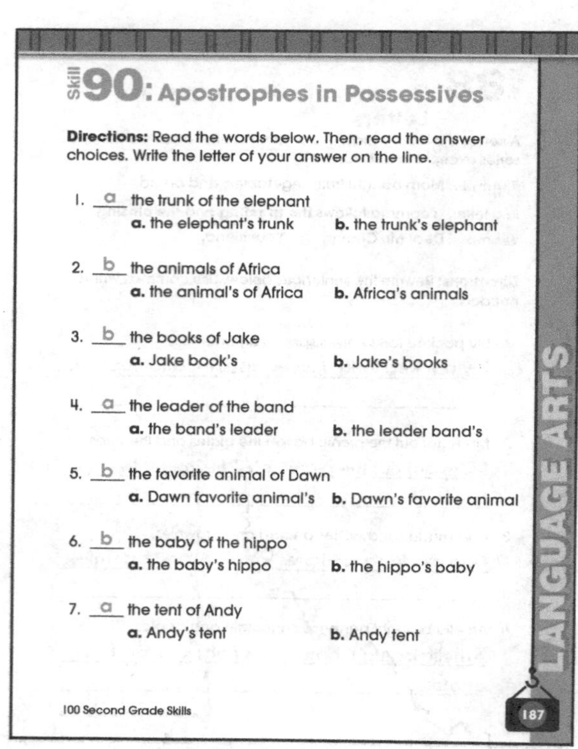

Skill 90: Apostrophes in Possessives

Directions: Read the words below. Then, read the answer choices. Write the letter of your answer on the line.

1. a the trunk of the elephant
a. the elephant's trunk **b.** the trunk's elephant
2. b the animals of Africa
a. the animal's of Africa **b.** Africa's animals
3. b the books of Jake
a. Jake book's **b.** Jake's books
4. a the leader of the band
a. the band's leader **b.** the leader band's
5. b the favorite animal of Dawn
a. Dawn favorite animal's **b.** Dawn's favorite animal
6. b the baby of the hippo
a. the baby's hippo **b.** the hippo's baby
7. a the tent of Andy
a. Andy's tent **b.** Andy tent

LANGUAGE ARTS

100 Second Grade Skills 187

Page 187

Answer Key

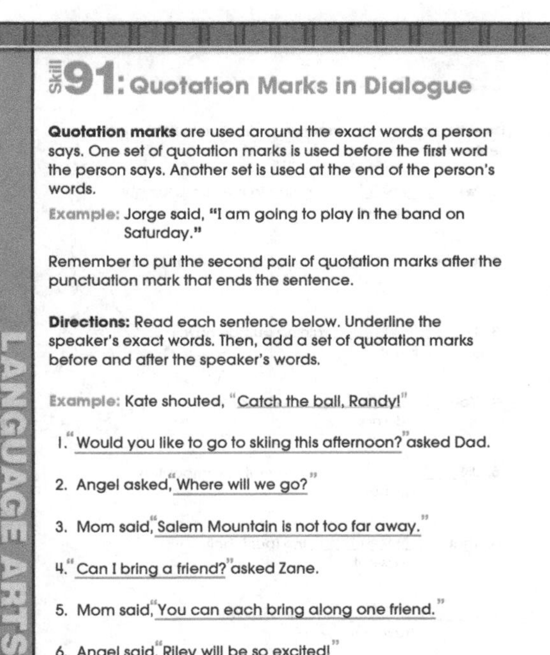

Skill 91: Quotation Marks in Dialogue

Quotation marks are used around the exact words a person says. One set of quotation marks is used before the first word the person says. Another set is used at the end of the person's words.

Example: Jorge said, **"**I am going to play in the band on Saturday.**"**

Remember to put the second pair of quotation marks after the punctuation mark that ends the sentence.

Directions: Read each sentence below. Underline the speaker's exact words. Then, add a set of quotation marks before and after the speaker's words.

Example: Kate shouted, "Catch the ball, Randy!"

1. "Would you like to go to skiing this afternoon?" asked Dad.
2. Angel asked, "Where will we go?"
3. Mom said, "Salem Mountain is not too far away."
4. "Can I bring a friend?" asked Zane.
5. Mom said, "You can each bring along one friend."
6. Angel said, "Riley will be so excited!"

LANGUAGE ARTS

188 100 Second Grade Skills

Page 188

Skill 91: Quotation Marks in Dialogue

Directions: Read each sentence below. Write the sentence again. Add quotation marks where they are needed.

1. Have you ever been sledding? Zach asked his friend.
   "Have you ever been sledding?" Zach asked his friend.
2. Jacob said, No, but it sounds like fun.
   Jacob said, "No, but it sounds like fun."
3. Tamara said, My grandpa taught me how to ski.
   Tamara said, "My grandpa taught me how to ski."
4. She added, He lives near the mountains in New York.
   She added, "He lives near the mountains in New York."
5. Mr. Jones said, I have a meeting at noon.
   Mr. Jones said, "I have a meeting at noon."
6. I want to go to the mountains on vacation, said Katrina.
   "I want to go to the mountains on vacation," said Katrina.

LANGUAGE ARTS

100 Second Grade Skills 189

Page 189

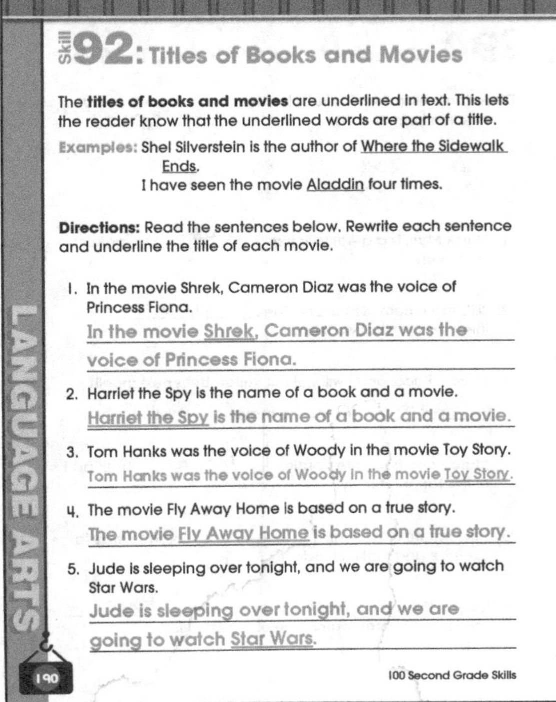

Skill 92: Titles of Books and Movies

The **titles of books and movies** are underlined in text. This lets the reader know that the underlined words are part of a title.

Examples: Shel Silverstein is the author of Where the Sidewalk Ends.
I have seen the movie Aladdin four times.

Directions: Read the sentences below. Rewrite each sentence and underline the title of each movie.

1. In the movie Shrek, Cameron Diaz was the voice of Princess Fiona.
   In the movie Shrek, Cameron Diaz was the voice of Princess Fiona.
2. Harriet the Spy is the name of a book and a movie.
   Harriet the Spy is the name of a book and a movie.
3. Tom Hanks was the voice of Woody in the movie Toy Story.
   Tom Hanks was the voice of Woody in the movie Toy Story.
4. The movie Fly Away Home is based on a true story.
   The movie Fly Away Home is based on a true story.
5. Jude is sleeping over tonight, and we are going to watch Star Wars.
   Jude is sleeping over tonight, and we are going to watch Star Wars.

LANGUAGE ARTS

190 100 Second Grade Skills

Page 190

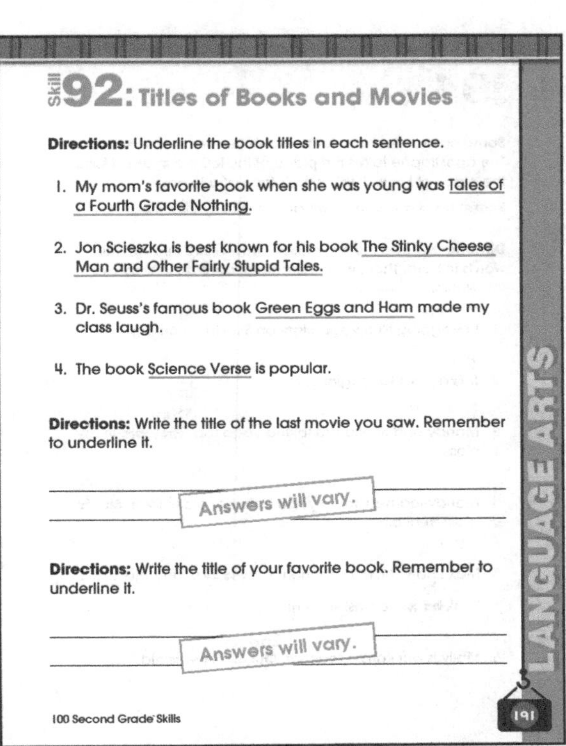

Skill 92: Titles of Books and Movies

Directions: Underline the book titles in each sentence.

1. My mom's favorite book when she was young was Tales of a Fourth Grade Nothing.
2. Jon Scieszka is best known for his book The Stinky Cheese Man and Other Fairly Stupid Tales.
3. Dr. Seuss's famous book Green Eggs and Ham made my class laugh.
4. The book Science Verse is popular.

Directions: Write the title of the last movie you saw. Remember to underline it.

Answers will vary.

Directions: Write the title of your favorite book. Remember to underline it.

Answers will vary.

LANGUAGE ARTS

100 Second Grade Skills 191

Page 191

Answer Key

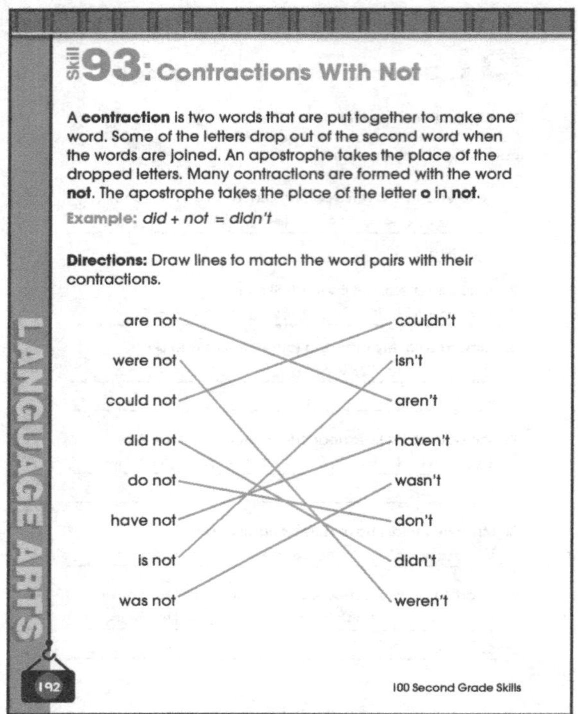

Skill 93: Contractions With Not

A **contraction** is two words that are put together to make one word. Some of the letters drop out of the second word when the words are joined. An apostrophe takes the place of the dropped letters. Many contractions are formed with the word **not**. The apostrophe takes the place of the letter **o** in **not**.

Example: *did + not = didn't*

Directions: Draw lines to match the word pairs with their contractions.

are not	couldn't
were not	isn't
could not	aren't
did not	haven't
do not	wasn't
have not	don't
is not	didn't
was not	weren't

LANGUAGE ARTS

192 100 Second Grade Skills

Page 192

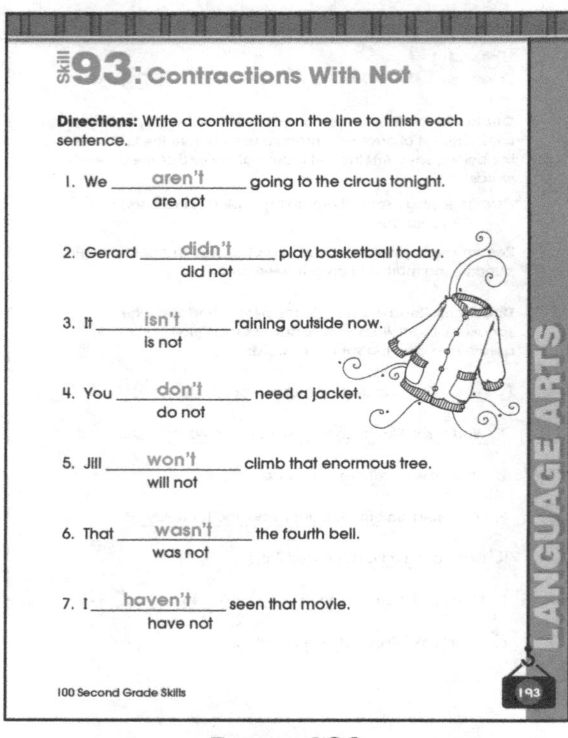

Skill 93: Contractions With Not

Directions: Write a contraction on the line to finish each sentence.

1. We aren't going to the circus tonight. (are not)
2. Gerard didn't play basketball today. (did not)
3. It isn't raining outside now. (is not)
4. You don't need a jacket. (do not)
5. Jill won't climb that enormous tree. (will not)
6. That wasn't the fourth bell. (was not)
7. I haven't seen that movie. (have not)

LANGUAGE ARTS

100 Second Grade Skills 193

Page 193

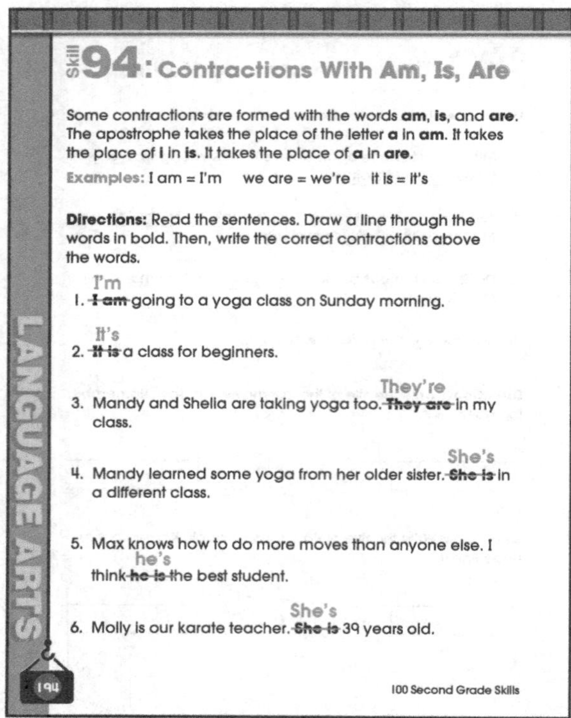

Skill 94: Contractions With Am, Is, Are

Some contractions are formed with the words **am**, **is**, and **are**. The apostrophe takes the place of the letter **a** in **am**. It takes the place of **i** in **is**. It takes the place of **a** in **are**.

Examples: I am = I'm we are = we're it is = it's

Directions: Read the sentences. Draw a line through the words in bold. Then, write the correct contractions above the words.

1. ~~I am~~ (I'm) going to a yoga class on Sunday morning.
2. ~~It is~~ (It's) a class for beginners.
3. Mandy and Shelia are taking yoga too. ~~They are~~ (They're) in my class.
4. Mandy learned some yoga from her older sister. ~~She is~~ (She's) in a different class.
5. Max knows how to do more moves than anyone else. I think ~~he is~~ (he's) the best student.
6. Molly is our karate teacher. ~~She is~~ (She's) 39 years old.

LANGUAGE ARTS

194 100 Second Grade Skills

Page 194

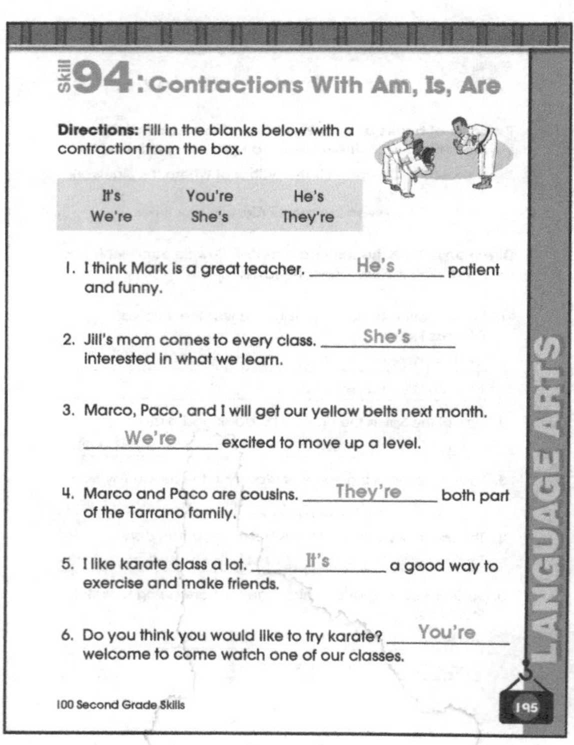

Skill 94: Contractions With Am, Is, Are

Directions: Fill in the blanks below with a contraction from the box.

It's	You're	He's
We're	She's	They're

1. I think Mark is a great teacher. He's patient and funny.
2. Jill's mom comes to every class. She's interested in what we learn.
3. Marco, Paco, and I will get our yellow belts next month. We're excited to move up a level.
4. Marco and Paco are cousins. They're both part of the Tarrano family.
5. I like karate class a lot. It's a good way to exercise and make friends.
6. Do you think you would like to try karate? You're welcome to come watch one of our classes.

LANGUAGE ARTS

100 Second Grade Skills 195

Page 195

Answer Key

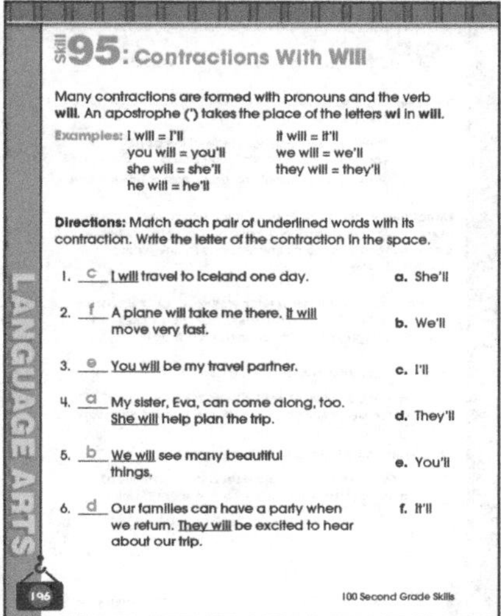

Skill **95**: Contractions With Will

Many contractions are formed with pronouns and the verb **will**. An apostrophe (') takes the place of the letters **wi** in **will**.

Examples: I will = I'll, you will = you'll, she will = she'll, he will = he'll, it will = it'll, we will = we'll, they will = they'll

Directions: Match each pair of underlined words with its contraction. Write the letter of the contraction in the space.

1. c I will travel to Iceland one day. — a. She'll
2. f A plane will take me there. It will move very fast. — b. We'll
3. e You will be my travel partner. — c. I'll
4. a My sister, Eva, can come along, too. She will help plan the trip. — d. They'll
5. b We will see many beautiful things. — e. You'll
6. d Our families can have a party when we return. They will be excited to hear about our trip. — f. It'll

LANGUAGE ARTS

196 100 Second Grade Skills

Page 196

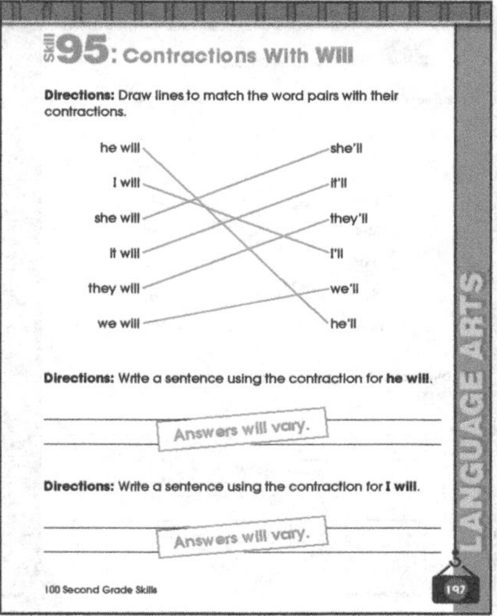

Skill **95**: Contractions With Will

Directions: Draw lines to match the word pairs with their contractions.

he will — she'll
I will — it'll
she will — they'll
it will — I'll
they will — we'll
we will — he'll

Directions: Write a sentence using the contraction for **he will**.

Answers will vary.

Directions: Write a sentence using the contraction for **I will**.

Answers will vary.

LANGUAGE ARTS

100 Second Grade Skills 197

Page 197

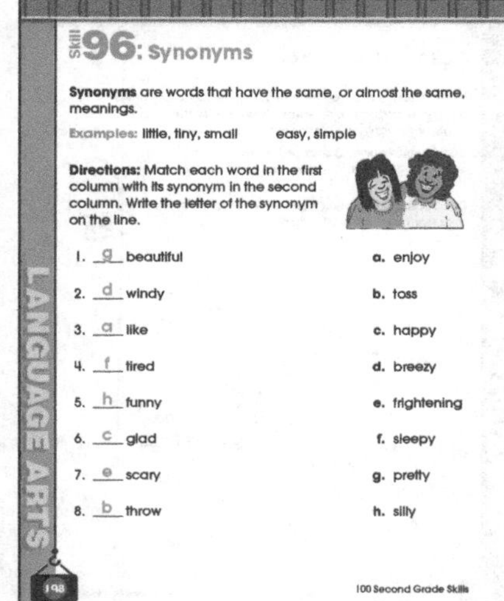

Skill **96**: Synonyms

Synonyms are words that have the same, or almost the same, meanings.

Examples: little, tiny, small easy, simple

Directions: Match each word in the first column with its synonym in the second column. Write the letter of the synonym on the line.

1. g beautiful — a. enjoy
2. d windy — b. toss
3. a like — c. happy
4. f tired — d. breezy
5. h funny — e. frightening
6. c glad — f. sleepy
7. e scary — g. pretty
8. b throw — h. silly

LANGUAGE ARTS

198 100 Second Grade Skills

Page 198

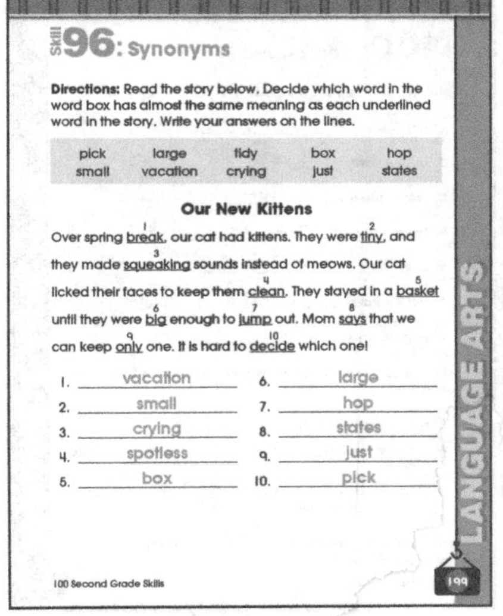

Skill **96**: Synonyms

Directions: Read the story below. Decide which word in the word box has almost the same meaning as each underlined word in the story. Write your answers on the lines.

pick	large	tidy	box	hop
small	vacation	crying	just	states

Our New Kittens

Over spring break[1], our cat had kittens. They were tiny[2], and they made squeaking[3] sounds instead of meows. Our cat licked their faces to keep them clean[4]. They stayed in a basket[5] until they were big[6] enough to jump[7] out. Mom says[8] that we can keep only[9] one. It is hard to decide[10] which one!

1. vacation
2. small
3. crying
4. spotless
5. box
6. large
7. hop
8. states
9. just
10. pick

LANGUAGE ARTS

100 Second Grade Skills 199

Page 199

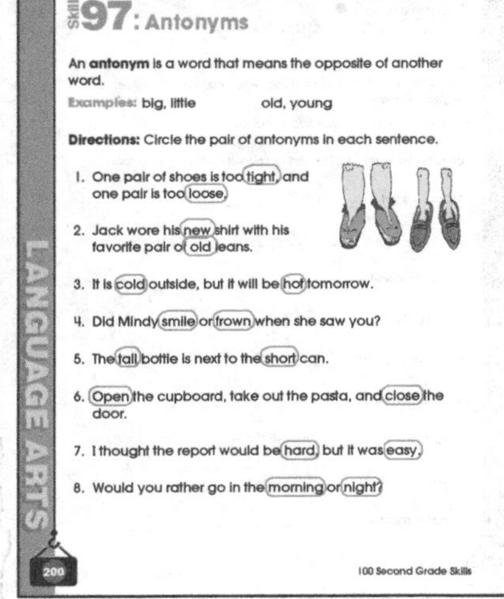

Skill **97**: Antonyms

An **antonym** is a word that means the opposite of another word.

Examples: big, little old, young

Directions: Circle the pair of antonyms in each sentence.

1. One pair of shoes is too (tight) and one pair is too (loose).
2. Jack wore his (new) shirt with his favorite pair of (old) jeans.
3. It is (cold) outside, but it will be (hot) tomorrow.
4. Did Mindy (smile) or (frown) when she saw you?
5. The (tall) bottle is next to the (short) can.
6. (Open) the cupboard, take out the pasta, and (close) the door.
7. I thought the report would be (hard), but it was (easy).
8. Would you rather go in the (morning) or (night)?

LANGUAGE ARTS

200 100 Second Grade Skills

Page 200

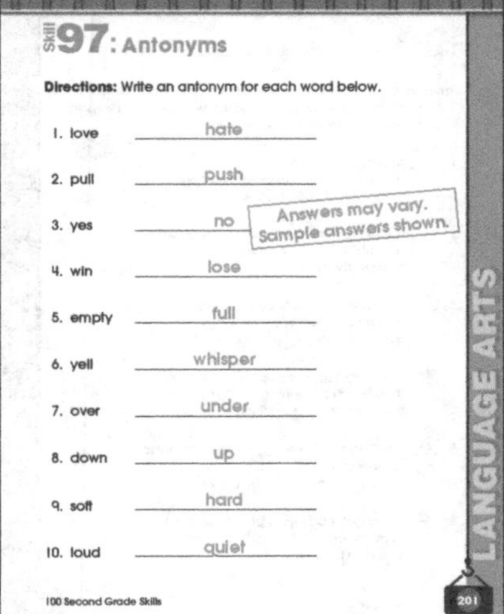

Skill **97**: Antonyms

Directions: Write an antonym for each word below.

Answers may vary. Sample answers shown.

1. love — hate
2. pull — push
3. yes — no
4. win — lose
5. empty — full
6. yell — whisper
7. over — under
8. down — up
9. soft — hard
10. loud — quiet

LANGUAGE ARTS

100 Second Grade Skills 201

Page 201

Answer Key

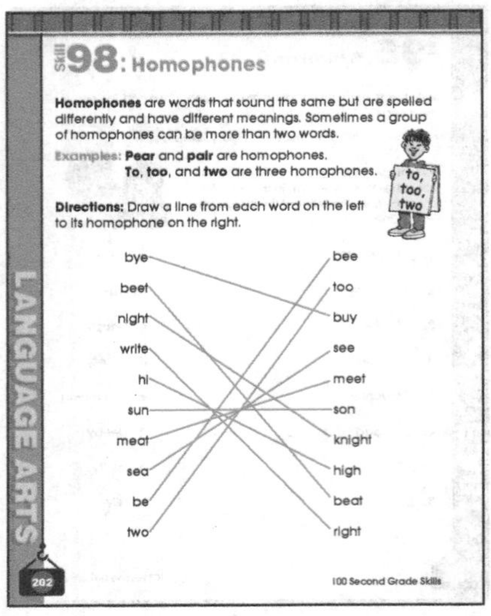

Skill **98**: Homophones

Homophones are words that sound the same but are spelled differently and have different meanings. Sometimes a group of homophones can be more than two words.

Examples: **Pear** and **pair** are homophones.
To, too, and **two** are three homophones.

Directions: Draw a line from each word on the left to its homophone on the right.

bye	bee
beet	too
night	buy
write	see
hi	meet
sun	son
meat	knight
sea	high
be	beat
two	right

LANGUAGE ARTS

202 100 Second Grade Skills

Page 202

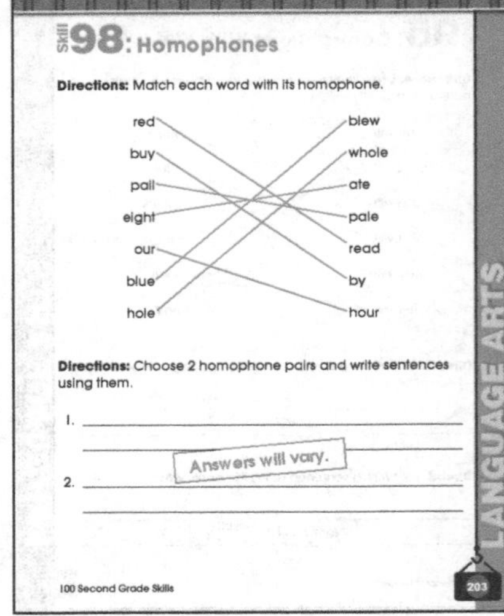

Skill **98**: Homophones

Directions: Match each word with its homophone.

red	blew
buy	whole
pail	ate
eight	pale
our	read
blue	by
hole	hour

Directions: Choose 2 homophone pairs and write sentences using them.

1. ______________________

Answers will vary.

2. ______________________

LANGUAGE ARTS

100 Second Grade Skills 203

Page 203

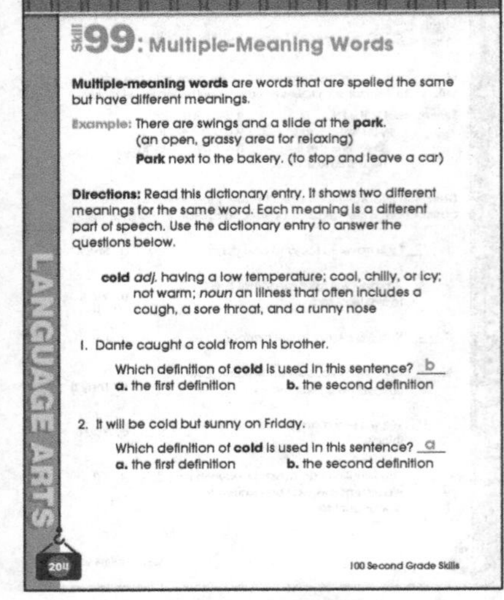

Skill **99**: Multiple-Meaning Words

Multiple-meaning words are words that are spelled the same but have different meanings.

Example: There are swings and a slide at the **park**.
(an open, grassy area for relaxing)
Park next to the bakery. (to stop and leave a car)

Directions: Read this dictionary entry. It shows two different meanings for the same word. Each meaning is a different part of speech. Use the dictionary entry to answer the questions below.

cold *adj.* having a low temperature; cool, chilly, or icy; not warm; *noun* an illness that often includes a cough, a sore throat, and a runny nose

1. Dante caught a cold from his brother.
   Which definition of **cold** is used in this sentence? b
   a. the first definition **b.** the second definition

2. It will be cold but sunny on Friday.
   Which definition of **cold** is used in this sentence? a
   a. the first definition **b.** the second definition

LANGUAGE ARTS

204 100 Second Grade Skills

Page 204

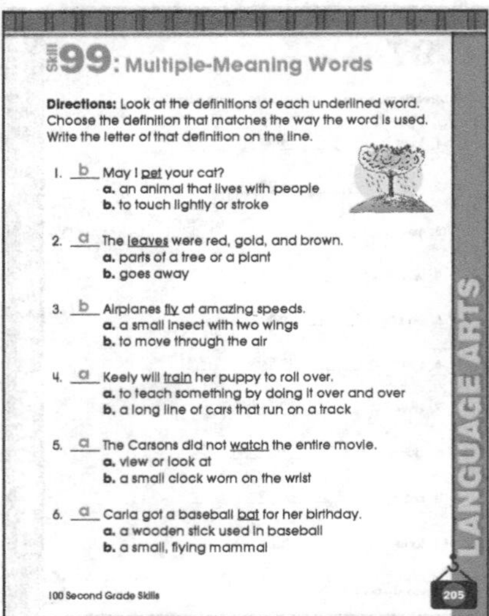

Skill **99**: Multiple-Meaning Words

Directions: Look at the definitions of each underlined word. Choose the definition that matches the way the word is used. Write the letter of that definition on the line.

1. b May I pet your cat?
   a. an animal that lives with people
   b. to touch lightly or stroke

2. a The leaves were red, gold, and brown.
   a. parts of a tree or a plant
   b. goes away

3. b Airplanes fly at amazing speeds.
   a. a small insect with two wings
   b. to move through the air

4. a Keely will train her puppy to roll over.
   a. to teach something by doing it over and over
   b. a long line of cars that run on a track

5. a The Carsons did not watch the entire movie.
   a. view or look at
   b. a small clock worn on the wrist

6. a Carla got a baseball bat for her birthday.
   a. a wooden stick used in baseball
   b. a small, flying mammal

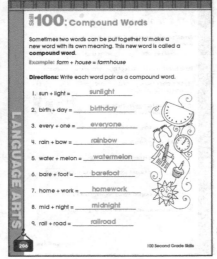

LANGUAGE ARTS

100 Second Grade Skills 205

Page 205

Skill **100**: Compound Words

Sometimes two words can be put together to make a new word with its own meaning. This new word is called a **compound word**.

Example: *farm + house = farmhouse*

Directions: Write each word pair as a compound word.

1. sun + light = sunlight
2. birth + day = birthday
3. every + one = everyone
4. rain + bow = rainbow
5. water + melon = watermelon
6. bare + foot = barefoot
7. home + work = homework
8. mid + night = midnight
9. rail + road = railroad

LANGUAGE ARTS

206 100 Second Grade Skills

Page 206

Skill **100**: Compound Words

Directions: Write each word pair as a compound word.

1. after + noon = afternoon
2. back + yard = backyard
3. class + mate = classmate
4. break + fast = breakfast
5. flash + light = flashlight
6. oat + meal = oatmeal
7. pop + corn = popcorn

Directions: Use a compound word from above to finish each sentence.

8. Nate saw fireflies in his backyard.
9. Ricky will need a flashlight when he camps outside.
10. Claire likes to eat popcorn at the movies with her grandmother.

Directions: Underline the other compound words used in the sentences above.

LANGUAGE ARTS

100 Second Grade Skills 207

Page 207